MUST *love* COWBOYS

CHERYL BROOKS

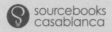

sourcebooks
casablanca

Published by Sourcebooks Casablanca, an imprint of Sourcebooks, Inc.
P.O. Box 4410, Naperville, Illinois 60567-4410
(630) 961-3900
Fax: (630) 961-2168
www.sourcebooks.com

Printed and bound in Canada
MBP 10 9 8 7 6 5 4 3 2 1

For Lynne

Chapter 1

Bunkhouse cook wanted.
Experience preferred.
Must love cowboys.

"YOU'RE LOOKING FOR *WHO*?" THE EYES BENEATH HIS dark, forbidding brow were an indeterminate hazel, yet I'd never seen a more intense gaze—or one that was more intimidating.

"Mr. Douglas," I replied. "Calvin Douglas. He's supposed to work here. This *is* the Circle Bar K Ranch, isn't it?"

"Yeah. He's here. Just never heard him called 'Mr. Douglas' before."

Anyone else would have smiled at that point, but his expression didn't soften in the slightest. From beneath the brim of a dusty brown cowboy hat, his eyes bored into me like a pair of drills, setting off an attack of nerves that made my hands shake and my throat go dry. He was precisely the kind of man I tended to shy away from.

Who am I kidding?

I shied away from all of them.

"M-may I see him?"

Getting out of my car had already taken most of the courage I possessed, even with Ophelia by my side. A mix of German shepherd and several other breeds, Ophelia had been rescued from an abusive home and taken to the shelter where I had worked as a volunteer during my senior year in high school. For the most part, she was fairly timid and tended to cringe at loud noises. But she could turn into a fierce, growling protector whenever she thought I was in danger—as several suspicious characters I'd encountered while walking near the park could attest. Surprisingly, she didn't growl at this man.

Obviously, she didn't consider him a threat.

I disagreed. I couldn't even look him in the eye, much less argue with him.

Not that he was arguing.

He nodded toward a long, one-story building near the enormous barn. "He's in the kitchen fixing dinner."

That occupation certainly fit with what little I knew about my grandfather's old Army buddy. According to the letter I'd received from him, their friendship had begun in boot camp and continued on through active duty. Calvin had served his unit as a cook, while Grandpa became a combat soldier. While I could only guess at Calvin's current state of health, Vietnam and Agent Orange had certainly left their mark on my grandfather.

Grammy had been pregnant with my mother when Grandpa was drafted, and she'd had no other children even after he returned. Five years later, unable to deal with the way the war had changed him, she divorced him and remarried. As Grandpa's only child, my mother eventually wound up being the one to deal with the mood swings and poor health that were the legacy of his tour of duty. Although Grandpa wouldn't talk about the war, I'd seen the scars and witnessed the sickness, both mental and physical, that had only worsened with the passage of time.

All of that was over now, and his ashes had been scattered in the Tetons as he'd requested. When his demons got to be too much for him, those mountains had been the only place he could find peace. I had often wondered why he'd never gone there to live, but I suspected even they were only a temporary fix. No doubt he became immune to their effect after a while, just as he'd become tolerant of so many of the drugs used to control his illness.

The tall cowboy tipped his hat in a gesture that struck me as being more dismissive than polite and headed back toward the barn without another word, leaving me to find the kitchen on my own. I watched him go, wondering what his story was. Why he had been so abrupt and unfriendly.

Not that it mattered. I wouldn't be there long enough to find out anyway. I was simply there to fulfill yet another of my grandfather's dying wishes.

"Come on, Lia," I said, giving my dog a pat on her broad head. "Let's do this and get going."

I wrapped my coat more tightly against the chilly wind. Grandpa had died the first of September. No doubt autumn in Wyoming would've been fine weather-wise, but with so many things to do in the aftermath of his death, I wasn't ready to pack up and go before winter set in. Even he had suggested I wait until spring to scatter his ashes.

"Go in April," he'd advised in one of his more lucid moments. "The weather will be better then." As cold as it still was in the mountains in late April, I wished I'd waited until July.

I stared at the building the cowboy had indicated, unable to decide which of the three doors led to the kitchen. Scanning the roofline, I spotted a wispy vapor rising from a vent above the door near the center and headed toward it.

Grandpa had come to live with us when I was a child, and since his bedroom and mine shared a wall, I often heard the rattling of my closet doors as he pounded away on the old Woodstock typewriter he'd inherited from his father. I had always known he corresponded with someone on a regular basis, I just hadn't known who he was writing to until I read his will.

To be honest, I hadn't expected the address to be current, but my letter to Calvin Douglas had received a reasonably prompt reply. In it, he thanked me for informing him of Grandpa's death and offered his condolences, stating that he hadn't heard from his old friend in more than two years.

I hadn't been surprised to learn that—the timing was about the same as when I'd given up my job and my apartment and moved back home to help care for my deteriorating grandparent. By then, he'd been in no condition to write letters, his dementia having progressed to the point that we probably should have put him in a nursing home. Mom simply couldn't handle him. God knew I was no nurse, but I'd managed fairly well until a few weeks before the end.

Despite being too weak to get out of bed, he was still a danger—to himself and everyone around him. I could never decide which hurt worse, his grip on my arm— and once around my neck—or the maniacal hatred in his eyes when he'd been overcome by a bout of paranoia.

The memory made me shudder as I climbed the two steps up to a small wooden landing.

In response to my knock, a tall, rail-thin man with sparse gray hair opened the door. "Tina Hayes?"

I nodded, holding out a hand that was still trembling from my encounter with the cowboy. "You must be Mr. Douglas."

"Calvin," he corrected. He looked even older than Grandpa had when he died, but his handshake was firm and he was at least smiling. Smiling men had become something of a rarity in my life, except for those who existed solely in my imagination. I'd become accustomed to Grandpa's wild-eyed glares, his doctor's solemn mask, and then there was the funeral director's grave countenance. Even the lawyer hadn't smiled much. On the other hand, my favorite firehouse fantasy had seen me through many trials and tribulations. Cooking for a bunch of handsome, hunky firemen, laughing with them, making love with those who weren't married, and flirting with those who had wives.

I wish...

"Thanks for your directions," I said, yanking my thoughts back to the present. "I might not have made it here without them—even with the GPS on my phone."

I'd driven across the country with Grandpa's ashes in a box in the trunk and Calvin's letter taped to the dashboard. Having lived in Kentucky all my life, Wyoming's vast open spaces and rocky terrain were completely foreign to me. Now that I'd finally seen the Tetons in person, I wished I'd found the time to accompany Grandpa on some of his trips out west. Unfortunately, school and work had always gotten in the way.

Always too busy.

And now it was too late.

"Those fancy gadgets don't help much out here," Calvin admitted. "Come on in. Dinner will be ready shortly."

Ophelia whined and gazed at me with anxious eyes, just as she'd done when we'd arrived at the lodge in Jackson Hole. "Don't worry, sweetie," I'd said. "I'm not gonna make you climb those mountains."

As if I would even consider it. My dog was my best friend, and she wasn't getting any younger. I wasn't about to risk losing her in the wilderness. Her life had been tough enough before I adopted her.

"I'm sure we can find something for her to eat too," Calvin added.

"I have food for her in the car. Besides, I hadn't planned on staying that long." I hesitated. I had no desire to sit down to dinner with a bunch of rowdy, uncouth cowboys. If the one I'd met was any indication, they wouldn't want me to—nor did I want to seem rude.

I'd had no idea how this meeting would go. Calvin hadn't heard from Grandpa in two years. A lot had happened in that time, and none of it good. Surely he wouldn't want to hear all the gory details. I certainly didn't want to talk about them, especially over dinner.

"Do you really think I'd let John Parker's grand-daughter come all this way and not stay for dinner?" Narrowing his eyes, Calvin gazed at me from beneath bushy gray eyebrows and shook his head. "Ain't gonna happen, young lady."

I started to protest being called that. Granted, twenty-eight wasn't old, but the last two years had seemed like triple that number, and no doubt they showed in my face. Still, Grandpa had been sixty-eight when he died, and since he and Calvin had been drafted at the same time, I assumed they were fairly close in age. Given the way the draft had been organized, they might've even been born on the same day.

The more I thought about it, the more peculiar selecting soldiers on the basis of their birthdays seemed. Imagine an entire platoon of Geminis or Capricorns. Clearly, an astrologer hadn't taken part in the decision-making process.

I caught myself smiling for the first time that day.

Calvin apparently took my smile as acceptance of his dinner invitation. "That's more like it. In honor of your visit, I'm making my famous chili and cornbread." He shot me a wink. "It was your granddad's favorite, although I work with better ingredients now than I did when we were in the Army."

I had the strangest feeling this man knew my grandfather better than anyone. I'd never noticed Grandpa having a preference for that particular meal. But then, perhaps none of us made chili the way Calvin did. What sort of things had they discussed in those letters? I hadn't a clue, but I'd found three full shoe boxes of them in Grandpa's closet after the will was read.

A will that instructed me to do what I was about to do now.

"Sounds great." Several moments went by before I found the words. "I guess you're wondering why I'm here."

He shook his head. "Not really. You have something to give me, don't you?"

I nodded. "In his will, Grandpa asked that I give you

back the letters you'd sent him, and these." I handed him the two small boxes I had tucked in my purse.

Tears filled Calvin's eyes. "He saved my life, you know. Saved a bunch of us." He opened one box and then the other. "He got this one for saving us, and this one for nearly dying in the process."

I blinked back a few tears of my own. "A Purple Heart and a Silver Star." I shook my head slowly. "I never even knew he had them."

"John was like that. Kinda shy, really. Never one to toot his own horn."

That description also fit his granddaughter. However, I kept that tidbit to myself.

"I really looked forward to his letters. When they stopped coming…" Grimacing, Calvin pressed his fist to the center of his chest. "I knew I'd lost the best friend I'd ever had."

"I guess it's true what they say about brothers-in-arms."

"It sure is."

"The letters are in the car," I went on. "There are quite a few of them."

"I kept the ones he sent me too. Funny, us both keeping them." He smiled. "Your granddad certainly had a way with words. He wrote some great letters."

That much I knew. I'd kept some of the letters he'd written to me when I was in college. Now I wished I'd kept them all.

Calvin slid the two medals into his pocket, then went back to his stove and began stirring a huge pot of chili. The heavenly aroma of chili combined with baking cornbread soon had my stomach growling, making me very glad I'd agreed to stay for dinner.

I hadn't cooked anything like that for Grandpa in a long, long time, if indeed I ever had. Special diets and a steady decline in appetite had made pleasing him nearly impossible. Knowing I liked to cook, Mom had finally given up and left it to me. Sometimes he ate what I fed him, and sometimes he spit it in my face.

I tried to remember him the way he'd been when I was younger, but even that person wasn't the one Calvin knew.

Voices from the next room broke the silence, accompanied by the scuffling of booted feet and the scrape of chair legs on the wooden floor.

"That'll be the men coming in for dinner," Calvin said. "Go on into the mess hall and have a seat."

Mess hall. I doubted the term was exclusive to the military, making me wonder what the dining room had been called before Calvin had taken charge of the kitchen. "Can I give you a hand?" I didn't want to admit that being the lone woman in a room full of strange men brought out the nervous Nellie in me like nothing else could.

"Sure." His smile suggested he either understood my reluctance or at least acknowledged the reason for it. "I'll dish up the chili if you'll get the cornbread."

Grateful for a task to occupy myself, I took off my coat and laid it on a chair next to a small corner table, then snatched up a pair of slightly singed oven mitts. One by one, I removed two cast-iron pans from the oven, each of which was divided into seven sections containing round loaves of lightly browned bread.

"Smells great," I said. "Love the pans."

Calvin snorted a laugh. "Keeps the men from fighting over who gets the most. They each get two."

That meant there were at least six other men—including the surly fellow I'd met first.

Oh, joy…

"Don't worry," Calvin added. "You can have one of mine."

Since the miniature loaves were easily twice the size of the typical muffin, I doubted I would go hungry, but that wasn't what concerned me. I cleared my throat, hoping to ease the tightness that anxiety had caused. "Nothing wrong with their appetites, huh?"

"It's practically a full-time job keeping them fed." He grinned. "Kinda like keeping the hogs happy."

"I heard that!" someone shouted from the mess hall. Good-natured laughter followed.

"You boys get on in here and grab a bowl," Calvin called back. "Or should I just pour the chili in the trough?"

"We're coming." After more scraping of chairs and scuffling of boots, the men descended upon the kitchen.

I should have turned around and smiled, but I simply couldn't face them. I would be gone in an hour anyway. No need to make friends with everyone. Not that I *could*…

Apparently, Ophelia wasn't interested in making friends, either. With a whine, she darted between me and the stove, sending me stumbling backward only to slam into a rock-hard body and be gathered up by a pair of strong arms.

"Good thing you'd already set down that cornbread." His breath stirred the hair lying against my neck and morphed the tickles into goose bumps that skittered down my back. "Wouldn't want to make a mess."

This wasn't the same cowboy. The voice was as different as the attitude. Heat flooded my cheeks.

He relaxed his hold but didn't let go. Nuzzling my neck, he drew in an audible breath. "Mmm...your hair smells even better than the bread."

"Oh, way to go, Dean," another man jeered. "That's sure to go down in history as the best pickup line ever."

"Give me a break, Nick," the one called Dean said. "I wasn't expecting a gorgeous blond to fall into my arms."

Positioned as I was, he couldn't see my eye roll or my red face—yet. I stiffened as he spun me around. My gaze landed on the base of his neck where it met the open collar of a plaid shirt. Placing a loosely fisted hand beneath my chin, he tilted my head back.

His smile stole my breath before the other details even registered. Freckles, dimples, big blue eyes, and an unruly thatch of sandy hair. Men might have made me nervous as all get-out, but that didn't mean I never looked at them. This one was worth a second glance. And a third. And a fourth...

"Enough of that, now," Calvin barked. "Tina's my best buddy's granddaughter. I won't have you teasing her."

"Didn't know you had a best buddy, Calvin," another man said. "Always thought we were your best buddies."

"Me and John go back to way before you were born, Sonny," Calvin snapped. "You don't know nothin' 'bout it."

In response to Calvin's reprimand, Dean released me, although he certainly took his time doing it. Another wave of tingles raced over my skin as he traced the length of my arms with his fingertips.

He scanned my face with appreciative eyes then glanced at Calvin. "Never woulda guessed an old coot like you would be friends with a girl like this."

In the space of ten minutes, I'd been called a *young lady* and a *girl*. Clearly, these guys didn't get out much.

"Yeah, well, I just met her myself." Calvin waved his ladle at Dean as though about to swat him with it. "Back off and I'll introduce you." Placing a hand on my shoulder, he used the ladle to point at each man in turn. "Let's see now… I imagine you've already figured out which one is Dean—his last name is Wayland, by the way. The bald guy with the handlebar mustache is Bull Russell. Sonny Ferguson is the kid with the curly hair. Nick Reno's the one with the ponytail and the smart mouth." He pointed at a rather tall, homely fellow. "That's Joe Knight, the foreman." I followed his gesture to the last man, who stood framed in the doorway. "And that mean-looking varmint over there is Wyatt McCabe."

Without his hat, he was even more formidable, and his eyes weren't the only feature contributing to that impression. Tanned skin, dark beard stubble, and thick black hair in a crew cut gone wild with a rather prominent widow's peak marked him as the rugged outdoor type. The sharp planes of his nose and the grim set of a small mouth with a full lower lip that should have been sensuous but wasn't—at least, not at the moment—suggested he was not a man to be crossed. And then there were the eyebrows. Now that I could see them clearly, they reminded me of a seagull's outstretched wings—if there was such a thing as a black seagull.

One of those extraordinary eyebrows rose ever so slightly. "We've met."

Chapter 2

"REALLY?" CALVIN SHOT ME A QUESTIONING GLANCE. "When?"

"About twenty minutes ago," I replied, ignoring the peculiar sensation deep within my pelvis as goose bumps tingled along my spine. "He's the one who told me where to find you. Although we didn't get around to introducing ourselves."

So his name was Wyatt. Too bad I'd already heard his last name and couldn't make the obvious "Earp" joke. He probably got that a lot—probably didn't like it, either.

"McCabe" also had a certain Wild West flavor to it. Regardless of his name, he certainly looked the part of a tough lawman—or maybe one of the outlaws. Without a sheriff's badge pinned to his vest, it was difficult to say.

"Well then, this is Tina Hayes," Calvin said. "You men watch your mouths while she's here."

"Sure thing, Calvin." The bald guy mimed zipping his lips, then smoothed out his mustache, twirling up the ends.

Nick snickered. "Which means Bull can't say another word." More laughter rippled through the group as they queued up with their plates and bowls.

Apparently Bull's vocabulary consisted mostly of swearwords, which didn't concern me very much. I doubted there were any I hadn't heard on a regular basis.

Grandpa's language had been pretty colorful, especially when he got confused and combative.

I'm not going to think about that.

I found a pair of tongs and served up the cornbread as the men passed by, hoping my blushes weren't too obvious. I'd never been able to control that response, and with six young men in close proximity, the heat in my cheeks was almost continuous. I counted myself lucky to have the excuse of standing next to a hot oven. Too bad I couldn't *stay* in the kitchen.

After the men had all filed into the mess hall, I picked up a plate and bowl and Calvin dished up my chili.

"They're a good bunch of guys," he said. "Nothing to worry about."

My blushes must've been more noticeable than I thought. "I'm not worried. Just a little…shy." A *lot* shy, actually.

"I know."

I looked up from my plate to find him smiling at me. "How did you—"

"Your granddad told me."

A grimace accompanied my blush. "I hadn't thought of that."

All those letters… Calvin had known Grandpa since long before I was born. I wasn't the only grandchild—I had two younger brothers—but Grandpa had obviously mentioned a thing or two about me.

"You're a lot like him," he said, echoing the thoughts I'd had earlier. "Same hair color, same green eyes. Same way of avoiding eye contact."

I glanced away, giving credence to at least one of those observations. "I'm worse about that than he ever was."

"Maybe." He nodded toward the doorway. "Better get on in there and eat that before it gets cold."

I followed him into the mess hall, wondering what else he'd learned in those letters. Had Grandpa reported every scraped knee, passing grade, and graduation? If so, it was a safe bet he'd never mentioned anything about my boyfriends because I'd never had one. Had he actually told Calvin that, or had the men in my life been conspicuous by their absence?

Needless to say, I didn't ask.

I might have had the occasional schoolgirl crush on a handsome classmate, but that's as far as I'd ever gotten. I was always too shy to let anyone know what I felt or how much I cared. On the other hand, my fantasy men didn't frighten me. I was able to engage in all sorts of sexy, flirtatious activities with them. Too bad the real thing had the opposite effect.

The mess hall appeared to be used as much for recreation as it was for dining. A large rectangular room with a plain wooden floor and stuccoed walls, it contained a pool table, an enormous flat-screen television, a coffee table, and a couple of couches and recliners on the far end. In the center of the room, a potbellied stove radiated welcoming warmth, and a sturdy wooden table with seating for ten stood in the area closest to the kitchen.

To my dismay, the men had arranged themselves around that table in an alternating pattern, making it impossible for me to avoid sitting next to at least one of them. I wouldn't even have the option of sitting beside Calvin. Had they done it deliberately or did they simply like having plenty of elbow room? I felt as if I'd landed in the middle of a game of chess or tic-tac-toe with opponents who were far savvier than I ever claimed to be.

That's your imagination, Tina.

Calvin took a corner seat next to Bull, leaving me to sit between two men, which I did *not* want to do, or on the opposite corner. I chose the corner, thinking it would give Ophelia room to sit on the floor beside me. The moment I sat down, however, I realized my error.

I was across from Dean, next to Nick, with Wyatt on my left at the foot of the table.

Crap.

The only things I dared look at were my dog and my plate.

After all I'd been through lately—taking care of my dying grandfather, helping Mom make funeral arrangements, executing his will, and driving halfway across the country and into the Tetons with my dog riding shotgun—I should've been more confident, but I wasn't. I closed my eyes, marshaling my courage.

When I finally glanced up and raised my head, Bull immediately gasped, crossed himself, and uttered a fervent "Amen!"

Nick burst out laughing. "Since when are you Catholic?"

Bull's face was as flushed as mine had undoubtedly been a few minutes before. "I'm not," he mumbled. "Just thought Tina might be."

I wasn't, but they didn't need to know that. Letting them think I'd been silently blessing my food was much easier than admitting the truth. "Thanks for the prayer, Bull." I certainly needed one.

Squaring his shoulders, Bull lifted his chin.

"You're welcome. I'm actually an ordained minister of the Church of the Holy Evangelical Society for the Spiritually Deprived."

"Oh, Lord," Dean said with a roll of his eyes. "Here we go again…"

"That's nice," I said. "Never heard of that one." Bull seemed sincere enough, although I couldn't help wondering if his credentials hadn't been obtained via the Internet.

Chuckling, Dean picked up his spoon and dug into his chili. "Neither has anyone else."

"It's real!" Bull protested. "You're just jealous. You damn well better—"

Since Joe was the foreman, I would've expected him—or perhaps even Calvin—to be the one to censure Bull's outburst, but Bull had just glanced in Wyatt's direction when he snapped his mouth shut.

I stole a peek at Wyatt and caught a glimpse of his piercing scowl before he returned his attention to his dinner.

"How d'you like that chili, Tina?" Calvin asked in a blatant attempt to change the subject.

"It's wonderful," I replied, despite the fact that I hadn't tasted it yet.

"That chili was her granddad's favorite," Calvin went on, speaking to the group at large. "He always came back for more."

The conversation shifted away from me after that, allowing me to relax enough to finally eat something. The chili was pretty tasty, although the cornbread was a little on the dry side.

"Have you been to Jackson Hole yet?" Nick asked me.

I had no idea how he knew anything about that part of my journey. Clearly, I'd missed something. "Yeah. I went there first. I'm on my way home now."

"Cool place, isn't it?"

"Yeah. Sort of like a Wild West ski resort." I probably would've enjoyed it more if I'd been there for a vacation instead of a funeral.

"I love that town," Nick went on. "Go there every chance I get."

Throughout the meal, Wyatt's plate had been directly in my line of sight, and I'd been aware of every spoonful the man put in his mouth. Even with my head turned toward Nick, I could still see him out of the corner of my eye. After buttering a piece of bread, he took a small bite, then slipped his hand beneath the edge of the table.

A moment later, I heard the unmistakable sound of Ophelia's mouth opening followed by a slurp of her tongue.

My sidelong glance revealed nothing more than an innocent cowboy wiping his fingers on a napkin before taking a sip of iced tea.

His eyes met mine over the brim of his glass. Again, no smile, no acknowledgment, no nothing. Just that same intense stare that made me drop my gaze, despite the peculiar fascination it triggered.

I really need to get back on the road.

If I left right away, I could make it to Rock Springs before dark and check into one of the nice, impersonal, dog-friendly hotels I'd discovered in the course of my online searches. If I couldn't find a room there, I could go on to Laramie or Cheyenne. I wasn't crazy about driving at night, but I'd done it before, and an interstate highway in good weather didn't pose much of a challenge.

I had to admit, I'd enjoyed passing through places I'd only heard about in history or geography class, and the names had gotten more interesting since I'd left Nebraska and crossed into Wyoming. I'd even considered taking a detour through Denver on the return trip, just so I could say I'd been there. I wasn't too far from Salt Lake City, either. I could even go on to Las Vegas if I wanted.

No. Vegas wasn't my kind of town, although the Grand Canyon was certainly worth visiting. I could take the southern route home and see that big crater in Winslow, then go on through Albuquerque, Amarillo, Oklahoma City, and Nashville before heading up I-65 to Louisville.

I'd spent a good part of the winter studying maps, and pored over them even more while recovering from a bout of flu in mid-March that knocked me down hard for over a week. Mom insisted that caring—and grieving—for Grandpa had made me more susceptible, but I blamed the worthless flu shot that I heartily wished I hadn't bothered to get. I still hadn't regained my usual stamina and had to stop more often on my journey than I would have liked, but I was finally making the journey—one I should've taken with Grandpa long ago.

"You've gotten awfully quiet."

I glanced up from my musings to find Dean smiling at me from across the table. After our little scene in the kitchen, he hadn't said much. "So have you."

He shrugged. "Not sure what to say."

Somehow I doubted that. "Don't worry. I'll be out of here pretty soon and you guys can get back to normal."

"You mean you aren't staying the night?"

I frowned. "Why on earth would I do that? I hadn't even planned on staying for dinner. This isn't exactly a hotel."

"Oh. Right." He sounded almost disappointed. "Where are you going from here?"

"That's what I've been thinking about," I replied. "Rock Springs or maybe Cheyenne. Depends on whether I can find a room in a place that allows dogs." Despite having compiled a list, without a set itinerary, I hadn't bothered to make any reservations.

"This may not be a hotel," Wyatt said. "But we do have an extra room, and we don't object to dogs."

The chatter at the other end of the table stopped abruptly. The fact that Wyatt's deep tones had startled me wasn't too surprising, but evidently they'd had a similar effect on everyone else.

"That's right," Dean said after a moment's hesitation. "I'd forgotten about that." My questioning frown prompted him to add, "It's the old foreman's quarters on the other side of the kitchen."

I glanced at Joe. "You're the foreman, right? How come you don't use that room?"

Joe shrugged. "Just never saw the need to move out of the bunkhouse after I got promoted."

Sonny chuckled. "Spends most nights with his girl-friend anyway."

"Oh, I do not," Joe protested, smiling.

Dean's disappointment had vanished. "We could clean it up for you real quick and you wouldn't have to be on the road all night."

"It won't take me all night to get to Cheyenne. Just—" I paused, doing some rapid mental calculations. "Okay, so it would take about five hours, but—"

"We can have a room ready for you a helluva lot quicker than that!" Nick said. Apparently Dean's enthusiasm was catching.

I didn't know what to say, although the prospect of a nighttime road trip to Cheyenne was rapidly losing its appeal. "Don't you have a boss of some kind? Someone who might not want you letting a strange woman spend the night in the bunkhouse?" That didn't sound right. "I mean, the foreman's quarters?"

"Are you kidding?" Dean was already on his feet gathering up the empty plates. "Angela would rip us new ones if we let you leave now."

"Angela, huh?" Clearly she had more nerve than I did. With the exception of Sonny, the Circle Bar K cowboys all towered over me, and at five-foot-ten, that didn't happen to me very often. Unfortunately, my height had never done much to alleviate my shyness. Not like spending an hour or so in the company of a bunch of cowboys. While I couldn't claim that sitting down to dinner with them had worked wonders, my blushes had definitely subsided.

"She's the boss," Dean explained. "Along with her father and her husband."

"You aren't in any hurry to get home, are you?" Calvin asked. "Be nice if you could stick around for a day or two."

I hated to admit it, but I wasn't in any hurry at all. For the first time in my life, I actually had time to spare and a fair amount of money to burn, which was why I'd given some thought to taking a few side trips along the way.

Time. I'd never known what it was like to have any

extra, and I still hadn't quite figured out what to do with it.

The main reason I didn't like the idea of staying at the ranch was that I didn't want to discuss the last two years with Calvin. I truly hoped he wouldn't ask. Better for him to remember Grandpa the way he was before.

"No. I'm not in any hurry." I exhaled a short, mirthless laugh. "I quit my job to take care of Grandpa. Haven't tried to find another one yet." Nor had I done any apartment hunting, putting off both of those tasks until my pilgrimage to the Tetons was over.

"What kind of work did you do?" Dean asked.

"I'm an IT specialist. I took some classes during the winter to bring me up to speed on the latest in the field, but I wanted to get this trip over with before I started filling out applications."

I hated how that sounded. *Over with.* Made it sound like an ordeal of some kind when I should've seen it as an adventure—although as adventures go, this one had been pretty tame. I'd driven fifteen hundred miles without a hitch, seen a lot of the country, and even found a relatively remote Wyoming ranch without any trouble.

"Computers, huh?" Nick said. "Think you could clean the viruses out of mine?"

"Maybe. I can take a look at it. Can't promise anything, though." I laughed again, this time with a touch of actual humor. If he'd been surfing the kind of sites I suspected he had, he needed a serious, up-to-date firewall.

"It's those goddamned porn sites," Bull said, echoing

my thoughts. "Trust me, you're better off making a date with a fu—*freakin'* hooker."

"Yeah, well, you can get other kinds of viruses doing that shit," Nick shot back. "Some that can't be cured."

Although I'd warned guys away from porn sites before, I'd never thought to suggest replacing that dubious pastime with an actual prostitute. Judging from the amount of laughter rippling around the table, neither had anyone else.

Calvin shot a scathing glance at Bull before addressing Nick. "You need to find yourself a nice girl, not a hooker."

Nick stood up, spreading his arms wide. "Do *you* see any nice girls around here?"

I bowed my head, unable to stop my smile. From the look of him, Nick couldn't have been long out of high school. As far as he was concerned, I was nothing more than an old maid, proving that at least one of these guys had the proper perspective.

Wyatt cleared his throat. "None that are your age, anyway."

Nick spun toward me, his eyes wide as he gaped at me in abject horror. "I didn't mean you. You seem really nice and all, but—"

I nodded. "I'm too old for you. No problem. I'm not in the market for a boyfriend anyway."

Dean was still collecting the dirty dishes. Two spoons slipped through his fingers to clatter on the table. "You mean you've already got one?"

The fact that I was in no hurry to get home should have made the answer to that question fairly obvious. "No."

"No husband?" He glanced at my left hand for verification.

I should have thought that was obvious too. "Um, no."

Dean exhaled with patent relief. "Glad to hear it. Wouldn't want any husbands or boyfriends pounding my head into the floor."

"You need to ask her another question while you're at it," Wyatt advised.

"What's that?" Dean asked, a befuddled frown furrowing his brow.

Wyatt aimed a challenging gaze at me, a trace of amusement quirking the corner of his mouth in the closest thing to a smile I'd seen on him yet. "You need to ask her if she has a *girl*friend."

Chapter 3

So. Wyatt *did* have a sense of humor.

"I'm a geek, not a lesbian," I said, arching a brow. "Although I do love my dog, who happens to be female." I got to my feet. "Not sure that counts."

Dean's frown dissipated. "Well, now that we've cleared that up, I should tell you that none of us are married or have girlfriends, except Joe."

I couldn't help chuckling. "Thanks." Unless one of these guys was interested in a one-night stand—which I most definitely wasn't—I doubted I would have any use for that information. "Wouldn't want any wives or girlfriends pounding *my* head into the floor."

"That sounds promising." The gleam in Dean's eyes was impossible to miss.

"Not really. Sorry."

The gleam faded. "What's the matter? Don't you like cowboys?"

Every woman I'd ever known had a soft spot for a guy in boots and chaps—even *I* had been to a rodeo in my youth—but I saw no need to encourage this bunch, especially since I wouldn't be there long enough for any preference of mine to matter. "Cowboys are okay, I guess." I shrugged. "I've always been partial to firefighters."

On the word, six pairs of eyes slid toward Wyatt.

"I'm not a firefighter anymore." With a scowl as ominous as a tornado-spawning storm cloud, he got up from the table, aimed a curt nod in my general direction, and stalked out of the room.

The inevitable flush stung my cheeks as I watched him disappear through a doorway that presumably led to the men's sleeping quarters.

Nick leaned closer. "He's a little touchy about that fireman thing," he said in a confiding whisper. "Don't worry about it."

A *lot* touchy was more like it. I wished someone had warned me.

"I'll go get my computer," Nick went on. "You can look at it while we get your room ready. Then maybe we can play pool or cards or watch a movie or something."

"Hey, now," Calvin said. "Is anyone going to help with the dishes?"

"I'm pretty sure it's Wyatt's turn," Dean grumbled.

"I'll do it." Joe scooted his chair back from the table. "Might be best if we left Wyatt alone for a while."

There was a story in there somewhere. I, of course, would never have the nerve to ask for the details.

Story of my life.

Nick set his laptop at the head of the table. "You'll be warmer sitting over here by the woodstove."

Rising from my chair, I came around the table and took the seat Joe had just vacated, opened the computer, and pushed it toward him. "Go ahead and type in your password and I'll work on it."

His hesitation told the tale.

"You mean you don't even have this thing password protected?"

Nick hung his head. "No. I never thought it was necessary. It's not like I have anything worth stealing."

I shook my head sadly. I'd seen the dish on the roof of the bunkhouse, so I could safely assume they had Internet access. "Ever buy anything online?" If he was visiting porn sites, chances were good he'd paid for something.

"Well, yeah. Sometimes."

"Then you have something worth stealing. And you can pick up a virus anywhere." Figuring that what Bull had already said was chastisement enough, I skipped the lecture about porn sites being the most notorious source of malware. "Does your wireless access have a password?"

He nodded. "It's bunkhouse7—all lowercase."

"My, how original." At least it wasn't 123abc.

Seeming to ignore my sarcasm, he said, "It started acting weird a couple of months ago—loading pages real slow and then going somewhere other than where I wanted to go. Now, anytime I connect to the Internet, it just keeps opening page after page after page. Can you fix it?"

"Probably. I'll start out in safe mode and see what I find. Worst-case scenario is that I may have to take it down to zero, boot from the disk, and install a new operating system, which means you'd lose all your data. Is there anything on here you can't live without?"

He hesitated. "Naw. Not really. Can't do anything with it now anyway."

"I'm guessing you don't have any antivirus software installed on it, right?"

The blank look I received answered my question. This kid obviously needed a crash course in computer protection.

"Okay. Let me play with it and see what I come up with."

"Great!" Nick said. "I'll go help Dean and Sonny clean your room."

Bull said something about going out to water the horses and left the room. Joe and Calvin were tidying up the kitchen, which left me alone in the mess hall. I was grateful for the quiet seclusion. I had always done my best work without anyone hanging over my shoulder, and I'd certainly never had to wonder what a computer thought of me. Dogs were the same way. Simple, straightforward, no hidden agendas.

Must be why I like them so much.

Nick was right about his computer being infected. It was an absolute mess, in addition to being full of dust. Several of the keys were sticky—a sniff suggested he'd been eating strawberry jam while surfing the net. Figuring I needed more equipment, I went out to my car and gathered up a few things along with my own laptop. After cleaning the keys and blowing out the dust with canned air, I got to work on the virus problem. It wasn't hopeless, but after about thirty fruitless minutes, I downloaded an antivirus program onto a thumb drive from my own computer, ran it on his machine, quarantined and deleted several nasty bugs, and rebooted.

"Yes!" Clearly, I hadn't lost my touch. I set up two user accounts, one with administrator privileges and one without, and defragged the machine. It was still acting a bit sluggish, and after scanning the memory usage, I opened his pictures file and wished I hadn't.

Nick stuck his head in about the time my blush was subsiding. "How's it going?"

"Fine," I said. "But you have some work to do."

"What do you mean?"

"Your pictures file is seriously slowing down the performance speed. You need to divvy them up into folders."

"You've been looking at my pictures?" His voice was a barely audible squeak.

"No," I lied. "Just noting the vast number of them."

"Oh." He sounded relieved, as well he should. The brief glimpse I'd had showed me some things I would have thought were physically impossible. Maybe they were. With the advent of digital photography, the old saying that pictures don't lie didn't hold much water anymore.

"You need to come up with a password—two, actually. One for your regular user account and one for an administrator account. They need to be fairly complex. You can write them down if you need to. It's unlikely anyone would ever break into your desk and find them, but once you go online, you're fair game."

He pulled up a chair and sat down beside me. "Why two?"

"You've been surfing the net using an admin account and no firewall, which amounts to computer suicide. Most viruses can only take over your machine if they get into it on the admin level."

Nick nodded as though he understood, but whether he would take any of it to heart remained to be seen. I'd given enough computers a second and third debugging to know that not everyone heeded my advice.

Dean and Sonny returned. "Your room's all ready," Dean announced. "Want us to bring in your stuff?"

Unlike most women my age, I already had the most essential items with me, namely, my dog and my computer.

I'm such a nerd.

However, similar to most women my age, I'd over-packed. "Don't bother. I'll get it. I won't need much." A toothbrush, my allergy meds, pajamas, and a change of socks and underwear would be plenty—and would save having to lug it all back out to the car in the morning.

Dean's mutinous expression said otherwise. "You will if you're staying more than one night."

I'd never known any men to be so anxious for my company before. Generally speaking, unless they needed me to fix something, I tended to go unnoticed. I'd been told there was nothing wrong with my appearance, although Dean's "gorgeous blond" remark was unusual—and he'd been standing behind me when he said it.

Then I remembered what Nick had said. These guys weren't horny. They were lonely.

They probably never had much in the way of company. Never anyone to liven up their lives with a visit. Never anyone new, whether that person was male or female. Even though they were probably more interested in women than men, I doubted that was their only reason for wanting me to stick around. Case in point, Sonny and Nick, who were roughly the same age as my much-younger brothers, and Calvin, who was my grandfather's contemporary. Aside from that first meeting with Wyatt, everyone had been very hospitable—not at all like I'd expected them to be.

I gave in. "If you insist. Just don't fuss when I ask you to carry it all back out to the car."

"Wouldn't dream of it," Dean said with a wicked grin. "I'll even help you unpack."

Discovering what he thought of my rather plain underwear wasn't high on my list of priorities. I wondered if the foreman's quarters had a lock on the door.

"No need for that," I said quickly.

"Ah, but if we unpack your stuff, you'll stay longer."

His logic was a tad faulty, even if it did make me smile. "Yeah, all of the twenty minutes it'll take me to stuff everything back in my suitcase."

"Touché." His smile broadened. "I'll help you anyway."

"And I owe you something for fixing my laptop," Nick said. "You gotta give me time to pay you back."

Dean let out a derisive snort. "What are you gonna pay her with? Rides on your horse?"

"Actually, I was thinking this might be more appropriate." With no further warning, Nick snaked out a hand to cup my cheek and turn my head toward him. His lips immediately fastened on mine, triggering a full-body blush that left me too astonished to protest. A swipe of his tongue brought me to my senses, and I pulled away.

"Son of a bitch," Dean exclaimed. "I thought you said she was too old for you."

"I didn't say that," Nick said. "She did." Grinning, he added, "Besides, I need all the practice I can get."

His cheeky grin reminded me of Tom Cruise and how the friends of his older sisters reportedly used him for kissing practice. If that was what these cowboys thought I was good for, I probably shouldn't complain— especially since the kiss Nick had just given me was only the third I'd ever received from anyone outside my family. A more adventurous woman would've gone back for another round.

Too bad I wasn't adventurous.

Still, as cures for shyness went, being repeatedly kissed by a bunch of handsome cowboys wouldn't be half bad. It might even work.

Then my thoughts jumped to what kissing Wyatt would be like, and my gut tightened in a way I'd only read about in romance novels. Somehow I doubted he would need any practice, and I certainly didn't intend to ask him for lessons.

"You aren't the only one who needs help," Sonny declared. "I could use some of that myself."

"More like the blind leading the blind," I muttered.

Considering the amount of laughter in the wake of Sonny's remark, I doubted anyone other than Nick could have heard me. And if his wide-eyed expression was any indication, he'd not only heard my mutterings, he'd understood them.

Our eyes met, and the quick shake of my head stopped whatever he'd been about to say. I should've been used to that sort of thing, but I wasn't. A pang of regret knifed through my chest and tears filled my eyes. With a sniff, I looked away and reached into my pocket for the ever-present package of Kleenex. "Damned allergies."

Oddly enough, my sinus and allergy troubles hadn't bothered me much during the course of my journey. Apparently the Ohio Valley's bad rap for those conditions was well deserved. Wyoming, on the other hand, seemed to agree with me.

I am not *staying here.*

Certainly not long enough to warrant going off my meds.

A subtle clearing of Nick's throat drew my attention again. His puzzled frown prompted me to explain.

"I haven't dated much," I finally said. "Twice" would've been closer to the truth, but he didn't need to know that.

"Me either."

Poor kid. If he stayed on this ranch only working with other men, he probably never would. He obviously wasn't shy. The kiss he'd stolen proved that much.

Not like me. I'd worked with dozens of men and rarely spoke to any of them beyond what it took to do my job. Tongue-tied, my mother always said. Now that I'd solved Nick's computer issues, we probably wouldn't have anything to say to one another.

Calvin came in from the kitchen. "You boys aren't bothering Tina, are you?"

"No way." Nick crossed his heart. "She fixed my computer."

The trace of awe in his tone was something I'd heard many times before. The way computers worked was like magic to a lot of people. Being able to fix them made me a magician by default, although it was never that easy. If only I could banish viruses with a wave of my wand and a shout of *"Expelliarmo Virioso!"* But then, I'd never received an acceptance letter from Hogwarts.

"That was nice of her," Calvin said. "Got her room ready?"

"Yep," Sonny replied. "Clean as a whistle. We're just on our way out to bring in her stuff."

I caught a whiff of cigarette smoke as Calvin sat down in a nearby chair, coughing until he was visibly winded.

"You've gotta quit that nasty habit, old man," Dean advised him. "Those smokes are gonna kill you."

"We're all gonna die someday," Calvin said. "Just a question of when."

My grandfather had shared that same attitude. Although he'd never explained it to me, I'd heard somewhere that the most valiant soldiers were those who considered themselves dead even before they went into battle. At first, that mind-set seemed rather fatalistic. But if you had to rationalize risking your life to save the lives of others, what better way to do it than to deem it already lost?

What I didn't understand was why that outlook persisted even after the war had ended. Was it because they'd convinced themselves of their death to the point they couldn't cope with survival? Grandpa had never listened to his doctors and only took his meds when I insisted. Perhaps he'd believed it pointless to try to save a man who was already dead and buried.

Shaking off my morbid thoughts had become increasingly difficult of late, and today was no different. I'd been on such a roller coaster of emotions. One minute I was up, thankful that Grandpa's suffering was finally over. The next, I was down, wondering how his life would have turned out if he'd been born on a different day and never been drafted into the Army.

In that moment, fatigue slammed into me like a runaway train, not creeping up on me the way it normally did. I was thankful for the bed I'd been offered, although truth be told, I would have been perfectly content to sleep in my car.

Ophelia nudged my hand. No doubt she was as tired as I was. This was the letdown after the taut wire I'd been stretched into finally snapped now that my tasks were complete. Silly. I was young enough to be able to handle the physical strain. It was the mental part that was sapping my strength.

"Wanna watch a movie?" Dean asked.

I stifled a yawn. "Sure. Although I'll probably nod off before it's over."

What kind of movies would cowboys enjoy? Probably not Westerns. Like any romanticized group of people, their lives were nothing like those depicted on the silver screen. I knew the feeling. I had to laugh at the way computer geeks on TV instantaneously hacked into someone else's machine when in reality it was a fairly time-consuming process. The one thing the screenwriters did get right was the lack of romantic liaisons among geeks.

And then there was Wyatt's firefighter thing. I could think of at least one popular series he certainly wouldn't want to watch. I couldn't help wondering what the deal was with that, although I had an idea it was destined to remain one of life's great unsolved mysteries.

I rose from my chair. "Ophelia needs to go out." To be honest, so did I. I hoped the foreman's quarters included a private bathroom or this arrangement would end right quick.

"You can show us what you want us to bring in for you." Dean nodded at Nick. "C'mon, Nick. Let's go get her stuff."

"Hold on a second." I darted a look between the two men. "This is voluntary, right? If I have to pay in kisses, I'll carry my suitcase myself."

The expression in Dean's eyes reminded me of the way Ophelia stared at me whenever she wanted to stay inside rather than go out in the cold. "Aw, come on, Tina. Nick got a kiss."

I arched a brow. "He was paying me back for fixing his computer. That was his choice of payment, not mine."

"Well, shit." He blew out a breath, then grinned. "Guess I'll have to work on my strategy."

I hoped his strategy wasn't anything like Nick's had been. Nick hadn't asked for that kiss. He'd taken it. Or given it. I honestly couldn't say which. If Dean wanted more than a kiss—and something told me he did—he'd damn well better be asking me first.

The trouble was, I had no idea what my reply would be.

Chapter 4

THE FOREMAN'S QUARTERS WERE ACTUALLY QUITE nice. In addition to a private bathroom, the room boasted its own television and recliner, a sturdy wooden desk and chair, along with a dresser, nightstand, and closet. I'd spent the night in a couple of hotels along my route that weren't as well appointed, nor had they been as clean. I wouldn't have expected a bunch of cowboys to be any great shakes as housekeepers, but they'd obviously had some practice.

I was surprised Joe hadn't taken advantage of the opportunity to move in there, although I was glad he hadn't. Somehow I couldn't see sleeping in the bunkhouse or bumping Joe or Calvin out of their room. I didn't even mind that the bed was only a twin.

The guys carried in my bags and thankfully didn't linger.

"We know you must be tired," Dean said when he caught me yawning. "We'll be in the mess hall if you decide you want some company." He pointed toward a door at the far end of the room. "That opens onto the hallway behind the kitchen so you can get to the mess hall without going outside. Calvin's room is next to yours."

"Thanks." My smile became another yawn. "Don't bother waiting up for me. I'm about done in."

He laughed. "And you were gonna drive to Cheyenne tonight."

"Yeah, well, best laid plans and all that." I said good night and closed my door.

Strange how quickly we slide into that mind-set. *My* room at the hotel. *My* room at home. *My* apartment— although I didn't have an apartment anymore and was essentially homeless. I couldn't see Mom throwing me out, but without a place to call my own, I felt as though I'd been set adrift, leaving me vulnerable to the entreaties of a bunch of cowboys who seemed to want nothing more than the pleasure of my company.

I didn't wonder why anymore, but this was no place for me. After their computers were debugged, they would have no need of me, and I certainly had no intention of becoming the bunkhouse whore.

As if I could. Bunkhouse virgin would be more like it. Anyone taking on the whore job would need far more experience than I'd ever had. I doubted that reading steamy romance novels and fantasizing about hot, sweaty firefighters qualified me for the job.

Exhaustion left my brain wide open for thoughts of that nature to creep in. Whether I was ever intimate with a man didn't matter in the greater scheme of things. No planets would go undiscovered. No grand plans for world peace would be derailed.

Then again, maybe they would. Perhaps my unborn sons and daughters would be the very ones to save the planet from global warming and terrorism.

Or not. God, I was going nuts. I needed to shed a layer of…something. I had no idea what. Inhibitions? My own persona and history?

Ophelia licked my hand as though she understood my problem—or at least wanted to help.

I considered joining the men in the mess hall. The bed, however, was much too inviting. Recalling that I'd traveled through several states and three time zones—plus gaining more than a mile in altitude—explained the weird feeling, wired but exhausted. I'd gotten jet-lagged without ever boarding a plane.

A knock at the door interrupted my thoughts. I opened it to find Calvin standing in the hallway, appearing to be even more exhausted than I was. Granted, I'd only met him a few hours before, but something about him seemed…different. I couldn't put my finger on it.

His smile hadn't changed, nor had his genial nature. "If you need anything, I'm right next door."

"I'm sure I'll be fine," I said. "Good night and thank you for dinner."

"You're welcome." He smiled wistfully. "I'm so glad you came."

"Me too." Mine was an automatic response, although, oddly enough, I meant it. How often did a woman get to spend the night in an honest-to-goodness bunkhouse anyway? I caught myself before the something-to-tell-my-grandchildren thought had a chance to become fully formed in my mind.

More like something for my memoirs. That was, if anyone wanted to read them.

After Calvin left, I washed my face and combed out my hair before changing into my pajamas. I could hear the men's voices and laughter from the mess hall, despite the fact that the kitchen lay between us. Apparently, the rooms all interconnected in one way or another. With no need for soundproofing in a building intended to house a bunch of cowboys who knew one another and worked together every day, I suspected the interior walls were relatively thin.

I turned out all the lights except for the lamp on the nightstand and crawled into bed with the latest romance novel on my TBR list, an erotic paranormal guaranteed to keep me awake half the night.

It didn't.

When I awoke several hours later, the lamp was still on and my book had fallen forward onto my chest. Ophelia lay curled up on the rug by the exterior door, her head up and cocked to one side. She looked toward me with her ears pricked, listening.

A moment later, I heard what must've awakened me. *Tap, tap, tap.* The sound was coming from the wall my room must've shared with Calvin's.

Mice?

I doubted it. Especially after my tired brain finally made sense of the pattern.

I rose from the bed and went out into the hallway, passing through the kitchen to peer into the mess hall. The room was still warm—no doubt the men had added more wood to the fire in the potbellied stove—and the moonlight streaming in through the window was more than enough to prove it was empty.

Frowning, I retraced my steps, pausing at Calvin's door.

Then I heard the moan.

I raised a hand to knock, hesitating as I recalled that Calvin had served in the same war my grandfather had and possibly suffered from the same sort of nightmares. As a child I'd learned to ignore the restless mutterings and occasional shouts coming from Grandpa's room.

Later, when his health deteriorated, I'd often gone in to check on him, never knowing what I would find.

When yet another moan broke the silence, I knocked without hesitation. "Calvin? Are you okay?"

The door must not have been latched very well because with my knock, it swung wide. The room was dark and silent, save for his raspy breathing.

"Calvin?" I said again.

Although I didn't know Calvin well at all, I knew enough to realize something was wrong.

I flipped on the light.

Calvin lay on his bed, his hands clasped to his chest, his eyes squeezed shut. A bluish tinge circled his mouth as he sucked in one long, shuddering breath and then another.

And then none.

"Calvin!" I was shouting now, praying someone would hear. I ran to the bed and shook him. Receiving no response, I screamed out the first name that came to mind. "Wyatt! Help!"

The thud of footsteps mingled with muttered curses. A pair of hands pulled me back, practically throwing me into the arms of someone else. Wyatt tilted Calvin's head back and leaned forward to listen.

"Not breathing," he snapped. "Sonny, call 911. Bull, bring the AED. Nick, give me a hand here."

I stared at him, unblinking, as he barked out orders and then, with Nick's help, pulled Calvin onto the floor and began chest compressions.

"I'll call the house," Joe said.

With all the other men accounted for, I realized I was in Dean's arms once again.

Regardless of who held me, my eyes were firmly fixed on Wyatt. Grim-faced and determined, he delivered the compressions with an ease that spoke of superior knowledge and skill. A white T-shirt stretched over his broad back, muscles bulged in his arms and shoulders, and his plain white briefs molded to his muscular buttocks.

I shook my head, trying to divert my attention from him to the dying man only to find that I couldn't do it. My eyes simply refused to watch another man die. Not Grandpa's friend. Not Calvin...

Wyatt was much easier to look at, along with Nick, whose ponytail was plastered to his bare back, a pair of navy blue boxers his only garment.

The two men worked together like a practiced team, Nick delivering breaths while Wyatt pumped rhythmically on Calvin's chest. When Bull came running in with the AED, Wyatt ripped Calvin's nightshirt open and applied the pads.

"Analyzing," the robotic voice of the AED announced. After what seemed like forever, the machine advised a shock and charged with a siren-like wail.

Wyatt shouted, "Clear!" and pressed the button.

A jolt shook Calvin's body. Another analysis followed.

Wyatt pressed his fingers to the side of Calvin's neck. "I feel a pulse."

Nick delivered another breath, then waited a moment. "He's breathing."

"An ambulance is on the way," Sonny announced.

"Sure glad you talked us into getting that AED for the bunkhouse," Bull said to Wyatt. Only then did I realize the only part of Bull that was adequately covered was his upper lip.

Too late, I glanced away.

What has been seen cannot be unseen.

"He's the reason I wanted it," Wyatt said. "I knew we'd have to use it on him someday."

"You okay?" Dean's voice in my ear nearly had me jumping out of my skin.

"Yeah. I heard him…tapping on the wall, moaning."

"Good thing you were here," Dean said. "Otherwise, we wouldn't have found him until morning."

Shivering, I turned in his embrace, making no protest as he held me against his bare chest, my arms folded over my breasts. Considering how scantily clad the rest of the men were, I was afraid to look down.

Wyatt sat back on his heels and pulled his shirt up to wipe the sweat from his face. "He's not out of the woods yet, and we're a long damn way from a hospital." He glanced at Sonny. "Better check his medicine cabinet and see what he's on."

"If he's anything like my grandfather," I said, "he has plenty of meds he doesn't take."

Wyatt nodded. "Wouldn't surprise me a bit. He's a stubborn old cuss."

Sonny returned a few moments later, an assortment of pill bottles stashed in a sling made from the front of his T-shirt. "He's got lots of them."

Wyatt examined the bottles, one by one. "Judging from the dates on these, he hasn't taken them in months."

There it was again—that fatalistic *I'm already dead, so why bother* attitude. Calvin obviously subscribed to it, but that didn't mean the rest of us had to like it. I could sense Wyatt's frustration—the expression in his eyes, the tautness of his stance. Oh, yes. I knew that feeling quite well. The utter futility of trying to save someone who didn't want to be saved.

Nevertheless, they had saved Calvin—at least for the moment. When he regained consciousness, he might thank them or he might hate them for interfering. Grandpa had threatened to come back and haunt us if we ever resuscitated him. I wondered if Calvin had voiced his opposition to having an AED in the building. Obviously it was there to be used on anyone who might need it. Bull and Joe both appeared to be in their forties, and though they seemed healthy enough, Bull was also a smoker, and it wouldn't be the first time a man their age had heart trouble. Calvin, however, was still the most likely recipient.

One glance at Wyatt proved he was itching to do more. Although firefighters had first responder training, Wyatt didn't seem satisfied even with that skill level. I could see the need in his eyes—even the way he breathed—he wanted to start an IV, whip out a scalpel, and perform open heart surgery right there on the bunkhouse floor.

And this man was a cowboy?

No doubt cowboys had plenty of opportunities to display their heroism. They rescued strays from ravines, killed rattlesnakes, and delivered calves and foals. Back in Wild West days, they went after rustlers and thieves. But Wyatt?

He might as well have had *To Protect and Serve* tattooed on his chest.

Perhaps there was a bit of Wyatt Earp in him after all.

I heard other voices, although no sirens as yet. Two of the cutest people I'd ever seen rushed in, the woman tiny and dark-haired and the man of medium height with longish blond curls. No doubt these were the owners of the ranch.

What a way to meet the boss.

"I checked on the ambulance," the woman said. "They're about twenty minutes out. How is he?"

"He's breathing and has a pulse, but that's about all I can say," Wyatt replied. He held up a prescription bottle and shook it. "Might be in better shape if he'd been taking these like he should."

The woman knelt beside Calvin and stroked his forehead. "Stubborn as an old mule." She blew out a sigh. "Just like Dad."

"He's not coming down here, is he?" Wyatt seemed slightly alarmed at the prospect.

"You think I could make him stay away?" she said with a snort. "He went to get the truck. I'm surprised he didn't beat us here."

The squeal of brakes and scattering of gravel heralded the patriarch's arrival.

"That'll be him now," the blond man said. He looked at me as though he had only just noticed me standing there. A frown flitted across his brow, then he held out a hand. "I'm Dusty Jackson. This is my wife, Angela." He paused as the epitome of the crusty old rancher came through the door, no doubt moving much slower than he would have liked. "And that's my father-in-law, Jack Kincaid."

Jack stared at Calvin, lying on the floor. "Is he dead?"

"Not yet," Wyatt replied. "I just hope that ambulance gets here soon."

"Think we oughta load him in the truck and meet them?"

"To be honest, I'd be afraid to move him," Wyatt said. "Better wait for the medics."

The old man nodded. Even he seemed to defer to Wyatt's authority, and he didn't strike me as the type to defer to anyone. Barely missing a beat, he turned toward me. "Now that we have that settled, will someone please tell me why this woman is in the bunkhouse snuggled up with a naked cowboy?"

Chapter 5

"I wanted to ask that question myself," Angela said. "Although I probably would've phrased it differently."

Under any other circumstances, my situation would've been funny. At the moment, however, it was awkward in the extreme. I started to draw away from Dean only to find he wasn't letting me go, despite the fact that he wasn't the only naked man in the room.

At least he hadn't been the only one a moment before. Bull's retreating footfalls sounded like, well, a stampeding bull. Dean probably would've joined him if he hadn't been using me as a shield.

"It was sort of…accidental," I said.

"She's here to see Calvin," Dean explained—which sounded even worse than being caught in Dean's arms.

I had to salvage this quickly or Jack Kincaid would probably run me off the ranch with a shotgun. "My grandfather left some things to Calvin in his will, so I stopped by here on my way back from scattering his ashes in the Tetons. I was asleep in the next room and heard Calvin tapping on the wall. Thought I'd better check on him."

"Good thing you did," Angela said. With a wag of her head, she added, "Poor Calvin. As if we haven't had enough trouble lately." Her lips formed a grim line that twitched into a tiny smile as her gaze slid past me. "Hold on a sec, Dean." Crossing the room, she snatched the covers from Calvin's bed. After tossing a sheet to Dean, she knelt beside Calvin and spread a blanket over him, then tucked a pillow beneath his head. She glanced up at Wyatt. "Has he said anything?"

"No." Grimacing, he blew out a sharp exhale. "Just wish we had some oxygen to give him."

"The ambulance should be here soon," she said. "I told them what to expect."

Dean finally backed away and wrapped the sheet around his waist, but not before I saw something else that couldn't be unseen. Despite being a head shorter than Bull, Dean certainly had him beat in the dick department. The muscles were nice too. Deciding it was safer to look at my dog, I turned toward her just as she sprang to attention.

"I hear sirens." I didn't, of course. I'd seen Ophelia's "siren" stance enough times to know that she heard them perfectly.

Wyatt arched a skeptical brow. "Who are you? Radar O'Reilly?"

Obviously I wasn't the only one who'd ever stayed up watching late-night reruns of *M*A*S*H*. My snappy comeback died on my lips as I finally heard the same thing Ophelia had, and so did everyone else.

Angela heaved a sigh. "Thank God."

Figuring the time had come for me to fade back into the woodwork, I was inching my way toward the door when the ambulance crew came bursting through it.

Dean must have had the same idea. Taking my hand, he pulled me out into the hallway as soon as the medics had cleared the threshold.

"Sorry about that," he said with a sheepish grin. "Sleeping in the nude sometimes has its drawbacks."

"Only sometimes?" I echoed. "Don't you get cold?"

He shrugged. "Not when I have you to keep me warm."

As suggestive remarks went, this was one of the more blatant I'd ever received, and the accompanying smirk added even more fuel to the fire. "True, but I've only been here for a few hours. Considering where you live, it's a wonder you haven't frozen to death."

His gaze swept me from head to toe. "No chance of that happening to you, is there?"

"Probably not." Oddly enough, now that the excitement was winding down, even my thick flannel jammies weren't doing the job. I was actually shivering, although I couldn't decide whether those tremors were due to the ambient temperature or the fact that I was talking to a man dressed in a sheet.

Or maybe it was because I'd seen his penis.

Until a few minutes before, I'd never laid eyes on a naked man unless he was incapacitated by age and illness or was still in diapers. In one fell swoop, I'd seen two of them. Despite the fact that spending the night in a bunkhouse with a bunch of cowboys was a bit like hanging out in the men's locker room—you have to be prepared to see some skin—with a lady sleeping nearby, I would've expected them to at least keep their undies on.

Guess not.

I peered through the doorway. The ambulance crew had already put Calvin on a stretcher, hooked him up to a monitor, and placed a mask over his nose and mouth that I recognized as the type that delivered 100 percent oxygen. One guy was taking his blood pressure and the other was starting an IV.

All of that should have pleased Wyatt, but judging

from his taut, anxious posture, he was still itching to do something—anything—to help the old man. After taking care of Grandpa for as long as I had, I understood the need. Unfortunately, while I was pretty well versed in emptying bedpans and urinals and changing soiled sheets, this sort of thing was way beyond my level of expertise. If I stuck around, I would only be in the way.

"Looks like you guys have everything under control. I think I'll go back to bed."

My comments had been intended for Dean's ears alone. Nevertheless, Wyatt must have heard them. His piercing gaze met mine. "You saved his life. You know that, don't you?"

The blushes I'd been spared earlier that evening returned with a vengeance. Unable to look him in the eye any longer, I shifted my focus to the indeterminate space between us. "I think you and Nick deserve the credit for that."

"Some," he admitted. "But you could've ignored the sounds you heard."

I shook my head. "Not after I realized he was tapping out SOS."

"You know Morse code?"

A short laugh escaped me. "Everyone knows that much, don't they?"

His eyes narrowed. "Maybe."

"We're just glad you did," Angela said. "What did you say your name was?"

Only then did I realize I had never introduced myself; I had merely explained my reasons for being there. "Tina Hayes. Calvin and my grandfather served together in Vietnam. They…kept in touch."

For the first time, Jack Kincaid looked at me with something bordering on approval. "I'm very sorry to hear of your grandfather's passing, ma'am." He drew in an unsteady breath. "Calvin is a good man. I sure don't want to lose him. Thank you."

Much more of that, and I would be in tears. I didn't even trust myself to speak. With a nod and a tight smile, I went back to my room.

I awoke the next morning wondering if Wyatt's fire-fighting skills might be the next ones he demonstrated because judging from the smoke and the beeping smoke alarm, the bunkhouse was on fire. Then again, nothing smelled quite like burned eggs.

When I dashed into the kitchen, my only consolation was that Dean wasn't naked.

Consolation? Hmm... I wasn't too sure about that, but he was the one holding the fire extinguisher while Sonny, Joe, and Nick were fanning the smoke out through the open doorway. Ophelia took the opportunity to make a hasty exit.

"Sorry about that," Dean said. "We were trying to fix breakfast for you."

A quick head count revealed two missing cowboys. "Where are Bull and Wyatt?"

"They followed the ambulance to the hospital and aren't back yet," Nick replied. He aimed a scornful glare at Dean. "Wish Bull had gone by himself. Wyatt actually knows how to cook."

"I'm sure he does." If Wyatt had been stationed in a firehouse, he'd undoubtedly done his share of kitchen duty. "It's nice of you to try, but once the smoke clears, I can fix my own breakfast."

Sonny gazed at me with hopeful eyes. "Could you cook something for us too?"

"You mean you haven't eaten either?" I glanced at the clock, which read eight thirty. By that time, I'd have expected a bunch of cowboys to be up and gone for the day.

"Not yet," Nick said. "We, uh, kinda slept in this morning."

"I don't blame you. None of us got much sleep last night." I paused, yawning as Ophelia trotted up the steps and into the kitchen. No doubt she also wanted breakfast. "And, yes, I can fix breakfast for all of us. Just let me get dressed, and I'll be right back."

"Great!" Joe said. "We'll have this mess cleaned up in no time."

I went back to my room and put out some food for Ophelia. I was about to change into my jeans when I realized I probably didn't need to.

Normally, the thought of four men seeing me before I'd washed my face and combed my hair would've embarrassed me half to death. But that was prior to last night's drama. Each of these guys already knew what I looked like in my pajamas, and I'd seen one of them naked. I reminded myself that I was wearing flannel jammies, not a slinky, see-through negligee. I put on my robe and slippers and returned to the kitchen.

"I'll get dressed later," I said. "Any idea where I might find an apron?"

All four men burst out laughing.

"You've got to be kidding," Dean said between chuckles.

"Yeah. Should've figured that." I heaved a sigh. "Okay. What do you all normally have for breakfast when Calvin's here?"

"Bacon, eggs, toast, and coffee during the week," Nick replied. "Pancakes on Saturdays, biscuits and sausage gravy on Sundays."

That didn't sound too bad—until I realized I had no idea what day it was.

Still lagging a time zone or two behind.

"Umm…my brain is kinda foggy. What day is it?"

"Thursday," Nick replied. "Although if you want to make pancakes, we're good with that."

I'd made plenty of chocolate chip pancakes for Grandpa. Quite often, that was the only thing I could get him to eat, and I hadn't made any since he died. This situation was different, but it still didn't take me long to decide to go with the usual Thursday menu, especially since I only knew how to make enough pancakes for one man. Something told me I wouldn't find any pancake mix in the pantry.

"Let's stick with bacon and eggs. If you guys will make the coffee and toast, I'll handle the rest. Just tell me how much you want."

The men each put in their order, which sounded like an awful lot to cook at one time until I remembered the restaurant-style griddle. I'd never used anything like it, but once I scraped off the burnt eggs and got it heated up again, I had to admit, it was freakin' awesome.

The eggs were about done when Dean sidled up behind me, smoothing his hands over my hips.

Amazingly, I didn't even flinch—a testament to what "snuggling up" with a naked man had done for me the night before. "Coffee's ready and the toast is toasting." He inhaled deeply. "And you smell good enough to eat."

Fortunately, I caught myself before asking him if he really wanted to eat me.

Talk about your suggestive remarks...

"Humph. That's what happens when you fry bacon without an apron."

He buried his face in my hair and inhaled again. "Doesn't smell like bacon to me. Smells like *you*."

"You just like my brand of shampoo."

"And you need to learn how to take a compliment. If I say you smell good, you smell good. Period." He followed that up with a kiss on the side of my neck that made me drop the spatula.

"Will you stop pestering her?" Nick snapped. "We've already had one fire in the kitchen this morning."

The steam from the griddle was reaching stifling proportions—at least I thought that was where the heat was coming from. I reached up and switched on the exhaust fan.

"Damn. Forgot about that fan," Dean muttered. "Would've gotten rid of the smoke a lot quicker. Probably should've had it on all along."

Nick practically growled his impatience. "Important safety tip. Now, will you please leave her alone? I'm starving!"

"Okay, okay, *okay*." Dean threw up his hands and backed off.

I chuckled as I spotted the warning label on the hood controls. "Apparently, the griddle is never supposed to be operated without the fan. Wish I'd noticed that sooner."

"Yeah, well, you live and learn," Nick said, stepping forward with a plate. "Three eggs and six bacons, please."

Chuckling, I retrieved the spatula and dished up his portion. "There you go, Nick. Chow down."

The others lined up for their share, and I doled out the remainder.

Joe was last in line. "Didn't you fix any for yourself?"

"I'm having an omelet," I replied, putting the last two strips of bacon on my own plate. "I want to see how well it works on this griddle." I cracked two eggs into a bowl, added some milk and seasonings, stirred it up, and poured it on the griddle. "This thing is awesome," I exclaimed as the eggs began to sizzle. "Wish I had one at home."

"You, um, like to cook?" Joe ventured.

"I *love* to cook," I replied. "I used to take cookies into work once or twice a month." I paused as I recalled that the days I'd brought in goodies were about the only times my male coworkers ever acknowledged my existence. That old saying about the way to a man's heart being through his stomach was bogus, though. I was living proof of that. "I've always had this fantasy about cooking for a gang of hungry firemen or construction workers or something. That way I could cook as much as I wanted and nothing would go to waste." Deeming it best to omit the wild, orgasmic fun-and-games aspect of that fantasy, I let out a sigh. "Feeding my sick grandfather wasn't any fun at all. He was hardly ever hungry and picked at anything I gave him. I probably threw away more food than he actually ate."

Joe hesitated before darting a quick glance at me. He seemed almost as shy as I was, which struck me as an odd personality trait in a foreman. "Don't suppose feeding a bunch of hungry cowboys would fill the bill, would it?"

I blinked, realizing that here was my ultimate fantasy come to life. Granted, they weren't firemen, but six cowboys out riding the range all day would work up one heck of an appetite. I could make all the pies and cakes and casseroles and pot roasts and bread I wanted—aside from the fact that I'd seen two guys naked and one had actually kissed me on the lips. "Yeah. I guess it would."

"Calvin's bound to be in the hospital for a while, and even when he comes home, he'll have to take it easy for several weeks." Although Joe was ordinarily rather homely, his smile made him look downright sweet. "Think you could stick around until he gets better? We'd pay you, of course. I'm positive Angela would agree to it."

I returned my attention to the omelet, adding a slice of cheese before folding it and transferring it to my plate. "I dunno... I'd have to think about it."

"No problem. Let me know if you have any questions."

"Okay."

Joe sauntered off to join the other men in the mess hall.

Six cowboys. Six healthy, hungry cowboys who probably weren't terribly picky about what they ate. Most people would consider that work. To me, it sounded like a dream vacation. I might change my mind after a week or two, but *still*...

I had no plans—nowhere else I truly wanted to go. Nothing I absolutely had to do. These guys needed me to cook for them, and I'd already moved in—sort of. I might even get paid.

Or laid...

I carried my plate into the mess hall. Taking a seat next to Nick, I reached for the toast just as Dean handed me the platter. Sonny got up and poured me a cup of coffee like he'd been waiting tables all his life.

I dug into my omelet, too occupied with my own thoughts to take part in the men's conversation as they wolfed down their breakfasts. Beyond noting that they were discussing the work that needed to be done that day, I paid them no heed.

I wasn't the only woman on the ranch, nor, if the men were to be believed, was I the only one who knew how to cook. Wyatt could easily take over for Calvin, although whether he would want to take on the extra job remained to be seen. He might be *able* to cook but not care for the idea.

After that first terse meeting, Wyatt was starting to grow on me. In the beginning, I'd only gotten a "get lost" vibe from him. I had no clue how he felt about me now, but I had earned at least a smidgen of his approval. Still, Joe was the foreman, and as such he had some authority. As long as Wyatt didn't make me too miserable and Dean didn't get too flirty, I figured I could handle the job.

The one thing I refused to do, however, was to stick around if there was any resentment toward me. I'd had to deal with enough of that in my previous job. Most of the men had ignored me, but some were openly antagonistic—like I was trespassing on their turf or some such nonsense. As a result, I'd been given some of the crappier jobs. My only consolation was that none of them had expected me to make the coffee.

These men, on the other hand, would probably only resent me if I tried to tell them how to take care of cows and horses. I didn't know a thing about ranching, and if I kept to myself, they could go on as they had before. All I had to do was feed them. Any kisses I might receive would simply be a perk. If I played my cards right, I might even get more than that.

Dream on, Tina.

I took a sip of my coffee, only to stop short as I realized every eye was on me. "What?"

"Thinking pretty hard, huh?" Dean asked.

"Evidently." They seemed to be expecting an answer to something. Too bad I hadn't heard the question— although I could probably make a good guess.

"I said, 'great breakfast,'" Dean explained.

"Oh…thanks."

"Could I have an omelet like that tomorrow?" Sonny asked.

"Me too," Nick said. "Looks great!"

I glanced at Joe. "What did I miss?"

"I, um, told them about the job offer."

"And?"

"They all approve and want you to start right now," Joe replied.

"Yeah," Nick said. "We think it's a terrific idea. Think you could make us some lunch to take with us?"

Clearly, I was hired. "Sure. What would you like?"

Chapter 6

NOT HAVING BEEN GIVEN MUCH TIME TO PREPARE, that first lunch was pretty ordinary. I made some ham and cheese sandwiches and packed up several bags of fruit and chips.

Dinner was a different story.

Joe must've called Angela and told her about me staying on as the cook because she came down to the bunkhouse soon after the men had gone off to do whatever it was cowboys did all day. Left to myself, I wouldn't have had the first clue as to how many chickens to fix for dinner or even when to have it ready. Thankfully, Angela had done some cooking for the men and was able to give me a few pointers.

"They usually eat at six, and you'll need at least three chickens," she said in response to my questions. "Four if you want leftovers."

"Wow. How on earth can you afford to feed them?"

"We raise most of the meat—the freezer is full of beef, pork, and chicken. We also grow some vegetables, and I do a lot of canning and freezing. I make a run into town once a week for anything else we need. Calvin gives me a list."

"How is he?" I asked. "Have you heard anything?"

"Wyatt called about an hour ago and said Calvin was back in the coronary care unit after an emergency cardiac catheterization. The cardiologist said he'd put in three stents and that Calvin's vital signs are stable. He's still not awake, though." She shrugged. "All we can do now is wait and hope for the best. Wyatt and Bull are on their way home. I'm gonna head over there later this afternoon. Sure wish he had some family we could call."

"I take it none of you has power of attorney for him?" Mom had been Grandpa's POA, which was a tough job even for a relative. To be POA for an employee would be strange to say the least.

"No. I wish we did. Right now, the doctors are making decisions on an emergency basis." She paused, biting her lip. "As far as I know, he doesn't have a living will, but I'm guessing he wouldn't want to be on life support."

"I don't doubt it. My grandfather didn't want any of that." Mom and I had made a point of having all the legal details in place long before they were needed. But then, we were family. This was different.

"It'd be nice to know for sure." She patted my arm. "I hope you're up to this. I'll be gone for a couple of days at least."

Recalling all the wide-open spaces I'd driven through to get to the Circle Bar K, I couldn't help wondering just where that ambulance had taken Calvin. "Where is he?"

"Salt Lake City," she replied. "They flew him out of Rock Springs in a helicopter." She paused, smiling. "Poor Wyatt. I can't imagine driving all the way to Salt Lake and back with Bull—but then, Wyatt is one of the few people who can get Bull to be quiet for more than five minutes."

I'd already picked up on the fact that Bull was quite a talker. Steering clear of both of them when they came back might be best. "They're probably too tired to talk much by now." I knew that feeling too, the mute numbness that came with total exhaustion. Toward the end of Grandpa's long illness, I'd gone for days grabbing snatches of sleep whenever I could, never truly getting enough rest.

She nodded. "At least they can take turns driving. Anyway, they won't be back until later this afternoon. Guess I'd better go get packed up myself, although I really hate to leave right now."

"You said something last night about having a lot of trouble lately. What kind of trouble?"

"Weird stuff," she replied. "Fences cut, cattle missing for a while, but then we find them straying. We fix the fences only to find another place cut a few days later."

"So nobody is actually stealing cattle, just cutting the fence?"

"Yeah. Like I said, it's weird because all it does is make more work for the guys."

"Ever seen any suspicious characters hanging around?"

Angela let out a mirthless bark of laughter. "Not yet. As big as this ranch is, it's damn near impossible to patrol all of it. At least, not with our limited manpower. Even having a couple of the guys ride the fence line every night wouldn't help much. The culprit could easily sit back and wait until they were gone and then cut the fence." She shrugged. "I guess some kids could be doing it as a prank, but I can't imagine why they would target this ranch in particular. None of the other ranchers I've talked to have had this problem."

"That *is* weird," I agreed. "Is there anybody who might be holding a grudge?"

"Not that I can think of, unless we've got enemies we don't even know about."

"That's doubtful. Most of us know who our enemies are." I smiled. "I'll keep an eye out for anything weird, although I have no idea what would be weird on a ranch. Never been on one before."

Angela smiled back at me. "You might be just the one to notice something we wouldn't." Her expression sobered. "Listen, thanks for agreeing to stay on and help out. Everything's gonna be kinda chaotic around here for a while."

"I'll try to keep the guys under control."

"Yeah, right," she drawled. "I can really see that happening."

I laughed. "I only said I would *try*."

"I can't ask for more than that. Guess I'd better get packing. If you need anything from town, Dad or Dusty can give you the money and one of the guys can go with you."

"Might take me a while to figure things out, but I'll do my best. Right now, I just have to do some poking around in the cabinets to see what's here."

"I certainly don't envy you *that* job." She pulled out her cell phone. "I'll call when I get to the hospital. What's your cell number?"

I gave her the number and she entered it into her phone. "Most cell phones don't work out here, so I'll probably call the bunkhouse phone—there's an extension in your room—but it wouldn't hurt for me to have it just in case. I'll keep you all posted on Calvin, and if you can come up with anything regarding his next of kin, give me a call. Hopefully, he'll wake up and they'll let him come home soon."

She didn't mention the other possibility, which was that Calvin wouldn't wake up and wouldn't ever come home. I hated to seem pessimistic, but after the way Calvin had looked when I found him, I wasn't holding out much hope.

I wished her a safe trip and got back to work. Having heard the "three chickens" thing, I figured I'd better start thawing out some stuff.

As Angela had reported, the huge chest-type freezer and the pantry were full. I might run out of a few things, but meat and vegetables weren't among them. Nor, I soon discovered, would we run out of flour or sugar anytime soon. I found a fifty-pound bag of each in the pantry. I couldn't imagine going through such quantities before the ants got into them, but then, I'd never cooked for a bunkhouse full of cowboys.

I found a few cookbooks to guide me on making meals for a crowd, picked out some recipes, and got started. I'd already made an apple pie and had the chickens marinating and a pot of green beans simmering on the stove by three thirty when Bull and Wyatt returned.

"I thought you'd be gone by now," Wyatt said, his tone carefully neutral. Perhaps he was regretting that comment about me being responsible for saving Calvin's life.

Heat of the moment and all.

"I fixed breakfast for the men, and Joe asked me to stay on as cook until Calvin comes home. Angela seemed to like the idea."

Wyatt responded with a flick of his brow, clearly debating the pros and cons of having a female in charge of the bunkhouse kitchen.

Bull was more direct. "Yes, but do we really need you? I can cook, and so can Wyatt."

"Yeah, well, you two went off in the middle of the night and left the guys to fend for themselves, none of whom can even fry eggs. Dean nearly burned down the bunkhouse before I took over."

Wyatt still wasn't saying anything. I didn't know him well enough to know if that was out of character for him or not, although he'd been pretty outspoken so far. I waited while his gaze swept the kitchen.

"Bull," he began, "when's the last time we had apple pie?"

"Shit, I dunno," Bull said, scratching his shaven head. "Christmas, maybe?"

Wyatt nodded at the corner table where the pie sat on a cooling rack. "I think we oughta let Tina do the cooking. We'll have enough to do being a man short, what with all the trouble we've been having with the fences."

Bull's jaw dropped as he followed the direction of Wyatt's gesture. "Damn! Calvin hardly ever makes desserts. Says fresh fruits are better for us. Won't let us eat white bread, either."

"He's right about that," I said. "But I'm guessing he didn't have the time to do much baking if he had other work to do."

"Maybe so," Bull admitted. "I kept telling him he should just stay here and cook. He said it would be too boring."

Calvin was probably right about that too. Still, a man who required three stents to unclog his coronary arteries probably hadn't had much energy of late. Of course, sitting around doing nothing might have made them clog up faster. I had a feeling that spending all day cooking and tasting would pack even more pounds on my hips. Ophelia and I were going to have to go for lots of walks.

Bull gazed longingly at the pie. "Don't suppose we could have some of that now, could we?"

"Help yourself. Just make sure you leave some for the other guys."

"I'll only eat a small piece," Bull promised, crossing his heart.

I glanced at Wyatt. "What about you? Are you hungry? Or would you rather wait until dinner?"

As exhausted as both men were bound to be, my first choice would've been a nap. Clearly these guys were made of sterner stuff.

"I'll save the pie for after dinner," Wyatt said. "Right now, I'd kill for a grilled cheese sandwich."

Of all the things I would've expected a man like Wyatt to ask for, grilled cheese wasn't among them. Then again, as a comfort food, grilled cheese was tough to beat. "No problem. Have a seat. Want something to drink? I made some fresh tea."

"Sounds good." He took off his hat and sat down. Rather than sagging with exhaustion, his shoulders seemed sort of stiff, like he needed a massage more than a sandwich.

Had he ever had someone to rub his back after a hard day? Would he even want that? God knew I would never ask—or offer.

Just fix him a sandwich, Tina.

That much I could do. While the skillet was heating up, I poured them each a glass of tea. As I set the tea in front of them, I eyed the pie askance, noting that a full quarter of it was missing. "Small piece, huh?"

"Couldn't help it," Bull declared as he scooped up another forkful. "This is the best thing I ever ate in my life."

"I doubt that," I said dryly. "You know what they say about hunger being the best sauce."

"He couldn't be *that* hungry," Wyatt said. "It's not like we haven't eaten since we left here last night."

"Yeah, but we didn't stop for lunch," Bull reminded him. "I'm not used to missing meals."

"I take it you'd also like a sandwich?"

His fork clattered on the empty plate. "Umm... could you make that two?"

I glanced at Wyatt. "What about you. Is one enough?"

To my surprise, he winked. "Yeah. But I think I'd better have a piece of that pie before it disappears."

"Guess I should've made two pies. I'll know better next time." No wonder Calvin seldom bothered to make dessert. If he had, he wouldn't have had time to do anything else.

I, on the other hand, had time to spare. I even had time to make another pie before dinner.

I could get used to this.

I gave Wyatt a plate and fork before returning to the stove. As I buttered slices of bread and put them in the skillet, I realized I had time to make homemade bread, pots of soup that cooked all day, and any other time-consuming recipe that came to mind. Calvin probably felt rushed no matter what he fixed.

While the sandwiches were grilling, I took the opportunity to pick their brains a little. "I didn't get much of an orientation to this job. What do you guys like besides grilled cheese and apple pie?"

"Are you kidding?" Bull said. "We'll eat anything."

A short chuckle escaped me. "Somehow I doubt that. What about the style? Italian, French, Asian, Indian? Or strictly American?"

Bull seemed impressed. "You know how to cook all that stuff?"

"Some of it," I admitted. "But with Internet access and a computer, I can find a recipe for just about anything." I plated up the sandwiches and carried them over to the table. "All I need are the proper ingredients."

I stopped short when I saw the pie. Or what was left of it. "Hmm…" Apparently all cowboys considered a fourth of a pie to be the standard serving. "Definitely need to make another pie." I couldn't complain. After the way Grandpa picked at his food, watching food disappear was a welcome sight.

"I doubt it would go to waste," Wyatt said.

I was standing right next to him, so when he stretched out his arm behind me, for a moment I thought he was going to wrap it around my hips and pull me in for a hug. I held my breath for a second or two, then blew it out, strangely disappointed when he lowered his hand.

"Guess I'd better get started on it then." I turned and walked away.

Had he meant to hug me and stopped himself? Or was I imagining things? Dean would've done it. I was sure of that. Wyatt was different—not nearly as free with his attentions or affections. That wink was probably all I would ever get from him. Funny how it seemed to mean more than a kiss from Dean.

A sidelong glance caught him rubbing his right shoulder, then stretching his arm out again.

"Something wrong with your shoulder?" The words were out of my mouth before I even had time to think.

"Yeah. Wrenched it a few days ago. Hurt like a sonofabitch while I was driving." He raised his shoulder and rotated it a couple of times.

Clearly he hadn't meant to hug me at all.

Story of my life.

"I keep telling you to go see a chiropractor," Bull said. "Why doesn't anybody ever listen to me?"

"When have I had time to go to a chiropractor?" Wyatt retorted. "Besides, you know how they are; they want you to come back twice a week or some such bullshit."

"It's not bullshit if it helps," Bull snapped. "But you always were a stubborn bastard."

"A heating pad or a massage might help." Once again, I spoke without thinking.

I really need to stop doing that.

"Maybe." What was going on in Wyatt's head was anyone's guess, but the look he gave me could've bored a hole through steel.

Obviously, I should've kept my mouth shut. If he was as stubborn as Bull claimed, he certainly wouldn't take any advice from me.

Electing to drop the subject before I irritated him any further, I started on the second pie. One nice thing about apple pie, it was pretty simple. I'd even found a nifty gadget that would simultaneously peel, slice, and core an apple with a few turns of a crank.

I was mixing the dough for the crust when the guys finished and put their plates in the sink.

Yawning, Bull announced, "I think I'll take a nap until it's time to feed the horses."

"Good idea," I said. "You guys must be exhausted."

Bull headed through the doorway to the mess hall, leaving me alone with Wyatt. I caught myself holding my breath again as he paused behind me. Heat flowed from him like a summer breeze.

"You don't have to do that." His breath tickled my ear, tightening my skin into tingling goose bumps. "We could eat the rest of the pie and no one else would ever know."

My laugh was as weak as my wobbly knees. He wasn't even touching me and I could barely stand up. I'd be dropping the pastry blender next. "Think you could get Bull to keep the secret?"

"I dunno. Maybe not."

"Really? Angela said you could—or that you could at least get him to be quiet."

"True, but there's a difference between being quiet and keeping a secret."

I couldn't argue with that, but I didn't think I could take much more of his close proximity without dissolving into a bundle of overstimulated nerve endings. My heart was already beating out of control, flooding my cheeks with warmth.

I wanted him to go away and yet didn't want him to leave. I knew I would relax and breathe easier without him there, but I craved his presence anyway.

So why was he still standing there?

"Uh, Tina," he began. "Listen, what you said about a massage… That actually sounded pretty good." He paused, seeming reluctant to admit he needed help and even more reluctant to ask for it. "Think you could…?"

I stared at the bowl of dough. I didn't need to invent a reason why I couldn't stop what I was doing and rub his shoulder for him. But at the same time, I had this itch to get my hands on something other than pie dough.

And some itches *must* be scratched.

"Sure. Just let me wash my hands." I put a plate over the bowl to keep the dough from drying out and turned on the tap. After letting the water run until it was good and hot, I washed my hands, then dried them with a dish towel. When I turned toward Wyatt, my worst fears were realized.

He'd taken off his shirt and stood facing me, the broad expanse of his muscular chest, lightly dusted with dark, curly hair, fully exposed. "Where do you want me?"

Right here. Right now.

Heat sliced through my pelvis, stealing moisture from my mouth to send it gushing from my core. My attempt to swallow failed utterly. "There at the table is fine."

He would probably smell bad after being on the road all night and most of the day. Bad smells usually put me off immediately. I figured I was safe. But when I moved closer, he smelled fine. Not freshly showered, perhaps, but nice. "Do you have any ointment to put on it?"

"There's probably something around here some-where, but for now, just use a little olive oil."

I was hard-pressed not to laugh out loud. Getting my hands on a hot, studly cowboy might make my tempera-ture soar, but by the time I'd smeared him with olive oil, he would smell like a salad.

Not sexy at all.

Unfortunately, after dribbling oil on his back and placing my hands on his shoulders, I was forced to revise that assessment. Wyatt would've been sexy even if he'd smelled like a barn. And salads, on the whole, were quite tasty.

I squeezed my eyes shut, trying to block out the image of the powerful-looking muscles in his back and shoulders, but I couldn't hide them from my hands. His hair, although relatively short, curled at the nape. Using the excuse of massaging his neck, I touched it. For some peculiar reason, that affected me even more than touching his skin had done—the gesture was more intimate, somehow.

Eventually, I found the sore spots in his upper back and shoulder and kneaded them hard. Wyatt's groans and sighs were like candy, enticing me to keep going until I'd thoroughly massaged every muscle in his body. Twice.

After a glance at the clock proved I'd been at it for about twenty minutes, I figured it was time to quit or I was bound to do something really stupid—especially since he was getting to me on a level no real man ever had. Surely twenty minutes was enough. Then again, he wasn't asking me to stop. If anything, I got the distinct impression he wanted me to keep going forever.

But I had work to do, a pie to bake, and chickens to roast. "H-how's that?" My voice was hoarse and hesitant, no doubt due to the parched state of my mouth.

Despite his long, shuddering exhale, his throat sounded tight when he spoke. "Good—um, better. Much better. Thank you."

I took a step back as he got to his feet. "Glad I could help."

Rather than staring at the floor like I normally did, I

made the mistake of tilting my head back and making eye contact. His gaze held mine for a long moment. Once again, what went on behind those enigmatic eyes was anyone's guess. He certainly wasn't giving me any clues.

A flick of his brow signaled the end of the interlude. "Well then. I guess I'll leave you to it." He slung his shirt over his shoulder. "I might lie down for a bit myself."

All I could do was nod. I waited until his retreating footsteps died away before letting out the breath I was well aware I'd been holding.

I would get used to him eventually.

Yeah, right. Maybe by the time my car was packed and I was two hundred miles down the road.

Men had always made me nervous, but when it came to getting under my skin, Wyatt McCabe took first prize. Closing my eyes, I breathed deeply for a few moments before resuming my task. I still had a lot to do in the next two hours. Letting Wyatt freak me out wouldn't help get it done.

Chapter 7

ALTHOUGH IT MIGHT HAVE BEEN OVERKILL CONSIDER-ing everything else I'd cooked for dinner, knowing how to make my own version of those awesome cheddar cheese biscuits they serve at Red Lobster is sometimes too great a temptation to resist.

Nonetheless, it was while I was making them that I thought of a way to find out who Calvin's next of kin might be. I had forty years' worth of letters between Calvin and Grandpa. Somewhere during all those years of regular correspondence, Calvin was bound to have mentioned a few of his relatives.

It was a daunting task, but at least I would only have to go through the letters Grandpa had received. While his letters to Calvin might be interesting, I doubted they would contain the kind of information we needed. Starting at the beginning would yield the best results. If Calvin was estranged from his family—and the fact that no one knew anything about them led me to believe he was— the more recent letters probably wouldn't mention them.

"Holy shit." Nick stopped short in the doorway just as I was dousing the biscuits with spoonfuls of hot garlic butter. "What *are* you doing?"

"Yeah, I know it looks kinda decadent, but this is a special occasion—my first time fixing dinner for you guys and all."

"Oh, I'm not complaining," Nick assured me. "They smell awesome."

I couldn't argue with him. I'd been known to wolf down one or two before they ever made it to the table.

"How many do we each get?"

"Two," I replied. "Just like the cornbread Calvin makes for you."

He frowned as he counted the biscuits. "Um, I don't think you made enough."

"What do you mean? There are six of you guys, one of me, and fourteen biscuits."

"Dunno how to tell you this, but Dusty and Mr. Kincaid are joining us since Angela's gone. They're already in the mess hall."

As a rule I'd never been one to use profanity, but the *F* word was the first thing that came to mind. "Nice of them to warn me. Guess they figured Angela had said something. Obviously I should've gone with four chickens."

"Don't worry. We'll make it stretch. If we get hungry later, we'll make popcorn or something." He snickered. "I heard Bull and Wyatt already had their share of the pie." He peered at me through narrowed eyes. "You aren't gonna let them have any more, are you?"

"Do you really think I could stop them?" I scoffed. "Although with two extra mouths to feed, the serving sizes are gonna be pretty small."

Note to self: Never, ever let the guys help themselves to a pie.

I did some quick mental geometry and came up with a solution. "If we cut each pie in sixths, everyone gets a piece."

He hesitated just long enough to have verified my calculations. "That works."

"So how do you all usually do this? Line up with your plates like you did last night, or put everything on the table?"

"We usually line up, but putting it all on the table sounds good." A smile quirked his lips. "More like home."

I smiled back at him. "Then we'll do it family style. See if you can dig up some serving bowls."

Granted, it might cause some squabbling and make more dishes to wash, but having eaten at least one dinner with them, I knew they had a dishwashing rotation set up. No way was I doing the cooking *and* the cleaning—not all of it, anyway. I wondered if Wyatt would help out since he'd been slated for dishwasher duty the night before.

Great. Yet another occasion to bump elbows with him.

I still hadn't recovered from the back rub.

Nick found a huge platter and some serving bowls that didn't look as though they'd been used in a very long time. "Better wash these real quick. They're dusty as hell."

I stuck my head through the door to the mess hall. "I need somebody to set the table." The blank stares I received were proof that this serving style wasn't typical. "Come on now. All you have to do is put the plates and silverware on the table. If you can ride horses and rope calves, surely you can do that."

To my surprise, the old man let out a guffaw that sounded much stronger than he appeared. "Angela said you were gonna try to keep these boys in line. Looks like you've got the hang of it already."

Dean raised a hand. "I'll do it. Wouldn't want you to think we were a bunch of savages."

"I'm sure she doesn't think that," Dusty said. "Although Angela probably does."

"Oh, she does not," Bull argued. "She loves us."

If I'd had to choose the one cowboy Angela probably *didn't* love, it would've been Bull, although he was bound to have a few endearing traits. The fact that he'd gone with Wyatt to the hospital proved how much he cared about Calvin. Hopefully that wasn't his only attribute.

"I wouldn't be a bit surprised if she did," I said. "How about the rest of you come on in here and grab a dish?"

One nice thing about this job, at least at breakfast and dinner, there was plenty of manpower. Once the table was set, we sat down to eat.

Despite being seated between Nick and Dean with Wyatt directly across from me, I felt considerably more comfortable than I had the night before. My only wish was that when I'd met Mr. Kincaid and Dusty, I hadn't been in the arms of a naked man. Still, as first impressions went, it was certainly memorable.

The good-natured banter between the men died down once everyone was served. I couldn't decide if that was a good sign or not. I thought everything tasted okay, but it wasn't until Dean let out an orgasmic moan that I figured they probably approved.

Mr. Kincaid was more polite. "This is a fine dinner, ma'am."

"Wait 'til you taste the pie," Bull said around a mouthful of chicken. "Best thing I ever ate—although this chicken runs a close second."

"Yeah, well, that's what you said before," Wyatt drawled. "We'll see if you still feel that way when your stomach's full." He arched a brow at me. "That is, if Tina lets us have any."

Something in Wyatt's eyes made me feel as though he was referring to something other than pie. With a blush rising in my cheeks, I was too tongue-tied to respond.

Fortunately, Nick answered him. "We've already got that figured out."

Avoiding Wyatt's gaze, I focused on my plate as that peculiar awareness of my erogenous zones assailed me once again. Dean might have been sitting as close to me as the situation allowed—I was conscious of his body heat and every move he made—but that one look from Wyatt *did* something to me.

Was he aware of his effect on me? If so, had he been pulling my chain by asking for that massage? Even though Bull obviously knew about the injury, Wyatt could have exaggerated his pain.

I doubted it. As a general rule, men didn't invent reasons to get my hands on them, and I had certainly never offered my services. I didn't need to look any further for a motive. He had a sore shoulder, and, stupid me, I'd mentioned a massage.

"Is there any news about Calvin?" Bull asked.

Dusty shook his head. "Not much. Angela called before I came down for dinner. He's moving around a little but still hasn't said anything."

"Think he might have brain damage?" Sonny asked.

"Maybe," Wyatt replied. "Although he was down for less than a minute before we started CPR, and we only had to shock him once."

"He's pretty old, though," Sonny observed. "And

he's a smoker. Might not take as long for that to happen to someone like him."

Recalling the bluish tinge around Calvin's mouth was reason enough to expect the worst. Even I knew that was a pretty ominous sign.

Wyatt shrugged. "We'll just have to wait and see."

"Angela said she wanted to try to locate Calvin's family," I said. "She didn't seem to think he had any." I glanced at the men gathered around the table. They had all worked with Calvin—some of them for many years. He was bound to have said *something* about his family. "Do any of you know who his next of kin might be?"

"He had a wife and kids once," Joe said. "They were killed in a car accident. Never heard him mention anyone else."

"His whole family?" I exclaimed. "How awful! But you say that like it happened long ago."

"Before he ever came here," Mr. Kincaid said. "He told me about it when I hired him. I'd never seen a man look so defeated. He's a good man and a hard worker, but I don't believe a body could ever get over something like that."

"No kidding." With that much loss, it was a wonder he'd been able to function at all. Then again, "riding the range" might've been therapy for him. Or a way to avoid getting close to anyone else.

Still, he'd corresponded with Grandpa for years— probably ever since returning from Vietnam. That was one connection he'd maintained. Surely there were others.

"I thought I'd take a look at the letters he sent to my grandfather. He's bound to have some cousins at least—maybe even a sibling or two. He might've mentioned them."

"If he does, I'm guessing they don't get along," Joe said. "He never talks about them. At least, not to me."

I glanced at Wyatt. He hadn't offered any ideas on locating Calvin's family, and judging from his expression, he never would. His gaze appeared unfocused but filled with such pain, he should have been crying out in agony. Was his shoulder bothering him again, or was it something else? Something much deeper and more lasting than mere physical pain? I recalled the way he'd reacted when the firefighter issue had been raised. Calvin wasn't the only man there who'd suffered. I could see it in Wyatt's eyes as clearly as if he'd been telling us his own life story.

As if he ever would. As little as anyone knew about Calvin's past, I had a pretty good idea nobody knew much about Wyatt's history, either.

"I'll start going through those letters after dinner," I said. "Even if I don't find anything there, I can do an online search of the census data or one of the genealogy sites. Does anyone know his full name and where he was born?"

"I can tell you his full name," Mr. Kincaid said. "Calvin Joseph Douglas. But as to where he was born or where he grew up…" The old man shrugged. "We might have it written down somewhere, but I couldn't say offhand."

I groaned. "There are probably a bajillion people in this country with the same name. Wish we at least knew which state he came from."

"We might find something in his room," Dean suggested. "Pictures or letters or something."

I smacked my forehead with the heel of my hand. "We've already *got* letters—tons of them—and they're probably still in the original envelopes. There's bound to be a return address on some of them. Calvin told me he'd kept all the letters he received from Grandpa too."

"Shouldn't be hard to find," Dean said. "He's only got a dresser and the one closet."

"I'll check the letters I brought with me first. I don't like digging around in other people's stuff." It had been tough enough going through Grandpa's things. Mom and I had chuckled over a few items, but there were so many more that had made us cry. Reading the letters he'd sent to Calvin would probably have me bawling in no time.

Then I remembered that a search of Calvin's room would be unnecessary because the letter-filled shoe boxes were still out in my car. *Great.* I'd hauled those boxes all the way from Louisville and hadn't bothered to deliver them.

Yet.

Wyatt cleared his throat, drawing the eyes of everyone present. "If I had to guess, I'd say Calvin was originally from Texas. Considering how long he's lived in these parts, his accent has probably faded some, but he still has traces of it."

I was pleased to note that Wyatt's stricken expression had been replaced with something more normal for him. Although he still seemed a bit grim, for the time being, he appeared to have overcome whatever ghosts from his past had reared their ugly heads.

"Thanks," I said. "That'll give me someplace to start in a search—if it comes to that."

Wyatt's gaze had nearly reduced me to jelly yet again when Dean gave me a nudge. "I'll give you a hand with those letters."

As I thanked him for the offer, I couldn't help wondering why someone as blatantly flirty as Dean didn't have a similar effect on me. Being unused to male attention, I couldn't explain the difference.

To my surprise, when I rose from the table, each and every one of the men practically leaped to his feet. The sudden display of manners was probably due to the presence of two of the ranch's owners, although I doubted they would've behaved the same way if Dusty had been there without Mr. Kincaid.

"It's very kind of you to take an interest in Calvin," Mr. Kincaid said. "I realize you don't know him very well, but..." Despite his gruff tone, there were tears shimmering in his eyes.

I had to blink back a few tears of my own. "He was my grandfather's friend—one of the few, actually— and probably the one he'd known the longest. Grandpa would want me to do whatever I could to help him."

"You're a good girl, Tina." The rough edge to his voice was even more pronounced. "I'm sorry I doubted you last night."

"No worries," I said. "Given the circumstances, your reaction was understandable."

Nodding, he glanced at Dusty. "Think I'll head back to the house now."

Dusty evidently took the hint. "I'll walk back with you."

I wished them both good night and watched them leave. Jack Kincaid must've been a tough dude in his day. The remnants of his commanding nature were still there, although softened by time and age. Twenty years ago, he probably would've thrown me out on my keister and booted Dean out the door if he'd caught us together like that. Now he shuffled toward that same door on the arm of his son-in-law. I didn't have to think long to conclude that he didn't like the idea one little bit.

After clearing the table and confirming that Wyatt and Bull were doing the dishes, I went out to get the letters from my car.

Dean followed me, taking the boxes as I handed them out to him. "Sorry we missed those last night. We didn't figure they were anything you'd need."

"That's okay. I'm just sorry I forgot to give them to Calvin." Needing to voice some of the unsettling thoughts I'd been having, I added, "I hope I get the chance."

"You think he won't make it?"

I closed the car door and leaned back against it. "Being unconscious for so long kinda worries me. That can't be a good sign."

"About all we can do is hope for the best." He set the boxes on the roof of the car and took a step closer. He must've showered and changed before dinner. I hadn't picked up on the scent of sweat—human, equine, or otherwise—while sitting next to him. He smelled clean, without overpowering me with cologne. Just a touch to entice...

He only gave me a moment to wonder whether he'd worn it specifically for me before easing closer still. "Nice evening, isn't it?"

A shiver wormed its way up my spine as I nodded. The sun had already set behind the hills, tinting the sky with a turquoise hue. "A little chilly, though. Wouldn't want to stay out very long without a coat."

"Don't worry. I won't keep you." With that, he moved even closer to place a finger beneath my chin. "And I certainly won't let you get cold."

Tipping my chin up, he lowered his head until our lips were only a breath apart. "Thanks for fixing us such a great dinner." He slid his arms around me, pressing his palms to my back. "You've been at it all day. You must be tired."

"Um…maybe a little."

He began rubbing my back, reminding me of the way I'd massaged Wyatt's sore shoulder that afternoon. Wyatt hadn't exactly melted beneath my touch, but I came dangerously close to melting beneath Dean's.

"Dunno about you, but I didn't get much sleep last night. Not after holding you like that."

Clearing my throat with difficulty, I figured I should say something, although I had no idea which words to use. "We were all a little…upset."

"About Calvin? Yeah, maybe. But that wasn't why I couldn't sleep." His hands moved lower. "I was thinking about *this*."

He'd barely finished his sentence before closing the last whisper of space between us. My head swam as his soft, warm lips pressed against mine. Strong hands stroked my back, skimming my hip. Another step forward had me pinned against the car. With his body so snug against my own, I could feel his heart beating. Feel his lungs expanding. Feel his erection pressed against my stomach.

Only a few minutes before, Jack Kincaid had called

me a "good girl." I'd been referred to in that manner all
my life. I knew it wasn't the right time or place, but just
this once, I wanted to be bad.

Very bad.

Chapter 8

DEAN SEEMED MORE THAN WILLING TO ACCOMMODATE me. Deepening the kiss, he teased my lips with the tip of his tongue. Somehow, my hands were on his shoulders, sliding down to grip his upper arms. I could have pushed him away, but instead I pulled him closer, letting his tongue slip into my mouth. Gliding a hand to the back of his neck, I threaded my fingers through his hair. Earlier that day, touching Wyatt there had done something to me. Something I felt again. Only this time, I recognized it for what it was.

Intimacy. Passion. Desire.

I kept telling myself this was happening simply because Dean was as lonely as the other guys living in that bunkhouse. Joe might've had a girlfriend, but the others were starved for female companionship to the point that a woman like me, who'd been virtually ignored all her life, was now receiving more attention than she knew what to do with.

If movie plots were anything to go by, the next step would find Dean in my bed—or in the backseat of my car—making wild, passionate love to me. We would be tearing each other's clothes in our haste to get down to business. Funny, I'd never felt that kind of urgency about much of anything. Nor did I feel it then. Although I was perfectly willing to let nature take its course, I saw no need to rush.

Dean was right about one thing: I certainly wasn't

cold. On top of that, he tasted like apple pie. Would I compare this kiss to others I received in the future? I had no idea.

You're thinking too much, Tina.

Maybe the fact that I was doing so much thinking was a bad sign. Surely I should have been kissed senseless by now.

Or maybe I was already senseless. After all, I was on a ranch in the middle of Nowhere, Wyoming, leaning against my car while a handsome cowboy attempted to kiss my lips off. If that was sensible behavior, I'd obviously been following the wrong rules.

Following those rules was probably why I'd never had a boyfriend. I had always expected Prince Charming to ride up on a white horse and fall in love with a woman too shy to say a word or even look him in the eye. Thus far, he hadn't bothered to put in an appearance.

Still, whether I craved it or not, I was too straitlaced for a whirlwind romance. Resigning myself to the inevitable, I turned my head, effectively ending the kiss.

"Sorry," I whispered. "I'm not any good at this."

"I think you're doing fine." His voice was tempered with a thick, husky timbre. "But maybe I'm pushing too hard."

"Well…considering I only met you yesterday, you might be."

"Look, I know you think I'm just a big flirt, but I really like you, Tina."

I nodded slowly, wondering how many women he'd said that to. I was so naive. But there was one way to overcome that failing.

Experience. The amount I'd had thus far would fit

through the eye of a needle. "I like you too. Only I don't know how much yet."

His deep sigh contained a slight quaver. "Me either." A smile curled his lips as he traced the contour of my cheek with a fingertip. "I'd sure like to find out."

"And how do you propose we do that?"

"Whatever you want. I'm game."

Gulping in a breath, I took what was, for me, quite a plunge. "A little fun and games, maybe?"

His eyes lit up. "Really?"

"I'll only be here for a couple of weeks at the most. Nothing serious, of course, and no strings attached, but…"

Somehow, I doubted Dean had ever been serious about much of anything. The odds were much greater that I would be the one to fall for him. He was cute and likable. What more could a woman want in a man? Money? I didn't expect to marry a millionaire or even date one. The romance novels I'd read should've had me believing that young, sexy, single billionaires fell from the sky like rain in April.

For that matter, handsome cowboys were supposed to be as plentiful. I didn't doubt there were hoards of them in Wyoming alone, but cowboys who met the young, sexy, and single requirements were bound to be pretty rare. Aside from the fact that most women probably didn't envision living out their happily ever afters in a bunkhouse.

None of those things mattered because I was only there to help out for a short while. When Calvin recovered and returned to the ranch, I would go home. If he couldn't resume his position as cowboy and cook, the owners would hire someone else who could take on both jobs. Replacing one man with two people made no sense whatsoever.

"No strings, huh? I can handle that." Dean retrieved the shoe boxes from the roof of the car and offered me his arm. "What do you say we start by spending the evening in your room reading old letters?"

His sly grin led me to assume there would be more than letter reading going on, although I had absolutely no idea what to expect.

As we strolled back to the bunkhouse, I became aware of something I couldn't recall ever having felt before—a slick, wet sensation between my thighs. I'd never been around a man who'd even attempted to elicit that response from me. Evidently, I wasn't incapable. Dean had proved that with one kiss.

He climbed the steps to the porch and held the kitchen door open for me. As soon as I stepped inside, I wished we'd used the door that opened directly into my room. Wyatt and Bull were at the sink, washing dishes, and the scowl Wyatt aimed in my direction made me suspect him of spying on us. I couldn't have named all the emotions reflected in his eyes, but at least one of them was disgust—or maybe annoyance. Whatever it was, it certainly wasn't jealousy.

In that instant, my anger flared. Who was he to judge me anyway? I was a grown woman who'd rarely even been kissed. Didn't everyone deserve a little passion in their life?

Determined not to let Wyatt make me feel guilty, I lifted my chin and walked past him with a purposeful stride. "Dean and I will be in my room reading through these letters if anyone wants to give us a hand."

I could have sworn I heard Wyatt let out a snort, but Bull was the one who spoke up. "I don't envy you that job. I never *could* read Calvin's handwriting."

Having been more accustomed to reading printed texts and emails, I wasn't much good at deciphering such things myself. I paused by the doorway to the hall. "Hopefully we'll have better luck. If not, I'll start searching online or read the letters my grandfather sent to Calvin. I'm sure they're all typewritten, although I don't believe they'd be as useful."

"Probably not," Dean agreed. With a smug grin, he placed a hand on the small of my back and steered me into the hall. "Y'all know where to find us."

I could scarcely contain my giggles until we reached my room. "Do you think they saw us?"

"I dunno," Dean replied, chuckling. "But if looks could kill, Wyatt would be facing murder charges."

"What's his problem anyway?"

He shrugged. "Maybe he wants you for himself."

My thoughts touched on the back rub episode. If Wyatt had wanted more than a massage, he'd had plenty of opportunity to ask me, and he hadn't. "I doubt it." I was a breath away from making the usual self-deprecating remark when it occurred to me that I now knew of at least one man who was anxious to be my—what was he, anyway? A sort of temporary boyfriend? The whole idea seemed rather shallow. Still, I certainly wasn't going to turn down a little male attention, particularly when the man in question was as cute—and willing—as Dean.

Wyatt struck me as the unattainable type. Sexy and tempting, perhaps, but ultimately beyond my reach.

Unfortunately, dismissing him from my thoughts wasn't easy. Putting my hands on him had done things to me I couldn't begin to explain.

"His loss." Waggling his brows, Dean dumped the boxes on the bed and sat down, patting the space beside him. "Have a seat."

Something told me if I were to sit that close to him, we wouldn't get much reading done. I opted to perch near the head of the bed with the letters between us.

"Chicken," he chided.

I grimaced. "If it's all the same to you, I'd rather not have to listen to any teasing from the rest of the gang. Not yet, anyway."

He glanced toward the door. "I'm guessing it'll be a while before anyone decides to join us."

Once again, I was far more adventurous in theory than in practice. On the other hand, unless he sneaked into my room late at night, this was probably our best opportunity. I couldn't see meeting him in the barn. For one thing, it was much too cold. "Okay, but make it quick."

"Don't believe anyone's ever said that to me before." Smiling, he shoved the boxes aside and pulled me into his arms. "But I'll do my best."

The kiss was better this time. Soft. Sensuous. Heady. We were even on a bed. Never having come that close to having sex in my life, I wouldn't have been too surprised if his kisses had triggered an orgasm.

They didn't, of course, although his lips did make me forget the possibility of being observed.

Until the image of Wyatt's scowl popped into my head.

I broke off the kiss. "Better not press our luck."

"Damn. I was just getting started." To my surprise, he seemed a bit breathless. Had kissing me really done that to him?

Amazing...

Breathing quite heavily myself, I scooted sideways and slid the boxes between us. Heat flooded my cheeks as my erogenous zones screamed in protest. Swollen lips, tingling nipples, and that sexy moisture between my legs.

He lifted the lids on the boxes and then handed one set to me. "These look like the oldest of the bunch."

"If I know my grandfather, they're probably in order." Doing my best to steady my nerves without making a big show of it, I chose a letter from one end of the box and studied the envelope. "This one's postmarked Saigon. Doubt if it would help us much."

Suddenly, I had no desire to read any of those letters, especially after noting the address on that first one—a missive Grandpa must've received while recovering from the wounds that earned him a Purple Heart. Those boxes had been in my possession for months, but beyond a quick check to verify their contents, I'd kept their lids firmly shut. Even now, when I had a valid reason to go through them, I was reluctant to do so, knowing full well how painful the task would be.

"You okay?" Dean asked. "You've been staring at that for a long time."

I glanced up. "I'm not sure I should be the one to do this."

He nodded as though he understood. "Too close to the recipient?"

"Yeah." I turned the letter over in my hand. "I wasn't

even born when this letter was mailed. Calvin was still serving in Vietnam. The war hadn't been lost yet. Saigon hadn't been renamed Ho Chi Minh City. And Grandpa was in an Army field hospital in Da Nang."

Goose bumps prickled my skin as I spoke those last words. Grandpa had come very close to dying in that hospital. Mom had told me that much. I didn't want to know any more.

Dean took the letter gently from my hand. "Maybe all we need to look at are the return addresses."

I nodded slowly. "I can do an online search once we know where Calvin lived during a census year. The 1980 census would be best."

"Then we'll just look for a letter with a 1980 postmark."

"Okay." That much, I could do.

In the end, Dean was the one who found the letter we needed. Calvin might not have been born there, but in 1980, he'd been living in Liberty, Texas. Apparently Wyatt's ear for accents was spot-on.

If Calvin and Grandpa were indeed the same age, Calvin would've been thirty-three years old then. Had his wife and kids already been killed in that accident? I caught myself staring at yet another envelope without daring to examine the contents. I knew finding Calvin's next of kin was important, but a letter written in the wake of the worst tragedy of his life was one I had no desire to read.

I went over to the desk and pulled up the census data on my computer but didn't get very far. If I'd ever known about the seventy-two-year blackout on census data, I'd forgotten about it. The most recent information

I could get to was from 1940—perhaps as many as ten years before Calvin was born.

"Looks like I'm going to have to sign up for one of the genealogy sites to find anything. Too bad we don't know his father's name. He would've been on the 1940 census along with any of Calvin's older siblings." That alone would've given us the information we needed, especially if he had any brothers. Any sisters would, of course, have been listed under their maiden names, which would make them difficult to track down if they had ever married.

Still, we knew Calvin had lived in Texas after the war. I tried a White Pages search, but all I learned was that Calvin probably knew everyone who lived and worked on the Circle Bar K Ranch.

"My, how helpful," I muttered.

"Need a hand?"

I glanced up to see Wyatt standing in the doorway. The condemning scowl was gone, possibly because I was sitting at the desk while Dean lay sprawled on the bed, evidently absorbed in the letter he was reading.

"Sure," I replied. "All I've come up with so far is that Calvin lives here in the bunkhouse with you guys."

"How come you aren't reading the letters?" he asked.

"I couldn't do it. I—" My voice faltered as I turned back toward the computer screen. My nice, impersonal link to the world. A link that didn't include the kind of troubling emotions I was bound to find in those hand-written letters.

"Hits too close to home," Dean supplied for me. "I don't blame you, Tina. This stuff is tough to read, and I'm not talking about the handwriting."

Without a word, Wyatt crossed the room, picked up a handful of letters, and took a seat in the recliner. I watched out of the corner of my eye as he very methodically chose the first letter in the stack, removed it from the envelope, and settled down to read.

Wow. Two cowboys in my bedroom. I would have entered that momentous bit of data into my diary, if I'd ever kept one. I'd flipped through one of Grandpa's journals after he died. He had diligently recorded the high and low temperatures and the amount of rainfall every day along with a list of the things he'd done, but he never mentioned his thoughts about what was happening.

Not like those letters Dean and Wyatt were reading. I was still hesitant to start poking around in Calvin's belongings, but continuing a fruitless search when I could be doing something productive was a waste of time.

"I'm going to look for the other letters," I announced.

"Think you'll find anything useful in them?" Wyatt asked.

"Probably not, but I can't read the letters Calvin wrote. I just can't."

He shrugged. "I'm sure Calvin wouldn't mind if you read the others. At least, not any more than he'd mind us reading these."

"Feels intrusive, doesn't it?"

"A bit." It was nothing like reading letters written in another century, even if the correspondents happened to be my ancestors. I barely knew Calvin, but I had known my grandfather quite well.

I glanced at Dean. As riveted as he was to what he

was reading, Wyatt and I might not have even been on the same planet.

With a nod, I rose from the desk and headed down the hall to Calvin's room.

Nothing had been touched since the ambulance crew had left the night before. The bed was stripped, the mattress still askew on its frame. The pill bottles sat on the desk, leaving me to assume that the medics had made a list of them. Choosing one at random, I read the label, just as Wyatt had done. That particular prescription had been filled several months prior, and the bottle was practically full—sufficient evidence to prove he hadn't been taking them.

I returned the bottle to the desk and glanced at the bed. Tidying up his quarters was the least I could do. I had just shoved the mattress back into place when I heard something hit the floor. A tiny glass bottle rolled across the bare wooden surface. Curious, I stooped to pick it up.

The cap was screwed on tight, but the bottle was empty. I stood there, staring at the label for several long moments.

Nitrostat.

Once again, I didn't have to be a medical professional to know nitroglycerine was used to treat chest pain. According to the expiration date, the tablets would still have been good if there'd been any left. Had he taken the last one right before I found him? Or had the bottle been empty to begin with? And if so, for how long? Surely if he'd been using them often, he would've refilled the prescription.

Unless he'd been putting it off. Still, anyone with

a known heart condition would understand the importance of having those tablets on hand at all times. He might've even carried them in his pocket.

I stared at the meds on the desk. Had this bottle been among them?

Only one way to find out.

Returning to my room, I handed the bottle to Wyatt. "I found this on the floor just now. Was it with the other medication bottles you checked last night?"

His brows knit together in a satyr-like frown. "No, but the fact that it's empty explains a lot."

Dean looked up from the letter he'd been reading. "What's that?"

"Nitrostat," Wyatt replied. "Used to treat angina. It won't stop a full-blown MI, but if he'd taken them, last night's episode might've turned out differently."

"Maybe he did take them," Dean said. "And that's why the bottle is empty."

"But why put the cap back on an empty bottle?" I asked. "Seems kinda odd, doesn't it?"

"Not necessarily," Wyatt replied. "Most people would probably recap an empty bottle without even realizing they'd done it." He hesitated for a moment, his slight frown suggesting an inner debate regarding the wisdom of voicing his thoughts. "What's weird is that your grandfather died and then you came to see Calvin right before he had a heart attack."

I stared at Wyatt, aghast at what he seemed to be inferring. "Are you suggesting that I had anything to do with either of those things?"

He shook his head. "No, but you have to admit, the timing is peculiar."

I certainly couldn't argue with that. If I hadn't arrived when I did, Calvin might have been dead before I ever had the chance to give him Grandpa's medals. "Do you think my visit caused Calvin's heart attack?"

"Probably not," Wyatt said with a shrug. "But stranger things have happened."

"And if you hadn't been here," Dean said, "he wouldn't have stood a snowball's chance in hell. Don't forget that part." Returning his gaze to the letter in his hand, he let out a gasp. "Holy shit! I think I've found it. Listen to this: *Jeannine married some rich guy from Houston while I was in Nam and doesn't want anything to do with the likes of me anymore. But then, she always did have a fondness for the finer things.* Figure this Jeannine is his sister?"

"Could be," Wyatt said. "Unless she was an old girlfriend."

"Would've been nice of him to mention the rich guy's name," I said, grumbling. "Even if she wasn't his sister, she probably knew Calvin's family."

"I guess that means we keep reading." Not surprisingly, Dean didn't sound as excited as he had a few moments earlier.

"Yeah." Reminding myself that Calvin's tragedies were his own, not mine, I grabbed a stack of letters and carried them over to the desk. With Wyatt in the room, sitting on the bed with Dean seemed like a bad idea.

Then again, perhaps that was why he'd offered to help.

Chapter 9

AFTER READING THROUGH SEVERAL YEARS' WORTH OF Calvin's letters, my brain was fried and my eyes felt like I'd been caught in a sandstorm. "Okay, guys. You can keep on if you want, but I'm going to bed."

Dean responded to my announcement with a huge yawn.

"I could use some sleep myself," Wyatt said. "Been a long day."

I started to remind him he'd had a nap in there somewhere, but since I wanted him to get a move on, I didn't argue. "I'll read some more tomorrow while you guys are out riding the range."

Dean snorted in disgust. "Riding the range, hell. Seems like all we ever do anymore is fix fences. I'd like to get hold of whoever's been cutting them and give him a swift boot up the ass."

"I'm sure it would be well-deserved." I returned my share of the letters to the box, marked my place, and closed the lid. So many memories were contained in those envelopes, some had been joyous, but others…

I'd found the one written after the accident that claimed the lives of Calvin's wife and children. Figuring that if Jeannine had been his sister, Calvin might've mentioned her name, I forced myself to read it. Jeannine was mentioned all right—and she was definitely his sister—but apparently Calvin had seen no need to identify her by her married name, even though her daughter, whom Calvin referred to as "my niece, Carla," had also been killed in the crash.

If Jeannine hadn't already decided she didn't want to associate with Calvin, that tragic turn of events probably would've been sufficient cause for their estrangement. According to the letter, Jeannine believed that Carla wouldn't have died if she had steered clear of Calvin and his family. While that assessment was probably true, it had undoubtedly compounded Calvin's pain.

That letter sapped my mental energy to the point that I didn't even make it through to the end. Some things were best taken in small doses.

After Wyatt departed with a rather abrupt "G'night," Dean lingered in the doorway long enough to kiss me one more time, setting my senses awhirl with anticipation, especially when his hands strayed downward to cradle my bottom.

"So, does 'fun and games' include sex?" he whispered. "I'd love to get you naked and *really* have some fun." He paused long enough to lick my earlobe, an act that nearly buckled my knees. "I have some condoms. Six of them."

Oh my...

That question in itself constituted a first. "Umm... not sure. Maybe."

Dean's hands continued their exploration of my backside as his lips drifted down to the base of my neck to nip and suck at my skin, making me long to throw caution to the wind and rip his shirt off. "But not tonight?"

"Seems a bit hasty, doesn't it?" True, I wouldn't be staying in Wyoming any longer than it took for Calvin to get out of the hospital, but was I really willing to take the plunge with a virtual stranger so soon? I doubted it, although for all I knew, I might be missing out on the opportunity of a lifetime.

Still, I'd gone my entire life without sex. One more night of chastity wouldn't kill me.

To my relief, he nodded. "Okay. I'll be good. But not for long." He gave my bottom a squeeze. "Good night, Tina."

"Good night, Dean."

Stifling a giggle, I closed the door with the squeak of a hinge that could have stood a quick shot of WD-40.

Tina and Dean. We sounded like a figure skating team. *Hayes and Wayland—or would it sound better as Wayland and Hayes?*

Still giggling, I let Ophelia out one last time, took a quick shower, hit the sack, and then lay awake for the next two hours fantasizing about what might have happened if I'd had the guts to act on Dean's suggestion.

He had six condoms. Would he use them all in one night?

Oh, surely not…

I could almost hear the squeak of the hinge again, imagining the lock clicking into place followed by the creak of floorboards as he crossed the room. The thump of Ophelia's tail would be muted by the doormat she had adopted as her bed. A tremor of excitement set off a strange ache in my core.

Or should I think of it as my pussy?

Probably. Vagina sounded too technical, although if I was truly intent on being bad, I could go for the *C* word. Unfortunately, I wasn't ready for that any more than I was ready to screw around with a man I barely knew.

What would it be like to be in bed with a naked man? Would we talk first or would he get right down to business? I flipped over in bed one more time, noting the twanging of bedsprings and the screech of casters on the floor. A round of energetic sex would have made enough noise to wake up everyone in the bunkhouse, no doubt prompting them to charge into my room to discover the source of the racket. That is, if they hadn't already noticed one of their number was missing.

Talk about embarrassing.

Perhaps I was better off sleeping alone. After all, fantasies had never placed me in compromising situations, infected me with nasty germs, or gotten me pregnant. I didn't have to put up with a man's whims on a regular basis, either. I'm sure there were plenty of perks associated with having a boyfriend or husband, but I'd been on my own long enough to know I could handle most things by myself.

But those kisses had done something to me, and so had rubbing Wyatt's shoulders. In fact, that episode with Wyatt had affected me more strongly than kissing Dean. Was I kissing the wrong man, or was his lack of a shirt the only reason?

Probably not. I'd seen Dean completely naked. Wyatt had my nerves doing jumping jacks from that first meeting.

The mere thought of him sent another gush of moisture from my vagina. I squeezed my legs together, savoring the slickness.

Closing my eyes, I imagined his calloused hands teasing my nipples. I'd never been touched in that manner by another person. Granted, I could do that sort of thing to myself, but a man's lips and tongue? I couldn't begin to duplicate the sensation of being licked and kissed all over, starting with my nipples and ending with my clitoris. Did guys actually stick their tongues inside a woman's vagina? I'd read about it in books, but did they really do that, or was it something women only wished they would do? I didn't know. I hoped it didn't exist exclusively in the realm of fantasy because the reality would be absolutely fabulous.

I'd also read a number of novels in which the heroine had sucked the hero's penis. I wasn't convinced I would like it, but I wanted to give it a try someday. I wanted to know what it was like to have a man's cock, big and warm, in my mouth as I sucked the plum-shaped head, listening to the groans of pleasure that proved how much he appreciated my efforts.

Okay. So there *were* perks to having a man around. Simply because I'd gotten used to the idea of not having a lover didn't mean I didn't want one.

All I needed was a smidgen of courage and I could have a man. Right here. Right now. He might not be the firefighting hero I'd dreamed about, but cowboys were good—better than I'd expected them to be—and most women thought they were hot. I'd envisioned smelly, tobacco-chewing, gun-toting outlaw types, and these guys weren't like that at all.

Too bad the cowboy I was leaning toward hadn't been the one to make the offer.

———

The following morning, despite my gritty, sleep-deprived eyes, I managed to get dressed and make my way to the kitchen without running into a wall. Putting the coffee on was my number-one priority, after which, I started on the rest of the meal.

The bacon was already sizzling on the griddle and I was rolling out biscuit dough when Dean sauntered in.

"Sleep well last night?"

"Not really." I gave him the once-over. "And you'd better get rid of that grin or the others will know what we were up to last night."

"I'll take full responsibility." After darting a quick glance toward the doorway, he gave me a kiss that could've melted an iceberg. "Need any help?"

I took a moment to regain my composure before nodding at the stack of plates and cutlery on the counter. "You can put those on the table if you like."

"Will do."

Dean had barely left the room when Nick wandered in, his long, dark hair free of its usual ponytail. "Biscuits? On a Friday? You're gonna have us so spoiled…"

"That's the idea," I said. "Calvin can put you all on a diet when he comes back, but I'm enjoying this too much to be stingy." I would have welcomed the opportunity to fatten Calvin up a bit as well. In my opinion, he was much too thin. Nick, on the other hand, was just about right. "I don't think I'm coordinated enough to make omelets for everyone just yet, so I'm making scrambled eggs with cheese. Think you could crack some eggs into that bowl for me?"

He didn't seem at all disappointed. "Sure thing. How many?"

"That depends. Are Dusty and Mr. Kincaid joining us for breakfast?"

"Probably," he replied. "I'm guessing the boss could fry up some eggs, but Dusty isn't much of a cook."

"Better make it two dozen then." The amount of food these men could put away still astonished me. They obviously had enough hens to keep them supplied with eggs, but I couldn't help wondering just how big the chicken coop was.

After cutting out the biscuits and arranging them on a pan, I paused for a moment to study Nick as he cracked egg after egg with considerable panache. I don't know why I hadn't keyed on it before—perhaps it was simply because his hair was loose now—but his dark eyes and skin finally clicked, along with features that tagged him as having more than a dash of Native American blood. Although with a name like Reno, I doubted it was on his father's side.

"You look a lot different without the ponytail," I observed.

He shot me a wicked grin. "More like a wild Indian, you mean?"

"I wouldn't have worded it quite like that, but yeah."

"I come by it honestly," he said. "My mom is half Shoshone. Her mother's people live on the Wind River Reservation." He chuckled, adding, "My parents met in a casino there, if that tells you anything."

I'd seen the sign for the reservation—and the casinos—at the turnoff in Rawlins. I returned his grin with a wink. "I suppose it does." Whatever his bloodline, he was a handsome devil, if a bit cheeky, and I liked him a lot. He'd even kissed me. There weren't very many guys I could say that about.

These cowboys were really starting to grow on me.

Sonny seemed like a nice kid, and Joe struck me as being an honest, dependable man. Next thing I knew, Bull would begin showing some endearing qualities.

I still didn't know what to make of Wyatt. I'd stolen a few peeks at him while we were reading Calvin's letters. He'd been so intent on what he was doing, he probably hadn't noticed my stares. What went on in that head of his? Even Calvin had referred to him as "that mean-looking varmint." But did he only look mean? Or did the meanness go deeper than that?

Who knew?

Having read some of Calvin's more emotional letters, I had a better grasp of who he was and the life events that had shaped his character. Wyatt, on the other hand, remained a mystery. Somehow, I doubted I would ever be privy to enough of his thoughts to even begin to understand what made him tick.

"All done," Nick announced, interrupting my musings.

"Thanks." I popped the biscuits in the oven and set the timer, then stared at the bowl of eggs, momentarily stymied by the vast quantity until I realized all I had to do was multiply my usual recipe by twelve. Fortunately, mental math was one of my strong suits, and I measured out salt, pepper, and milk as though I whipped up two dozen scrambled eggs every day of my life. I only hoped the end result justified my confidence.

After heating up an enormous iron skillet, I melted a whole stick of butter and added the eggs. I had just given them a few stirs with a wooden spoon and was reaching for the tongs to flip the bacon when another hand met mine.

"I'll do that."

Wyatt's voice in my ear shattered the poise I'd worked so hard to achieve, and my heart leaped sideways an instant before my body followed it. "Oh... okay," I said, thankful that I hadn't been holding anything hot or fragile.

A blush prickled my face and goose bumps tightened my skin as I picked up the spoon and continued stirring the eggs, amazed my trembling hands didn't botch the job. Did he have any idea how intimidating he was? Probably. Even if his goal hadn't included making me jump out of my skin, his deft movements reminded me that he was much more comfortable cooking for a crowd than I had any right to be.

"I guess you're used to helping Calvin with the cooking, huh?"

"Some," he replied. "Not often."

So why was he helping me now? Did he think I was totally incompetent?

I reminded myself that Nick and Dean had offered to help, and I'd given them each a task. Wyatt hadn't asked, and I hadn't told him what to do. He'd simply taken on the job. That should've pleased me, but once again, his motivation was unclear—unless he couldn't stand the idea of overcooked bacon. Perhaps it had taken him years to teach Calvin to fry it up the way he liked.

Of all the stupid, ridiculous reasons to invent...

Truth be told, Wyatt made me feel more inept and nervous than any man ever had—and that was saying quite a lot. What *was* it about him?

Several slow, calming breaths later, I decided the eggs were done. I was adding the grated cheese when Dean returned from setting the table. Stopping short in the doorway, he aimed a puzzled frown at Wyatt before darting a questioning glance at me. All I could do was shrug.

Apparently unperturbed, he pulled butter and jam from the fridge just as Sonny and Nick came into the kitchen and got out a jug of orange juice and some glasses. Wyatt was transferring the last of the bacon to a platter when I grabbed a couple of pot holders and started to pick up the skillet, intending to carry it into the mess hall.

"I'll do that," he said again. "You take the bacon."

Oh, so now he thought I was too weak to lift a skillet? Damn the man for making me feel like a…a what? A fragile flower? A weakling? I was taller and stronger than most women and certainly capable of hoisting however many pounds the thing weighed.

I was sputtering a protest when he actually pulled the pot holders from my hands. He wasn't even giving me a choice. After that, I took a step back and simply stared at him, openmouthed, as he carried the skillet from the kitchen. When the oven timer dinged, I nearly screamed.

Only now I didn't have a pot holder to take out the biscuits. Gritting my teeth in annoyance, I snatched up the platter of bacon and marched into the mess hall. After plunking it down on the table, I flipped my hair back over my shoulders and aimed a tight smile at Wyatt. "Seeing as how you have the pot holders, would you mind getting the biscuits, please?"

Evidently impervious to sarcasm, all he did was nod before heading back into the kitchen.

I took a seat beside Dean, wishing I had glared rather

than smiled—and possibly included the word "confis-cated" in there somewhere.

A quick survey of the table made me glad I hadn't done anything of the sort. Each and every one of the men seated there—and for the record, there were seven of them—was staring at me, although Mr. Kincaid seemed more puzzled than curious.

Not surprisingly, Bull spoke up first. "Who gave you the hickey?"

Chapter 10

SO MUCH FOR KEEPING SECRETS.

Not that it really needed to be kept hush-hush, unless secrecy was important to Dean. He was the one who was actually employed at the ranch. I was temporary help at best.

Seated at the end of the table to my immediate left, Joe cleared his throat before aiming a tiny smile somewhere in the vicinity of his plate. "Obviously not you."

Sonny nudged Nick. "You kissed her. Must've been you."

The twinkle in Nick's eyes suggested he would've been pleased to claim responsibility, but in the end, he shook his head. "I only kissed her on the lips, not on the neck."

"Guess that leaves Wyatt or Dean," Dusty said with a chuckle. "My money's on Dean."

"For what?" Wyatt asked as he returned with the biscuits.

"For giving Tina a hickey," Bull replied. "Big one too. Must've taken him a while."

Fortunately, Wyatt had set the pan down before anyone could enlighten him. Otherwise, if his clenched fists were any indication, he might've thrown it against the wall. He scowled at me, then at Dean, his satyr-like expression more pronounced than ever.

A moment later, every trace of anger or annoyance had vanished. "I'm sure it did." Without another word, he sat down in the chair across from me and took a sip of his coffee.

"This all looks great, Tina," Joe said. "Let's eat while it's hot."

Out of the corner of my eye, I caught a glimpse of Dean's smirk before he snatched two biscuits from the pan, then dropped one of them on my plate. "Hot is good."

I bowed my head, pressing my lips together and trying very hard not to laugh. Apparently there weren't many secrets in a bunkhouse.

What was I thinking?

Dusty broke the silence. "Um, if you'll all pass me your plates, I'll dish out the eggs."

I handed over my plate and simply sat there, waiting for the other shoe to drop.

It didn't. The bacon platter went around the table, followed by the butter and jam. Pretty soon the men were too busy eating to say much, and they certainly weren't talking about me.

Perhaps I'd misjudged them—unless they didn't intend to gossip about me to my face.

Great. Actually, I would've preferred that to the sort of locker room discussion that was bound to commence as soon as I was out of earshot. We might not have done the deed, but Dean had gotten farther with me than anyone else ever had. Sneaking another peek at Dean, I was relieved to see the surreptitious shake of his head.

I should've known. Despite not having established the need for secrecy, he wasn't going to kiss and tell.

At least, not anymore than he already had. I still

hadn't figured out when he'd given me the hickey, or why I hadn't noticed it when I brushed my hair. Then again, I'd been half asleep at the time.

I cleaned my plate and hopped up from the table. "Gotta get started on lunch for you guys. Any requests?"

Bull gazed at me with longing in his eyes. "Apple pie?"

"Sorry," I said. "No time for pie, but I could make some cookies today. That way you'd have them for lunch tomorrow."

"Better make a big batch," Sonny advised. "Or else they won't last that long."

I didn't have to look far to find evidence to back up his statement; there wasn't a particle of food left on the table. Even the jam jar was empty. I wondered what it would take to actually fill them up to the point of having leftovers.

Four chickens, Angela had said.

I glanced at Dusty. "Heard anything from Angela?"

He shook his head. "She said she'd call if there was any change in Calvin's condition."

Obviously there hadn't been. "I'll look through those letters some more today. Hopefully, I'll find something useful."

I headed toward the kitchen, leaving the men to clear the table. So far, the lunch thing was turning out to be the hardest part of the job. Perhaps I needed to start a day ahead.

In the end, I wound up packing them a lunch that was essentially the same as I'd fixed the day before. I doubted they would complain, especially after I made cookies and chicken salad for Saturday's lunch.

I'd found two partially thawed pork roasts in the meat

compartment of the fridge that Calvin must have taken out of the freezer at some point, possibly intending to cook them today. After sprinkling them liberally with a couple of dry rub mixtures from the spice rack, I put them in a large slow cooker, set it on low, and went to work on the chicken salad.

Never having made it using anything but canned chicken before, I opted to cook two chickens and go from there. Fortunately, huge pots were easy to come by in that kitchen and I had the chickens simmering in water seasoned with salt, pepper, and bay leaves before the guys had even left for the day.

Dean made a point of being the last to leave, giving me a hug and a kiss before donning his hat and heading out. "Have you thought any more about what I said last night?"

I didn't have to ask what he meant. "Yeah. Still not sure I'm ready for that. But I'll let you know if I change my mind."

If he was disappointed, he hid it well. His gaze flicked toward the base of my neck. "Sorry about the hickey. Guess I got a little carried away. Of course, if Bull had kept his mouth shut, it wouldn't have been a problem."

Somehow I doubted Bull had been the only one to notice it. "Yeah. Not sure I'll ever live that one down— not that it's anyone's business. Speaking of which, do we really need to keep our, um, 'fun' a secret?"

He paused for a few moments as though weighing the pros and cons. "Might be best," he finally said. "Especially with the way Wyatt's been acting."

I didn't need to question him about that, either.

"Okay, then. You and the guys have a good day. Be careful out there."

"Will do."

I spent the rest of the morning making cookies. Unable to find any chocolate chips, I whipped up a double batch of peanut butter cookies, then put together another batch using oatmeal and raisins. I should've had plenty of time to read while they were baking, but it wasn't until the last tray was in the oven that I finally got around to reading the rest of the letter I hadn't been able to finish the night before.

Apparently Calvin's niece, Carla, had been unmarried at the time of her death but had left behind a six-month-old son. Calvin might have lost his own wife and kids, but somewhere out there, he had a great-nephew named Tom.

The next letter included an account of a custody battle between the boy's biological father, whom Calvin had only referred to as a "no-good scoundrel," and Calvin's sister, Jeannine—a battle Jeannine had lost.

By the time I'd read through the next ten or twelve letters, I had a pretty good handle on the family's troubles. A severely depressed Calvin had found his way to Wyoming, vowing never to marry or get close to anyone ever again. Jeannine and her husband, Richard—Calvin had finally mentioned his name—had divorced, the stress of their daughter's death and losing custody of their grandson having taken its toll on the marriage.

The boy, Tom, along with his scoundrel of a father, had essentially disappeared.

This left me with two choices: keep reading, or sign up for one of the genealogy sites. Considering the tiny amount I knew about Calvin's lineage and background, I decided I would have more luck reading the letters. With a resigned sigh, I opened another envelope.

I hadn't been reading long when the bunkhouse phone rang.

"Figured you'd be the best one to call since the guys are probably out," Angela said when I answered.

"Yep. Been all by myself since breakfast." I shot an apologetic glance at Ophelia, who sat panting quietly by the door. She never seemed to mind being discounted unless there was food involved. "How's Calvin?"

"Better, I think," she replied. "He's moving around more, and he's said a few things. Nothing I can make any sense out of, but they're actual words now, and I've managed to get him to eat a little bit. The doctor seems optimistic."

In my experience, doctors usually were, and quite often that optimism was totally unfounded. "That's good news. We've been reading through the letters he sent to my grandfather, trying to find his next of kin. He mentioned some family members, but never included a surname. It's almost like he was trying to keep his family a secret."

"He was never one to reminisce about the past," Angela agreed. "Probably because most of it wasn't good."

Considering what I'd read so far, I couldn't argue with that. "No kidding. Apparently he has a sister whose daughter was killed in the accident along with Calvin's wife and kids." I went on to relate what I'd learned, including the existence of the great-nephew Calvin had presumably never met.

"That's interesting," she said when I'd finished. "The

nurses told me there was a guy here asking questions yesterday. He said he was a friend of the family, but visiting hours were over, so they didn't let him in. They're pretty strict about the visiting times here."

"Did they get a name?"

"Duane something," she replied. "Said he was a tall guy in his late twenties. As far as I know, Calvin doesn't have any friends other than the guys on the ranch, and I've never heard him mention anyone named Duane."

"Friend of the family, huh? Tom would be about that age," I mused. "His father could've easily changed his name after gaining custody."

"True." I thought she hesitated. "But even if it was Tom, I can't figure out how he would've known Calvin was here, what with the HIPAA regulations and all. He couldn't have spotted Calvin's name on a list of patients—even if he'd known where to look. God knows Calvin didn't call him up and ask him to drop by. Seems kinda strange."

"Very strange," I agreed. "Guess I'll keep reading through the letters."

"Let me know if you find anything. Who knows? If that guy really is a family friend—or even a long-lost relative—he might know who to contact if Calvin doesn't pull through. I'm only his employer, and I'd rather not have to deal with those kinds of decisions."

"I don't blame you for that," I said. "One other thing, though. I found an empty nitroglycerine bottle on the floor under Calvin's bed. That in itself wasn't strange—we figured he'd either taken them all that night or had forgotten to refill the prescription—but the cap was on the bottle. Weird, huh?"

Her sharp laugh contained very little amusement. "We've got a monopoly on weird at the Circle Bar K. When I get home, remind me to tell you about all the stuff that's happened over the past few years."

"I will." If it was any weirder than the current situation, it would probably give me nightmares.

"So...how're you getting along with the guys?"

I couldn't help rolling my eyes, even though I could've predicted she would ask that question. "Okay, I guess. They seem to like the food."

This time, her giggle was genuine. "I'll bet they do. Calvin's a good cook, but he isn't terribly creative. You can usually tell what day it is by what's on the table."

That certainly jibed with Nick's rundown of the weekly breakfast menu. "Hopefully they won't get too confused."

"I wouldn't worry about it. They aren't giving you any trouble, are they?"

I was *so* not going to tell her about my adventures with Dean. Or Nick. Or Wyatt. "Not a bit," I declared, although any number of things they'd done could've been construed as troublesome. "They seem quite willing to help me out."

"I'll just bet they are." Her dry tone spoke volumes. "I guess that's it for now. I'll give y'all a call tomorrow. Let me know if you find anything in the letters."

"Will do."

I hung up the phone, still somewhat bewildered by the idea of any strangers trying to visit Calvin—especially someone claiming to be a friend of the family. Even if Calvin had been in contact with Duane, unless he came to the ranch and found him gone, he wouldn't have known where to look for him. Granted, any heart attack victims from the surrounding area would probably end up in the same hospital, but *still...*

I blew out an exasperated breath. Nothing about this trip had gone according to plan—at least, not once I'd set foot on the Circle Bar K. Prior to that, my journey had been smooth sailing all the way. Perhaps Angela was right about the ranch having a monopoly on weirdness.

A glance at the clock proved I needed to stop reading and start cooking, otherwise there would only be two pork roasts and a boatload of cookies for dinner, although I doubted anyone would complain. I was beginning to understand why Calvin had adopted a regular menu. It certainly eliminated the guesswork.

The chicken had cooled by then, so I made the chicken salad, pleased that, if nothing else, I had the next day's lunch taken care of.

After rummaging through the pantry, I decided on macaroni and cheese, stewed tomatoes—of which there were enough jars to prove *someone* liked it—and a spinach salad.

My, how colorful. I was considering a dessert of blue raspberry Jell-O as a way to include all of the primary colors when a wave of bittersweet nostalgia swept over me.

Grandpa's favorite. Funny how the crazy old man he'd become had such a fondness for blue Jell-O. Perhaps there was some truth in the whole "second childhood" adage.

Shaking off the memory, I went on with my work and had just popped the mac and cheese in the oven when Wyatt came in.

Alone.

I tried to seem nonchalant, but I had no idea how successful I was at hiding my dismay. "Where's the rest of the gang?"

"They'll be here in a bit." He shrugged his right shoulder, wincing. "This shoulder was killing me, so I came on ahead."

"You really ought to have that looked at," I advised. "Might be a torn rotator cuff."

"Maybe." He stood there, staring at me for a long moment. "Feels more like a pulled muscle."

If I'd ever known how to tell the difference, that knowledge escaped me. I cleared my throat. "You could take some ibuprofen."

He nodded. "That's the plan—unless you wouldn't mind working on it some more." His piercing gaze sought mine from beneath a raised brow. "Or do you think Dean would object?"

There was no mistaking the challenge in his tone—a challenge a more confident woman would've met with a serene smile and a witty rejoinder. Completely inexperienced in banter between the sexes, I had no idea how to respond. As always, Wyatt had managed to get under my skin, sending my heart skittering into overdrive and tying my tongue in knots. "I-I don't know what you mean."

He took a step closer, reminding me of the way Dean had pinned me against the car. Lifting a hand, he brushed my neck with his knuckles, triggering a swarm of goose bumps. "I mean, anyone who would do that to a woman might not like it if she put her hands on another man."

Ah, yes. The infamous hickey. Dean and I had agreed not to get too involved, but should I tell Wyatt that or let him believe ours was a more serious attachment? Did it matter? In desperation, I glanced at the clock.

Five fifteen. The other men probably wouldn't be back for at least another half hour. "I can spare you twenty minutes."

A tiny smile quirked the corner of his mouth, making me wonder which of us had won that round. "I'll take it."

This time I was watching as he stripped off his shirt—or rather, he was watching me. I'd seen Dean completely naked, and I'd seen Wyatt in his underwear. The sight of him peeling back his shirt to reveal his bare chest shouldn't have affected me.

But it did. My mouth went dry and the pulse pounding in my chest moved farther down to center on my clitoris. I doubted he had any motive beyond relief for a sore shoulder—certainly nothing sexual—but having recently gotten a tiny taste of what could happen between a man and a woman, my body had other ideas.

Fortunately, if I didn't tell him, Wyatt would never know—and somehow, I couldn't imagine myself ever putting those feelings into words. Not with him, anyway.

Not with anyone, come to think of it.

With a look that said he knew exactly what I was thinking—and feeling—he took a seat much the same as he had the day before.

I stared at his bare back. "I don't suppose you found any liniment, did you?"

"Horse liniment, you mean?" he asked. "No. That stuff smells terrible."

Somehow, I doubted the smell was the only drawback. "It might help, though."

He shook his head. "Stings too much. The olive oil was fine."

A man in pain shouldn't be critical of horse liniment. Once again, I wondered if he was toying with me— faking the pain simply to gain attention.

Despite knowing there was one other man on the ranch interested in spending time in my bed, the same argument I'd used before won out.

Twenty minutes. Surely I could handle anything for that long.

But with my hands on his skin rapidly turning a therapeutic massage into a more erotic one, I didn't think twenty minutes was anywhere near enough. Dry-mouthed no longer, I was practically drooling with the need to lick the side of his neck before sinking my teeth into it.

My latent vampire instincts must be surfacing.

Yeah, right. The thought of him recoiling in pain and glaring at me as though I'd lost my mind was quite enough to stop me.

"Oh, yeah," he groaned. "Right there."

His muscles knotted beneath my fingers. He wasn't faking.

Doggone it.

"Doesn't that hurt?"

"Some," he replied. "It's a good kind of pain, though."

"Like a bite on the neck, you mean?"

I blinked. Who said that? Certainly not me. I never said such things. I rarely even thought them—until now—nor could I explain my reasoning for comparing a pulled muscle to being bitten.

"Maybe." Turning his head, he peered up at me from the corner of his eye, a sly smile curving his lips. "Why don't you give it a try?"

My fantasy came alive as I parted my lips and swept my tongue over his skin. Salty with dried sweat and fragrant with oil, his skin covered enticingly firm muscles. Even in the act of pressing my teeth into his flesh, I couldn't believe I was actually doing it.

In one swift move, he pivoted in his chair, snaked a hand behind my neck, and pulled me into his lap. With a kiss as forceful as it was abrupt, he instantly melted me into a compliant mass of mushy muscles and jangling nerve endings.

The slam of a door brought me at least partially to my senses. Leaping to my feet, I staggered toward the shelter of the nearest major appliance, which happened to be the fridge—an appropriate choice, considering how hot I was. Opening the door, I stood facing the shelves, hoping whoever had just walked into the bunkhouse would suspect me of nothing beyond getting out spinach for the salad. An even more desirable side effect would be for the icy air to fade my blush and force the blood back into my brain where it was so desperately needed.

I stared blankly at the contents of the fridge. I hadn't been on the Circle Bar K for three full days, and I'd already been kissed by three cowboys.

Clearly, I should have headed west long ago.

Chapter 11

I HAD JUST TAKEN THE INGREDIENTS FOR THE SALAD from the fridge when Nick blew into the kitchen like a raging tornado. "Wow, Tina! Dinner smells great!"

Apparently the scent of roasting pork was far more remarkable than Wyatt sitting at the kitchen table without a shirt. On the other hand, the chances of me ever getting used to such a sight was about as likely as my feet touching the Martian landscape.

"Hopefully it'll taste as good as it smells." I dumped the vegetables on the cutting board, then ran a quick eye over Nick's dusty, disheveled form. "What happened to you?"

"My horse spooked out from under me." His eyes lit up as he snatched a handful of cookies from the platter.

With the apple pie debacle still fresh in my mind, I'd hidden the bulk of the goodies, only leaving out the number I considered expendable—an amount already significantly diminished from having been within Wyatt's reach.

"Oh, yum." After scarfing down one of each flavor in rapid succession, he added, "Landed on my ass and rolled down the hill a ways."

With Wyatt's kiss still sizzling on my lips, I wasn't about to offer my massage therapy services to anyone— especially a man with a sore behind.

I stole a peek at Wyatt. Drat the man, he wasn't even trying to conceal the evidence, but sat idly chewing on a

cookie as though he hadn't just sent the woman responsible for the bite on his neck into oblivion by annihilat-
ing her with a kiss.

Clearing my throat, I aimed my gaze resolutely
toward Nick. "I take it you survived the fall."

"Of course, I did," Nick said. "That was nothing. I've
been hurt lots worse. One time I—"

I put up a silencing hand. "Please. Spare me the
gory details."

"Hey, at least I haven't asked you to rub my butt."
Grinning, he darted a glance at Wyatt. "I see you've been
working on his shoulder." His grin shifted from merely
wicked to diabolical. "Just like he told us you would."

"Is that right?" I drawled. "I didn't realize I was so
predictable—or that easily manipulated." I aimed what
I hoped was a stern glare at Wyatt.

Wyatt spoke up. Finally. "All I did was ask. You
could've said no."

Although this was true, and I said so, saying no to
Wyatt was becoming increasingly difficult.

"Yeah." Nick snickered. "You didn't have to bite
him."

Oh, great. Now I had a reputation for biting *and* getting hickeys. "Actually, he asked me to do that too."

Wyatt stood and slung his shirt over his shoulder.
"Yet another time you could've said no."

His arched brow made me long to slap him, and I was
about to do just that when a tiny grin twitched the corner
of his mouth. He was teasing me, of course. But why?
First impressions being what they were, I'd gotten the
idea that teasing wasn't in his nature.

I reminded myself that this was the sort of thing an

unmarried woman could expect when she began hanging out with a bunch of equally unattached cowboys. I should simply take it in stride and laugh it off.

But I wasn't used to being teased by men. The grandfatherly type, perhaps, but certainly not eligible bachelors. The snappy rejoinder I should have made simply wouldn't materialize. I directed a pleading glance at Nick.

A quick nod of comprehension followed his puzzled frown. "Um...if we want dinner, we'd best not be pestering the cook."

"Right." Momentarily emboldened, I flapped a hand at both of them. "Go. Now."

"Sure you don't need any help?" Despite Wyatt's innocent tone, I could see mischief lurking behind his eyes.

"You can set the table and pour the tea if you like. Otherwise, if I need help, I'll ask for it."

As I picked up a knife and began chopping cherry tomatoes and olives for the salad, I could almost feel Wyatt's eyes on me. The hair on the back of my neck prickled in anticipation of an attack from behind.

The attack never came. Moments later I heard the clatter of plates mixed with the murmur of male voices.

Were they talking about me? Dean might have wanted to keep our kisses hush-hush, but Wyatt and Nick had made no such promises. And where was Dean, anyway? He should have been there to protect me from Wyatt.

Nothing serious... Did that mean no staking of claims? No territorial disputes? No protection of property? Clearly, there were pros and cons to both types of relationships.

Did I really want protection from Wyatt? He unnerved me more than any man ever had—and that kiss had done things to me I didn't even want to think about—but I couldn't imagine him ever deliberately hurting me.

My grip slackened, causing the knife to slip from my fingers. Whether he would hurt me wasn't what concerned me. Trust and surrender were the issues at stake. I wasn't ready for either of those things—especially not with Wyatt. I might have trusted Dean, but I didn't intend to give myself to him, body and soul. Somehow I knew Wyatt wouldn't be content with anything less than my all.

Nope. Not ready for that.

Not now, and possibly not ever.

A shiver crept up my spine, tightening the skin on my back. My hands trembled to the point I didn't dare pick up the knife.

Nick was right. It really didn't pay to pester the cook.

Although I managed to get my roiling emotions under control enough to finish preparing the salad without losing a finger, my focus remained inward for quite some time. The guys raved over the meal, and I'm certain I accepted their praise graciously enough, but I said very little until Mr. Kincaid brought me out of my reverie.

"Any news about Calvin?" he asked.

I nodded, grateful for a neutral topic to divert my troublesome thoughts. "Angela called. She said Calvin was talking some, although he wasn't making much sense, and she got him to eat a little bit."

"Do they think he'll come out of it?"

"She said the doctors were optimistic." I left it at that, not wanting to dilute any hope the men might have.

"Sounds great," Joe said. "What about you? Did you find out anything?"

"I sure hope so," Dean declared. "I was about to go blind reading those letters."

"As a matter of fact, I did," I replied. "Although I'm not positive it will help." I gave them a brief account of what I'd discovered, ending with Duane's attempt to see Calvin. "He said he was a friend of the family, but I can't help thinking he's Jeannine's grandson. From the description the nurses gave Angela, he was about the right age. What really has me bugged is how he knew Calvin was in the hospital."

"Seems kinda fishy," Bull said as he shoveled in a forkful of pulled pork.

"Yeah," Dean agreed. "Nobody besides us even knew he was sick."

Bull swallowed and leaned forward with the air of a master detective about to reveal the solution to the greatest mystery of our time. "Except whoever it was who put him in the hospital to begin with."

I stared at him, puzzled. "What? You mean the ambulance crew?"

"No." With a dramatic lift of his brow, he glanced at each of us in turn. "I mean whoever it was who tried to kill him."

Silence reigned for the space of three heartbeats.

"Yeah, right," Sonny snorted. "Who would want to kill Calvin?"

"And why?" Mr. Kincaid added. "He's been living

on this ranch for years, never harmed a soul, and didn't have any enemies—at least none that we know of. Why now?"

"Why, indeed?" Now that Bull had the floor, he obviously intended to milk his moment for as long as possible. He shot a suspicious glare at me. "Maybe *she* had something to do with it."

"Oh, come off it," Dean snapped. "She's no murderer."

I sat back in my chair, letting the full weight of the implication sink in. Wyatt had said something about the timing of Calvin's illness being peculiar. Perhaps he was right, but in a different way. "I certainly didn't kill Calvin, nor did I have any reason to. But what if someone knew I was coming to see him and followed me here? Someone who wanted him dead but didn't know where to find him?"

"That makes some sense," Dean said. "But who knew where you were going?"

"As far as I know, only my parents," I replied. "That doesn't mean someone else couldn't have found out. Someone who expected me to come here and was simply biding their time."

Wyatt cleared his throat. "We're letting our imaginations run away with us. Calvin wasn't shot or stabbed. He had a heart attack."

"Wouldn't be the first time a murder was made to look like a death from natural causes," Bull insisted.

"But what about motive?" Wyatt asked. "Why would anyone want him dead?"

"No clue." Dean let out a long sigh. "Guess that means we need to keep reading those damned letters, huh?"

I nodded, but my mind had already gone sprinting off

in a new direction. What were the motives for murder? Money, love, hate, revenge... Who would hate Calvin enough, or blame him enough, to want him dead? Some other soldier he'd known in Vietnam? The family of a comrade who'd died as a result of something Calvin had done?

It wasn't until I reminded myself that Calvin had been a cook rather than a foot soldier that I realized how unlikely such a scenario would be. Fatal mistakes and bad judgment during combat weren't unheard of, but I doubted anyone had died simply from eating the food he'd prepared.

But there were a number of deaths in his past. His wife and children, along with his niece. From what I'd gathered from the letters, the accident had been just that: an accident. His wife's family would've been very upset, but they certainly couldn't have blamed Calvin for her death.

Jeannine was a different story. She and Calvin were already estranged before the accident, and after all the losses she'd suffered—her daughter, her grandson, and ultimately, her husband—her hatred could've festered for years before finally coming to a head.

My own possible involvement, I discounted. No one beyond Grandpa's lawyer and our immediate family knew what was written in that will, let alone known when I would carry out Grandpa's wishes. No one except Calvin, and I'd gotten the distinct impression he hadn't told anyone on the ranch about my upcoming visit. Hence Wyatt's belligerent attitude when I first arrived.

Wyatt... His voice of reason had effectively shot

down Bull's murder theory. That and the fact that Calvin wasn't dead.

Which only made it *attempted* murder.

By giving a man alone in his own bed a heart attack? And if so, how? By stealing his nitroglycerine tablets? Maybe. That empty bottle could be explained a dozen different ways—including the fact that the cap was on it. As dark as the glass was, it might be hard to tell it was empty at a glance. He might not have realized he'd taken the last one until it was too late.

My thoughts returned to the present, only to discover that while I'd been sitting there staring at my plate, the conversation had gone on without me, ultimately arriving at the same conclusion. Until Calvin could tell us what happened that night, we couldn't prove anything, sinister or otherwise.

Which meant that Dean, Wyatt, and I—and anyone else we could recruit—would be reading through more letters that evening.

Oh, joy...

I now had four cowboys in my bedroom. Sonny, Nick, Wyatt, and Dean were scattered about the room—Sonny and Nick having brought in more chairs while the others resumed their positions from the night before. Bull, Joe, and Dusty were in Calvin's room reading the letters sent by my grandfather. If I'd had to guess, I would have said there had never been a time when every ranch hand on the Circle Bar K was engaged in reading a letter of any kind, let alone some that were forty years old.

Mr. Kincaid had opted out of the search, using his

increasingly poor eyesight as an excuse, although I could see his inability to join in fretted him a bit. Grandpa had reacted to infirmity in much the same way—although in Grandpa's case, I would have used the word "angered" rather than "fretted." No doubt there were plenty of former soldiers who slid gracefully into old age, but most probably went there entirely against their will.

The guys had all had a pretty tiring day—Nick's tumble and Wyatt's sore shoulder thankfully being the worst of it—and their exhaustion was evident after an hour or so of squinting at Calvin's handwriting. Judging from all the yawns and bleary eyes, I doubted Dean would be awake enough for more than a quick kiss or two after the others had gone.

I was about to call it a night when a line of text practically jumped off the page and bit me.

"Holy cow! Listen to this: *Jeannine went and married another rich bastard. This time she snagged a Caruthers from Houston. Never ceases to amaze me how she manages to find them, let alone get them to marry her.* A rich guy from Houston… How many Jeannine Caruthers could there possibly be in Houston?"

"At a guess, not very many," Wyatt said.

"Rich dude, huh?" Dean said. "Wonder if she stayed married to that one."

"Only one way to find out." Swiveling my chair around to face the desk, I logged on to my computer. "Although if she married into a rich family, she might have forgiven Calvin for his involvement in her daughter's death—at least enough to not want him dead."

Wyatt frowned. "I thought we'd already ruled out Bull's attempted murder theory."

I'd forgotten I'd kept my own thoughts about possible motives to myself. "Maybe. It's an interesting theory, though. Jeannine lost more than a daughter as a result of that accident. She might've been the type to hold a grudge."

Nick's eyes lit up. "And if she married a rich guy, she could afford to hire a hit man."

"You've been watching too many cop shows," Sonny scoffed. "Working on a ranch must be real boring for you to come up with that idea."

I didn't know much about Nick's viewing habits, but he did strike me as the adventurous type. A suggestion like Bull's could easily have had his imagination working overtime, just as it had done with mine.

"There was absolutely no evidence of foul play," Wyatt said firmly. "We all knew he had a bad heart. It was just a matter of time before it caught up with him."

"Yeah, but his sister might've known that too, you know," Nick countered. He peered at the envelope in his hand. "We've only made it to the mid-nineties in these letters. They might've been in contact with each other more recently."

He had a point. "You guys keep reading while I run a search." The name Caruthers had an "old money" ring to it. A woman who married someone like that would have undoubtedly been in the news at some point. If nothing else, their marriage records would pop up.

They did.

"Bingo! Jeannine D. Anderson and Franklin W. Caruthers were married on September 26, 1995, in Houston, Texas." I clicked the back link and scrolled down the page. "Lots of newspaper stories listed. We're talking stinking rich. Maybe not along the lines of the Rockefellers or the Vanderbilts, but plenty well-off." I opened another file and scanned it quickly. "Apparently Jeannine didn't settle down to live a quiet life in the country. She's done a lot of charity work, most of it involving support services for single mothers, which, given her history, isn't too surprising."

Farther down, I found a mention of her husband and brother-in-law. "Looks like Franklin is some sort of oil tycoon, and his brother, Harold, owns a pharmaceutical company called Larosa Biotech."

"Ooh," Nick exclaimed. "Plenty of money for a hit man—and access to all kinds of drugs."

I couldn't help chuckling. "You're definitely wasted on a ranch, Nick. You should run for sheriff or join the police force or something."

"Don't encourage him," Sonny advised. "He's hard enough to live with as it is."

Nick's unabashed grin was even more cocky than usual. "I'd probably make detective in a year."

"Sure you would," Dean drawled. "Solving all sorts of imaginary crimes."

Wyatt aimed a withering glance at Nick and Dean before nodding at me. "Don't stop there, Tina. Keep going."

I gaped at him for a long moment as my subconscious mind put a sexual spin on his terse directive. The mere thought of him saying those same words in a more intimate setting made me feel like I'd swallowed an entire bag of cotton balls.

His piercing gaze somehow erased everyone else from the room, triggering a fantasy so real I could almost feel it. Wyatt lay naked on my bed, kissing me the way he had earlier that afternoon—a kiss I had somehow managed to avoid thinking about during dinner, although how I'd done it was a mystery.

No. That was a lie. I'd been thinking about it. Constantly. I'd only pretended to forget it.

My hands were on his stiff cock, feeling its heat and girth. His own lubricating fluid flowed from the head, allowing my palms to glide easily along the length of his shaft. He was telling me to keep going until—

A hand passed in front of my face. "Earth to Tina."

I blinked. Hard. "Sorry, Nick. I was...thinking."

"Thinking, hell," Dean remarked. "You looked like you'd seen a damned ghost."

"It was nothing. I'm just...tired." I tried to shake it off, but the dregs of the fantasy lingered, slowing my thought processes to the flow rate of frozen molasses. I turned back toward the computer, focusing on the screen, placing my fingers on the keyboard—fingers that a moment before had been caressing Wyatt's rock-hard penis. And he was telling me not to stop...

"Okay," Dean said. "Maybe we should call it a night. These letters aren't going anywhere."

"Yeah. Might be best." I started to close the laptop when another entry caught my eye.

Franklin Walter Caruthers's obituary.

Chapter 12

SUDDENLY, I WASN'T THE SLIGHTEST BIT SLEEPY. Opening the file, I scanned the entry while Sonny went over to Calvin's room to tell the others what I'd discovered.

"Thank God," Bull exclaimed when they joined us. "I found out all sorts of things about you and your folks, but not a damn thing about Calvin's family."

I couldn't help cringing a bit. Having Bull privy to my childhood escapades was unsettling to say the least. Fortunately, none were particularly embarrassing—at least, none that I could recall.

Putting those thoughts aside, I reported the news. "Jeannine's husband must've been a good bit older than she was. He died in 2001 at the age of seventy-seven. Says here he's survived by Jeannine, two daughters from a previous marriage, and several grandchildren. No telling how much of his money Jeannine wound up inheriting."

"With that kind of fortune involved, they probably would've had some sort of prenuptial agreement." As always, Wyatt was the voice of reason.

"Yeah, but he still could've left her a bundle, couldn't he?" Nick asked, obviously still hanging on to the hit man idea.

"Maybe." Without any clues beyond Calvin's vague references to his sister liking "the finer things," we had few insights into her character—although a woman who'd made a name for herself aiding the plight of unwed mothers probably wasn't the type to hire hit men. "Let's see what else we've got here."

I went back to the search and found something even more interesting. "Oh, dear. According to *her* obituary, Jeannine died this past January. Sorry, Nick. Doesn't look like she would've hired any hit men."

"And nobody told Calvin?" Sonny asked.

"They probably would have if they'd known where to find him." I scratched my head. "Surely they could've found his address. I mean, *I* found it when I did that White Pages search."

"Yes, but you knew which state to look in," Wyatt pointed out.

"True. But there are only fifty states. He would've turned up in a determined search—although they would've had to rule out about a bajillion other guys with the same name. Maybe her family is having the same problem we are—either that or they don't care. Wonder who Jeannine's lawyer is…"

I read through the rest of the article, hoping to discover a contact person of some sort, but I didn't find anything other than the name of the funeral home. "Looks like calling the funeral home is our best bet. Somebody had to make her funeral arrangements. If we could contact them—"

"Not much point in that, is there?" Wyatt said.

"What? Oh, yeah. I see what you mean. None of the Caruthers family is related to Calvin in any way—they've probably never even met him—so they wouldn't have a say in any health-care decisions." Seeing no reason to put a further damper on the evening, I chose not to mention the need for funeral arrangements. "The only person who might is Jeannine's grandson, and God only knows where he is—unless that Duane character really is him."

"There's something else we haven't considered," Wyatt began. "Maybe someone did contact Calvin when his sister died. Maybe he just didn't care enough to tell us about it."

Dean stuffed a letter back into the box beside him on the bed. "Either way, we sure have wasted a lot of time on this."

"Not really," Dusty said. "At least we know there isn't anyone to contact. Until he can speak for himself, it looks like Calvin is our responsibility."

Dusty was right, of course, but I found it hard to believe that a man like Calvin could have lived so much of his life estranged from the few relatives he had. Although from the look of it, he'd found a new family on the Circle Bar K—one that seemed to care a whole lot more about him than his real family did. Small wonder he'd kept in touch with Grandpa.

After they returned the letters to their respective boxes, the guys filed out of my room.

Class dismissed.

I felt the loss almost immediately. My shyness had never allowed me to interact with a group of men on a daily basis, and with no choice now but to do so, I discovered that I actually liked them. Although Dean and Nick were my favorites, Sonny could've been my younger brother, while Joe seemed like a sort of uncle. Bull was an experience unto himself. I still wasn't sure how I felt about Wyatt.

Having two brothers should've made me comfortable with men in general, but I'd been old enough to babysit by the time they were born. I hoped they wouldn't be the ones making the kinds of decisions for me that Dusty and Angela now had to make for Calvin.

Ophelia whined softly and started toward the door. I got up and let her out. She was only gone for a few moments before coming back up onto the porch. She had yet to venture much beyond the stable yard, and in an area undoubtedly crawling with rattlesnakes, the fact that she stayed close by was as comforting to me as it probably was to her.

I took a shower and was about to climb into bed when a tap at the door heralded Dean's return. I probably shouldn't have, but I let him inside and into my arms. Instantly, his lips covered mine with the kind of warm, wet kisses guaranteed to turn any sensible female into a blithering idiot.

Apparently, I wasn't sensible. All I could think about was how different his kisses were from Wyatt's. When Dean had first approached me, my experience was essentially nil. Now I wanted to scream in frustration. There was nothing wrong with Dean or the way he kissed. He simply wasn't Wyatt. Wyatt, whose one earth-shattering kiss had done more to me than all of Dean's combined.

"I really need to oil that hinge," he whispered against my lips.

"Might be a good idea."

Then I remembered what Nick had said. He probably wasn't the only one who knew of Wyatt's plans to have me work on his shoulder. But did any of them know about the kiss? I wasn't completely sure Nick did, although he'd obviously spotted the bite on Wyatt's neck. What either of them had said to Dean was anyone's guess.

I opted for a circuitous approach to my original question. "Do the other guys know you're doing this?"

"I haven't said anything, if that's what you mean. Although they probably have their suspicions."

I waited to see if he would add anything to that, but he didn't, his lips being otherwise occupied with the exploration of my face. "I'm kinda surprised to see you tonight. You all seemed really tired."

His chuckle vibrated against my chest. "Some things you're never too tired for."

My body was already responding to the warmth of his touch. Funny how a woman's body could know things she didn't know herself. I liked that. I slid my hand down the center of his chest, but the memory of my fantasy about Wyatt made me hesitant. What was wrong with me? Why could I have a heart-stopping moment simply thinking about Wyatt when it took so much more than that with Dean?

I returned his kiss. He tasted good, smelled good, and the feel of his arms around me was marvelous. I sank into a comfortable, idyllic state. Not urgent or frantic, just…nice.

There was nothing wrong with nice. Nice was good, although not as shockingly spectacular as my fantasy about Wyatt had been. Would I be disappointed if I were to live out that fantasy with Dean?

Somehow, I doubted I would ever have the courage to find out. I had never reached into a man's jeans to wrap my fingers around his penis, nor had I ever been presented with the opportunity.

As though he'd read my thoughts, Dean skimmed his fingertips over my breasts, teasing my nipples through the flannel of my pajama top. "Think we could lose some of these clothes?" His soft tread proved he'd removed his boots, but other than that, he was still fully dressed.

Nerves made my hands cold and my voice unsteady. "I-I don't think so. I mean, I wish I could be that uninhibited, but I'm not."

He nodded as though he understood. "The condoms are in my pocket. Let me know if you want to use them."

"Still not sure that's a good idea." The mere mention of condoms had my throat so constricted with anxiety, it was a wonder I could make an intelligible sound.

With a quiet chuckle, he pressed his lips to my neck. "Saving yourself for marriage?"

"I wouldn't say that, exactly. I'm just…chicken."

"Maybe we can fix that."

"I doubt it," I said under my breath.

Another knock at the door triggered a sharp inhale that sent me into a coughing fit. Fortunately, Dean had the good sense to pull away and press himself against the wall.

"Hold on," I said when I recovered enough to speak. Opening the door with yet another loud screech of the hinge, I found myself face-to-face with Wyatt. "D-did you, um, forget something?"

His eyes swept the interior of my room. "Just wondering if you'd seen Dean."

Dean stood with his back against the wall, vigorously shaking his head.

I bit back a smile. "Not since you all left."

My, how easy it is to lie. Folding my arms, I returned his regard with a steady gaze, my hip cocked to shift my weight onto one foot. I had nearly convinced myself that my thoughts were as nonchalant as my pose when my mind drifted, ultimately landing on something it shouldn't have: the image of Wyatt, naked, with my hand wrapped around his stiff penis.

Was he the stuff of dreams or was he real? He might've made me nervous in the extreme, but somehow I suspected he would be the star of every fantasy I would have from that point onward.

I tried, but my thoughts refused to shift and neither did my gaze. His eyes. Those intense, brooding, hazel eyes. The line of his jaw and the twitch of his lips reminded me of his smirk when he left me, still reeling from that incredible kiss.

A kiss that had been so astonishingly real. I hadn't imagined it the way I'd imagined my hand on his cock, stroking it as he begged me not to stop. Would he kiss me again? My heart nearly stopped at the thought of him mentioning the previous incident. Somehow, I couldn't see Dean keeping quiet after hearing something like that. I drew in a breath, wondering how in the world I could get them to switch positions with any degree of diplomacy or tact.

Finally concluding that such a feat simply wasn't possible, I added, "Is there anything wrong? What I mean is, are you worried something might've happened to him?"

Wyatt shook his head. "No. He's a grown man. He can take care of himself." He paused, sweeping the doorjamb with his gaze. "I'll oil that hinge for you in the morning."

"That's very kind of you." Somehow, I managed to keep from stammering, although my chattering teeth probably betrayed me.

He continued to stand there, staring down at me as though intimidation were his ultimate goal. A moment passed before he gave me a curt nod. "Okay, then. Let me know if you need anything."

Anything? Was he hoping I would ask him in? Or had that squeaky hinge made enough noise earlier for him to suspect that Dean was hiding behind the door? Not wanting an answer to either of those questions, I began closing the door. "Don't worry. I will. Good night, Wyatt."

Fortunately, he didn't read too much into my reply. "Good night, Tina. Sleep well."

I watched him turn to go, wishing I had the guts to call him back.

What a stupid idea.

When the sound of his footsteps faded, I closed the door the rest of the way.

Dean let out a sigh of apparent relief. "Whew. That was close. Good thing I still had my pants on."

I looked at him with surprise. "I know Wyatt makes me jumpy as all get-out, but are you saying you're afraid of him too?"

"Oh, no way," Dean insisted. "I just don't want to put you in the middle of another scene."

A moment passed before I recalled the "scene" to which he was referring. "Oh. Yeah. I see what you mean. That would be…awkward."

"No shit." Grinning, he pulled me into his embrace and kissed me again. "See you at breakfast." He nodded toward the exterior door. "Guess I'd better leave this way and come back in through the bunkhouse. Probably shoulda used that door to begin with. More discreet."

All I could do was nod.

After he left, I finally went to bed. I didn't fall asleep for quite a while, but when I did drift off, I certainly didn't dream about Dean.

No, my dreams involved a dark, brooding, ex-firefighter cowboy with a sore shoulder, orgasm-inducing kisses, and uncanny timing.

Unfortunately, they were only dreams.

Chapter 13

THE NEXT THING I KNEW, IT WAS SATURDAY MORNING.
Time to make the pancakes.

Fortunately, I'd had time to flip through a few cookbooks before being faced with the task, although after I finished, I had to wonder why Calvin didn't make them more often. Either he didn't like pancakes or he considered them unhealthy because with that huge griddle and a nifty gadget that dispensed the correct amount of batter with the press of a button, making a bajillion pancakes was quite literally a piece of cake.

"By George, I think she's got it," Bull exclaimed as he sauntered into the kitchen. Grabbing a plate, he got in line behind Sonny and Dean.

Nick, having been first in line, had already kissed the cook and was no doubt in the mess hall, chowing down on a stack of pancakes that would have choked a horse. That is, if horses ever ate pancakes, which I doubted. Ophelia, on the other hand, ate a proportional amount with no difficulty whatsoever.

I was a little surprised at how well my timid pet had settled in at the ranch—and the entire journey, for that matter. Beyond her initial reaction to the men, she seemed tolerant of them, even affectionate at times—especially toward Wyatt. I could only assume it was because he sneaked her treats at dinnertime, but I'd seen the others doing the same thing.

She liked him. *Go figure.*

I shooed the guys out after breakfast. Without any letters to read, I would have more than enough time to wash the dishes.

Calvin's refusal to give up his cowboy chores in favor of becoming the full-time chief cook and bottle-washer didn't surprise me a bit. Now that I was getting into the swing of things, my free time had grown to the point that boredom was a distinct possibility. At least I had a car and could make a run into Rock Springs now and then.

That being said, I was reluctant to leave the ranch, mainly because I thought Angela might call, and I didn't want to miss any news about Calvin. As weak as the signal was on my cell—most of the time it was nonexistent—I'd stopped carrying it.

But I was getting restless. Dean had told me there was a phone extension in the barn, so I figured I could at least go out there and visit the horses.

I'd never been around horses much, but I soon discovered I liked them almost as much as dogs. They were friendly and inquisitive, nuzzling me whenever I drew near. I was bonding with a pretty reddish brown horse with a white star and a black mane when I heard the phone.

"Figures," I muttered as I headed toward the sound. Fortunately, it was in the tack room, which wasn't far away, and I caught it on the third ring. "Hello?"

"Hey, Tina," Angela said. "Still getting along okay?"

"Sure. Made a ton of pancakes this morning and the guys are all happy as clams." *Some more than others.*

"Great. I've got good news too. Calvin is doing much better. He actually recognized me this morning, and so far, he seems fairly coherent. His speech is a little slurred and he's still pretty weak, but other than that, everything looks good."

"Slurred speech?" I echoed. "Do they think he had a stroke?"

"The CT of the head was negative, but they said sometimes strokes don't show up right away. His hand grasps are equal, though, so they don't think that's the problem. One of the nurses said he acts kinda like he might've overdosed on something."

"That's doubtful, considering his pill bottles were all full—except for the nitroglycerine tablets."

"That's what I told them. Anyway, the doctor talked like he might release him tomorrow or the day after if he continues to improve." She hesitated for a second or two. "Dad doing okay?"

"Seems to be," I replied. "He and Dusty haven't missed a meal in the mess hall since you left."

She giggled. "I'm not surprised. Dad only cooks when he feels like it, which isn't very often these days. He hasn't been going out with the men, has he?"

"Not as far as I know. I only see him at mealtimes."

"Dusty must be keeping an eye on him then. He's next on my list of people to call—unless you've found any of Calvin's family."

"We found out his sister's name was Jeannine Caruthers, but she died back in January. There doesn't seem to be anyone else, unless that guy who tried to visit him really is his long-lost great-nephew, which is doubtful. The best we could tell from Calvin's letters, even Jeannine didn't know what happened to the kid."

She blew out a sigh. "Calvin and I obviously need to have a talk about what to do the next time something like this happens. It's been tough trying to figure out what he would want me to do."

"Good luck. Getting my grandfather to sign the POA papers wasn't easy."

"Yeah. Most men don't like the idea of giving up control."

In my experience, neither did most women. "After this, I'm guessing he'll understand the need for some sort of contingency plan."

"I sure hope so," she said. "Guess I'll give Dad a call. Y'all take care, now."

"You too."

I hung up the phone, unsure whether to be happy or sad. I was pleased to hear of Calvin's improvement, but his recovery would ultimately mean my departure. I was already starting to feel at home—*cue the guitars and fiddles*—on the range, even though I had yet to actually explore the places where the deer and the antelope play. I hadn't ridden a horse, and I hadn't seen a cow—not up close, anyway.

With those omissions in mind, I strolled out beyond the stable and found where the pigs and chickens were housed. I noticed a few eggs in the chicken pen, along with the basket I'd seen Sonny use to carry them into the kitchen. Cooking and debugging computers weren't the only things I could do. I had no burning desire to tend the hogs, but I could certainly feed chickens and gather eggs. Just because I hadn't been raised on a ranch didn't mean I couldn't learn.

I had the basket on my arm and was unlatching the gate when movement on the hillside beyond the out-buildings caught my eye. A blink and a stare revealed nothing more than the wind blowing through the tall brown grass. I glanced at Ophelia standing beside me. If she'd seen the same thing, she made no sign.

"Probably just a bird," I muttered. Certainly not anyone responsible for cutting fences, especially not in broad daylight.

As I gathered the eggs, I considered the fence-cutting mystery. As Angela had said, all it did was make more work for the men, forcing them to ride the fence line twice as often as they usually did and spend a great deal of time searching for stray cattle. As far as I knew, no fences had been cut since my arrival, but—

My thoughts broke off as I racked my brain for any mention of cut fences in the past two days. There had been grumblings about previous episodes, but none that were current.

What had changed? Calvin was in the hospital. Angela was in Salt Lake City. Mr. Kincaid was alone up at the main house most of the time. Dusty and the hands were out during the day, which, if I hadn't been there, would have left the bunkhouse unattended.

If I hadn't been there. Without my presence, anyone wishing to search the premises and steal anything that wasn't nailed down would have had ample time to do so. The trouble was, fences were being cut even before my arrival and nothing had been stolen—at least, not that anyone had noticed. Try as I might, I couldn't come up with anything that would explain everything—or even connect the dots.

I carried the eggs back to the kitchen and washed them before placing them in one of the cartons stacked in a bin beside the door. After stowing them in the fridge, I took three pounds of hamburger from the freezer and set it out to thaw along with a dozen store-bought buns. The kitchen was equipped with a good-sized deep fryer, but by the time I realized how many potatoes I would have to peel and slice to make fries for nine people, I opted to make potato salad instead. Having packed the balance of the cookies with the men's lunch, I knew I couldn't count on there being any left for dessert. So, after eating my own lunch, I dug around in the freezer and found some blackberries.

As I stared at the label on the package, a wave of nostalgia hit me like a freight train. Grandpa and I had picked blackberries every summer for as long as I could remember, and blackberry cobbler was one of the first things I'd ever baked. I should cherish those kinds of memories and let them crowd out the more recent ones.

An odd thought struck me then. Was that his reason for sending me on this trip? To help me remember the good times and forget the bad? If so, his ploy had worked. In my mind, I could see the glossy berries, rich with color and flavor as they ripened in the sun. I could hear the drone of bees and other insects as I fought them for the berries. Feel the sting of the thorns scratching my arms, leaving battle scars of which I'd actually been proud. Inhale the heavenly scent of blackberry cobbler while it baked in the oven, and see Grandpa's blissful smile as he took that first bite.

Those were the things I needed to remember. Episodes I could look back on with fondness and joy rather than regret or despair. Time was supposed to heal all wounds, but those few short days in Wyoming had already done more for me than all the months that had passed in the wake of his death.

So it was with a much lighter heart that I made the most recent in a long line of blackberry cobblers. Neither Grandpa nor his friend Calvin would be there to share it with me, but there were others who would enjoy it just as much as they would have. I was content with that.

Once the cobbler was in the oven, I chopped up and boiled a mountain of potatoes. After they cooled, I made the potato salad, adding my own flourishes to a recipe I'd found in one of Calvin's cookbooks.

I had just reached the point of simply waiting for the guys to show up, when it struck me that while Wyatt had seemed to think there was no longer any reason to contact Jeannine's family, and there probably wasn't, something about her obituary bugged me. In searching for other people to contact, I'd overlooked the fact that there had been no mention of the one person we did know who had survived Jeannine.

Fortunately, I'd bookmarked the page and was able to pull it up without any trouble. Sure enough, Calvin wasn't mentioned. Only the relatives on the Caruthers side of the family were listed.

"Still at it?"

With a gasp, I swiveled around to see Wyatt standing in the doorway. Clad in boots, jeans, and a dusty denim jacket over a dark blue plaid shirt, he might've been the template from which every sexy cowboy had been cut.

"Sorry," he said, removing his hat. "Didn't mean to startle you."

I shot an admonitory glance at Ophelia, who was supposed to warn me when someone was sneaking up behind me. Apparently Wyatt didn't rate that response.

"No problem," I lied. "C'mere and take a look at this."

As much noise as his boots made on the bare wooden floor, I couldn't believe I hadn't heard his approach. *Sneaky fellow.*

"What's up?"

I scooted my chair sideways and gestured at the computer. "Read that."

Tossing his hat onto the recliner, he placed a hand on the edge of the desk and leaned toward the screen. The last time I'd been that close to him, he'd kissed me senseless. At the moment, however, his nearness only allowed me to observe his satyr-like frown up close and personal. Crossing my arms, I hugged my chest, doing my best to suppress the inevitable shiver.

"So?"

"Notice anything missing?"

"You mean beyond Calvin's name?"

"Nope. That's my point. Either Jeannine's break with Calvin was complete to the point of denying the connection altogether, or whoever wrote her obituary didn't know she had a brother."

"So no one would've contacted him." He nodded. "Yeah. Probably not."

"Which means he probably doesn't even know she died." I tried to move my chair back to put a little more space between us only to find it was already against the wall. "Not the best news to give a man as soon as he wakes up after nearly dying, is it?"

"Not really." Arching a brow, he aimed his unnerving glare at me. "You mean he's awake?"

"Yeah. Angela called. She said he seems more coherent—he actually recognized her—but he's still pretty weak and his speech is slurred." When I added the part about him acting like someone who'd overdosed, Wyatt's reaction was similar to what mine had been.

"Not like him to take too many pills. More like not enough."

"That's what I thought." I shrugged. "There isn't any evidence of that, really. Just the opinion of one of the nurses."

"As much as nurses see, I wouldn't discount that suggestion."

"Me either." I shrugged again. "Guess that's something we can ask him about. Angela said they might release him in the next day or so if he continues to improve."

Wyatt took a quick step backward and drew himself up to his full height. His gaze softened for an instant before his usual enigmatic expression slid back into place. "You'll stay on for a while, won't you?"

Once again, I'd caught a brief glimpse of some indefinable emotion in his eyes. As good as he was at hiding his feelings, it was a wonder I'd seen it at all. "Sure," I replied, keeping my tone light. "I can stay as long as you need me to."

I started to add something about room and board being all I really needed at that point, but he seemed satisfied with my response, giving me a brief nod before a frown once again creased his brow.

"Look, I'm sorry about yesterday," he began. "I shouldn't have done that. Kissed you, I mean."

Somehow I doubted he was the type to apologize very often—or even need to. Moistening my lower lip, I caught it in my teeth, completely at a loss for words.

Should I tell him what that kiss had done to me? Or should I tell him about Dean? I wanted to laugh it off, but I couldn't bring myself to do it. A heated flush crept up my neck to sting my cheeks. "I, um, didn't mind. Not really."

As encouraging responses went, that one was pretty mild. Wyatt, on the other hand, reacted like a horse that simultaneously felt spur and curb, taking a step toward me before stopping short.

Until our eyes met.

In seconds, I was in his arms with my back against the wall, his kiss crushing any shred of resistance I might have offered. What he'd done the day before seemed tame in comparison. Thrilled, aroused, and terrified at the same time, I couldn't fight the emotions; I could only let them flow through me like floodwaters through a broken dam.

The notion that the door to my room was standing wide open flitted through my mind and was immediately dismissed. I flat-out didn't care. Wyatt might've scared the bejesus out of me.

But I liked it.

This time, no door slammed, no boisterous voices broke the silence. My strength and will returned, but instead of pushing him away, I curled my arms up around his neck and clutched the back of his head, a move somehow inherently erotic. My knees sagged. If I'd been against anything less than a wall, I would've pulled him down on top of me.

A moment later, the wall was gone, its solid form replaced by something soft and yielding. My head swam in protest of the sudden shift from vertical to horizontal, but Wyatt's lips never left mine. His hands gripped my head as though ensuring my continued cooperation, then released me to strip off his jacket. My only wish was that he'd gotten rid of the shirt along with it.

He pressed a knee between my legs, nudging them apart. Despite being fully clothed, that intimacy made me feel exposed and vulnerable. Searing need knifed through my core, releasing yet another emotional flood, this one of passion and desire. I wrapped my legs around him, pulling him closer, pressing his erection hard against the ache between my thighs.

A deep, gut-wrenching groan emanated from his chest, heralding the sound he'd undoubtedly heard an instant before I did. Booted feet. Slamming doors. Male voices.

Suddenly, he was on his feet, pulling me upright before practically throwing me into the chair.

He stood there, staring at me, controlling his rampant breathing with a visible effort. "Next time, remind me to lock the damned door."

Chapter 14

SO THAT'S WHAT IT'S LIKE TO BE MANHANDLED.

Scary, but exhilarating, and definitely not the sort of thing I'd ever thought I would enjoy—although I wasn't sure *enjoy* was the right word to describe the way I felt.

Oddly enough, the entire situation seemed rather funny. The more I thought about it, the harder I giggled. By the time Dean stuck his head in the door, tears of laughter were streaming down my face. Wyatt had at least had the good sense to pick up his jacket, but my bed was slightly rumpled. God only knew what my hair looked like.

"What's the joke?" Dean asked.

Wyatt shot him a grin. "You kinda had to be here."

Thankfully, he hadn't been.

When Dean asked about Calvin, I gave him the rundown of the day's events, ending with the news that Calvin would be coming home soon.

His reaction was similar to Wyatt's. "You won't leave right away, will you?"

Oh, dear... "Like I told Wyatt, I'll stick around as long as I'm needed."

Nick's head popped up over Dean's shoulder. "If that's the case, you'll never leave. Calvin's a great guy, but you're a better cook."

"Thanks, Nick. But for heaven's sake don't tell Calvin that." I rose from the chair, pleased to note that the rubber in my knees had once again been replaced with bone. "Nothing too exciting on tonight's menu, anyhow. Just hamburgers and potato salad."

"And blackberry fuckin' cobbler," Bull added as he joined the crowd at my door.

The way things were going, I was glad Wyatt had moved as fast as he had. Otherwise, we would've had quite an audience. I glared at Bull, forcing myself to keep a straight face. "Bull, if you so much as touch that cobbler before dinner, I'm gonna knock knots all over your bald head."

"Damn if you don't sound just like my mother," Bull declared. "You'll be telling me to watch my language next."

"I might," I snapped. "It's about time someone did." I wasn't sure what to make of sounding like Bull's mother. Seemed a little weird. Even weirder was the fact that I sounded a lot like *my* mother.

Bull chuckled, obviously enjoying the banter. "Good luck. If I didn't cuss, I probably couldn't talk at all."

"Somehow, I don't think she'd see that as a problem," Wyatt drawled.

Once again, I was overcome with helpless laughter. "You guys are killing me."

"Well now, we can't have that," Wyatt said, his drawl still quite pronounced. "You're the best cook we've got." Snatching a tissue from the box on my desk, he used it to wipe the tears from my cheeks.

I was still giggling when it struck me just how intimate that gesture was. On top of that, he was smiling at me in a very disturbing manner—a smile quite unlike that of a casual acquaintance.

I stole a glance at Dean just as he muttered, "Aw,

hell," turned on his heel, and stomped off, clearly displaying his annoyance—and also the fact that he'd recognized both intimacies for what they were.

He was being replaced, ousted, and bested—something I'd never intended and certainly never expected. Hurting Dean's feelings was the last thing I wanted to do. He'd been so sweet, so understanding.

If you hadn't kissed him, you wouldn't be in this... situation. I couldn't call it a mess. Not yet.

"What was that all about?" Bull demanded.

"Oh, shut up, Bull," Nick growled. "For once in your life, just shut the fuck up."

Either Bull was too dense to pick up on the vibes between Dean and me or he'd forgotten about the hickey he'd so graciously brought to everyone's attention. Then again, perhaps he'd assumed Wyatt had been the culprit. Or not. As befuddled as I was, I couldn't remember.

I had only myself to blame. Well, no. That wasn't completely true. Dean and Wyatt had both initiated everything. At least I thought they had. I certainly hadn't been the one to kiss either of them first. Granted, I'd bitten Wyatt, but—

But what? I'd bitten him and he'd kissed me. What was that? Some sort of mating ritual I knew nothing about?

Oh, bloody hell!

Bull would have undoubtedly said something far more colorful, but that expletive was as profane as I ever got, and I rarely said it aloud.

If I'd had to guess, I'd have said Wyatt knew exactly what he was doing, and also what Dean and I had been up to. Case in point, his irritable reactions when Dean and I started getting chummy.

I wasn't sure "chummy" was the right word, either.

I'm so confused...

Heaving a sigh, I strode from the room, bypassing Nick and Bull and leaving Wyatt to make his own explanations. Before anything else happened, I needed to have a talk with Dean.

I hurried through the kitchen and into the mess hall. Sonny and Joe were both in the process of hanging up their hats and jackets, but there was no sign of Dean.

The door to the men's sleeping quarters stood ajar. Peeking inside, I spotted Dean sitting on a bunk, picking out a melody on a guitar like he knew what he was doing.

"Hey, you," I said softly. "Can I come in?"

"Sure. Why the hell not?"

I thought it best to ignore the question and take him at his word.

I'd never been in that section of the building before and was a little surprised at how nice it was. Laid out like a dormitory with windows at regular intervals, the long, narrow room had rows of beds arranged along both exterior walls. The amount of space between each man's "room" suggested the bunkhouse had been built to accommodate a lot more men than it currently housed. A hodgepodge of patterns, colors, and mismatched furniture reflected a variety of personal tastes. A doorway at the far end presumably led to the showers, while another appeared to open out toward the stable yard.

Dean's area contained a leather recliner, a small oak dresser, and a nightstand topped with a rather rustic-looking lamp. A Navajo rug lay on the floor, and the quilt covering the bed was crafted in a similar style.

For the first time, I realized how little these men had. I assumed they were paid a decent wage, but their needs were obviously simple; the size of their bank accounts probably didn't mean much to them.

They were certainly a breed apart from any men I'd dealt with in the past. They didn't seem ambitious or greedy, but did they dream of more? A home of their own? A family? In his letters to my grandfather, Calvin had made it clear that he'd chosen this kind of life—mainly because he'd lost the ones he loved most and couldn't stand the thought of losing anyone else. However, despite his determination to avoid family ties, his illness had proven just how important those connections could be—and I had an idea he'd found another family here on the ranch. Dean was part of that family, and I didn't want to hurt him any more than I would Calvin.

"I didn't know you played the guitar."

He shrugged. "Ever since I was a kid."

"Sounds pretty good." I sat down in the recliner opposite him and leaned forward, unsure how to begin. "Talk to me, Dean. Tell me what you're feeling."

He strummed a few chords before he spoke, his gaze directed toward the floor. "I don't know how I feel. Angry, maybe." When he looked up at me, disappointment showed in his eyes, but no anger, and certainly no tears. "I probably shouldn't be. After all, we did say no strings."

"Seemed like a good idea at the time, didn't it?" I paused, grimacing. "I'm not so sure anymore. This is all so new to me. You of all people should know that."

A tiny smile touched his lips. "Yeah. Guess it's a good thing we never got around to using those condoms." His eyes drifted back to mine. "You've never slept with a man before. Have you?"

"Um…no. Was it that obvious?"

"Yeah. I was kinda nervous about that," he confided. "I've never done a virgin. It's a little scary."

I couldn't help smiling. "Imagine how it feels from my perspective."

"Good point. I really didn't like the idea of hurting you." The concern in his eyes left little doubt as to his sincerity. "Looks like Wyatt'll be the one to do the honors."

"Maybe. I don't know if that's what he wants. He's not what you'd call talkative. I mean, I can't see having the kind of casual arrangement with him that you and I have."

"Had."

I eyed him curiously. "Is that it? One hint of competition from Wyatt and you're throwing in the towel?"

"I was never even in the ring." He sounded more realistic than defeated, which was good in a way and really rotten in another. I tried not to think about that.

"To be honest, I don't even know if Wyatt's in the ring. But I think I owe it to myself to take the time to figure it out."

"Well…you know where to find me if you need me."

Somehow, I wouldn't have thought it would be that easy, and I still felt as though I owed him an apology. "I'm sorry, Dean. I never dreamed any of this would happen. None of it. From the moment Calvin insisted I stay for dinner, I might as well have been on another planet. And you know how it is with us aliens. We tend to make mistakes."

He arched a brow. "You think what we did was a mistake?"

"No, and I don't regret it for a second. But I do regret hurting your feelings. I never meant to do that, and no matter what happens between me and Wyatt, I want us to be friends." The tears I'd searched for in his eyes finally welled up in my own. "I really like you guys. All of you. I've never had any male friends before. I was always too darn shy."

"Not anymore." His wry grin gave me a glimmer of hope. "I mean, you've seen me naked."

"And you've had your hands on my boobs." It was a testament to my steadily diminishing shyness that I was actually able to say that without stammering or blushing. I still had more to learn, but I'd come a long way in three days, and I'd enjoyed every minute of it.

"Yes, I have." His smile broadened, then slowly faded. "I'm gonna miss that." He played an intricate riff, one I recognized. "There's gotta be a song in there somewhere."

"If so, you be sure and write it. Just don't tell everyone where your inspiration came from."

The wicked grin I remembered finally put in an appearance. "I'll call it 'She Was Almost My Fuck Buddy Sweetheart.' Sure to be a huge hit."

"Don't quit your day job yet," I advised, laughing—with relief as much as amusement. "Speaking of jobs, I have hamburgers to grill and tomatoes to slice. Hungry?"

"Always."

"What do you like on your hamburger?"

"Lettuce, tomatoes, onions, and pickles."

"Hmm…" I tapped my chin. "Onions, huh? Kinda makes me glad I won't be kissing you later on."

A wistful smile replaced his grin. "So we're really calling it quits?"

"I think it's best."

Once again, his gaze drifted toward the floor. "Sure was fun."

Reaching out, I lifted his chin with a fingertip, forcing him to look at me. "Dean, those moments I spent with you were the most fun I've ever had, and if we'd kept on, you might've had the chance to use those condoms."

"You really mean that?"

"Absolutely." I wasn't lying, either. Kissing Wyatt was thrilling, but making out with Dean was a blast.

"They say you never forget your first fling—or is it your first love?"

"Doesn't matter. I won't forget any of this, Dean. Not until I'm old and senile, and probably not even then." Would he be content with that? Being unfamiliar with the mysteries of the male mind, I could only hope.

I had just risen from my chair and started for the door when he began to play a long, wailing riff, complete with enough bends and sustains to satisfy the most discriminating country music fan.

"Do me a favor?" he asked, punctuating his request with a slide. "If Wyatt's a better kisser, don't tell me."

Then again, some workings of the male mind were astonishingly transparent.

"Fair enough."

———

I went back out to the kitchen and started on the hamburgers, trying to focus on the job at hand rather than all the crazy emotions zinging around in my head. I'd never had a boyfriend—casual or otherwise—therefore, I'd never broken up with one man because another guy was hitting on me. What did I say to Wyatt now? *All clear? I'm yours?*

For the moment, I decided it was best not to say anything. Wyatt was messing with my mind in ways I couldn't begin to understand, or even count. Jumping into anything with him, be it my bed or whatever sort of relationship he had in mind, seemed inadvisable. I wasn't technically brokenhearted or even on the rebound, but a slower approach was bound to be less confusing.

Maybe.

Wyatt at least had the good sense to leave me alone with those thoughts. Otherwise, I probably would've burned the burgers. I wasn't exactly in competition with Calvin for best bunkhouse cook, but I suspected that working cowboys could be counted among the ranks of hamburger connoisseurs, unless they ate them often enough to be sick of them. Or disliked the smell of cattle enough to never want any part of them on their plates.

Surely not...

After only our third dinner together, the guys already seemed to be pretty well-trained. Sonny and Nick set the table without being asked, then came back to collect the serving dishes as I filled them up with fixings for the burgers. Bull hadn't so much as stuck a finger in the cobbler.

The mood was different, though. Calvin's improvement should have raised their spirits—they had all seemed pleased to hear the news—but after that, their behavior was more subdued, even somber. I doubted it was because the food tasted bad. Bull looked like he'd died and gone to heaven when he bit into his hamburger, and he didn't mince words when it came to describing the potato salad as the "best goddamned thing I ever ate in my life."

"You said that about the apple pie," Nick reminded him. "Can't have it both ways."

"I sure as hell can," Bull argued. "That pie was the best until now. I'm guessing that fuckin' cobbler will be next."

"Maybe you just need to be more specific," I suggested. "You know…the best pie or the best salad rather than the best *thing*."

"Good point," Bull said with a nod. "I'll do that."

I thought the atmosphere would lighten up some after that, but it didn't. If anything, the guys seemed even more morose.

"You guys are awfully quiet this evening. Anything wrong?" Dean's silence was easily explained. It was the others who had me stumped. Even Dusty and Mr. Kincaid weren't saying much, and I was pretty sure they didn't know anything about the shifting interpersonal relationships.

"No," Nick replied. "Everything's fine."

"Fences intact, cows all accounted for?"

He helped himself to more potato salad. "No problems. Just another day on the Circle Bar K."

"Oh. Okay." I'd had a pretty uneventful day myself before Wyatt showed up. Things got a lot more interesting after that.

The subject seemed to be closed until Joe—who, being the exact opposite of Bull, rarely said anything at all—spoke up. "We, um, kinda like having you around, Tina."

"I see," I said with a slow, dubious nod. "And that explains all the gloomy faces?"

"Well, yeah," Sonny said. "We sorta hoped you'd stay on even after Calvin came home."

"I already said I would. I'm sure Calvin won't feel like doing much for a few weeks."

Sonny shook his head. "We meant forever. But if you aren't gonna marry Dean, I guess there's no reason for you to stick around."

Despite being rendered momentarily speechless, I was about to protest that those two outcomes weren't mutually exclusive when Nick added, "Unless she marries Wyatt."

Chapter 15

THIS TIME I *REALLY* DIDN'T KNOW WHAT TO SAY.

Fortunately, Bull filled in the gap in the conversation. "No need for her to marry anyone. I mean, since when does our cook have to be married?"

"Well," Mr. Kincaid began, "seein' as how we've never had a female cook before, her bein' married couldn't hurt."

If I'd taken on a permanent position, I could understand that—up to a point. But for a temporary job, I couldn't see that it mattered. "Yeah, well, I'm *not* married, and I don't plan to be anytime soon." I couldn't even imagine a shotgun wedding being appropriate in this situation. No doubt my father would be pleased if I decided to marry, but he certainly wouldn't force the issue by brandishing a twelve gauge. Dean and I hadn't done anything the average teenager wouldn't do, and probably less than that. "Can we talk about something else?"

"Hey, you're the one who fussed at us for being too quiet," Nick said. "We're just spicing up the conversation."

I put up a hand. "Sorry I said anything. From now on, I'll keep my mouth shut and enjoy the silence." I'd had plenty of practice doing both of those things—as opposed to only three days worth of making small talk with a bunch of cowboys.

Now I was stuck sitting at the table with them when

all I really wanted to do was disappear—preferably through the floor. Unwilling to risk making eye contact with anyone, Dean and Wyatt in particular, I stared at my plate.

I'd only been there for three days and they were ready to marry me off? How weird was that? On the one hand, I should be thanking my lucky stars. On the other, I ought to be running for my life.

Or getting drunk. Maybe that was my problem. I didn't drink enough. Didn't loosen up enough.

No. That wasn't true. Comparatively speaking, I'd loosened up quite a bit, despite not having actually done the deed with a sexy cowboy. Then again, there was plenty of alcohol on hand. I'd seen beer in the fridge and tequila in the pantry—along with a bottle of rum that was dusty enough to have been hidden away in there for a very long time. Who knew what might have happened if I'd taken a shot or two for courage?

"Can I have some cobbler now?" Bull sounded almost meek.

"Sure. Help yourself." I rose from the table. "I'm kinda tired. Would you guys mind cleaning up?"

They all looked at me like I'd sprouted antlers. I'd forgotten that the dishwashing rotation was part of their routine.

"Sure," Joe said. "No problem."

Muttering my thanks, I beat a hasty retreat.

No matter who came knocking on my door that night—and I doubted anyone would—I was *not* letting him in.

But Ophelia needed to go out.

I wasn't the slightest bit sleepy, despite having taken a long, hot shower and reading nearly a third of the book I'd downloaded. Figuring a bit of exercise and fresh air couldn't hurt, I donned a jacket and went with her.

We didn't go far. The moon was so bright I could easily have found my way even without the security light mounted above the barn door. Ophelia trotted alongside me as I crossed the stable yard, the loose gravel crunching beneath my shoes. She was sniffing around the edge of the chicken pen when I glanced up at the open hillside.

A beam of light caught my eye. At least I thought that's what it was. It disappeared so quickly, I wasn't even sure I'd seen it.

"That's your imagination, Tina." Nonetheless, with all the fence cutting troubles, not to mention the movement I thought I'd seen there earlier that day, I figured I ought to tell someone.

Great. Now I had to stick my nose in the bunkhouse and wake everybody up.

Wake was right. I hadn't realized how late it was. The bunkhouse windows were dark, and another security light was all that shone from the main house.

Goose bumps prickled my nape, and I glanced over my shoulder more than once as I hurried inside, half expecting someone to pounce on me from behind. Entering through the kitchen, I passed through to the mess hall, my footsteps echoing loudly in the empty room. The door to the men's sleeping quarters stood open. I tiptoed closer and peered inside.

"Hey," I stage-whispered. "Anyone awake?"

"Yeah." Bedsprings creaked somewhere in darkness, and a tall figure loomed against the moonlit windows. "What's up?"

Of course it had to be Wyatt. It couldn't possibly have been Joe or Bull or anyone else.

When he stepped into the mess hall, my breath caught in my throat. I'd seen him in a T-shirt and briefs before—and make no mistake, it was an impressive sight even then—but that was before I'd gotten a taste of his heart-stopping kisses and massaged those broad, muscular shoulders.

The deep breath I took to settle my nerves didn't completely eliminate the tremor in my voice. "I just went out with Ophelia, and I'm pretty sure I saw a light up on the hill. Might be your fence-cutting friend."

"Show me where."

He caught my arm as I started toward the kitchen.

"Not that way," he whispered. "Through the window." He gestured toward the south side of the mess hall, then put a finger to his lips.

Understanding the need for stealth, I slipped off my shoes, and we crept silently across the room. The warm pressure of his hand on the small of my back made me acutely aware that I was alone in the dark with a man clad only in his underwear—a man who'd kissed me senseless only hours before.

Keep breathing, Tina.

When we reached the window, I stood at an angle to the pane, pointing toward the east. "There. Near the top of that hill."

"Hmm… No fences up there, but following that ridge is the quickest way to the road on foot."

"I thought I saw something moving up there this afternoon. I couldn't tell what it was, though."

He nodded. "Anyone wanting to keep an eye on the place could see a helluva lot from up there."

"Yes, but why? I mean, I can understand why someone might want to watch what's going on during the day, but what is there to see at night?"

"That's what we need to find out."

I stared up at him, aghast. "You're not going out there alone, are you?"

"Why? Would that worry you?"

His inflection suggested he either found that idea amusing or it pleased him. I wasn't sure which, but I saw no reason to deny my concern.

"Of course it would." I started to add that I didn't think it was safe for anyone to go out alone, but his grin stopped me.

"Yeah, well, I did say *we*."

My cheeks tingled with warmth, making me glad neither of us had turned on a light. "Yes, you did."

He tipped my head back with a finger beneath my chin. "Be right back." Though brief, the kiss was astonishingly sensuous, setting off a full-body blush and a telltale ache at the apex of my thighs. "Keep a lookout for anything suspicious."

He'd been gone several moments before I convinced myself that continued surveillance was indeed vitally important—far more so than contemplating stolen kisses in the dark. Turning back toward the window, I gazed out into the distance.

Wyatt returned with Nick a few minutes later, both of them carrying their boots. "Seen anything?"

"No," I replied. "How are you going to get out of here without anyone seeing *you*?" To be perfectly honest, what he'd said about what could be seen from that hilltop kinda had me spooked—especially if whoever was up there had a rifle equipped with a night-vision scope.

"We'll go out through Calvin's quarters," Wyatt said with a nod in that direction. "His room has the same sort of exterior door that yours does, only his lets out toward the pasture. We'll circle around the outbuildings and head up the hill farther to the north."

My eyes widened as I noted that our potential sniper wouldn't be the only one armed. Each man wore a holster slung low on his hip, the pale moonlight casting a gleam on a pair of pistols that wouldn't have been out of place at the OK Corral.

I was pretty sure Wyatt Earp had survived that fight. Whether Wyatt McCabe would come back alive was less certain.

Get a grip, Tina. This isn't the Wild West.

Wyatt must've caught my wide-eyed stare. He patted the holster. "In case we run into any rattlers."

I couldn't decide which was worse, a sniper or a snake. "Gee, thanks, Wyatt. That makes me feel *so* much better."

Nick chuckled. "Don't worry, Tina. He's a pretty good shot—and I'm better than he is."

I glanced at Wyatt for confirmation.

"Sometimes," he conceded. "But not tonight."

While I had no clue what he meant by that, I suspected the explanation would be lengthy, and time was something we couldn't afford to waste. "You guys be careful."

"We will," Wyatt said. "Mind keeping watch 'til we get back?"

As if I would do anything else. "Sure."

The two men barely made a sound as they disappeared through the doorway. Ophelia whined and started to follow them. I grabbed her collar and held on until I heard the soft click of the outer door closing.

"No way, Lia." On any other occasion, I might have let her go, but not now. Not when stealth was required.

I carried one of the dining room chairs over to the window and sat down to watch. Ophelia curled up at my feet and began snoring almost immediately. Given the edgy state of my nerves, I never expected to get sleepy, but after a bit, I had to lean against the wall to keep from falling out of the chair.

A hand on my shoulder woke me with a yelp. "Warn me next time, will you?"

"I did," Wyatt said, chuckling. "Fired warning shots and everything."

"Oh, you did not." I rose from the chair, rubbing my right arm, which had also fallen asleep. "Where's Nick?"

"Gone back to bed." Having already divested himself of everything but his T-shirt and jeans, Wyatt appeared to be headed in that direction himself.

"I take it you didn't find anything."

"Nope. Whoever it was must've been heading for the road when you saw that light. I bet we find some fences down in the morning."

With no evidence to support my claim, most men would have told me that flash of light was nothing but a product of my overactive, hormone-driven imagination. Wyatt, on the other hand, still believed me. Granted, they'd already dealt with enough fencing problems for my story to have been plausible, but he didn't even qualify his response.

"Guess you'd better get some sleep." I hesitated, unsure whether it was safe to press my luck. "Sorry for sending you out on a wild-goose chase."

"Don't be. That was the first decent lead we've had."

The silence between us stretched out long enough to feel awkward. "Good night," I finally said. "Thanks for believing me."

"Why wouldn't I believe you?" He sounded genuinely puzzled.

"Oh, you know—" I was about to say *you know how men are* until it struck me that I was talking to the one man to whom the general rules didn't appear to apply. "Most guys would tell me I was imagining things."

He shrugged. "Maybe. But I don't think you were. I'd be stupid not to go take a look."

"You're anything but that." I must have been really sleepy because I hadn't intended to say that aloud.

His next words proved I had.

"I'm glad you think so." He grazed my cheek with his fingertips. "I'd *really* be stupid if I didn't do this."

Oh, God...

Spearing his fingers through my hair, he tilted my face upward, his searing gaze locking on to mine. The moment our lips touched, my eyelids fluttered down, and he ravaged my mouth with his kiss.

He didn't stop there. My face, ears, and neck were all easy targets for his scorching kisses. Kisses that robbed me of breath, sapped the strength in my legs, and destroyed every scrap of willpower I possessed.

There had to be valid biological reasons for those reactions—hormones and foreplay combining to turn women into willing participants in a less than equitable arrangement. Perhaps females only crumpled in male arms to enable the guy to have his wicked way with her—or carry her off somewhere.

Which is exactly what Wyatt did.

By the time my back touched the mattress, I'd forgotten all about biology and willpower. Sleep was unimportant. Nothing mattered but the man in my arms.

The urgency that had been missing with Dean finally surfaced. I wasted no time yanking off Wyatt's shirt, my palms and fingertips itching to make contact with his skin. Massaging his shoulders was nothing compared to this. The contours of his body were like classical sculpture beneath my hands, although unlike the cold hardness of marble, he was still hot from the exertions of the search.

The search. I didn't care about that, either. Didn't care that some imaginary fellow with an infrared scope could probably see our heat signature through the window. Very little could have stopped us now.

Drunk on his scent and his touch, I didn't even consider offering any resistance. I was enhanced by him, made stronger, more complete, more *real*.

I didn't have to be shy anymore, didn't need to be. I could touch and caress any part of him I wished. His hair, his neck, his face, and the rest of that amazing body. They were mine now. I licked the side of his neck, tasting his salty skin before sinking my teeth into the taut muscles beneath. Biting him had gotten me kissed once before. What would it get me now?

A deep, guttural growl issued from his throat, transmitting the vibration to my lips.

"You're playing with fire, Tina."

I smiled against his neck when I really felt like laughing. If he thought I didn't want him insane with passion, he had a lot to learn about me. I'd been hesitant with Dean, and now I understood why.

I wanted to be fucked—hard and fast and deep—by this man and this man only. But could I say it? Or should I simply make it impossible for him to do anything else?

"Am I really?" I whispered. "What else should I do? What makes you crazy?"

"You do," he replied. "*You* make me crazy. I never thought it could happen to me. But from the first moment I laid eyes on you..." Another kiss dipped lower, and suddenly a button came undone. And another and another... "I thought I could stand back and let Dean have you, but I couldn't do it. Just...couldn't."

One swipe of his tongue over my nipple sent me soaring. Every sensation was amplified—the touch, the sights, the sounds. Wyatt's hands left a fiery trail as he slid them down my sides and under the waistband of my pajamas. Skimming my hips, he pushed my pants to my thighs. My body tingled as though his touch had exposed raw nerve endings. Cool air ruffled the curls between my legs.

His jeans went next, along with his briefs. It didn't matter how; all I cared about was that he was naked. The hard ridge of his cock pressed against my stomach, leaving a trail of slick moisture as he moved downward, kissing his way from my lips to my breasts. Nudging my legs apart with his knee, he hesitated, his cockhead poised at my entrance, waiting.

For what? Permission?

"Go ahead, Wyatt," I urged. "Make me scream."

The first plunge did it, invading me with a shocking, exhilarating force. Ignoring the brief pain as my hymen gave way, I sucked in a breath and grabbed his shoulders, anticipating the next wave of incredible delight. Thrust after thrust stretched and stimulated as stars came and went behind my shuttered eyes. My moans were real and insuppressible; I could neither fake nor stop them—or even stifle the sounds. He went on and on—pulsing, pounding, penetrating.

I opened my eyes to find his gaze riveted to my face, his expression fierce and exultant, yet tender, perhaps even vulnerable. I'd never seen such a jumble of emotions before, but the one thing I didn't see was regret. Nor could he have seen it in my eyes because I had no regrets. None.

I was well aware that no barrier stood between us, and that the result of such an omission might well be a baby I would have to carry for nine months and then look after for the next eighteen years. I accepted the risk as well as the responsibility. Whether he felt the same remained to be seen.

His pace slowed to a heavy thud, the smack of our bodies occurring less often, but with no less enjoyment. My eyes rolled back in my head and were drifting shut when he spoke.

"I didn't have a condom."

He hadn't said he'd forgotten to put it on or asked if he needed one. He'd been as unprepared as I was. "I noticed that."

"Does it matter?"

I caught myself before saying the first word that came to mind, opting for the second and far more responsible reply. "Probably."

He nodded. His speed didn't change; only the force and depth of his thrusts increased. Three thrilling strokes later, I reached a euphoric plateau and hung there, suspended in space, delirious with joy.

"Sorry." With what could've been a gasp or a sob, he withdrew.

The absence of his body inside mine was such a tremendous loss; I barely felt the spurt of semen on the back of my thigh.

I never wanted to feel either of those things again. Unless Dean was willing to give up his stash of condoms—and I had no intention of asking for them—I really needed to go to the store. It was either that or risk getting pregnant.

Abstinence was not an option.

Chapter 16

Despite having just been nailed by Wyatt McCabe, I was already anxious to do it again—immediately, if not sooner.

I say "nailed" because I couldn't think of any other word that accurately described the experience, and even that one came up short. I couldn't say we'd made love, because to the best of my recollection, love hadn't been mentioned, no matter how much I suspected—or hoped—it would eventually be brought into play.

For the moment, I was more stunned than anything, and I had absolutely no idea what to say. Being a man of few words, I doubted Wyatt would start spewing poetry, or whatever it was men did in the wake of mind-blowing sex.

Unless it hadn't been as mind-blowing for him. If it wasn't, I really didn't want to know.

But he did say I made him crazy, and I was pretty sure that was a good thing. Of course, now that we'd done the deed, he might not be crazy anymore. Perhaps he'd been cured.

Hmm... Clearly, I was thinking too much. Reminding myself that actions did, after all, speak louder than words, I turned on my side to give him more room to lie down, hoping he would take the hint.

He did.

God bless him.

As much as I hoped he would kiss me again, I knew

I needed to be the one to initiate it. I touched his cheek with a gentle caress, then skimmed my fingertips through the hair at his temple. Reaching around to cup the nape of his neck, I pulled him closer. Had I ever done that to Dean? I honestly couldn't remember. But I knew for a fact I'd never kissed Wyatt first. Until now.

The kiss we shared in the aftermath of sex was no less satisfying than those that preceded it. But the tone had changed somehow, becoming sweeter, more poignant. I didn't know what to make of that, although it didn't strike me as standard fuck-buddy stuff.

Knowing so little about him was frustrating when I wanted to know everything. Why he was so touchy about certain subjects. Why he was working on a ranch instead of in a fire station. Why he'd never thought "this"—whatever it was—would happen to him. Why the sexiest man I'd ever met wasn't already taken. Why it scared me to think I might not be able to keep him.

Breaking off the kiss, I drew back, drinking in the sight of him. Moonlight twinkled in his eyes, highlighting the sharp planes of his nose, the arch of his brow, and the sensuous fullness of his lips. I'd never seen a stronger, more handsome face.

"What're you lookin' at?" he asked.

"You," I replied, tracing his uniquely shaped eyebrows with a fingertip. "Just you."

A tiny smile dimpled one cheek. "Like what you see?"

"Very much."

He acknowledged the compliment with a self-conscious clearing of his throat. "Never figured I'd get this lucky, especially after you left the mess hall in such a hurry."

"I *was* feeling kinda picked on."

"Sorry about that. We don't know how to behave around a woman like you." His smile became a grin that creased the corners of his eyes. "Or as Dean once put it, a gorgeous blond."

I doubted Dean would put it quite like that since I'd called off our no-strings deal. "What's he calling me now? A two-timing bitch?"

"If he did, Nick and Sonny would pound him into the dirt and Bull and Joe would finish him off."

"Why on earth would they do that?"

Wyatt's sudden burst of laughter made him look so boyishly handsome, I barely recognized him as the man who'd been so brusque with me when I first arrived. "In case you haven't noticed, you're pretty popular with all the guys. Bull's even talking about nominating you for sainthood in that crazy religion of his—patron saint of cowboys or some such bullshit."

I gaped at him for the space of about three heartbeats. "He must've really liked that cobbler."

"Come on now, Tina. It's more than the food, and you know it."

Actually, I didn't—unless I'd passed through some sort of transformational portal during the drive from Louisville. "I've never known any guys to be that"—I hesitated, searching for the right word—"fond of me."

He shrugged. "Maybe that's because you never gave them the chance. I'm guessing your grandpa was pretty *fond* of you."

I wasn't convinced. "Yes, but he was family, and I used to cook for him too."

"Whatever. None of that matters right now anyway."
Leaning forward, he kissed me again, effectively putting
an end to the discussion. "Guess I'd better get going or
neither one of us will get any sleep tonight."

He was right, of course. For one thing, the bed wasn't
big enough for two people. For another, Wyatt's kisses
weren't exactly conducive to sleep, nor was having his
shockingly male body within arm's reach. If we ever did
find ourselves in a larger bed, actually sleeping with him
would take some getting used to.

I would also have to get used to seeing him naked. At
the moment, however, watching him climb out of bed
and bend over to snatch his clothes from the floor was
an event in itself. Being a spectator while he pulled on
his T-shirt and briefs was more erotic than I ever would
have imagined.

With another kiss and a quick "'Night, darlin'," he
headed for the door.

"Good night—" I stopped short as I found myself on
the horns of a new dilemma. What on earth should I call
him? Sweetie? Honey? Cupcake? None of those seemed
to fit. For now, his name would have to suffice. "Wyatt.
Sleep well."

As he closed the door behind him, I glanced at
the clock, wincing at the late hour. With so little left
of the night, falling asleep quickly was advisable.
Unfortunately, with all the food for thought he'd given
me, my brain refused to shut down.

Sainthood, huh? I didn't want to be a saint. Following
that first kiss with Dean, I'd wanted to be bad. I hadn't
quite made it to the finish line, but my shyness had dissipated considerably, enabling me to say and do things I

might not have had the nerve to do otherwise. The question now was, could I be bad with Wyatt?

I was still trying to decide whether I'd already done that when my alarm went off.

Time to make the biscuits.

At least, I thought that was what I was supposed to do that day. To be perfectly honest, I was a little fuzzy on exactly which day it was.

Pancakes yesterday meant biscuits and sausage gravy today. The menu seemed a bit lacking in vitamins, so I figured I'd chop up some fruit for a salad.

Have to keep my cowboys healthy.

If I didn't die from lack of sleep first. Blinking against the sunlight already streaming in through the window, I sat up, feeling around for my slippers. It occurred to me that without Wyatt in my bed as proof, I might've dreamed it all—even that first trip to the bathroom after he left. Having heard a few horror stories about "honeymoon" bladder infections from my friends, I'd had sense enough to get up and empty my bladder. My torn hymen had stung a bit at the time, but at the moment, I suspected I would have more trouble walking than peeing.

Perhaps I hadn't dreamed it after all.

I glanced at Ophelia. "Think I ought to do some stretching exercises before breakfast?"

My spayed and presumably virgin dog replied with a noncommittal yawn before strolling over for her morning dose of affection.

"Guess not." I ruffled her ears. "You're such a brave girl. You would've gone out with Wyatt and caught the bogeyman last night if I'd let you. Wouldn't you, Lia?"

Her response was a soft whine that I took for a yes,

but which probably only meant she needed to go out *right now*. Staggering to my feet, I stumbled to the door and opened it. "Watch out for rattlesnakes," I advised as she trotted past me. Closing the door, I shivered from the morning chill. I still hadn't come to terms with the Wyoming weather. Back home in Louisville, Derby week was about to commence. Horse races were being run, tulips were in bloom, and mint juleps were the drink of choice. Although Derby Day was occasionally wet and chilly, the first Saturday in May usually meant warmer temperatures.

Not so in Wyoming. The guys had built a fire in the mess hall stove every night since my arrival, and if there were any tulips planted around the bunkhouse, they certainly weren't blooming. With plenty of blankets on my bed, I hadn't been cold, but the thought of snuggling up with a nice, warm cowboy had a definite appeal. If I was going to stay forever, as Sonny had suggested, I would have to look into getting a bigger bed so Wyatt could stay all night.

But first, I had to go shopping for condoms.

Imagine that.

I'd already pulled on jeans and a sweater when Ophelia scratched at the door. After letting her in, I stepped out onto the porch and peered up at the hill to the east. At the moment, anyone hiding out up there would be rendered invisible by the blinding glare of the sun.

Shaking off the creepy feeling of being watched, I went into the kitchen and put the coffee on.

—⁂—

Despite downing two cups of coffee that was strong enough to lift weights, I could barely keep my eyes open at the breakfast table. Wyatt, on the other hand, was as bright-eyed and bushy-tailed as a young squirrel.

Bad analogy. He's more like a—oh, bloody hell, I don't know.

I needed that tequila, and I needed it now. As soon as the guys headed out for the day, I was downing a shot and taking a nap. Then I realized I hadn't done my "day ahead" preparation for lunch. My brain was so fried, I couldn't think of a single thing to fix.

"Don't suppose you all would mind giving me some lunch ideas, would you?"

"Just throw together some sandwiches," Nick replied. "I'll help you."

I squinted at him, wondering how much he knew about Wyatt's activities after the search for the bad guys.

Or was "outlaws" a better word?

Wyatt McCabe and his trusty sidekick, Nick Reno, searched the premises to no avail. The outlaws remain at large. They could have been characters in an old Western. Wyatt would be the sheriff and Nick could be his deputy.

My God, I need sleep.

"Sounds good." Yawning, I leaned forward, resting my chin on my hand. I knew there was cheese and lunch meat somewhere, probably in the fridge.

Yeah. That's it. The fridge. And bread. We definitely have bread.

"There's plenty of fruit salad left," Bull said. "We'll take that with us."

I nodded. I must've fallen asleep at some point during

the preparations because by the time my mind cleared, I'd chopped up every apple, orange, grape, and strawberry in sight. It was a wonder I hadn't lost a finger. For the edible nature of the biscuits and gravy, I could only credit divine intervention.

At least, I assumed it had been edible. There wasn't any gravy left and only a few crumbs marked the plate where the biscuits had been.

Not even enough to send to the lab for testing if someone gets sick.

That someone would probably be me. I already had a dull sort of stomachache. Probably from the vigorous sex. Apparently sex with Wyatt and the subsequent lack of sleep weren't good for my mental or physical health. I wondered how he would react if I were to tell him never to visit my bedroom again.

No. I wasn't *that* messed up. I would get used to it eventually, and if the heated looks Wyatt was giving me over the breakfast table were any indication, he intended to give me plenty of practice.

"I, um, need to go to the store," I said during a momentary break in the chatter. "We're out of…stuff."

Dusty seemed oblivious to the nuances of the conversation, the light I'd seen on the hillside during the night having been so thoroughly discussed, no one had much chance to speculate on what might've happened afterward. "Yeah. Angela usually goes shopping on Fridays. We kinda missed that this week. One of the guys can go with you if you need help."

I nodded, then waited to see who would volunteer.

No one said a word.

Dean was bound to be a little miffed with me. Wyatt

probably didn't want to draw attention to the fact that we had become an item. I was pretty sure that Joe, being the foreman, couldn't be spared from duty. Bull had yet to mention the possibility of my sainthood, but being his sole companion for several hours might bring it to the fore. Nick and Sonny had probably never been grocery shopping in their lives.

I felt like I had the night before when I'd left the mess hall so abruptly. I wanted to curl up and disappear, or get on the road and head for home. This thing with Wyatt wasn't going to be my happily ever after. I was stupid to even think it. People's lives didn't change that much in only a few days.

"I can go by myself. You all have enough to do. Guess I'd better get started on lunch." I didn't give them the chance to make another offer. I rose from my chair and headed for the kitchen. Snatching up a loaf of bread, I yanked off the twist tie and began laying out slices in a row across the counter. Filling their stomachs was the only thing I was good for. That and the occasional fuck. Not being loved. No one had ever said anything about love.

I slapped together the sandwiches and had them packed up and ready to go before anyone bothered to carry their empty plates into the kitchen. Did they take Sundays off? Probably not. Livestock had to be fed no matter what day it was. Maybe their dishwashing rotation didn't include Sundays. That was fine with me. I was nothing but a drudge anyway. I could do it myself. I didn't need help. I didn't need anyone.

I glanced at Ophelia, who was looking up at me as though hoping I would drop a tasty morsel at any moment. *Even my dog only wants food.*

Just to prove my point, I tossed her a piece of roast beef, which she gobbled up in seconds.

"See? That's all anyone wants from me." I dashed angry tears from my eyes. Oh, yes. I was hot stuff when Calvin was in the hospital and the guys were hungry. They couldn't fool me. They were only buttering me up so I wouldn't leave before he came home.

Speaking of which, he might be coming home that day. I would clean his room some more, then I could pack my suitcase and get on the road to—

Where was it I'd wanted to go? Vegas? Denver? In my current mood, Vegas wasn't a good idea. I would gamble away all of the ready cash and end up begging on the street. Or selling my services.

Yuck.

The rational part of my brain finally spoke up. None of that would happen. I had a credit card that wasn't anywhere near to being maxed out. I would stay until Calvin felt like cooking again. Of course I would. This crazy mood was just—

Oh, bloody hell.

Quite literally, in fact. I wasn't crazy. I had only been suffering from an unusually severe case of PMS.

No sex tonight.

Chapter 17

NO WONDER NONE OF THE GUYS HAD OFFERED TO GO shopping with me. They must have figured the "stuff" I needed involved the current phase of my menstrual cycle, which was understandable considering my vague terminology and halting speech. Condoms were probably the last things any of them would have guessed.

Well, maybe not everyone. Wyatt should've known what I needed, and Dean probably suspected. How much the rest of them knew was unclear. In a way, I wanted to come clean and confess, thus eliminating the need for secrecy and nipping any misunderstandings in the bud, especially if one of the requirements for sainthood in Bull's religion was chastity.

Nah, probably not. After all, Bull had been the one to notice the hickey.

Once lunch was taken care of, I plopped three chuck roasts in the slow cooker along with some red wine and mushrooms so I could make the drive into town without having to worry too much about dinner.

It occurred to me then that whoever was watching the bunkhouse might simply be waiting for everyone to leave. Nighttime surveillance was explainable pretty much the same way; anyone wishing to sneak in unnoticed could only do so when the lights were out and everyone was asleep.

And do what? Raid the freezer? The best I could tell, there wasn't anything of significant value in the bunkhouse, unless it was something that was valuable only to our prowler. The barn, on the other hand, was probably full of expensive items. Saddles weren't cheap, and I'd seen several of them in the tack room.

I dismissed that idea after realizing the fence-cutting episodes required the men to be out for long periods of time during the day, and the best saddles were probably those in use. Additionally, nothing had been reported stolen before my arrival, when presumably the bunkhouse had been empty for much of the day and the barn was unattended.

But what if the perpetrator was waiting for *me* to leave? Going to the store would allow ample time for someone to break in and search the place, although actually breaking in wouldn't be necessary. Each door might have had a lock, but I was probably the only one who used them, and only on the doors to my room.

I glanced up as Dean entered.

"Lunch ready?" he asked.

I nodded. "It's all there in the cooler. Listen, I'm wondering if maybe one of you guys shouldn't stick around here until I get back. With me gone, whoever's watching the place could easily come in and search at their leisure."

He scratched his chin. "You think that's the reason for the cut fences? So someone could search the bunkhouse?"

"Seems the most obvious, doesn't it? The fence problems stopped about the time I arrived, and I doubt it was because they'd already found what they were looking for. Not if someone is still prowling around."

"Maybe. That's about the only explanation that makes any sense." He hesitated, frowning. "Especially since Angela and Mr. Kincaid are nearly always up at the house. They might not notice someone sneaking in down here, although I can't imagine why anyone would want to do that."

The phone rang, interrupting any further discussion. "That's probably Angela." I wiped my hands on a dish towel, then reached for the receiver.

"Hey, Tina," Angela said. "Just calling to let y'all know Calvin is being released today. Not sure when, and it'll take us about four hours or so to get home after we leave here, but I'm guessing we'll be there by dinnertime."

"Great! I'll tell the guys. I'm going into Rock Springs today. Anything you need from the store?"

"Not that I know of." She giggled. "If we time it right, we'll pass each other on the highway."

"I hadn't thought of that." Knowing that Angela had more experience shopping for a crowd, I was about to suggest they pick up the groceries when I realized Calvin probably wouldn't feel up to it, nor did I want to ask Angela to buy the "stuff" I needed.

She gave me the name of the store where she normally shopped and told me how to get there. "Have Dusty give you some grocery money before you go."

"Will do." I certainly wouldn't be using any of that money for condoms. That is, if I could bring myself to actually buy them in the first place. I consoled myself with the fact that I'd never been to Rock Springs before. No one would know me or remember me after I left.

I had just hung up the phone, thinking that with two additional mouths to feed, I'd better up the number of chuck roasts to four, when a tap on my shoulder reminded me I wasn't alone.

With a quirky grin, Dean took my hand, placed a small package on my palm, and closed my fingers around it. Pressing a finger to his lips, he mimed silence, then picked up the cooler and sauntered out.

When I opened my hand, a strip of three condoms wrapped in what appeared to be a rather extensive shopping list unfolded on my palm.

He might have kept the other three hoping to use them himself, but his willingness to share proved that Dean was nothing if not a good sport.

———

After receiving a huge wad of cash from Dusty and learning that Mr. Kincaid planned to hang around the bunkhouse and wait for Angela and Calvin's return, Ophelia and I set out.

Only about an hour away, Rock Springs was a good-sized town and not at all difficult to navigate. I found the store Angela had suggested and proceeded to buy more food in one day than I normally purchased in two months. Interestingly enough, I discovered that buying condoms was no more embarrassing than buying tampons, especially when they were purchased together. My dilemma was in trying to decide which type to get.

In the end, I bought the same kind Dean had given me, hoping he'd at least had enough experience with such things to know which brand was the best.

I grabbed lunch at a drive-through before heading back to the ranch, feeling almost, but not quite, like I was going home. I'd been living there for several days, and in that time, I'd taken on a new job, been kissed by three cowboys, lost my virginity, and learned more about Calvin and his family than I would be comfortable having anyone know about me. Perhaps Calvin and I were even now. Grandpa had obviously reported on my progress from time to time, and I really didn't mind that, but the letters he'd sent had been intended for Calvin's eyes only. With Calvin incapacitated, reading his letters to Grandpa had seemed like a reasonable course of action. Now that he'd improved, it only seemed nosy.

Had Angela informed Calvin of his sister's death? Somehow I doubted it. Better to let him come home and settle in before getting hit with the bad news.

I arrived at the ranch, having followed a vehicle that turned out to be Angela's.

"Looks like we didn't pass on the highway after all," she said when I pulled up alongside her truck. She opened the passenger door and waited while Calvin climbed down from the cab.

For a man who had recently been through a near-death experience, he looked surprisingly good. His color was certainly better, although he moved more stiffly than before. Ophelia approached him cautiously, tilting her head as she sniffed the air around him, just as she'd done when we brought Grandpa home from the hospital for the last time.

Calvin gave her a pat and then smiled at me. "Been keepin' the boys fed?"

"Sure have," I replied. "Dunno how you did it and still had time for riding and roping."

"Can't say I've been doin' as much of that sort of thing

as I used to. Not lately, anyway." Somehow, I suspected that was as close to an admission of weakness as he intended to give. "Hope they haven't given you any trouble."

"Not a bit," I insisted, although any number of things they'd done could be construed as such. My hymen would certainly never recover.

He held out a hand. "I understand I have you to thank for me not bein' six feet under."

"You're welcome," I said as I shook his hand. "But I can't take all the credit. Wyatt and Nick are the real heroes. All I did was yell for help."

"Which you couldn't have done if you'd ignored what you heard."

I shrugged. "Naturally curious, I guess." Did he truly recall tapping out SOS on the wall, or had Angela filled him in on the details?

"That wasn't all you did, young lady. I'd been feeling a lot worse lately and figured my time was coming, but seeing you here and knowing your grandpa had died, well, that made me want to take better care of myself. Guess I left it a little too late."

"You seem to be on the right track now," I said. "You look much better, anyway."

Angela beamed. "He hasn't smoked a cigarette since he woke up."

"Yeah, well, in a smoke-free hospital, that's not hard to do," Calvin said, chuckling. "Need help with those groceries?"

I laughed along with him, pleased to see he hadn't lost his sense of humor. "Nope. I got this. Besides, I'm guessing you aren't supposed to be doing any heavy lifting." I glanced at my watch. "You've got plenty of time to rest before I have to start on dinner. We can talk more after I get this stuff put away."

He patted my arm. "Your grandpa always said you were a good girl, Tina."

"I'm sure he did." I let out a short laugh. "Just don't believe everything you hear."

Mr. Kincaid opened the kitchen door and stepped out onto the landing. "Well, look who it is," he said, grinning. "Get on in here, Calvin. I've got a nice fire goin' in the mess hall."

Truth be told, I wouldn't have minded a little help. My car's cargo-carrying capacity had been stretched to the point that if I'd taken one of the guys with me, he would've had to ride home on the roof. Nevertheless, I waited until Calvin and Angela were inside before popping the trunk lid. I had gathered up several grocery bags when a peculiar prickling sensation on my nape made me steal a glance at the hillside. No movement this time, but I still felt like I was being watched.

Anger flared and I whirled around, blatantly staring at that spot and shouting, "I know you're up there, you creep! You'd better get lost before I sic my dog on you!"

"You tell 'em, Tina!" Nick chuckled as he emerged from the barn, leading a dark brown horse. "Although I'm not sure that's much of a threat."

To my credit, I somehow managed not to scream or jump out of my skin. "She only seems timid. She's actually quite fierce."

"Uh-huh," he said with a skeptical nod. "*Sure* she is."

"Don't make me prove it," I snapped. I was just

rattled enough to be a bit testy. "What're you doing here anyway?"

"My horse went lame. Had to bring him back and get another one."

His innocent tone and bland expression seemed almost rehearsed, making me wonder whether the men had been returning at regular intervals to keep an eye on the bunkhouse. "Any fences down?"

He shook his head. "Haven't found any so far. Didn't see anyone up on that hill, either." He nodded at the grocery bags dangling from my fingers. "Need help?"

"Yes, please."

Dropping the reins, he left the horse and started toward me. "Don't worry," he said, obviously noting my gasp of surprise. "He won't run off."

"I'll take your word for it." I watched the horse for a few moments anyway. Nick was right, though. He didn't budge an inch.

Nick opened the rear door on the passenger side. "What'd you do? Buy out every store in Rock Springs?"

"It's not my fault," I said defensively. "Dean gave me a pretty long list."

The only things I'd bought for myself were tampons, condoms, a bottle of personal lubricant, and dog food. I'd considered getting a home pregnancy test and a one-dose treatment for yeast infections, but I figured those things could wait until I actually needed them. Hopefully, I never would. Drawing attention to myself certainly wouldn't have been an issue. I could've bought all that, plus another six boxes of condoms, and the yawning, gum-popping cashier probably wouldn't have noticed, much less commented.

I wasn't that jaded. The cashier couldn't have cared less about my purchases, but as hot as my face felt, my blush must have been epic.

By the time Nick and I had lugged everything inside, Mr. Kincaid had gone back to the main house and Angela had Calvin settled in front of the mess hall television with a cup of coffee and the remote. Somehow, I doubted spending Sunday afternoon in a recliner was typical behavior for him. The trick would be to keep him there.

Nick had just left when Angela came into the kitchen. "Want some help putting all this stuff away?"

"Absolutely." I surveyed the mountain of bags on the corner table with dismay. "It's a little overwhelming."

"I know the feeling. Whenever I go to town for supplies, I try to time it so the guys are here to help out when I get back."

"Good plan," I said. "Wish I'd thought of it."

"You'll know better next time."

We'd been busy for several minutes when she peered into the mess hall. "Looks like Calvin's doing okay out there." She sighed. "Bet he'll be glad when the men come in for dinner. He's probably sick to death of me."

"I doubt that."

She shrugged. "Maybe not, but I've been hanging around his bedside for days. He's bound to be ready for some male company. I was hoping Dad would sit with him for a while longer, but he seemed kinda worn out himself." She didn't say it aloud, but no doubt she suspected she would be hanging around her father's bedside before long.

"Does Calvin know we read his letters trying to find his family?"

"No," she replied. "I couldn't bring myself to ask if he knew his sister had died, either."

"I don't blame you. Talk about bad timing."

"No shit. We did discuss setting up a power of attorney for health care and a living will so we would know what to do if this sort of thing happened again. He seemed agreeable."

"That's good." I wasn't surprised. Until that first brush with death, most people didn't think too much about dying. Fortunately, Mom had seen the need for that sort of planning with Grandpa long before I did.

"We'll have to break the news to him at some point. Might be best if we play that by ear."

"I guess so. Although I should probably tell him we read his letters before one of the guys lets it slip." I was already wishing I hadn't promised to sit down for a chat with Calvin before dinner. Considering those letters had been sent to my grandfather, I was the one who needed to confess. Then again, Grandpa had never said I shouldn't read them. He'd only asked me to give them to Calvin along with his medals.

Hmm...

Then there was that old adage that you might as well tell the truth because people were bound to discover your secrets anyway.

I finished up in the kitchen and headed into the mess hall where Calvin was watching CNN.

He glanced up when I came in and muted the sound. "Hey, Tina."

I took a seat in the chair across from him. "You look comfy."

"I'm a whole lot more comfortable here than I was in

that hospital," he declared. "They were real good to me, but I'm happy to be home."

"I know what you mean," I said. "The guys will be glad to see you. They've been pretty worried."

His eyes misted slightly. "They're a good bunch."

I certainly couldn't argue with that. In a very short time, they'd not only grown on me, they had nearly cured my shyness. "Yes, they are." Resting my hands on my knees, I leaned forward. "While you were in the hospital, Angela asked us to try to locate your family. The guys helped me read through the letters you sent to Grandpa in the hope that we might find some names."

He reacted with a disgusted snort. "Like anyone would care. Besides, I'd much rather have Angela or Dusty making decisions for me than someone I haven't seen or spoken to in years."

"Then you need to write that down and make it perfectly clear what your wishes are. Don't leave any room for guesswork." I started to quote all the things Mom and I had done with respect to Grandpa's affairs, but I doubted I would need to.

He nodded. "I told Angela I would. I've already caused her enough worry."

One obstacle left to overcome… "We did find out a few things about your family—some I think you should know."

"Go on." His tone was casual—even disinterested— but I caught a glimpse of curiosity in his eyes.

"Once we figured out your sister's name, I ran a search to see if we could contact her."

He snorted again but didn't comment.

"We found several things—the record of her

marriage to Franklin Caruthers, newspaper articles about charity work she'd done, stuff like that. In the process, we ran across her husband's obituary." I paused, letting that sink in. "And then we found hers. She died this past January."

A slight frown was the only visible indication he'd even heard me. "S'pose I could've expected that. She was a good bit older than me. Would've turned seventy-four this year."

"She was your only relative?"

He nodded. "Far as I know, she was—'cept for that grandson that got taken away from her." Arching a brow, he added, "But I guess you read about that in my letters."

"Yeah. Sorry for invading your privacy, Calvin. But those letters were all we had to go on. Under the circumstances, we felt it was justified."

Smiling, he leaned forward and patted my arm. "I'm not fussin' at you, Tina. I know how much pain it probably caused you to read them."

"No kidding, although reading them helped me understand a few things about Grandpa." I sat up straighter, shaking off the tendrils of melancholy that threatened to bind my lips together. "There's one other thing I ought to tell you. In Jeannine's obituary, you weren't listed as one of her survivors. It made me wonder if the Jeannine Caruthers we found really wasn't your sister after all."

"Married to Franklin Caruthers, the oil baron, or whatever they call themselves these days?" He nodded. "Yeah. That's Jeannine, all right."

"Seems pretty tacky not to even mention you."

His indifferent shrug suggested the initial pain, if

any, had already worn off. "Maybe whoever wrote the obituary didn't know she had a brother. To be honest, I'm not too surprised." A fleeting frown furrowed his brow. "I'd like to take a look at it, though. Just to be sure."

"No problem." I rose from my chair. "I'll get my computer and be right back."

Rushing into my room, I unplugged the laptop with trembling fingers. I shouldn't have been nervous about any of this—after all, it was nothing to do with me—and yet I was. Returning to the mess hall, I set the computer on the coffee table and clicked the bookmark.

"Here," I said, turning the screen toward him. "The only survivors mentioned are from the Caruthers side."

He studied it carefully. "Yep. Every last one is a Caruthers. 'Course, without knowing that grandson's name and ignoring me for most of her life, there aren't any others she could've listed."

"No cousins or anything?"

"I'm sure there are some, but none we ever knew. As I recall, my mother had a brother who lived somewhere back east with the rest of her family. I never saw any of them, and my dad was an orphan."

I reminded myself once again that not all families were alike, and that family ties could sometimes be more irksome than comforting. Some were downright danger-ous. Spotting a link to an online guestbook, I clicked on it, without giving a thought to whether Calvin would want to add anything to it or not.

As soon as the page loaded, my jaw dropped—and not only because of the vast number of entries in the book. At the top of the page in bold red lettering was a request for Calvin Joseph Douglas to please contact the legal firm of Jamison and Markovitch. There was even a hyperlink.

A glance at Calvin proved he was as astonished as I was. "Interesting," he said after a few moments' scrutiny. "Wonder what they want me for?"

"No telling. What I can't figure is why this would be on the guestbook when there was no mention of you in the obituary. Do you…" I hesitated, unsure how to put it. "Do you think the reason you weren't mentioned in the obituary was because no one knew you existed until after her will was read?"

This time, *his* jaw dropped. "What? You think she actually left me something?"

"Kinda seems that way, doesn't it? After all, you *are* her nearest living blood relative. And she was a very rich woman."

Chapter 18

"BUT WE HAVEN'T SPOKEN IN YEARS," CALVIN PROTESTED.

I shrugged. "Maybe she wanted to reconcile but didn't know how to contact you. She could've stipulated in her will that you needed to be found."

"Seems like she could've done that before she died, doesn't it?"

"Maybe she tried and couldn't find you—or died before she had the chance. I found you in a White Pages search without any trouble, but I had a recent address to begin with. She wouldn't even have known which state you were living in."

"I'll grant you that," he said. "I never told anyone where I was headed when I came here, except your grandpa. Far as I was concerned, he was the only one who needed to know."

No wonder they'd kept in touch. "If you were one of Jeannine's beneficiaries and she'd left a record of your address, the executor of her estate would've sent you a letter when she died." I'd had some recent experience with wills and such, my current whereabouts being the result of another document in which Calvin had been named. "That is, *if* she named you as a beneficiary. If so, I can't believe this is all they've done to try to find you. I mean, what are the odds you would ever see this?"

"Not very good," he agreed. "'Specially since I didn't even know she died."

"There's one way to get all the answers." I slid the

mouse pointer over the hyperlink. "All we have to do is email her lawyers."

I might've been dying of curiosity, but Calvin didn't seem particularly interested. He leaned back in his chair, looking a bit more haggard than he had earlier. "Let me think about it for a while."

Given his current state of health, I didn't want to push it. After copying the law firm's web address, I closed the computer. "No problem. I bookmarked the page. We can go back to it anytime."

God only knew what Jeannine might have left Calvin, although I seriously doubted it would have been her entire fortune. Her husband had children and grandchildren from his previous marriage, which meant she would only have the portion she received after his death. Still, even that could've been pretty substantial unless there was a really stringent prenuptial agreement in place.

I couldn't wait to hear Wyatt's take on the matter.

"Guess I'd better get back to the kitchen." I picked up my computer and nodded at the television. "See anything interesting on the news?"

"No," he replied. "Nothing good, anyway."

No news is good news. There was a boatload of truth in that. Happy times and status quo had never been newsworthy. Unfortunately, reporters rarely had to look very hard to find something to talk about, even on a peaceful ranch in Wyoming.

I paused in the doorway. "Ever make Yorkshire pudding to go with the roast beef?"

"Might have," he replied, grinning. "That is, if I knew what it was."

"It'll be a surprise." Never having made enough for

a bunkhouse full of cowboys, I figured I might even surprise myself if it turned out okay.

I knew the recipe by heart, but mentally doubling the quantities as I headed back to my room was a bit of an eye-opener. At least I knew there were enough pans and sufficient oven space in which to bake such a huge amount.

I had the second batch in the blender when the door swung open and Wyatt stepped inside. One glimpse of his tall figure—hat, boots, chaps, and all—had my uterus twisting into a tight knot that suddenly burst, flooding my senses with a shot of nirvana that doubled me over.

A spontaneous orgasm? Was there really such a thing?

I had no idea, but any man whose mere presence could do that to a woman was a force to be reckoned with. Dean had certainly never had that effect on me. No wonder Wyatt had made me so nervous in the beginning. How on earth had I ever kept from throwing myself into his arms?

However, instead of being pleased to the point of cockiness, he seemed concerned. "You okay, babe?"

Not wishing to give him any more power over me than he already had, I gasped out the first word that popped into my head. "Cramps."

Under the circumstances, it might have actually been true. But if I'd ever had a cramp like that one, my monthly period would've been something to look forward to rather than grudgingly endure.

A moment later his hands gripped my shoulders, pulling me upright and into his arms. The kiss that followed turned me to mush and would have relaxed any internal spasms my uterus could dish out short of labor pains. I was floating, drifting on a cloud—until I realized my feet truly had left the floor.

"Been waitin' all day to do that," he said as he set me back on my feet.

His voice sounded rough, almost desperate. Was he really as anxious to see me and make love with me as I was to be with him? It seemed impossible. I'd had enough to keep me busy for most of the day, but during the drive to Rock Springs, he'd been on my mind constantly.

"Me too."

He kissed me again, then leaned forward, touching his forehead to mine. "Cramps, huh? Does that mean I can't, um, see you tonight?"

His disappointment was transparent, but thanks to the sexy novels I'd read, I knew all sorts of things a woman could do to a man without actually having intercourse. I aimed what I hoped was a beguiling smile at him and nodded. "Unless you're out chasing bad guys all night."

"Don't plan to be, but you never know." He seemed to hesitate, shifting his weight from one booted foot to the other. "If it wasn't for bad guys, we might not have had any reason to get together."

Now it was my turn to hesitate. What did he mean by that? Was he thinking the passion had only sparked between us because of all the mystery and intrigue? Maybe. To be honest, I'd wondered about that myself— what with the whole heat-of-the-moment thing and all.

I opted to play it cool. For once. "I'm sure we would've found an excuse eventually." I followed that up with a wink. "Can't fight fate, you know."

His posture relaxed slightly. "Is that what you think this is? We're fulfilling our destiny or something?"

"Could be," I replied. "Either way, I'm not looking a gift horse in the mouth."

There. I'd said it. I was leaving myself wide open to whatever happened between us—and I hoped it wouldn't end anytime soon.

A glimmer of a smile enhanced his slow nod. "Me neither."

He drew in a breath as though about to make an additional comment, but seemed to think better of it, stopping before his mouth formed the first word. With a barely perceptible shake of his head, he leaned closer and kissed me again, momentarily disrupting my train of thought and eliminating anything else I might have said.

My lips tingled and my heart was still doing flip-flops as he turned and sauntered from the room.

It didn't take a mind reader to know there was something he wasn't telling me—or at least didn't *want* to tell me—and he certainly knew the best way to keep me from plaguing him with questions. Those kisses of his were enough to silence a magpie. Still, I couldn't help wondering whether his secret had some bearing on his decision to give up firefighting to become a cowboy.

Maybe.

Probably.

Oh, bloody hell... I didn't have the first clue as to what went on in his head. Men might claim their thoughts were simple and straightforward, but I knew better. They could twist events and react to them in even more bizarre ways than women did. Wyatt would tell me what the problem was at some point. Until then, I would simply have to wait. Whatever happened, I had no intention of holding that lack of communication against him.

Considering our first meeting, it was a wonder we'd come this far.

I finished fixing dinner with the scent of Wyatt McCabe filling my head, which might have been responsible for the enormous salad I threw together. I preferred to chalk it up to Calvin's return, especially since I wound up making a broccoli and cheese casserole in addition to the roast beef and Yorkshire pudding. After all, it wasn't every day a guy got out of the hospital after nearly dying. He needed at least one option that didn't contain enough fat and cholesterol to give him another heart attack.

With a sigh, I realized the days of cooking without regard to anyone's health were over. From now on it was back to the heart-healthy diet I probably should've been serving up from the start. No more pie and cookies for dessert. No more baked potatoes with butter and sour cream. I drew the line at eliminating red meat—not that I could've gotten away with that on a cattle ranch—but the other restrictions would take a lot of the fun out of the job. I wondered how many accolades I would receive for serving up sugar-free Jell-O for dessert instead of peach pie.

Maybe if I made Jigglers...

I reminded myself that when it came to heart disease, Calvin's smoking habit was probably his most significant risk factor. Now that he'd quit, his next hurdle would be to avoid gaining weight, although as skinny as he was, I doubted it would be a problem, at least not at first. Maybe the sugar-free Jell-O could wait for a bit.

I was mulling over recipes with "healthy" ingredients when the guys came in to get the plates.

The pudding came out perfectly—puffy, buttery, and lightly browned—and I carried the first dish into the mess hall with pride, leaving Nick to follow with the second batch.

Mr. Kincaid peered at it with interest as we set the pans on the table. "What the devil is that?"

I glanced at Calvin, who had probably guessed what it was from our earlier exchange. However, it was Wyatt who spoke.

"Yorkshire pudding," he said with a touch of nostalgic fervor. "Haven't had that since I was a kid." He stole a peek inside the ceramic pitcher sitting next to the platter of roast beef. "I see you made plenty of gravy to go with it."

"You betcha." I smiled, absurdly pleased that Wyatt had been the one to correctly identify one of my favorite, if somewhat obscure, side dishes. A flush rose in my cheeks before drifting downward to create a warm, cozy sensation around my heart. At one time, I wouldn't have dared look such a man in the eye, but I was able to do it now, further enhancing the connection between us. Unlike the intimidating glare I knew him to be capable of, his gaze was gentle and inviting, combining with a smile so genuine, they stole my breath and comforted me at the same time.

I could almost feel myself falling in love with him, and I didn't want to look away. Didn't want to break the spell...

"Have a seat, Tina," Bull urged. "I gotta try that stuff."

The spell might have been broken, but there was an empty chair beside Wyatt. I wondered if he'd saved it for me.

The pressure of his hand on my knee as I sat down told me he had done just that. The cozy feeling intensified to the point I was surprised Bull didn't remark on what was surely a visible change in my aura. Fortunately, his eyes were aimed at the food rather than at me.

"Pudding, huh?" Sonny said with a dubious frown. "Doesn't *look* like pudding."

"It's more of a bread, actually," I said. "You make it with eggs, flour, and milk like a pudding, only it isn't sweet."

"It's British," Wyatt said, as if that explained everything, and perhaps it did. "Trust me, you'll like it."

Mr. Kincaid gave an official welcome-home speech for Calvin's benefit, and after that, we dug into dinner like the celebration it was. Sonny declared it the best meal he ever ate in his life. I doubted Calvin appreciated that sentiment, but he didn't fuss about it. For once, Bull didn't say much of anything, being too busy making the last of the pudding and peach pie disappear.

The warm fuzzies persisted throughout the meal, becoming even more pronounced when Wyatt followed me into the kitchen to help with the dishes. The whole evening had a happily-ever-after vibe to it. I could actually see myself living here with these men for the rest of my life—especially Wyatt. I cautioned myself that I was thinking such thoughts much too soon. This entire episode might simply turn out to be the one bright spot in my otherwise humdrum existence that I would look back on with fondness in my later years. I might fall in love with Wyatt only to have something horrible happen to him.

My, how optimistic.

I reminded myself that I often engaged in tragic

fantasies during that particular phase of my menstrual cycle. I'd learned to see it for what it was and put a lid on it, but I wasn't always successful.

"Calvin looks pretty good," Wyatt said, interrupting my morbid ruminations. "Did you tell him about us reading his letters?"

"Yeah. Figured it was best to come clean. I told him about his sister dying too."

"How did he take the news?"

"Pretty well, I think. He didn't know she'd died, which made me wonder if maybe she wasn't the right Jeannine Caruthers." I set a stack of plates in the sink, then turned to face him. "I showed him the obituary. He said the woman we found was definitely his sister, but we stumbled on something else—something that puts a completely different spin on several things."

"Sounds interesting. What is it?"

Someday I would get used to Wyatt's uniquely shaped eyebrows, but for the moment, I was still fascinated by them, especially when arched in surprise. I shook my head. "I'd rather show you. I want to get your gut reaction."

"I'm *really* curious now."

I glanced at the sink. "Come on, then. This won't take long, and the dishes could stand to soak for a bit."

I led the way to my room and logged on to my laptop. I'd left the browser open on the guestbook page, and it only took Wyatt a few moments to scan the contents.

"Definitely interesting," he said. "Although I can't imagine why anyone would ever think he would see this."

"That's what I thought, but I suppose it's better than nothing."

He nodded. "Hiring a private investigator would've made more sense, but I can see where this could actually work. That is, if he ever got wind of her death. I mean, he did see it eventually."

Not having considered the private detective angle before, another possibility occurred to me. "I wonder... Do you think the guy asking about Calvin at the hospital could've been a detective? He might've only pretended to be a friend of the family in order to gain access to him."

"Seems odd for it to take a detective this long to find him. I mean, his sister died nearly five months ago."

"What if they only hired the guy recently, hoping that notice would work?"

"That makes sense, but why would a detective pretend to be a family friend?" He shook his head, frowning. "Seems like he would've gotten more attention if he'd told them who he really was."

"I doubt it. I got the impression that hospital was really strict about limiting visitors in the critical care units. I'm a little surprised they let Angela see him, although as his employer, she's probably the closest thing to family he has around here."

"That's why Bull and I followed the ambulance to Rock Springs and then drove on to Salt Lake. We told them Angela would be coming to stay with Calvin. Trust me, he wouldn't be the first cowboy to be dragged into the ER by a couple of his buddies." Wyatt paused, cocking his head to one side, his gaze aimed toward the computer screen. "What if the reason they've made so little effort is because someone *doesn't* want him to be found?"

"A secondary beneficiary, you mean?" I'd had similar thoughts myself. Hearing Wyatt say it made my own suspicions seem less preposterous.

"Yeah. Think about it. If Jeannine had named Calvin as her heir with the provision that her estate would go to someone else after a certain length of time, that person would have plenty of reasons to hope he was never found." He paused again, his frown becoming more ominous by the second. "Or to *make sure* he was never found."

His tone of voice made the implication clear. "I thought you didn't put much stock in Bull's murder theory."

"I didn't." He tapped the bold red lettering at the top of the guestbook page. "*That* changed my mind."

Chapter 19

"Motive was the main thing missing from Bull's murder theory," Wyatt went on. "We have that now. Unfortunately, what we *don't* have is a method or a suspect." His frustration was as plain as the furrows his fingers left in his hair. "It'd be different if he'd been shot. It's pretty hard to prove attempted murder when the victim had a heart attack."

"What about that empty nitro bottle?" I said. "What if someone emptied it knowing he might die without them?"

"It's possible," he conceded. "Incredibly hard to prove, though. A murderer would've worn gloves, but our fingerprints are all over that bottle." He blew out a breath. "We're still jumping to conclusions, and I sure as hell don't want to worry Calvin with our suspicions. Might be enough to bring on another attack."

After seeing the way he'd reacted to Jeannine's passing, I suspected Calvin was tougher than that, but Wyatt knew him better than I did. "Calvin didn't seem too interested in finding out more. Said he'd think about it."

"Could be he knows something he isn't telling us. We only know one of the reasons he cut himself off from his sister. Maybe there's something more sinister going on."

I couldn't help chuckling. "With imaginations like ours, we should be writing crime novels instead of working on a ranch."

"Oh yeah? I can think of several other ways to use

my imagination, all of which are a helluva lot more fun than sleuthing." His choice of terms accompanied by a Groucho Marx–style eyebrow waggle sent me over the edge into all-out laughter.

"Sleuthing?" I echoed when I had enough breath to speak. "I haven't heard that word since I outgrew Nancy Drew mysteries."

"Ah, so you *do* have a background in sleuthing."

"Not sure I'd call it that, although I've read my share of whodunits. The trouble is, we not only don't have a suspect, we're not even sure we have a crime."

"You're forgetting the fence-cutting episodes."

"Hmm…so I am. Speaking of which, I was talking to Dean about that this morning. Did he say anything to you?"

"Just that you were thinking it might have been a means of keeping us out of the way long enough for someone to search the bunkhouse."

I nodded. "And that person could've done enough searching to know how badly Calvin might need those nitro tablets."

"The fences haven't been cut since Calvin had his heart attack…" His expression grew thoughtful. "Wonder if that'll start happening again now that he's home."

My eyes widened to the point of discomfort. "You think the murderer will try a more direct approach this time?"

"Like actually taking a shot at Calvin? Maybe. Depends on how desperate he is."

I stared at the link to the law office, wishing Calvin had shown a little more interest. For me to contact them without his consent felt wrong—far worse than reading his letters. "I sure hope Calvin decides to contact those lawyers. They could probably answer a lot of our questions."

"Or stir up a hornet's nest full of trouble. Like I said, Calvin knows those people better than we do, and rich folks can be pretty ruthless when it comes to hanging on to their assets. Did you tell Angela about this?"

"No. I thought I'd wait until Calvin made a decision. You're the only one I've told." Calvin hadn't sworn me to secrecy, so I wasn't exactly betraying a confidence. Nevertheless, having Wyatt to swap ideas with made keeping quiet that much easier.

"I'm glad you did," he said. "Calvin may not want to admit it, but he needs protection."

With a nod, I closed the computer and got to my feet, wondering just how far Wyatt would go to keep the old man safe.

To protect and serve...

Memories of that awful night returned with a vengeance. At the time, Wyatt's own life hadn't been at risk, but if even half of what we suspected was true, that could change in a heartbeat. "I guess that's all we can do for now," I said, failing to suppress a shudder.

His eyes narrowed in concern. "You aren't scared, are you?"

"I dunno. Maybe a little." As if to prove it, my body gave another involuntary quiver.

Wyatt eased me into his embrace. He felt so solid and warm. So capable and strong.

But even a strong man could be brought down by a bullet. Grandpa had once been a healthy young soldier. Near the end when he could no longer even bathe himself, I'd been the one to do it. I'd seen and touched the scars from the bullets that nearly killed him.

"No one's gonna hurt you," he whispered. "I won't let that happen. I *can't* let that happen." He tightened his hold on me as though the shelter of his arms would somehow be all the protection I would ever need.

"It's not me I'm worried about." I'd been nervous enough when he and Nick had gone out in the middle of the night in search of a prowler. The possibility that someone wanted Calvin dead boosted my anxiety to a substantially higher level. "I'm worried about Calvin, you, and all the guys. When someone is bent on murder, other people—innocent people—sometimes get in the way."

The words had scarcely left my lips when I felt Wyatt stiffen around me. The warmth was still there, but he seemed…frozen.

I drew back in surprise. One glimpse of his stricken expression confirmed my suspicion that there was something else going on. Something that had nothing to do with Calvin. "What's wrong?"

Wyatt had once been a firefighter, and now he was a cowboy.

To protect and serve…

Of course. Somehow, somewhere, there'd been at least one person he couldn't protect. Someone whose memory haunted him like a ghost.

"I thought coming here would make a difference." Although he was speaking to me—at least I thought he was—his gaze was focused on some distant, indefinable point. "And most of the time it does. I ride horses. Round up strays. Feed cattle. Fix fences." A frown creased his forehead. "It follows me, though. Wherever I go, whatever I do, there's always someone I can't protect. Someone I can't save. Something beyond my control."

I touched his cheek. "What happened, Wyatt? Can you tell me?"

As if my touch had flipped the switch that brought him back to the present, he blinked. His eyes were once again focused on me, but they were filled with enough anguish to make anything I'd ever endured seem trivial.

"I'm not sure." His short bark of laughter contained no amusement whatsoever. "Does it change anything for you to know I was once so helpless, I could only watch? I couldn't do anything to stop what was happening. I couldn't even yell for help."

"Stop what?" Despite his intense, penetrating gaze— one that should've had me shaking in my shoes—my knees held firm, although my voice sounded soft and breathy.

"My father," he snapped. "Does it help you to know I could only crouch in a corner and watch while he beat my mother to death?"

I stared back at him for the space of as many heart-beats as it took me to realize my mouth was hanging open. "Oh, Wyatt…"

What else was there to say? To be honest, I was surprised I was able to say what little I had. Then it dawned on me that in all the years since then—no doubt he'd been a child at the time—he'd probably never said those words to anyone.

Except *me*.

I tried to lick my lips with a tongue that had gone bone dry. "Yes, it does help. Because it helps me to know who you are." My tremulous smile lasted less than a second. "I want to know everything about you,

Wyatt. Everything. Can you do that? Can you tell me everything?"

He stared at me with eyes now devoid of expression. My heart slid to my toes as he lowered his head, obviously preferring to face the floor instead of me.

With a slow exhale, he glanced up. "I think I just did."

I watched as tension flowed from him like a receding flood. My own anxiety, on the other hand, didn't abate one iota. Even my teeth were chattering.

With a shrug, he continued, "Everything that matters, anyway. The rest is only what came afterward—police, counselors, foster homes. My last foster father was a firefighter, and he was everything my real father wasn't. Someone to look up to and emulate. I followed in his footsteps the best I could, but there were still fires I couldn't put out fast enough, still people I couldn't save." He paused, rubbing the back of his neck with a hand that appeared to be shaking as much as I was. "After that last big fire—all those people we couldn't rescue—I knew I had to quit. I got in my truck and started driving until I wound up here." He smiled. "I'd never been on a horse in my life, but I learned. It felt right, like this was where I belonged."

"I know at least one person you saved."

He shrugged again. "That was only basic life support training. Anyone could've done it."

"True, but *you* were the one who saved Calvin's life, and you aren't just anyone. Not by a long shot. You're a good man, Wyatt McCabe," I said with absolute conviction. "No matter where you go or what you do, that part of you still shines through."

"I'm glad you think so. If you didn't—" He squeezed

his eyes shut, whether in a wince or to blink back tears, I couldn't tell. "I don't know what I would've done. From that first moment, there was something about you, Tina. Something that shook me up like nothing else ever has, which is why I was acting like such an asshole. I'm sorry about that."

"No worries," I said. "I was kinda shook up myself. Guys like you usually have me shaking in my shoes." Wyatt had made me tremble before he even opened his mouth. "In case you haven't noticed, I'm a little on the shy side."

Finally, he smiled. "You think?"

"Yeah. I didn't realize you were different until I saw you feeding cornbread to Ophelia. Although the fact that she didn't growl at you should've been my first clue." I glanced at my trusty dog, who was currently asleep on my bed. "She's a pretty good judge of character." Turning back toward Wyatt, I studied him for a moment. "You okay?"

He nodded. "For now. I never know when the flashbacks will hit me or what will trigger them."

If memory served, I was pretty sure I'd witnessed a few of those episodes already, and I'd been the inadvertent cause of at least two of them, including the most recent. "If you ever need to talk, I'm a pretty good listener."

"I've noticed that too."

The smiles we exchanged were evolving into a kiss when I heard footsteps coming down the hall.

Nick stuck his head through the doorway. "Sorry to break up the party, but those dishes aren't gonna wash themselves, and I'm sure as hell not tackling that mess alone."

"Be right there," Wyatt said. "Tina had something she wanted to show me."

"*Sure* she did," Nick scoffed. "Listen, you two can play show-and-tell later. Right now, I want to get my chores done before I conk out from eating that huge dinner." He aimed a grin at me. "Which, by the way, was fabulous."

"Glad you enjoyed it," I said. "Any requests for tomorrow?"

"I dunno… The stuff you come up with on your own is damn good. Surprise me."

"You're a big help," I grumbled. "Guess I'll just ask Calvin what he usually does on Mondays."

Wyatt cleared his throat. "I can tell you that—any of us could. The usual weekday breakfast, sandwiches for lunch, and pork chops for dinner."

I was almost afraid to ask. "How many pork chops apiece?"

Nick licked his lips.

Oh, here it comes…

"I can eat three," he said. "Unless they're the big thick ones. And then I usually only eat two."

"And what would you like with your pork chops?" After the day I'd had and as tired as I was, no telling what weird combinations I might come up with if left to my own devices.

"Anything," he replied. "Use your imagination."

"You might be sorry you said that when I serve Swiss chard ice cream for dessert."

For a moment there, I thought Nick might actually gag. He put up a placating hand. "Okay, okay. Green beans and mashed potatoes." The resignation in his voice and posture suggested that those two dishes comprised the remainder of their standard Monday night fare.

"Not terribly imaginative," I said. "But doable."

"Baked sweet potatoes instead of mashed?" Wyatt suggested.

I nodded. "That's better. What about a salad?"

Wyatt arched a wicked brow. "Caesar?"

"You got it."

"Wait a minute," Nick said. "What about dessert?"

I grinned. "Sugar-free Jigglers."

Nick stared at me, unblinking. I could've sworn there were tears in his eyes. "You're kidding me, right?"

"For now," I replied. "Although I'm pretty sure it'll come to that eventually."

"I'll give up a pork chop if it means having pie," he declared.

"What kind?" I prompted.

"Doesn't matter," he said. "Just as long as you don't make it with Swiss chard."

———

After the guys left to wash the dishes, I took Ophelia out for a short walk. A surreptitious glance at the hillside where I'd seen a light the night before revealed nothing, although it wasn't yet fully dark.

I came back inside to find Calvin waiting for me. "I hate to put more of a burden on you," he began. "But I could really use your help making sure I'm taking my pills right—at least 'til I get the hang of it."

Among those people currently residing in the bunk-house, no doubt he envisioned me as the closest thing to a nurse. While I couldn't claim to be an RN, I could read and understand a prescription label. If I had any doubts or questions about his medications, I had a computer and I knew how to use it. "No problem. Do you need help tonight?"

"There might be one I'm supposed to take at bedtime. Not sure."

I followed him into his room, noticing a slight shuffling of his feet as he walked. I couldn't recall that he'd moved that way when I first arrived, although at the time, I hadn't been paying any attention to his gait. I probably would now; I'd watched Grandpa like a hawk for years.

Old habits die hard...

Calvin retrieved a sack full of medication bottles from his dresser and handed it to me. I was thankful to see a full bottle of nitroglycerine tablets in there along with several other prescriptions.

"Hmm...metoprolol succinate, Plavix, and simvastatin." That last one I recognized as a medication Grandpa had taken to lower his cholesterol; the rest I would have to look up. I handed him the simvastatin. "You should take one of these tonight and the others in the morning. If you don't have a pill organizer, I can run into town and get you one. Grandpa was on so much stuff, putting it in an organizer was the only way I could keep it all straight."

"Thanks, Tina. I'd appreciate that." With a rueful smile, he added, "Guess I should've paid more attention to my blood pressure and cholesterol before now. I knew they were both high, but I really hate taking medicine. It's my own damn fault I wound up in the hospital."

Given the discussion I'd had with Wyatt earlier that evening, I wasn't sure whose fault it was. However, until we found further proof, I saw no point in giving Calvin anything else to worry about.

"Don't be too hard on yourself, Calvin. You're not the only man who doesn't like to take his meds. Half the time I had to disguise the stuff I gave Grandpa, especially toward the end when he was having one of his bouts of paranoia. Even when he was perfectly lucid, he wasn't what you'd call compliant." I sometimes wondered why he'd been so resistant. Was it a refusal to admit weakness, or was it simply a matter of not wanting to rely on a bottle of pills to keep him alive? Never having asked the question, I didn't know.

"I'll just bet you did. John always was a stubborn fellow." Smiling somewhat reminiscently, he set the sack back on the dresser and headed into his bathroom.

A better nurse would've waited until he actually swallowed his evening dose, but I figured I could trust him to take it on his own. He'd learned that lesson the hard way.

Nick and Wyatt were still at the sink washing dishes when I went back to the kitchen. As I passed behind them, I did something I'd never done before in my life—to anyone. I grabbed Wyatt's ass.

Actually, it was more of a fondle than a grab, but he obviously felt it because he aimed a sly wink over his shoulder at me as I headed toward the freezer.

Nick's chuckle proved he'd either seen or at least guessed what I'd done. "Not shy anymore, are you, Tina?"

"I wouldn't say I was completely cured," I said. "But I'm getting there."

He nodded. "Are you two gonna be sneaky like you and Dean were? Or are you planning to openly bunk together?"

Clearly Dean and I hadn't been sneaky enough if Nick thought that. "Dean and I did *not* sleep together." On the other hand, the fact that I not only didn't blush but was able to form a rational reply was further proof of how far I'd come in my battle with shyness. "Besides, the bed is much too small."

"You could put two bunks together," Nick suggested, apparently undeterred by such a minor detail.

"And have one of us fall through the crack in the middle of the night? No, thank you." Opening the enormous freezer, I began digging around for pork chops. Unfortunately, since the different meats were all wrapped in white paper and many of the labels were smudged, they weren't easy to find.

"No, really," Nick persisted. "That wouldn't happen if we tied the bed frames together."

"I dunno if I'd like that or not. I'm used to sleeping alone." A glance at Wyatt, whose shoulders were now shaking with barely suppressed laughter, gave me an idea. "Besides, what with Wyatt's bad shoulder and all, he might have a hard time getting comfortable."

"Not if you massaged it for him real good," Nick said. "He'd probably sleep like a baby."

"Uh-huh. Sure." I finally found some pork chops, but the package was pretty small, so I rummaged around until I found three more. By this time, my fingers were practically frostbitten. "What kind of pie did you say you wanted?"

"I didn't," Nick replied. "And don't change the subject."

"I'll change the subject if I want to." I glared at my so-called boyfriend. Although I was very glad he had shaken off the demons of his past and regained his sense of humor—at least temporarily—his continued silence was a teensy bit exasperating. "Doggone it, Wyatt, will you please say *something*?"

Wyatt stopped laughing just long enough to say, "We could use baling wire to hold the beds together."

Chapter 20

"THANKS A BUNCH, WYATT," I SAID. "DO YOU REALLY think we can get away with anything that, that…blatant?"

"Sure. We're two consenting adults." He glanced at Nick. "Doesn't bother you, does it?"

I rolled my eyes. "Of course it doesn't bother him. He's the one who suggested it!"

"Hey, if an idea is good…" With a shrug, Wyatt snatched up a dish towel and dried his hands.

"Where are you going?" Exasperation coupled with fatigue and a bit of menstrual snappishness made my question sharper than necessary.

"To move one of the extra bunks into your room," Wyatt replied with perfect calm.

For a moment, all I could do was gape at him. "Right *now*?"

"We're finished with the dishes." Nick's tone and expression tacked the "well, duh" onto his reply.

"Oh. So you are." My brain was really beginning to protest the abuse it had taken over the past twenty-four hours. I needed sleep. Badly. Now my desire to dive into bed was being thwarted by two cowboys who were fixing to rearrange the furniture. "Guys, look. I'm exhausted. I didn't get much sleep last night—"

"Neither did we," Nick countered.

"I know, but I'm guessing you two actually fell asleep at some point." I looked Wyatt right square in the eyes. "I never did."

With a flick of his brow, he nodded. "We'll make it quick then."

That particular response wasn't exactly what I had in mind, but I figured he might be in need of a sympathetic ear. Spilling the beans about his childhood had to have been tough. Then again, he'd been living with his past for a long time. Maybe I was the one who needed to adjust.

I nodded my consent, wondering what the other men would make of the new arrangement, especially Calvin. With him home from the hospital and sleeping in the room next to mine, keeping quiet would be even more important than if Dean and I had ever actually spent a night together. Too bad it would also be more difficult.

But not tonight. Something told me I'd have my mouth too full of Wyatt to let out many cries of ecstasy.

Chuckling to myself, I transferred the frozen pork chops to the refrigerator and rummaged around for pie ingredients. At the rate I was making pies, I wouldn't have been too surprised to find I'd used up all the available frozen fruit. Maybe it was time for a cream pie—butterscotch was my specialty—or even a cake.

I was still pondering that decision when Wyatt and Nick came trooping through the kitchen with a bed frame. Considering they'd passed through the mess hall with it, I could hardly wait to hear the comments from the others, who were presumably watching TV.

I didn't have to wait long because Sonny and Dean were right behind them with a mattress. Bull brought up the rear carrying a stack of sheets. The only one missing was Joe, and I'd have bet anything he'd gone after the baling wire.

Oh, bloody hell...

"Y'all are bound and determined to get us"—I caught myself before saying *hitched*—"together, aren't you?"

"Self-defense," Dean said with a grin. "Wyatt has some pretty wild nightmares. You might have better luck calming him down than we do."

So...it wasn't so much a matter of getting us together as it was getting Wyatt into a different room. I had to wonder why they hadn't stashed him in the old foreman's quarters before now. But whatever the reason, apparently I was going to have to deal with another man suffering from post-traumatic stress disorder. I didn't mind, really, but some combat soldiers tended to come up swinging, especially when awakened by loud noises. Grandpa had been one of them.

On the other hand, it was a safe bet that Wyatt's worst nightmares revolved around a woman's scream. Dean was probably right about me being a better roommate.

It struck me then that Wyatt wasn't all that young— mid-thirties at least, and possibly older. Never having asked him, I didn't know for sure, but he should've been married with children a long time ago. So should I, for that matter. Shyness was my big issue. His was different.

Unless he'd been married before.

Once again I realized how little I knew about the man with whom I was about to start sharing a bed. He seemed to think telling me about his mother's murder said it all, and from his perspective, perhaps it did. I wasn't convinced; I needed to know more. A *lot* more.

Perhaps he *had* been married, and his wife couldn't deal with the horrors of his past. Or maybe he was like Calvin in that respect, avoiding attachments to keep from losing anyone else. He seemed to know what he was doing from a sexual standpoint, so I seriously doubted I was his first.

Had I told him he was *my* first? I didn't think I had, and in the heat of the moment, he could easily have missed the loss of my virginity. There hadn't been much of an opportunity for detailed confessions, either. Maybe that was why he didn't want to be sneaky about our relationship. He wanted everyone to know so there would be no excuse for us not to spend time together.

Guess the double bunk is a good idea after all.

I was fortunate to have reached that conclusion because in the next instant, Joe came through the kitchen with a coil of wire in one hand and a pair of pliers in the other. Why I had ever thought there would be any semblance of privacy in a bunkhouse was beyond me. Case in point, I'd had more men in my bedroom in the past few days than I had in my entire life—even taking into account that I'd lived in a home with a father, a grandfather, and two younger brothers.

I simply waved at Joe as he passed by.

Figuring it would be a while before I could crawl into my makeshift double bed, I made a big batch of tuna salad for the next day's lunch. I had no idea whether the guys all liked tuna, but it had been on the list Dean had given me. Surely someone would eat it.

At least no one was in my bathroom when I went to take a shower, although to be honest, I half expected Wyatt to join me there. I could've used someone to wash my back.

Yet another novel experience.

Someone should have stuck me in a bunkhouse years ago. If they had, my shyness would've been nipped in the bud and would never have blossomed into the evil entity it had become. Well…maybe not evil, but that was the way I was thinking at the time. Exhaustion did funny things to me—making me loopy and weird.

So much so that by the time I stumbled out of the bathroom and saw Wyatt stretched out on one side of my newly enlarged bed, I began laughing hysterically.

"What's so funny?" The glance he stole at the bulge in his briefs made me laugh even harder.

"You. Expecting me to sleep with you in that thing."

"It's sturdier than you think," he said. "We all but welded the frames together."

How sweet. He thought I was only worried about our personal safety. I had other concerns, most of which involved the whole happily ever after thing. So much had happened in a very short time. I hadn't had time to process it all.

Therein lies your problem, Tina. You think too much.

The voice in my head sounded suspiciously like Morgan Freeman. Or maybe it was Alec Guinness. I wasn't sure. Either way, it sounded venerable and wise. I thought perhaps I should listen.

"Does Calvin know you're in here?" Not only would hearing strange noises coming from my room disturb the old man's rest, I could see him trying to return the favor I'd done him by rescuing me from whatever varmint had crawled into my bunk.

He nodded. "Even if he didn't, I don't see how he could've missed what was going on in here earlier. We weren't exactly quiet."

By that I could safely assume Calvin had either okayed the project or acted in a supervisory capacity. I didn't know which was worse: the guys knowing what we were up to or getting caught in the middle of a steamy tryst. I felt like a new bride being teased by her husband's groomsmen.

Only there hadn't been a wedding. There'd been a—

A *what*? An understanding? Dean and I had started out with a no-strings relationship that, given time, might have gotten a lot more involved. What exactly did I have with Wyatt?

I blew out a weary, resigned breath. At least they'd put the headboards against the wall. If I had to climb over Wyatt to let Ophelia out during the night, whatever arrangement we had would probably end pretty quickly.

He held out a beckoning hand. "C'mon over here and lie down. You look worn-out."

In that moment, I realized what was bugging me. The night before, Wyatt had picked me up and carried me into my bedroom. Now it was up to me to voluntarily get into bed with him. The subsequent attack of nerves had my feet rooted to the spot. Earlier, I'd been thinking about sucking his luscious cock. Now, it seemed as if those thoughts belonged to another person entirely.

As though he understood my dilemma, he got up and came toward me. Simply watching him move was riveting. The play of muscles beneath his skin. The shock of dark hair, hazel eyes that could appear brooding and forbidding, and a moment later seem welcoming and kind. He gathered me into his embrace.

"You aren't scared, are you?"

The echo of his earlier question cleared my mind. "Not scared, exactly. Just a little out of my element."

A chuckle rumbled in his chest, soothing my ruffled nerves like a balm. "You aren't the only one."

Frowning, I took a step back. "Seriously?"

"Of course. Here I am, trying to figure out how, after all the horrible things that have happened in my lifetime, I could suddenly get this lucky."

I hadn't thought of it that way, but sooner or later, everyone's luck was bound to change. "The law of averages, perhaps?"

"Maybe. Remember what you said about not looking a gift horse in the mouth? I've been telling myself the same thing all evening, and I still can't believe I'm here with you." As if to prove the reality of it all, he tightened his hold on me. "But you're real. Sweet, warm, and adorably sexy."

The kiss that Nick had interrupted earlier began anew—as warm and intoxicating as hot chocolate laced with rum. From where our lips touched, a thrill began, then slid to my heart before spiraling downward to my core, igniting pangs of desire that probably wouldn't be satisfied.

Bad timing.

He lifted me off my feet and into his arms. A few steps later, I was lying on the bed, amazed that I couldn't feel the seam between the two mattresses. They must've padded it somehow.

Such resourceful fellows...

Wyatt's lips were on mine again. Soft and seeking, loving yet undemanding. As always, his kisses obliterated any resistance. I longed to open to him and welcome him inside.

After kissing his way across my cheek, he hesitated, his lips hovering over my ear. "Am I right in assuming those were menstrual cramps you were having this afternoon?"

His question snapped me out of my blissful state. I may have fibbed about having cramps, but the presumed cause was real enough. "Yeah. Sorry. Blame it on Mother Nature."

"At least we know my lack of protection last night didn't cause any problems."

A tiny giggle escaped me. "I'm not sure a pregnancy would faze anyone but me at this point. Everyone else seems to have decided you and me are a done deal."

"But we aren't a done deal, are we?"

My heart dropped at least two inches within my chest, stretching every major blood vessel like a bungee cord before snapping back into place.

Fortunately, he kept talking, eliminating the opportunity for me to say something I might later regret.

"You have a choice, Tina. You'll always have a choice. I don't ever want you to feel like you don't."

"Thanks. I appreciate that." Despite the speed with which everything had happened between us, he obviously wasn't going to force the issue. "The same goes for you. The guys may have booted you out of the bunkhouse, but that doesn't mean you have to stay here."

He sucked my earlobe into his mouth, sending goose bumps skittering down my neck. With a slow exhale, he let go. "I'm here because I want to be." His voice was like the rumble of distant thunder, deep and rough. "And the way I feel right now, I always will."

As declarations of undying love went, it wasn't bad.

However, I wasn't ready to make that decision yet, and I was very glad it hadn't been made for me. He was right about the importance of choices. A pregnancy at this stage could be disastrous for both of us.

"I want you to be here too," I said. "No pressure."

Another kiss averted anything else I might've said, which was fine with me. The time for words had passed.

I slid a hand down his back to delve beneath the waistband of his briefs. I'd fondled his buns while he was washing dishes with this very thing in mind. Cupping his muscular buttocks in my palm, I squeezed him, hard.

His subsequent groan was all the encouragement I needed. I pushed his underwear down as far as I could, and he took them the rest of the way.

Gotta love a naked cowboy.

I was emboldened by the knowledge that this was my show tonight. He couldn't take the initiative, so it was up to me. I liked that. Liked knowing I could make him groan and sigh. Trailing my fingertips over his buns, I gave them another squeeze before moving on to even better things.

His cock was hard and hot in my hand, and as much juice as he was pumping out, I doubted I would need to break the seal on my brand-new bottle of lube. I was going to suck him first anyway. I hadn't done that yet, and I was dying to give it a try.

I stroked the length of his shaft, marveling at the velvety feel of smooth skin stretched over firm flesh. Needing more, I pushed him onto his back and made a dive for his groin.

Despite his strangled-sounding "Oh, God," he certainly wasn't trying to stop me.

Not that he could.

I gave the tight head a lick, enjoying the salty taste of him and the slick fluid welling up from his slit. Opening wide, I slid my lips over his cockhead, taking him in as far as I could. His cock was big and warm in my mouth, and it didn't take me long to get creative, licking up and down the shaft before going back to sip the juice from the head. Saying it wasn't bad was a gross understatement.

I not only liked it, I *loved* it.

Any cramps I might've had were superseded by an ache that had its origins in passion and desire. If he had insisted on actual intercourse, I wouldn't have objected; I would have tucked a towel under my butt and yanked him inside me in a heartbeat.

But that was something new lovers probably didn't do. It was too intimate, too…knowing.

I trailed the back of my hand over his balls, delighting in the tickle of his scrotal hair against my skin. Reaching down, I cupped them in my palm, feeling their weight, wanting nothing more than to suck them until he begged for mercy. I kissed my way down his length until springy curls brushed my cheek.

Oddly enough, Wyatt didn't smell like a man who had been in the saddle all day. In fact, I caught a whiff of something—cologne, perhaps—on the soft skin where his torso met his thigh. A smile tugged at my lips as I leaned closer. The scent was subtle, as though he'd placed an infinitesimal drop of spicy fragrance precisely where he had known I would find it.

Was it enticement or reward? I didn't know and didn't care. I fully intended to suck him until he came in my mouth whether he expected it of me or not. His enjoyment was important to me, but this was something I suspected would give me as much satisfaction as actually being nailed by my big, handsome cowboy.

Between his drooling dick and my saliva, I had no trouble getting him wet enough to suck a nut into my mouth. Wyatt's gasp of surprise was followed by a guttural groan of pure pleasure, a response which served as both encouragement and reward. I continued on, stroking his cock while caressing his scrotum with my tongue. After a bit, I fisted my hand around his shaft and took up a steady rhythm, rotating my palm over his slick cockhead before plummeting to the base and back again.

Tingles washed over my skin as he slid a hand from my shoulder to the back of my head. Tangling his fingers in my hair, he lightly massaged my scalp as though attempting to return the favor by caressing the only part of me he could reach.

Anxious to savor more of his juice, I released his testicle and turned on my side. With my head pillowed on his stomach, I aimed his delicious dick at my lips and sucked him in. His hips rose in response, driving him in deeper still. My subsequent moan must have urged him to continue, because he kept on, each thrust becoming increasingly forceful until he was actually fucking my mouth.

Without warning, the orgasm I never expected to have began coiling up inside me like a cobra threatening to strike. I only hoped I could hang on long enough for Wyatt to reach his own climax because that was one event I did *not* want to miss. He had to be close; his cock was unbelievably hard, the flange catching my lips on the outstroke. As his pace slowed, I slackened my hold on him, letting it happen, letting him come.

Seconds later, his back arched and an inarticulate sound issued from his throat as his cock pulsed against my tongue, filling my mouth with his cream. I had barely begun to swallow when my own orgasm detonated, making my previous episode of "cramps" seem like a mere hiccup in comparison.

Apparently, there were orgasms and then there were *orgasms*.

Wyatt's cock slipped from my mouth, and from where I lay sprawled on top of him, I caught the next spurt of semen across my neck. My mind went blank as wave after wave of gut-clenching ecstasy passed through me, rendering me oblivious to my surroundings, save for the erratic rise and fall of his chest.

Slowly, the spasms began to subside, and I rolled onto my back, my uppermost arm flopping bonelessly onto the sheet. "Holy cow, that was good."

He let out a breathless laugh and patted the top of my head, ruffling my hair. "Glad you liked it. For a second there, I thought you were gettin' kinda grossed out."

"No way," I insisted. "That was absolutely fabulous."

In the past, I had always found that "Have a happy period" marketing strategy for feminine products to be rather annoying. Now I was beginning to suspect whoever came up with that little gem of having been fortunate enough to have a guy like Wyatt around to help her through it.

Nah. Prob'ly not.

Either way, I doubted I would ever refer to my monthly visit from Aunt Flo as "The Curse" again.

Chapter 21

I AWOKE THE NEXT MORNING WITH A MAN IN MY BED.

So many new things were happening to me, things most women my age took for granted. Every one of my high school chums had married. One had even tied the knot before graduation. I'm sure there were plenty of guys in my college classes who hadn't found the right woman, but they were geeks like me. Shy. Introverted. Nervous around the opposite sex.

Would I still be nervous around men with whom I wasn't sharing a bunkhouse? Maybe. That was one test I had yet to face, although I certainly would when I went back home.

Or would I? I had no job to return to. No apartment. No reason not to stay and cook for this gang of cowboys for the rest of my life. But did I really want that? Was it even possible? Calvin would undoubtedly be ticked if I stole his job, and now that he was out of the hospital, Angela might not want to keep me on the payroll.

Yet another decision that will probably be made for me.

Truth be told, I was getting a little tired of being on the receiving end of those kinds of decisions. Wyatt had told me I had a choice. I liked that idea. I could kick him out of my bed and send him back to the bunkhouse if I wished. I didn't want to, but knowing I could made a huge difference.

Rolling over, I sat up. Ophelia looked up at me from her post on the doormat, her tail wagging in greeting.

"Good morning to you too," I said. "Need to go out?"

Wyatt spoke up from his side of the bed. "Probably not. I let her out a little while ago."

Yet another first. No one had ever done that for me. At least, not within recent memory.

"Thanks." I was about to ask if he'd had trouble sleeping when I recalled that he had always been the one to answer my cries for help during the night. "You must be a really light sleeper."

"Yeah. Unlike *you*."

I turned toward him to protest, but one glimpse of his tousled hair, sleepy eyes, and boyish grin nearly detonated another orgasm. "Not my fault I was dead to the world." My comeback wasn't as snappy as I would've liked, but given the circumstances, I didn't think it was too shabby.

Chuckling, he ran a finger down my arm. "I slept better than usual myself."

"No nightmares?"

"Not a one," he declared. "Just sweet dreams about this beautiful blond who gets off on sucking my dick."

"Hmm…well, don't let it go to your head."

"I might if I'm the only one to have that effect." His gaze intensified, seeming to delve past my eyes to discover my thoughts. "Am I?"

This from a man who could make me climax simply by walking into the room.

"So far," I replied. "Actually, that was a first—and not just the orgasm."

"Meaning?"

Dean had already figured out the truth. It was only a matter of time before Wyatt reached that same conclusion.

"*You* were my first."

His mouth formed a soundless O, and for a long moment, all he did was blink. "I don't get it. You're beautiful and sweet and sexy as hell. Why—"

"I'm a computer geek, Wyatt. I thought I'd made that clear."

"What? You mean geeks never have sex?"

"The shy ones don't."

"You must've hung out with some real idiots," he said with a slow wag of his head. "I can't imagine any man not falling for you."

"It's sweet of you to say that, but Dean was the closest thing I've ever had to a boyfriend, and we didn't get that far."

As a long silence stretched between us, his satyr-like frown returned. "I'm not sorry I'm your first, but I hurt you. Didn't I?"

"Maybe a little," I admitted.

"You should have said something. I wouldn't have—"

"Been quite so rough?" I touched his cheek. "Wyatt, sweetheart, you didn't do anything I didn't want you to do. I've been waiting all my life for that moment, and my wildest dreams were nowhere near as fabulous as the reality."

He drew in a breath. "I'm glad you feel that way. You aren't the only one whose wildest dreams were put to shame. In many ways, that was a first for me too."

My jaw dropped. I couldn't imagine a man like Wyatt not being sought after by every single woman within a hundred-mile radius, perhaps even the subject of a determined chase. He was the kind of man most women dreamed about. Strong, dependable, and astonishingly sexy. Completely nonplussed, I just sat there for a few seconds. Then I decided I had to know.

"Okay. Spill it. If that's true, I'm guessing you've never been married, but you have to at least have had a girlfriend."

He shrugged. "I'm not saying I've never had sex. I dated a few girls in high school—even made the mistake of sleeping with one of them. I had a nightmare that freaked her out like you wouldn't believe. I never tried it again. Until now. It was...*different* with you—like it really meant something instead of just going through the motions." His expression grew wistful as he added, "And you're right. I've never been married. Not even close. After a while, you stop looking."

We had more in common than I ever would have guessed. "I can relate to that. I might've ogled a few hunky firefighters, but I never expected them to return the favor. Shy girls like me tend to be invisible."

"You're not invisible, Tina," he said. "Not to me or any cowboy on this ranch. We're all crazy about you; it's hard to believe we've only known you for a week."

Actually, I'd been there less than a week, but I saw no need to split hairs. I smiled, shaking my head. "I never would've thought we would get along so well. You guys made me nervous as all get-out in the beginning." Anticipating his next question, I added, "And no, there aren't any past traumas to explain my shyness. I just didn't inherit the flirting gene."

"Does that mean your mom's a flirt?" His teasing

smile took any sting out of his question. "Or was it your father?"

"No—well...they might've been when they were younger. I really don't know for sure. Neither of them is anywhere near as shy as I am. I mean, they found each other and had kids and everything. " I debated whether to add more to that, opting against it before ultimately deciding it was something I needed to get off my chest. "I never thought that sort of life was even possible for me. But being here with you, I feel almost...normal."

"Same here," he said. "Normal. Boringly, predictably normal."

I shot him a grin. "Doncha just love it?"

"Oh, yeah," he said with a sage nod. "Being different is highly overrated."

As both of us burst out laughing, I suddenly realized how happy I was. Deliriously so, like the heroine of a romantic movie, dancing the night away with the man who brought out the joy in her. I'd always been in the background, far too quiet and shy to join in the fun. Now I was giggling my head off while a handsome and completely naked cowboy pulled me back down on the bed and ruthlessly kissed me.

The banging on my bedroom door was a minor event, and even Nick's shouted, "I'm starving! Will somebody please fix me some breakfast?" didn't bother me.

I did, however, respond. "Keep your shirt on, Nick. I'm coming."

The sexual connotation of what I'd just said struck Wyatt and me at the same time, resulting in another spurt of laughter. Still giggling, I sat up and put on my slippers, then reached for my robe.

I could get used to being normal. Especially if it meant getting a rear view of Wyatt every morning as he headed toward the bathroom. The soft morning light accentuated the curves and planes of his body, the broad perfection of his back, which tapered to narrow hips, muscular thighs, and buns to die for.

Oh, wow...

I glanced down at my flannel pj's. Wyatt might appreciate it if I returned the favor now and then. Unfortunately, I'd never been comfortable wandering about in the altogether, and I hadn't made a habit of it even when I lived alone. Given the minimal privacy of the bunkhouse, I probably shouldn't start.

It would be different if Wyatt and I had a place of our own—

Whoa, Tina. Don't go there yet.

Without the benefit of a fairy godmother, our happily ever after was still a long way off. We barely knew one another. Could a lasting love be forged in such a short time? I doubted it, although the possibility certainly provided food for thought. If we ever decided to make a life together, would it be on the Circle Bar K? Living in the bunkhouse was fine now, but raising kids in that environment would pose quite a challenge.

Kids. Yet another adventure my shyness had denied me. Had I ever even considered what being a mother would entail? No doubt I had contemplated the joy of gazing into the trusting eyes of my newborn child. But the ups and downs, the challenges and the triumphs, not so much—probably because I considered the chances of ever having a family of my own to be so remote.

On the flip side, I was beginning to think of the ranch

as home and the people there as family. Wyatt had said he'd felt the same way when he first arrived. Viewed in that light, the whole fate and kismet thing seemed perfectly plausible, even without a magic wand to cast the spell.

At the moment, however, I had cowboys to feed and pies to bake. Any plans for the future would have to wait a while longer.

———

As the men lined up for breakfast, I was pleased to note that Calvin seemed to have improved overnight. The lines around his eyes had diminished, and he moved with greater confidence.

I dropped a heaping spoonful of scrambled eggs on his plate. "You're looking pretty chipper this morning. Sleep okay?"

"Sure did," he replied. "There's no place like home." His sly wink suggested that while he might have known Wyatt and I were sharing a bed, he hadn't been disturbed by any peculiar sounds coming from my room. "Throw a few home-cooked meals on top of that, and anyone would feel better."

Bull, who had been first in line, helped himself to three slices of buttered toast, then patted his stomach. "I dunno about that. Since Tina's been doing the cooking, I think I might've picked up a few pounds."

I arched a brow. "Now, Bull. Don't go blaming me. I never forced you to eat anything."

"Can I help it if you're such a damned fine cook?" He turned toward Calvin. "You just wait. She'll have you fattened up in no time."

"I'm sure she will." If Calvin's smile was to be believed, he hadn't taken offense at the implication that my culinary skills eclipsed his own. Either that or, after years of hearing Bull carry on, he probably knew better than to take him seriously.

Nick stepped forward and held out his plate. "Uh-huh. That is, if you stick around long enough."

There was no mistaking his meaning. "I'll stay as long as I'm needed." Keeping my tone neutral, I deliberately avoided Wyatt's gaze. If he had any sense at all, he would know that the "being needed" stipulation applied to him more than anyone.

Calvin was still smiling when he picked up his toast and followed Bull into the mess hall.

"Yeah, well, you know how we all feel about *that*." As though acknowledging his previous faux pas, Nick hung his head slightly while keeping his voice low.

I spoke in an even softer tone, hoping that Calvin hadn't overheard either of us. "And the less said about it, the better."

Angela hadn't mentioned the possibility that I might stay on indefinitely, and I doubted she would have said anything to Calvin, either. Stealing a man's job while he was in the hospital was pretty tacky. I'd heard of permanent replacements being hired during an extended sick leave, but Calvin had been gone less than a week.

I filled Sonny's plate in silence. Wyatt was next in line.

"You know why I said that, don't you?" I whispered after Sonny left the room. "I don't want Calvin to think I'm trying to snatch his job out from under him."

"He's a grown man, Tina," Wyatt said. "And he's also a realist."

"Yes, but what if he never recovers enough to work on the ranch with you guys? Being the full-time cook might be his only option." I glanced at Joe, who stood behind Wyatt. "What will happen if he turns out to be permanently disabled?"

Joe shrugged. "No telling. Although I'm pretty sure no one would kick him out of the bunkhouse—at least not right away. Come to think of it, I can't remember anyone ever actually retiring from this job."

I had no idea whether that was a commentary on the life span of the average cowboy or their tendency to drift from place to place, neither of which appealed to me.

What happened to retired cowboys? Did they live out their declining years in solitude or was there a special home for them? I could just imagine a bunch of crusty old cowhands sitting on a sunny porch swapping stories, but God only knew whether that was the best choice for them. In a more diverse group, they would undoubtedly brighten the lives of any elderly ladies who'd ever fantasized about riding off into the sunset with Gary Cooper or John Wayne.

The truth was there was nothing terribly romantic about what they did. From my perspective, it was a very lonely sort of existence. The camaraderie among the men on the Circle Bar K was clearly evident, but there were times when they might spend an entire day with only their four-legged friends for company.

I was no different, really. I spent most of my time with electronic devices. What did that make me?

Having filled their plates, I collected my own breakfast, but with a somewhat wistful, contemplative air rather than the more contented mood with which my day had begun. My feelings now were more akin to those I normally had in late summer or early fall, when the whirring voices of cicadas provided a counterpoint to chirping birdsong while soft, cool breezes blew in through my windows—enjoying those moments of peace knowing they wouldn't last and that winter would soon be upon us.

Kentucky winters were nothing like those in Wyoming. If I stayed where I was, I would be snowed in the bunkhouse for weeks, perhaps even months, with these guys. How would I cope with a life so far removed from my usual stomping grounds, a lifestyle so different from my own?

Finding no answers to my questions in my own head, I took a seat in the mess hall. A sweeping glance around the table revealed myriad expressions—some introspective, some laughing, some simply neutral as they ate their food. It struck me then that I truly could spend a winter with these men, and I doubted I would ever experience any boredom whatsoever.

That thought cheered me, and I caught myself smiling—or rather, Bull did.

"Someone looks mighty damned pleased with herself this morning," he said, his usual bombastic tone carrying a touch of suggestion.

In another phase of my life, I would have blushed. Now, I simply responded with a serene smile and a softly uttered, "With good reason," before returning my attention to my plate. I'd outdone myself on the scrambled eggs that morning, tossing in a few extra seasonings I'd never included before. Apparently sex with Wyatt had improved my creative spirit along with my mood.

Bull gaped at me, openmouthed. "That's all you're gonna say?"

"Yep." As a coworker, I was under no obligation to tell him anything, and I doubted I would have said very much, even to a friend. From a need-to-know stand-point? *Zip.*

I turned my still-serene smile on Sonny, who was giving his plate a very thorough scraping with the side of his fork. "Did you get enough to eat?"

"Yes, ma'am," he replied. "Just making sure I got it all."

"Glad to hear it." Recalling the one spurt of Wyatt's semen that wound up on my neck instead of in my mouth brought on a sudden bout of tingles. "We wouldn't want anything to go to waste."

I followed that statement with a meaningful glance at Wyatt, whose barely audible chuckle proved he'd understood me perfectly. Even a napkin pressed to his lips couldn't hide his grin.

I'd gotten a taste of the inside joke experience with Dean, but for some reason it was far more satisfying with Wyatt.

Some reason?

Who was I kidding? I knew exactly what that reason was.

I was falling in love with Wyatt McCabe.

Chapter 22

WITH BREAKFAST OVER AND DONE WITH, I FIXED LUNCH for the guys and sent them on their way. Wyatt gave me one heck of a smooch before he left. Apparently being sucked off by your girlfriend tended to put a guy in a grateful mood.

After I finished cleaning up the kitchen, I took a peek through the door to the mess hall. Calvin was sitting in one of the recliners, reading a book.

"Need anything?" I asked.

He shook his head. "Not unless you know how to turn the clock back twenty years."

"Sorry. No can do. Be a neat trick, though."

"That's the trouble with getting older," he said with a wistful smile. "The mistakes you've made tend to stand out more than the things you did right."

Although I hadn't reached that point and didn't share his perspective, I couldn't recall ever having made any glaring mistakes. On the contrary, staying that first night in the bunkhouse had turned out to be one of my better moves, and it had taken precedence over just about anything else I'd ever done—good or bad. A brief flashback to *It's a Wonderful Life* brought on a smile. Jimmy Stewart's character had wished he'd never been born. While that particular wish had never crossed my mind, neither had I ever considered my life to have had much of an impact on anyone else's.

But it had. The man sitting there comfortably reading a book was living proof of that.

"I've been thinkin' about Jeannine," he went on. "I never shoulda run off like that—cut myself off from the only family I had." He paused, frowning. "Too late now."

"Does that mean you don't want to talk to her lawyers?"

"Haven't decided yet," he replied. "If she did leave me something in her will, I'm not sure I should accept it. Just doesn't seem right to benefit from her death when I've done my best to avoid her for so long."

"If I read those letters correctly, your estrangement was as much her fault as it was yours. Maybe this is her way of trying to make amends."

Calvin shifted in his chair and fidgeted with a page of his book as though reluctant to put his thoughts into words.

"More like easing her conscience," he finally said. "My only mistake was in letting her have her way; letting her ignore her own kin while she pretended to be something she wasn't."

Obviously he still felt some animosity toward his sister, even after her death. "Wouldn't hurt to talk to them, though, would it? I mean, if you don't want any part of the inheritance, you need to tell them so. There might be a secondary beneficiary who's hanging from a limb waiting for you to be found." I didn't add my suspicions that if he refused the bequest, whoever that person was might stop trying to kill him.

I wished I'd known Calvin better. I'd barely met the man before he was carted off to the hospital, which made knowing what to say and when to say it that much more difficult. The suggestion that he might have been the victim of an attempted murder could cause all kinds of worries, many of which might prove to be groundless.

"True," he said. "I'm still not sure I want to get mixed up in any of it. You know how rich people are."

Never having known any, I could only guess at what he meant. However, if the news media reported anything accurately, Wyatt's comment about wealthy people hanging on to their money tooth and nail was probably spot-on.

"I don't blame you for not wanting to open a can of worms, but—" How on earth could I sound convincing without alarming him or seeming paranoid? I paused for a moment to regroup. "What if she just wanted closure of some kind? To put your mind at ease or even to apologize?"

"Could be. But once you've opened a can of worms, it's damn near impossible to put the lid back on."

I certainly couldn't argue with that. "True." I waved a conciliatory hand. "It's up to you to decide."

"I'll let you know if I change my mind." With a brief nod, he leaned back in his chair and reopened the book in a manner that announced quite clearly that the subject was closed.

And he thought my grandfather was stubborn.

"Any idea what you'd like for lunch?"

"Doesn't matter," Calvin said. "I'm sure it'll be delicious."

I was a little surprised that he was so…compliant. So willing to sit back and let me wait on him with minimal input. He'd obviously been a hard worker all of his life and had seldom heeded doctor's orders. Had his near-death experience changed him that much? "Did your doctor say how long he wanted you to take it easy?"

"I'm supposed to see him again in two weeks," he replied. "Guess I'll hear all about that then."

From that I could assume I would be staying on for at least another two weeks, which meant I wouldn't be home for the Derby. I could watch the race, of course, but it was a safe bet that Wyoming television stations didn't give it the same kind of all-day coverage we got in Louisville. Cowboys probably didn't have much interest in that sort of horse race.

When my trip was in the planning stages, I'd seen something about rodeos being held regularly in Jackson Hole during the summer, but I had no idea whether there was one big rodeo the entire state celebrated the way Kentucky did with the Derby. I made a mental note to look it up when I had the chance. In the meantime, I couldn't imagine Wyoming would have much going on in late April, unless it was the birth of about a bajillion calves, in which case everyone would be too busy to do much partying.

Fortunately, I had the day's menu planned out ahead of time, which eliminated a lot of time-consuming guesswork—until I remembered the pork chops. I could make butterscotch pies in my sleep, but the pork chops were another issue altogether. Fried, grilled, or baked? Breaded or plain? Barbecued or marinated? By the time I got around to contemplating this dilemma, the pies were already chilling in the fridge and the guys were gone for the day, so I asked Calvin.

"Fried," he replied. "I just throw them on the griddle with a little salt and pepper."

Somehow, I thought I could be more creative than that, but at least I knew what the men were used to.

"Sounds good. I'm going to run into Rock Springs this morning. Do you need anything besides a pill organizer?"

"Prob'ly not—unless you can find me some more books to read."

Judging by the cover, the book he held was a western. *Big surprise*. "I'll see what I can come up with." The thump of Ophelia's tail drew my eye to where she lay stretched out beside the potbellied stove. "Want me to leave Ophelia here to keep you company?"

He nodded. "She looks pretty happy there."

She would also provide some decent protection. At the very least she could warn him of any intruders. I was trying to think of an excuse for him to keep a gun handy when I spotted a pistol on the table beside him, along with a cleaning rag and a can of oil. Someone might have left it there intending to clean it later, but given Wyatt's concerns, I suspected its presence was as deliberate as the box of bullets sitting next to it.

"My cell phone has a good signal in town. Give me a call if you think of anything you need." I handed him the wireless phone from the extension in my room. "I put the number on speed dial. All you have to do is press zero-one."

"I'm impressed." He set the phone on the arm of the recliner. "Never did figure out how to do that."

I doubted he ever had much need to call anyplace but the main house. Nevertheless, I couldn't help chuckling. "Hey, I'm a computer geek. Remember?"

"I surely do." His eyes took on a wistful, faraway expression as though gazing back through time. "Your grandpa was mighty proud of you."

"He'd have been proud of me if I'd been a ditch digger."

"He would at that." With a nod and a fond,

reminiscent smile, he settled back and opened the book again, although his focus didn't appear to be on the page.

"Back in a bit," I said and left him to his thoughts.

The drive to Rock Springs already seemed shorter than it had the last time. I was also acclimating to the town, finding a pharmacy without any difficulty and not even missing the turnoff to the grocery. For someone who'd rarely ventured beyond the outskirts of Louisville, I wasn't doing too badly.

Calvin and Ophelia were both snoring when I returned, so I set three new books on the table beside him, then went ahead and filled up the pill organizer with the appropriate dosages. When I compared the mess of bottles in his medicine cabinet to his new prescriptions, I found two that had similar generic names, but none that were exactly the same. On closer inspection, I noted that some of the tablets didn't even match the descriptions on the labels. God only knew what they were. Having dealt with Grandpa's meds after he died, I figured the best thing to do with Calvin's pills was to return them to the pharmacy for disposal on my next trip into town. With that in mind, I put them in a bag and stuck it in a cubbyhole in the desk in my room. I doubted that Calvin would ever take the old ones by mistake, but I thought it best not to take any chances.

I fixed a cucumber and tomato salad for lunch, half expecting Calvin to turn his nose up at it. However, true to his word, he offered no complaint, cleaned his plate, and helped himself to more.

"Thanks, Tina," he said when he'd finished. "That was tasty...for a salad. Guess I should get used to eating stuff like that."

"Same here," I said. "I probably ought to stop making desserts too—although Nick about had a stroke when I mentioned sugar-free Jigglers."

He chuckled. "That boy has quite an appetite."

"I've noticed."

I was about to comment on *his* good appetite when he cleared his throat, seeming slightly embarrassed. "Thanks for the books, by the way—and the pill box. I'd have thanked you sooner if I'd been awake." He paused, grimacing. "Sorry I'm such lousy company."

"Don't worry about it," I said. "I don't need to be entertained. Besides, you need your rest."

He acknowledged his "need for rest" with a shrug and halfhearted nod. "Never realized how quiet it was around here during the day. You must've been lonely here all by yourself."

Of all the things he could have said at that moment, a remark about my loneliness was the last thing I would have expected.

It shouldn't have been, though—especially after the bed-making episode had made my liaison with Wyatt common knowledge. To say I'd been *entertained* was putting it mildly. No wonder he'd seemed embarrassed.

"Not really," I said. "I had plenty to keep me busy." Reading his letters to Grandpa had taken up any spare time I'd had. "Or is this about Wyatt?"

"Wyatt's a good man, Tina. You could do a lot worse. But he has…issues."

"Yeah. I figured that. Especially after the guys were so anxious to get him out of the bunkhouse and into my room."

"Has he told you anything about himself?"

I nodded. "Maybe not the fine details, but yeah. I know the gist of his past—what happened to his parents and why he gave up firefighting and came here."

Calvin put down his fork and leaned back in his chair while studiously avoiding my eyes. "You'd be taking on a lot with him. I just want to make sure you know that."

"I do, and I'm okay with it. Everyone has baggage, even someone like me who's led a relatively sheltered life. And, really, we've only known each other for a few days. No telling what sort of future we might have together. Maybe all we'll ever have is the here and now."

"Never knew you were such a philosopher." His smile and jesting tone both faded as he continued, "'Course that's all any of us ever have…the here and now. Never the when and if."

I longed to lighten the mood but had no idea how to do it. In the end, I simply got to my feet and began gathering up the dishes before stating the obvious. "Guess we'd better enjoy it while we can."

Calvin went on as if I hadn't spoken. "You're the kind of woman Wyatt needs, and you'll be good for him. I'm just not sure he's the right man for you."

Despite believing that Calvin had my best interests at heart, my temper rose slightly. "Yeah, well, so far he's the *only* man." I started to add *beggars can't be choosers*, but I didn't feel like a beggar. I felt like I'd been given a rare and precious gift—a gift I wasn't sure I deserved.

He raised a placating hand. "No need to get riled. I'm just telling you what I think."

"Objection noted."

I carried the dishes into the kitchen, trying to decide

whether I was truly angry. Wyatt had saved the man's life, and Calvin didn't think he was good enough for me? Geez, it was as if Grandpa had somehow been reincarnated in Calvin's body when he was resuscitated—although considering the fact that everything Calvin knew about me had come from that source, I shouldn't have been surprised to find they had similar opinions.

Then again, perhaps Calvin's reasons were different from the typical "no man is good enough for my little girl" stance, whether I was his granddaughter or someone else's. Did he object because he didn't believe I would stay on the ranch, or that Wyatt wouldn't want to leave? Or did he want me to go because he didn't want me taking his job?

A moment later, I recalled how Calvin had lost his family and the last shred of my anger evaporated. Grandpa hadn't lost his wife—not like that, anyway—and he certainly hadn't lost his daughter. No, Calvin's objections were based more on his own experiences and what he knew about Wyatt.

But I wasn't Calvin. I didn't have his past. I may have shied away from men in general, but not because I was afraid to love or feared it wouldn't last. I wasn't shy or timid anymore. Not with Wyatt or any of the others. Somewhere on the Circle Bar K, I had discovered my courage, which was perhaps the greatest gift of all.

I intended to make the most of it.

After washing a few dishes, I took Ophelia for a short walk. When I returned, I sat down at my desk and opened my computer, determined to find the most awesome pork chop recipe in existence.

As I perused the possibilities, I caught myself smiling.

Computers had always fascinated me, but cooking was a passion I'd never had the opportunity to fully explore. I loved cooking for this motley crew of cowboys. I loved watching them devour their food. I loved the creative outlet cooking provided. To top it all off, I actually *liked* these men. Each in his own way perhaps, but I could see living and working with them for many years to come.

In that moment, I realized I wasn't going back to Kentucky. I was staying right where I was—doing something I loved with people whose company I enjoyed.

And Wyatt McCabe was at the top of that list.

Chapter 23

IN THE END, I OPTED FOR THE HEALTHIER VERSION OF the most awesome pork chop recipe in existence, which was baked rather than fried. I was in the process of dipping the meat in seasoned flour, beaten eggs, and bread crumbs—in that order—when it struck me that Calvin might not know that someone had been asking about him at the hospital. I knew I hadn't mentioned it, but Angela hadn't said one way or the other.

Would knowing that someone was looking for him help to convince Calvin to contact Jeannine's lawyers? For that matter, would that same man eventually come knocking on the bunkhouse door? One thing for sure, if anyone did come knocking, I wouldn't trust him for a second.

But would Calvin trust him? He'd been alone in the bunkhouse earlier that morning. Anyone watching the place could have seen me leaving and taken the opportunity to visit. There were so many things going on that not everyone knew about. Case in point, Angela didn't know anything about the notice on Jeannine's guestbook.

I'd told Wyatt, but should I tell Angela? Without Calvin's permission, I had no right to tell anyone what I'd discovered. The trouble was, if the guy showed up at the house, no one would be suspicious of him, and somehow I felt that every one of us needed to be wary.

On the other hand, if our elusive visitor really was trying to kill Calvin—for his inheritance or any other reason—why would he risk showing himself at the hospital? To make another attempt on Calvin's life while he was unconscious? While that was a fairly standard dramatic plot twist, I seriously doubted it was as easy as television shows and movies would have everyone believe, mainly because practically every piece of medical equipment has an alarm or a lock on it. Still, it wouldn't be too hard to create a diversion of some sort...

A swift downward glance revealed that I'd dipped one chop in the bread crumbs without dipping it in the egg first.

Bloody hell... That's what I get for playing detective instead of master chef.

With that admonition in mind, I was able to complete the preparations without any additional mistakes. After the chops had spent about half an hour in the oven, their heavenly aroma convinced me I was a far better cook than I was a sleuth.

I scrubbed up several sweet potatoes and had just put them in the oven when a gust of chilly air blew in through the kitchen door as Angela came inside carrying a stack of magazines.

"Damn," she exclaimed. "Something sure smells good. Got enough to feed three more?"

I somehow managed to turn my gasp into a cough, which went a long way toward restarting my stunned heart. Apparently mulling over murder mystery plots had me jumpier than usual. "Sure do. I'm trying out a new pork chop recipe. Hope the guys like it."

"I've never seen anything yet they wouldn't eat, but they sure seem happy to have you doing the cooking."

She laid the magazines on the counter. "I brought these for Calvin. Thought he might want something to read."

"Good idea. He asked me to get him some new books when I went to town this morning." Recalling my earlier doubts, I considered her timing to be most opportune. "Have you told Calvin about his visitor?"

Angela's dark braids swung back and forth as she shook her head in reply. "To be honest, I'd almost forgotten about that. Guess I'd better tell him." She jerked her head toward the mess hall. "I take it he's in there?"

I nodded. "Might be napping, though. He's been dozing off and on all day."

"If he is, I won't wake him," she said. "Poor guy. This has to be hard on him."

And it might be even harder before it's all over. "What happens if he can't go back to work?"

"I've been thinking about that," she replied. "He's pretty close to retirement age, so it might not matter in the long run. We have pensions set up for all the guys, although no one's ever actually retired from here. They usually cash out the policy when they decide to move on."

"That's what Joe said." Since there seemed to be no way to segue into the question I really wanted to have answered, I wound up stating the obvious. "I'm glad Calvin has a pension."

"Social Security too," she said. "He's bound to have plenty in savings. He's never been the type to go out and blow his paycheck on whiskey and women." She paused, giggling. "Come to think of it, none of the men are—except Bull. To hear him talk, he never has any money."

Given Bull's suggestion that Nick spend his earnings on hookers rather than Internet porn, that didn't surprise me. "That's the stereotype though, isn't it? Seems like half the country songs I hear are about cowboys being hard-drinking, honky-tonkin' drifters."

"I suppose so." Her expression darkened slightly, making me wonder if, despite my best intentions, I'd said the wrong thing. "Most of the men who've worked for us haven't been like that. In fact, Dusty was one of the hands up until a couple of years ago. Dad wasn't too happy when Dusty and I got together. He's kinda old school."

"I noticed that." Particularly after the way he demanded to know what I was doing snuggled up with a naked cowboy on the night of Calvin's heart attack.

She acknowledged my dry tone with a grin. "Believe it or not, he's come a long way in recent years. We never used to eat in the mess hall with the men when I was a kid. Now it seems strange not to."

"More like family than employees?"

"Yeah. I really hate it when one of them decides to quit."

Now we were getting somewhere. "Why do they leave?"

She shrugged. "Lots of reasons. As you know, it's pretty lonely out here. Some guys like that sort of life, but others can't stand it. Some wind up on the rodeo circuit. A few have come and gone because of women they got involved with." She smiled fondly. "I picked one guy up on the highway after his girlfriend dumped him on the way to the Jackson Hole rodeo. He's married to the local veterinarian now."

"Sounds like he and Dusty both married well."

Marrying me certainly wouldn't be a step up for Wyatt if my only income was what I earned as the bunkhouse cook. I might have to do some computer work on the side. As long as I had Internet access, I could easily work from the ranch in some capacity or other—among other things, I was pretty good at website design. But of course, Wyatt hadn't said anything about marriage. Not yet, anyway.

I felt slightly ill at the thought of leaving any of these guys, and parting with Wyatt would undoubtedly break my foolish heart. I drew in a slow, calming breath, knowing I would never have a better opportunity. "I can't understand why anyone wouldn't want a job here. It's like working at home with your family or your best friends."

"Yeah. Seems sort of natural, doesn't it? Much better than getting in your car and driving off to work every morning. I remember my grandmother saying something like that once. She said ranching was hard work, but at least she and Granddad were together." She paused, nibbling at her lower lip. "Which brings me to something I've been meaning to ask you. The guys have made a...request."

"Oh?" As uncomfortable as she seemed, I was almost afraid to hear her out.

"They want you to stay on as their cook. Permanently."

My openmouthed surprise gave way to a chuckle. "They? Or was Bull the only one?"

"As usual, he was the most vocal, but the others all seem to agree."

"Even Calvin?"

She nodded. "To be honest, I think he'd be tickled

to death to leave the cooking to someone else. We used to have a guy who did all the cooking, cleaning, and laundry. I forget why he quit—maybe the guys wrecked the bunkhouse or complained about the food once too often—but it's been done before. Calvin sort of got drafted into it in the beginning, and if he does decide to retire…" She ended her sentence with a shrug.

"I'm already here," I finished for her.

"I know it's not the sort of work you've been trained to do," she said quickly. "And it doesn't pay a whole lot, although it does include room and board. The guys are used to doing their own laundry and keeping the bunkhouse clean—Calvin and our previous foreman had them pretty well-trained—so you wouldn't have to do that. You could just be the cook."

"I'll think about it." I'd already given it plenty of thought, almost to the point of volunteering to take care of the chickens as well. However, I didn't want to seem too anxious.

"I'd really be grateful if you did," she said. "Right now, we've got a good bunch of cowboys. All of them are honest and hardworking, and I want to keep them happy. I was afraid Joe would quit when he started dating my friend Jenny. He hasn't asked her to marry him yet, but it's only a matter of time before he goes off to help her run her ranch."

"Wyatt would make a good foreman. The guys seem to listen to him, anyway."

She frowned. "He doesn't have as much experience as Joe or Bull, but you're right. He's smart and very dependable. Sensible too." A breath of frustration stirred her bangs. "He's another one I don't want to lose. Just wish Dusty and I could help out as much as we used to. Looking after Dad makes it hard. I don't like leaving him alone for long."

"He could come down here and hang out with Calvin. That way I could keep an eye on them both." I smiled, hoping to lighten the mood a bit. "Unless you think they'd get too rowdy for me."

"I doubt it," she said, returning my smile. "Sounds like you'd be running an adult day care along with being the cook."

"There are worse jobs." At least neither man was crazy or incontinent. They'd be a piece of cake after Grandpa.

"True. I'll see what Dad and Calvin have to say about it. Like I said, Dad still has some old-fashioned attitudes." She picked up the magazines. "He might consider it beneath his dignity to hang out in the bunkhouse every day."

"He didn't act like he minded yesterday, although he did seem pretty tired."

"Hmm…" She paused, chewing on a thumbnail while the wheels turned in her head. "Maybe we could make up a place for him to nap here in the bunkhouse—God knows there are plenty of extra beds—and maybe get another recliner for the mess hall. I could tell Dad that Calvin could do with some company during the day to keep his spirits up. Might be good for both of them."

I nodded my agreement and went on with the dinner preparations, thankful that Wyatt had put in his Caesar salad request before I went to the store, otherwise we would have had to make do with makeshift croutons and less-than-authentic dressing. I measured out the ingredients for the dressing and put them in the food processor with my mind focused on the actual task for once. What happened next was up to Calvin and Angela. I would help them in any way I could, but the decisions weren't mine to make.

Oh, who was I kidding? I wanted to *do* something. I wanted to tell the police what I suspected and insist that they put out an APB for that Duane dude. I wanted to call Jeannine's lawyers directly and find out what, if anything, she had bequeathed to Calvin. Whatever decisions Wyatt and I made regarding our relationship would happen in their own time, and while I was as anxious to embark on my happily ever after as any single woman, knowing there was something I could do about Calvin's situation was about to drive me up the wall.

The search for Calvin's next of kin had been tedious and time-consuming, but at least I'd been actively doing something. Now I was in a holding pattern, leaving it all up to someone else to decide, and I didn't like that feeling one tiny little bit. I'd enjoyed the search, the chase, the challenge—perhaps I should've been a detective rather than a computer geek.

I scraped the salad dressing into a jar and put it in the fridge, then set about washing the food processor, all the while wondering what was taking Angela so long. Their conversation might be none of my business, but that didn't stop me from wanting to barge in on it. Instead, I got out the loaf of French bread I'd bought that morning and began cutting half of it into cubes. I was toying with the idea of using the remainder for cheesy garlic bread when Angela returned.

"I told Calvin about the guy asking about him at the hospital. He said he doesn't know anyone named

Duane." She hesitated. "He also told me his sister's lawyers are looking for him."

"I was hoping he'd tell you about that. He seemed
so reluctant to contact them. Said he'd think about it."

"Yeah, well, hearing about Duane must've helped
him make up his mind. He said for you to go ahead and
send them an email."

"Thank God." The sense of relief was overwhelming,
like getting the all clear after a near miss by a tornado
or a bomb threat. "Although it might be best if he called
them unless he has his own email address. Otherwise,
they might think I was poking my nose into something
that was none of my business."

"I'll let you two work that out," she said. "I've got to
get back to the house and finish up the payroll or none
of you will get paid on Friday. I'll see what Dad has to
say about the 'day care' idea." She giggled. "Of course,
I won't put it that way. I'll make it sound like he'd be
helping Calvin with his recovery and rehabilitation."

"Sounds good." I wiped my hands on the barbecue-
style apron I'd purchased that morning, which, unlike
some of the others I'd considered, was more service-
able than witty. It even had pockets and matching oven
mitts. "So Calvin didn't have any idea who Duane
might be?"

"No." She cocked her head to one side, putting me in
mind of an inquisitive robin. "But I'm guessing you do."

"It's all conjecture, of course. I mean, he might
simply be a friend of the family like he said. But he
could also be Calvin's great-nephew or even a detective
hired by Jeannine's lawyers."

She shook her head slowly. "He could be any of those

and it still wouldn't explain how he could've known Calvin was in the hospital without coming here first."

I sucked in a breath. "Yeah, well, some of us were thinking maybe Duane knew he was in the hospital because he had something to do with Calvin being there."

Her eyes widened. "Okay… The payroll can wait." Crossing to the corner table, she pulled out a chair and sat down. "Let's hear it."

I gave her a quick rundown of all the suspicions any of us had raised, ending with Wyatt's change of heart on the subject of attempted murder.

"It all fits, doesn't it?" she said. "The fences being cut…the men kept busy rounding up strays… And if Calvin's sister really did leave him a fortune, that provides a motive to go along with the opportunity. What I can't figure out is how you could make a man have a heart attack. Even dumping his nitro wouldn't necessarily kill him. Calvin could've gotten the prescription refilled before he needed them again."

"I know. Which means all of this could simply be a string of unlucky coincidences." I shrugged. "But it *feels* wrong."

"Yeah. If it wasn't for the fences being cut and some stranger knowing Calvin was in the hospital—let alone the one where he was actually being treated—I'd say Calvin simply picked the wrong time to run out of pills." She got to her feet. "Guess we'll all have to be on the lookout for anything suspicious."

"Do you think we should tell Calvin what we suspect? I mean, you know him better than I do…"

"Afraid of how he might react to the idea that someone is trying to kill him? Yeah. Might be best to hold off on that. After all, the man does have a heart condition. Don't want to go making it worse for no reason."

"Guess we'll know more after we contact those lawyers."

"I guess we will."

Chapter 24

NOT WISHING TO WASTE ANY TIME, I THREW THREE more sweet potatoes into the oven before making a bee-line for the mess hall. "Ready to call those lawyers?"

"Thought you were gonna email them," Calvin replied. "Not sure I want to talk to those bloodsuckers."

I, for one, didn't think I could stand the suspense any longer and was within a hairbreadth of pushing for the telephone option. "I can email them if that's what you want. Don't suppose you have an email address, do you?"

He shook his head. "Don't even have a computer. Never saw the need for any of that stuff."

"No problem. It only takes a few seconds to set one up."

"That'll be fine," he said. "What do you make of that guy at the hospital?" His tone was as abrupt as his change of topic.

"You mean Duane?" I practically had to bite my tongue to keep from calling the dude a murderer.

Innocent until proven guilty, Tina.

I cleared my throat. "I'm guessing he's a friend of Jeannine's. After all, he did say he was a family friend. If he's not your friend, he pretty much has to have been one of hers."

Calvin nodded, but he didn't seem convinced. "Kinda weird, though, isn't it? Him knowing I was in that hospital."

"Yeah. Never having talked to him, we don't have any idea how he found you, although it's possible Jeannine may have asked him to look you up." I waited half a beat before adding, "Those lawyers of hers might know who he is."

"If they do, they're probably in cahoots with him."

His attitude made me wonder if Calvin had reached the same conclusions Wyatt and I had, or if this was simply the snappish mood of an irritable convalescent—either of which rendered a phone conversation inadvisable. "Maybe. We'll never know unless we ask."

His sharp inhale was accompanied by a wince, reminding me that being resuscitated had repercussions of its own. "Go ahead and set up an email account for me and write that letter. I'm sure you'll know what to say better than I would."

"I'll do that right now, but I'll read you the message before I send it. Okay?"

"That'll be fine."

I refilled his iced tea glass and headed into my room. The email account took no time at all, but I gave it a better password than Calvin might've liked. I smiled, recalling Nick's online woes. Hopefully, he was steering clear of the porn sites.

After clicking the hyperlink to the law firm's email address, I wrote a short message, then carried the laptop into the mess hall and took a seat in the chair beside Calvin's recliner.

"How's this? 'My name is Calvin Joseph Douglas, formerly of Liberty, Texas, and currently residing on the Circle Bar K Ranch near Rock Springs, Wyoming. Although we have been estranged for many years,

Jeannine Douglas Caruthers was my sister, and I am saddened by the news of her passing. Please offer my condolences to the surviving members of the Caruthers family.' I figured it would be best not to ask about the will at first."

"Yeah," he said, nodding. "Let them do the talking."

"Okay to send it?"

He nodded again, and I clicked the send button, doing my best to downplay my sigh of relief.

"Be interesting to see how quickly they respond," he said. "Especially since they've prob'ly got someone else just itchin' to get their hands on her money." His laugh was a mirthless cackle. "Bet they'll be glad to hear I don't want it."

"None of it? Seriously? I'm guessing it'll be a pretty penny."

He shrugged. "What on earth would I spend it on— and who would I leave it to when I die?"

"Those are things you'll have to think about, but I wouldn't bother until we hear back from them. They may only want to send you a few family mementoes."

"Like what your granddad left me? Yeah. I wouldn't mind having those kinds of things."

I closed the laptop and stood. "In the meantime, I need to get back to the kitchen or dinner might end up being less than edible."

"Angela told me something else," he said as I turned to go. "She told me she'd asked you to stay on as the cook."

"And how do you feel about that?"

"Couldn't be happier," he declared, and from the way he was smiling, I was fairly certain he meant it. "I never did care much for the job, even when I was in the Army. Matter of fact, I told the folks at the draft board I was a pretty good shot with a rifle. Damn if the sonsabitches didn't turn around and make me a cook."

"Ah, the mysteries of the military bureaucracy," I said with a chuckle. "Then again, you were probably one of the few who weren't begging to be a cook."

"Hadn't thought of that." The twinkle in his eyes was the first I'd seen since his return from the hospital. "You might be right."

I took my computer back to my desk and returned to the kitchen with a much lighter heart than I'd had in some time. At least we were doing something instead of simply mulling over possibilities.

About half an hour later, I was chopping the romaine when the men came in from the barn. I glanced up as Wyatt came sauntering into the kitchen. No orgasm on sight this time—possibly because Nick was with him—but the hug and kiss he gave me nearly did the trick.

"Guess what?" Wyatt said. "We found another cut in the fence."

"Yeah, and it looks like the fence bit back this time." Nick's eyes glowed with ghoulish delight. "We found blood on the end of the wire."

"Serves him right," I said with a nod. "Don't suppose you scraped it off for evidence, did you?"

Wyatt shook his head. "No, I thought it best to leave it where it was, but I did cover it with a plastic bag. Maybe we can get a forensics team to take a look at it."

His tongue-in-cheek tone suggested just how unlikely he thought that event would be.

"You never know what'll turn out to be important." I shot Wyatt a look that heralded my own bit of news. "Calvin told me to send that email."

"What email?" Nick demanded. "What haven't I heard?"

"Bloody hell," I muttered. "I probably shouldn't have said that. We need to have a group discussion to bring everyone up to speed on all this stuff. I'm sick of trying to remember who knows what and telling the same story over and over again."

Wyatt nodded. "Might be the right time for that. I wouldn't want anyone to do something stupid just because we hadn't told them everything."

For the most part, Calvin was the only one whose feelings we had to consider, and he was the one we were trying to protect. I didn't think it would be a problem unless he decided to get stubborn about it, or had another heart attack after hearing our attempted murder theory. No one else seemed to want to tell him because of that possibility, but I had an idea Calvin was made of sterner stuff.

"Let me talk to Calvin," Wyatt said. "I'll see what he says and then we can go from there."

Nick looked like he was about to bust a gut with curiosity. "Oh, come on! You can tell me."

I figured it wouldn't hurt to let a least one cat out of the bag. "Remember Bull's cockamamie murder theory? We may have discovered a motive." I put up a hand. "That's all I'm saying, so don't bother asking me to tell you anything else."

"Hot damn," Nick exclaimed. "I knew it!"

I couldn't help chuckling as he darted off toward the mess hall, obviously taking me at my word. "You know, he really is wasted on a ranch. He needs to start working on a degree in criminology."

"He *is* pretty sharp," Wyatt agreed. "And his timing is excellent." Sidling up behind me, he wrapped his arms around my waist and pulled me against him. Heat transferred instantly from his chest to my back, and his erection snuggled nicely between my buns.

"Holy cow, that feels good. My back is killing me, and you're like a freakin' heating pad."

His breath on my neck triggered a mass eruption of tingles. "I can do a lot more than provide heat." He took a step back and settled his hands on my shoulders. "Might be time for me to return the favor."

He was obviously referring to the shoulder massages I'd given him. "Not sure I have time for that right now." I'd given him twenty minutes. At the moment, I didn't have that much leeway.

"Oh, yes, you do." His voice was a deep, caressing rumble that felt almost as good to my ears as his hands did to my aching back. Almost, but not *quite*…

I put down my knife and leaned forward, bracing my hands against the edge of the countertop as he kneaded my back muscles with his strong, warm fingers. "Mmm…" When he reached the spot between my shoulder blades, the orgasm I hadn't had earlier threatened to put in an appearance. "Ahh…yesss… Right…*there*…"

"Not hurting you, am I?"

"Maybe, but it's a good kind of pain."

"Like a bite on the neck?"

Laughter pooled in my chest before bubbling to the surface. "I'm getting a reverse déjà vu vibe here."

"Like I said, I'm just returning the favor." His hands slid to my lower back. "And later on, I'll return another favor."

"Mmm…promises, promises. I'm still a bit out of commission, you know."

"Not for what I have in mind."

"And what's that?"

He pulled me upright, his lips brushing the edge of my ear. "Total. Body. Massage."

"Ooh, sounds fabulous." I shivered in anticipation. "Will my masseuse be naked?"

"Absolutely. And you can do anything you want with him." A kiss landed on the spot where my neck and shoulders met, setting off another avalanche of goose bumps. "*Ask* him to do anything." His lips closed over my earlobe, the tip of his tongue providing an additional tease that threatened to melt me down on the spot. "*Tell* him to do anything."

"Oh my…" He was asking a lot from a notoriously shy woman. But then, he'd cured me of that affliction, hadn't he? "What if I told you to dance naked on the bed?"

His chuckle combined with his embrace was even more stimulating than the kiss, but in a different way, making me feel loved and cherished. "Not sure the bed could take that kind of abuse, but if you insist…"

I shook my head. "Hypothetical question. Too dangerous, anyway." I turned to face him. "And I want to keep you safe. Don't ever want anything bad to happen to you." I reached up to stroke his cheek, tracing the line of his firm jaw with a fingertip. My hands were still damp from the lettuce, but he didn't seem to mind as I cupped the back of his neck in my palm and pulled him down for a kiss. "Not even falling off a bed."

The moment our lips met, that same delirious, almost mystical sensation began swirling through me, touching my heart as well as my core and making my head swim. The things this man could do to me...

"Dammit all," Nick snapped from the doorway. "I leave you two alone for ten seconds and look what happens."

I broke off the kiss with a show of reluctance that wasn't the least bit feigned. "I thought you *wanted* us to get together. I mean, the whole double bunk thing was your idea."

He threw up his hands. "Hey, I'm fine with you two doing whatever it takes to make you want to stay on here. I just don't want it to interfere with dinner, which is probably getting burnt to a crisp. I need pork chops, and I need them now!"

His eyes twinkling with amusement, Wyatt folded his arms and leaned against the counter, seemingly content to sit back and watch the battle unfold.

"Keep your shirt on, Nick," I said, aiming a glare at the guy who was rapidly becoming my favorite cowboy—not counting Wyatt, of course. "You'll get your pork chops—although not as many as you might like since we're having guests for dinner."

"I know," Nick mourned. "I spotted the three of them heading down from the house just now. Hope you cooked a ton of chops."

"Not quite that many, but with all the stuff I put on them, I'm sure they'll fill you up good."

His expression brightened momentarily before morphing into a frown. "Did you make any pies?"

"Yes, I made pies," I grumbled. "Two of them."

"Hmm… Two pies cut into six pieces makes twelve servings." His eyes lit up again. "There are only eleven of us."

"Not counting my dog, who happens to have a fondness for butterscotch pie."

"Well, shit." Nick grabbed a stack of plates. "Guess I'll just go set the table." Muttering under his breath, he stomped off to the mess hall.

I could've easily split my pie with Ophelia and used the twelfth piece to placate Nick—as big as the chops were, I didn't think I'd have much room for dessert anyway—but while I doubted I would hear any complaints from Ophelia, I could only imagine the ruckus Bull would raise if Nick claimed the extra serving. I didn't think it was worth the drama, nor did I believe he deserved any kind of reward for interrupting a darn good kiss.

Wyatt grinned. "I thought he'd never leave."

Scooping me into his arms, he picked up where he left off, ravaging my mouth with lips and tongue and making me forget all about mundane things like pork chops and butterscotch pies.

Until the smoke alarm went off.

"Bloody *hell*…"

Further investigation revealed that while the pork chops weren't burning, some of the sweet potatoes had sprung leaks, allowing a fair amount of their sugary pulp to drip directly onto the heating element. Never having baked that many at one time, I was unprepared for the spectacular results.

Fortunately, I had a trained firefighter standing by.

I'd never seen a man move that fast. Wyatt turned off the oven, flipped on the exhaust fan, and had the fire extinguisher in his hands before I even had time to react. Not only was the fire out in a matter of seconds, he even managed to do it without causing any further damage to the potatoes.

I gazed up at him with frank admiration. "Damn, you're good."

His cheeky grin came dangerously close to starting an entirely different kind of fire. "I know."

Chapter 25

AFTER ALL THAT EXCITEMENT, DINNER SEEMED SORT OF anticlimactic. Being slightly caramelized, the sweet potatoes were quite tasty and so was the salad. However, I was a little disappointed with the pork chops. Although remarkably tender, they seemed a bit heavy with all the breading and the mushroom sauce—not that anyone else complained. Ophelia obviously considered them to be quite scrumptious, and no one had anything left on their plate except for the bones.

We were passing around the pies when Calvin spoke up. "So, what's this I hear about another fence being cut?"

After Wyatt and Joe gave their version of the latest act of vandalism, Calvin shook his head in mystification. "Still can't figure out why anyone would do that. It doesn't make any sense at all."

Angela and I exchanged a speaking glance. "There are a few other things we need to talk about," she began. "I want to make sure everyone knows the full story about what's been happening around here."

Bull let out a whoop. "Goddammit, I was right, wasn't I?"

Calvin stared at him, shaking his head in patent bewilderment. "About what?"

"About someone trying to kill you," Bull replied.

Given Bull's usual tactless manner, Calvin's frown was understandably skeptical. However, instead of asking Bull to explain, he shifted his gaze toward Wyatt. "What's your take on this business?"

If anyone thought it strange that he would direct his question at Wyatt, they didn't mention it. I, for one, wasn't a bit surprised. Wyatt had a persona that tended to put him in charge whether he was the owner of the ranch or one of the hired hands.

Wyatt's reply was direct and to the point. "We think the fences are being cut to keep us out of the way while someone searches the bunkhouse."

"What on earth for?"

"That's what I'm not sure about, although I'm guessing they were trying to find a way to make your death appear to be from natural causes. The first attempt having failed, our perpetrator seems to be looking to have another go."

If Calvin was ever going to suffer another heart attack, now was the time. Although from where I was sitting, I couldn't see that he so much as batted an eyelash. "So, someone is trying to do me in, huh? Seems pretty determined." He leaned back in his chair and waved a hand. "Go on."

Given his cavalier response, I couldn't decide whether Calvin believed any of it.

Wyatt, on the other hand, seemed willing to give him the benefit of the doubt. "Anyone watching the bunkhouse would know you usually come back to start on dinner at four, but the rest of us wouldn't be back until five thirty or six. Fences were being cut, keeping us out chasing strays with not much chance that any of us would come back during the day.

"Then Tina showed up, and you all know what

happened that night. Now, under ordinary circum-stances"—he cast an apologetic glance in Calvin's direction—"you would've died. But you didn't. Because of Tina, you survived and were taken to the hospital. Bull and I followed the ambulance to Rock Springs, and then went on to Salt Lake City after they told us they were flying you there for surgery. We hung around until you were out of danger and then we came on home."

"I left for Salt Lake the next day," Angela added. "But I wasn't comfortable making decisions for you, so I asked Tina to try to locate your next of kin."

She glanced at me, which I interpreted as the signal for me to chime in with my part of the saga. "I went online and did some digging but came up with noth-ing. Then I got the idea to read your letters, thinking you might've mentioned the names of some of your relatives. Through those letters, we discovered that your wife and children had died in a car accident along with Jeannine's daughter, Carla, whose illegitimate child survived the crash."

Calvin nodded. "That would be Tom Anderson—at least, that's what his name was before his father got custody of him. I wouldn't put it past him to change the boy's name to his own surname—although for the life of me, I can't remember what it was. As far as I know, Tom and his father pretty much dropped out of sight. The boy would be in his late twenties now. Jeannine and her husband split up after that."

I was surprised that the mention of his family's tragic past didn't draw more of a reaction from him. I waited a moment, then continued, "We kept reading the letters and found that Jeannine married Franklin Caruthers

a few years later. An online search revealed that both
Jeannine and Franklin had died. Since we'd eliminated
any next of kin who wasn't on the Caruthers side of the
family, we pretty much stopped looking."

Angela glanced around the table, speaking to the
group as a whole. "This afternoon, I told Calvin that a
young man who claimed to be a friend of the family had
tried to visit him while he was in the hospital. Visiting
hours were over, so he wasn't allowed into the unit. The
nurse said his name was Duane something—she didn't
catch his last name.

"Now, the hospital staff won't give out information
over the phone to just anyone. But they don't interro-
gate visitors or check their identification. If Duane had
shown up during regular visiting hours, they would've
let him in. The fact that he never came back again makes
me wonder if all he wanted to know was whether Calvin
was actually a patient there."

With a nod toward Calvin, Wyatt picked up the nar-
rative. "We couldn't figure out how he could've known
which state you were in, let alone which hospital. That's
when Bull first put forth his attempted murder theory,
saying the only person aside from us who could've
known you were in that hospital was the one who put
you there, meaning the person who tried to kill you."

Bull puffed out his chest, seeming rather pleased
with himself.

Wyatt acknowledged him with a grimace. "At the
time, the idea seemed pretty far-fetched. After all, it
wasn't as if someone had taken a shot at you, and as far
as we knew, no one had a motive for murder. I'll admit,
I blew it off.

"Then Tina thought she saw something moving up on the eastern ridge Saturday morning. Later that night, she spotted a light in roughly the same place. When Nick and I went out to check, we didn't find anything, but as I said at the time, that's a great spot for someone to spy on us, aside from being the most direct route to the main road on foot."

I spoke up. "From that, I got the idea that someone might be watching the bunkhouse, trying to catch it when it was empty—or when everyone was asleep—so they could sneak in, either to search the place or steal something."

"Any idea what?" Dean asked.

A quick look around revealed nothing but blank faces. "No clue."

Wyatt cleared his throat and directed his gaze back toward Calvin. "Then you came home, and Tina showed you Jeannine's obituary. Tina clicked on the link to the online guestbook and found a message asking you to contact Jeannine's lawyers. We still have no idea what was in her will, but if you were in line to inherit a fortune, that might give someone a motive for murder."

"So has anyone called about the will?" Nick asked.

I raised a hand. "I sent an email to Jeannine's lawyers right before dinner. As late as it was, they might not see it until tomorrow. I'll check again here in a little bit to see if they've sent a reply."

"So that's it? We just sit and wait to hear back from them?" As usual, Nick was itching for a share of the excitement—to the point that he hadn't even touched his pie.

"A lot depends on what they have to say," Wyatt said. "But in the meantime, we can go over the details. Maybe something will turn up."

"Let me get this straight," Calvin said. "You think someone is trying to kill me so they can inherit my sister's money?"

Wyatt shrugged. "Depending on how Jeannine's will is worded, it's possible. There could be a secondary beneficiary."

"And I suppose you think this Duane character is really my great-nephew, Tom?"

"Possibly," Wyatt replied. "Even if Tom wasn't named as a beneficiary, if he could prove he was your sister's grandson, he could contest the will. But only if you couldn't be found or were already dead."

"That gives us a motive for murder," Dusty said. "But it doesn't explain how it was done."

"No, it doesn't," Wyatt agreed. "Which brings us to the next evening when Tina found an empty nitro bottle on the floor in Calvin's room." He glanced at Calvin. "Any idea how it got there or why it was empty?"

"Not really," Calvin replied. "There were plenty of pills in it earlier that day. I know because I took one while I was making the chili." He hesitated. "I wasn't feeling too good—hadn't felt good for a couple of weeks."

That certainly jibed with the way he'd looked when he stopped by my room to say good night.

"What about later on that night?" Wyatt prompted. "Could you have taken all of them?"

Calvin shook his head slowly. "I can't remember taking any more at all. In fact, I don't actually recall going to bed."

I thought that sounded strange, but I also had an idea that nearly dying might wreak havoc with a person's memory. "Did you keep the bottle in your pocket or in your medicine cabinet?"

"Usually in my pocket," he replied. "But at night I set it on the table by my bed."

If he'd been doing that, he'd obviously been having fairly frequent bouts of chest pain. Without Duane's attempted visit, I'd have said Calvin's collapse and the fence-cutting episodes were completely unrelated.

"What about before that?" Wyatt prompted. "Did you do anything different?"

"Might've taken a couple of aspirins—but that wasn't unusual."

"What about your other meds?" I asked. "Did you take any of them?"

"Might have," he replied. "Like I said, I don't remember much about that night."

I tried a different tack. "Yesterday you told me that my visit had made you decide to start taking better care of yourself. Would that have included taking your meds like you were supposed to?"

"Maybe. You see, John's friendship meant a lot to me. When I stopped hearing from him, I thought, what the hell, if he doesn't care enough to write to me anymore..." The sag of his shoulders made his shrug seem more pronounced, more hopeless. "I dunno. Just seemed sort of pointless to go on living. Finding out he'd been sick for years and had died didn't help my attitude any. The man who'd saved my life was gone..." His eyes shimmered with unshed tears. "Then you came and gave me those medals. They reminded me that my best buddy had nearly been killed trying to save me and the others from the VC. I didn't want his sacrifice to have been in vain."

That part made perfect sense. "Okay then, let's say you did take your meds that night and set your nitro bottle on the table like always. If someone came into your room, would you have heard them?"

"I'm a pretty sound sleeper," he admitted. "And my hearing isn't what it used to be."

"So someone could've slipped into your room during the night and emptied out your nitro bottle, thinking you might die without them?"

"Could be," he said. "I've never locked that outside door. Didn't see the point."

I wasn't too surprised to hear that. The best I could tell, no one on the ranch ever locked up anything.

"Maybe it's time you did," Angela said. "Until we figure out what's going on around here, we should all start locking our doors and keep a lookout for anything suspicious. And I do mean *anything*." She nodded toward her father. "The more we stick together, the better off we'll be. Dad has agreed to stay here in the bunkhouse with Calvin and Tina during the day."

She made it sound as though her father would be helping to protect Calvin from any further harm. I knew that wasn't the only reason for the plan, but that rationale had to have made convincing him a lot easier.

Mr. Kincaid shifted in his chair, drawing my eye. He seemed tired and distracted, picking at the meringue on his pie with a fork and barely acknowledging what Angela had just said, leaving me to wonder how well he'd followed our convoluted discussion. I also wondered if, having essentially relinquished the running of the ranch to Angela and Dusty, he was beginning to tune out the finer points, either believing his continued input to be unimportant, or putting it on hold until one of his better days rolled around.

Whichever the case, this didn't appear to be one of his good days. I suspected that if Angela had already made up a bed for him in the bunkhouse, he probably would've taken a nap as soon as dinner was over. As it was, he would have to walk back up to the house.

"Mr. Kincaid," I began, "would you like us to set up a bunk for you in case you ever need to lie down and rest while you're here?"

For a moment, I didn't think my question had even registered. Then he nodded. "That'd be right nice of you." With a glimmer of a smile, he added, "And I think it's high time you were calling me Jack."

"I'll do that," I said, returning his smile with one of my own.

"I think we still have one of the newer mattresses left." Dean aimed a surreptitious glance at me, making it quite clear where at least one of those mattresses had gone. "We'll get it ready for you this evening." Then he rounded on Nick. "Right after I pound you into dust for stealing that last piece of pie."

No wonder it looked as though Nick hadn't dug into the pie yet. What I'd seen on his plate must've been his second helping.

"Hey, if it wasn't for me, we would've had sugar-free Jigglers for dessert," Nick declared. "I figure I earned it." Scooping up a hefty portion, he popped it into his mouth with gusto.

Nick's response was a welcome bit of comic relief after the serious turn the conversation had taken, and it had everyone chuckling, including Dean. I sincerely hoped we could solve this mystery without any further drama and get back to normal—whatever that was. I wasn't counting on it, though. Greed could be a pretty powerful motivator.

Unfortunately, when I checked the inbox on Calvin's email account after dinner, I didn't find anything. Not even spam.

Chapter 26

BY THE TIME MY HEAD HIT THE PILLOW THAT NIGHT, my back wasn't the only thing hurting. My feet were killing me, and my head was aching from trying to figure out whodunit, if indeed anyone actually had. The discussion hadn't ended with dinner, but was hashed and rehashed for what seemed like days without accomplishing anything. My only wish was that Wyatt's offer of a total body massage included therapy for a frazzled brain.

I felt a little better after a shower, but when Wyatt actually put his hands on me, my moans and groans were as much ecstatic as they were pain-related. As he dug his fingers into a particularly sore spot on the top of my shoulder, I pressed my lips together, trying hard not to yelp.

"Seems like someone put in more work today than the hired hands," he observed. "Your back and shoulders are all tied up in knots."

"If you think that's bad, you should be on this end of my feet. About the only time I wasn't standing on them today was during the drive into Rock Springs—although that may be the reason I'm so worn-out."

"I'll tell you what's wearing you out," he declared. "You're putting way too much effort into feeding us. Trust me, Nick will live long and well without having pie every day. You'll have enough to do looking after Calvin, even without having to ride herd on Jack."

Angela may have pulled the wool over her father's

eyes, but Wyatt obviously wasn't fooled. "Actually, I'm hoping they'll keep each other occupied—and out of trouble."

"Maybe," he said. "Don't count on it, though. I wouldn't put it past Jack to wander off."

"You really think he's in that bad a shape?"

"Sometimes," he replied. "The rest of the time he's sharp as a tack. It's deceptive."

I nodded. "That's the way Grandpa was. I never knew what to expect." The worst was the nighttime confusion, which resulted in a lot of sleepless nights—for both of us. At least I wouldn't have to deal with that.

"I wouldn't get too attached to him, either," he advised. "I have a feeling Jack isn't long for this world. He's failed a lot just in the time I've worked here."

"Angela said something similar. She's pretty worried about him."

I could've told her a few things that might have helped to improve her perspective. In particular, the relief she would feel when his suffering and the heartbreak she'd had to endure while watching him deteriorate came to an end. I wasn't sure she was ready to hear that yet. After all, he was still walking and talking and functioning reasonably well.

Funny how Wyatt suspected me of becoming attached to the old man, although I'd adopted a bunkhouse full of cowboys easily enough. Even Calvin already seemed like family, and he'd been in the hospital half the time I'd been there.

Boy, when I finally get over being shy around men, I do it in a big way.

Case in point, the man I was now sharing a room

with. While our relationship might have been new and uncertain in many ways, in others it seemed perfectly natural. I barely noticed when he began pushing up my pajama top, although the feel of his hands on my bare skin certainly got my attention.

"Mmm…that feels *so* good."

"That's the idea." The low, rumbling tone of his voice enhanced the thrill of his touch. "Feels pretty good on my end too."

I smiled into the pillow. "Sweet of you to say so."

"You do that to me, Tina. Bring out my sweet side, I mean."

I had a feeling that, similar to my aptitude for intimacy, that part of his nature hadn't been buried very deep. "Like the way you bring out my sensuous side?"

"Mmm hmm…" He smoothed his palms over my back in a slow, circular motion. "Guess that means we're good for each other."

"I believe it does."

I'd always known I was capable of intimacy. I'd simply never given myself permission to explore those feelings before. Perhaps ranch life had allowed our true feelings to surface.

Still, Wyatt had more reasons to be wary than I did. I couldn't even begin to imagine what he'd suffered. The miracle was that he hadn't been scarred to the point where redemption wasn't possible.

He'd been brusque with me in the beginning, but he was capable of such tenderness. I could imagine him cradling a newborn calf in his arms or soothing a nervous colt, much like he'd managed to alleviate my anxiety, making me feel safe.

And loved.

Whether that was his intention didn't matter; it was certainly the way I felt.

His hands moved lower on my body, taking my pajama bottoms with them until I lay practically naked upon the sheets. By the time he reached my feet, I was relaxed enough to fall asleep, but one particular part of me was wide awake, clamoring for attention.

I'd never suspected that a woman could have an erection every bit as hard and hot as a man's, but the tight, tingling need emanating from my clitoris had me convinced.

Wyatt rolled me onto my back and unbuttoned my top, exposing my breasts. His touch seemed purely therapeutic at first, but quickly slipped into a more erotic mode as his fingers brushed my nipples. My clitoris responded with a surge that made me tremble.

A nudge was all it took to spread my thighs apart, exposing my sex to his touch. A waft of air and the dip of the mattress was all the warning I had. He had to know that actual intercourse wasn't going to happen that night. Nevertheless, he eased up between my legs.

At that moment, I wouldn't have cared if he'd gone ahead and taken the plunge. However, it wasn't until his hot, wet cock met my engorged clitoris that I understood his intention. Kneeling between my outstretched thighs, he stroked my own tight bud with his erection. His lips and tongue had felt fabulous enough, but his firm cockhead pressed against my clit raised the pleasure to new heights. Although he was barely visible in the dim light, what I could see—broad, muscular chest and shoulders, along with his thatch of thick, unruly hair—enhanced the effect.

He moved the hot, slick head back and forth, up and down, and around in circles until I thought I would go mad with the desperate need to feel his cock on every part of my body in every possible manner. On my face, between my breasts, and another place I never would have dreamed I would consider. I drifted on, delighting in those sensations while anticipating others. I had a bottle of lubricant. Surely that was all that was needed.

What was it he'd said? That I could ask him to do anything...*tell* him to do anything?

Yeah, right. I could really hear myself telling Wyatt to fuck my ass.

Still, what he'd already done without being asked was nothing short of breathtaking. Should I let him continue or stop him now?

A sigh escaped my lips.

"Feel good?"

"Incredibly."

"But?"

How had he done that? Was there hesitation in my reply? An unspoken request? I had no idea, but he'd given me the opening I needed.

"Umm...I was thinking of something else you could do."

"Such as?"

Was he really going to make me say it? Probably. I doubted it was the sort of thing a gentleman would even suggest. Although I may have been wrong about that.

"I was thinking of an...alternative—" Alternative what? Approach? Method? "One that might be better for you."

"Anal?"

Once again, he proved just how adept he was at reading me.

I nodded. "I'm willing to try it if you are."

"I don't want to hurt you anymore than I already have."

"Sweet of you to say that." I racked my brain, trying to recall anything I'd ever read on the subject. The one detail aside from sufficient lubrication that stood out in my mind was not to be in too big a hurry. "I think you'd have to take it really slow."

"I can do that. With or without a condom?"

The mere thought of his naked cock inside me set off a quiver of anticipation. "Without," I replied. "But with plenty of lube."

His next question was bound to be about the position. I wasn't at all sure I wanted to be seen facedown with my butt sticking up in the air, but while Wyatt had never struck me as the dominant type, he *was* a bit on the alpha side. Chances were good that he would absolutely love it.

I retrieved the bottle of lubricant from the nightstand and handed it to him. After that, I removed my pajama top and rolled over onto my stomach, adopting a position far more vulnerable than any I'd ever dreamed I would assume voluntarily.

His softly uttered, "Wow" and the touch of his hand on my bottom was proof of his enjoyment. Even so, he didn't rush. The next thing I felt was his breath on my skin, then his lips, followed by his tongue. He stroked my clit with a calloused fingertip, scraping my emotions raw, making me long to be fucked so badly I could hardly stand it.

Positioned as I was, my nipples brushed the sheets,

tingling as they hardened while my pussy clamored
for his attention. The snap of the cap on the lube and
the swift outflow of air as he squeezed the bottle drove
me wilder still. Cool moisture on my anus followed—
soothing and oddly arousing—as he probed the opening
with a slick fingertip. While I hummed with pleasure, he
added more lube and another fingertip. My clit became
even more engorged, teetering on the brink of pain.

His fingers were soon replaced by the blunt head
of his penis. Slowly, with painstaking slowness, he
worked his way inside. He felt absolutely fabulous
right where he was, but I did my best to relax and let
him in. Eventually, I felt something give and he slid in
with no discomfort and very little effort. The outstroke
was even better, although my ecstatic sob must have
sounded like a cry of anguish because Wyatt came to
an abrupt halt.

"You okay?"

"Oh, God, yes," I said, practically panting out the
words. "Don't stop."

Apparently he didn't believe me because he dribbled
more lube on his cock before resuming the steady thrusts
that soon had me delirious with delight. Grasping my
hips, he shifted me side to side in a movement so slight,
if it hadn't been for the exponential increase in bliss, I
wouldn't have noticed it at all.

Wyatt's groan reverberated throughout my body as
he plunged in deeper than ever. When I tried to envision
how he would look at that moment, the mental image of
his balls bouncing off my pussy triggered a backward
shove that had me seeing stars.

The effect on him was immediate. I didn't need to

hear his ragged exhale to know he'd reached his climax.
I could feel it.

His hand slipped unerringly from my hip around to
my clitoris, and that one brief touch sent me screaming
into overdrive. I bit back a cry as my knees slid out from
under me, landing me flat on the bed and initiating an
abrupt withdrawal that set off shock waves of indescrib-
able ecstasy.

Until that moment, I'd never truly believed what
romance novels had to say on the subject of anal sex.

I knew better now.

Chapter 27

I CHECKED CALVIN'S INBOX FIRST THING IN THE morning—that is, after doing my best to kiss Wyatt's lips off—and again after breakfast and found nothing. The spammers hadn't even found him yet.

It wasn't until after lunch that I discovered an email from Jamison and Markovitch. I probably should have waited to let Calvin open it, but curiosity got the better of me—not that the message contained anything I hadn't expected to see.

Calvin was indeed Jeannine's heir, with one very interesting detail: the secondary beneficiary wasn't her grandson Tom, who wasn't even mentioned, nor was it anyone named Duane. It was the Mother's Haven Foundation, which had been Jeannine's favorite charity—one that it appeared she had already endowed with a small fortune.

I was somewhat surprised they would've put even that much information in an email, although they did attach a form for Calvin to fill out, which included a request for several documents to establish his identity— his military service record, driver's license, and birth certificate. After those documents had been received and approved, they would send him a copy of the will along with some additional information.

I was dying to hear Wyatt's take on it, but the men wouldn't be back for hours. Calvin, however, was there, and so was Jack.

Their impressions were polar opposites.

"Looks like you're gonna be a rich man, Calvin," Jack said, slapping him on the back. "Might have to find us a new cowboy."

Calvin, on the other hand, seemed less optimistic. "Might not turn out to be anything much."

"I dunno," I said. "There could have been a prenuptial agreement that returned the majority of her assets to her husband's estate when she died, but I can't see naming a charity as a beneficiary if there wasn't a good-sized chunk of change involved."

That being said, the fact that the secondary beneficiary was a charity effectively eliminated any motive for murder. Somehow, I couldn't see hordes of unwed mothers banding together to do away with Calvin in order to keep their shelter from closing.

No case now, Nancy Drew...

I hated to admit it, but I couldn't help feeling a teensy bit let down—and not because I wanted Calvin's heart attack to have been an attempted murder. I had simply viewed the matter from that perspective long enough to believe it.

Now we would have to abandon our sleuthing sideline in favor of ordinary ranch life—unless we could figure out who was cutting the fences. Unfortunately, catching the perpetrator red-handed would be more a matter of luck than detective work. Even finding blood on the fence wouldn't help unless we had a suspect for comparison.

So much for that.

"I'll print this form and you can fill it out and sign it. We can make copies of your other documents."

Calvin nodded. "Got all of that stuff in my desk."

I glanced at Jack. "I'm assuming you have a printer up at the house?"

"Yep," Jack replied. "Angela can show you where it is."

"If we can scan the documents and send everything as email attachments, they'll get them a lot faster."

"And we'll know something sooner," Jack said with a nod. "You know, sometimes these newfangled contraptions are pretty useful."

While Calvin went off to retrieve the necessary papers, I took the opportunity to get Jack's take on the matter, but I regretted asking the question almost immediately. Being somewhat deaf himself, Jack had a tendency to speak rather loudly.

"Be a good thing if Calvin were to inherit a bundle. He's worked damn hard all his life. He deserves an easy retirement."

"You don't think it'll cause him any trouble?"

"Nah. Not if he's careful."

I considered asking him to define "careful," but decided against it. For one thing, Calvin returned much too quickly.

"Great," I said. "I'll head up to the house and get these sent off. Think you two can hold the fort while I'm gone?"

"Absolutely," Calvin replied. "Although we might do it lying down."

"A nap sounds damn good," Jack agreed. "I believe I'll try out my new bed."

Despite the debunking of our attempted murder myth, I was tempted to say no—to tell them that at least one of them needed to stay awake while I was gone—but I wouldn't be going far, and I fully intended to lock the doors before I left.

"Right," I said. "Be back soon."

I gathered up the documents and headed up the hill to the main house with Ophelia at my heels. Although the weather was still relatively cool, daffodils were beginning to poke through the mulch in flower beds on either side of the steps leading up to the wide veranda, and a few crocuses were actually blooming. Built of logs that had been buffed and varnished to a high sheen, the house seemed fairly typical for the region except for the front door, which was comprised mostly of stained glass. A bit leery of tapping on the glass, I rang the bell.

Moments later, Angela opened the door. "Hey, Tina. What's up?"

"We heard back from Jeannine's lawyers. Looks like Calvin is in line to inherit something, and if he doesn't claim it, a charity for single mothers is the beneficiary."

"So our little powwow was for naught?" Clearly, she didn't consider a charity as a threat, either.

"Seems that way. Guess we let our imaginations run away with us."

"Can't say I'm sorry to hear that." She glanced at the documents. "Need to copy those?"

I nodded. "Jack said you had a printer."

"Sure thing." She led the way to an office that had windows made entirely of stained glass. Apparently, she caught me staring. "The stained glass is a hobby of mine. Keeps me sane."

"It's beautiful," I said. "Love the hardwood floors and the oak desk too. Very western." Despite the rustic decor, I was pleased to see she had a relatively new printer complete with a flatbed scanner. I printed out the form and scanned the other documents onto a thumb drive. "I'll have to come back and scan this one after Calvin fills it out and signs it."

"No problem. I'll be here." She hesitated for a second or two. "How are Dad and Calvin getting along?"

"Pretty well, I think. They've been playing checkers and watching CNN. They were fixing to take a nap when I left."

She nodded. "Dad usually naps in the afternoon. What with all the excitement, he probably won't wake up until dinnertime."

I hoped Calvin didn't sleep that long. Knowing how slow the legal process could be, I was dying to get that form signed and sent off—anything to get the ball rolling.

Nevertheless, I accepted her offer of a brief tour of the house, after which I collected Ophelia and headed back to the bunkhouse.

I was about halfway down the hill when I spotted a car parked in the stable yard and a tall, dark-haired man wearing a suit and tie standing on the kitchen porch. That in itself wasn't terribly disturbing. It was his energetic attempt to open the door that had me bugged.

"Where the devil is Wyatt Earp when I need him?" I had half a mind to go back and get Angela, but I did have a dog who had proven her worth as a protector on more than one occasion. I glanced at Ophelia. "Or for that matter, why didn't you warn me?"

My trusty canine companion's response was a non-committal pant. Therefore, I opted to do the safest thing, which was to keep my distance, stopping when I reached the gravel at the foot of the slope. "Can I help you?"

To his credit, the man's reaction was more along the lines of being genuinely startled than being caught trying to break into the bunkhouse. Whichever the case, he recovered his composure with apparent ease. "Yes, ma'am. I'm looking for Calvin Douglas. Does he live here?"

"That depends on who you are."

His subsequent smile was disarming enough— even a bit embarrassed. "Sorry. I knocked, but no one answered. I thought the door might be open."

Figured it was stuck, did you? Fortunately, I managed to keep from saying that aloud.

"We've been having some trouble lately, so we're keeping them locked."

"I see."

I couldn't help wondering just how much he did see—especially since the one time I'd left Jack and Calvin alone in the bunkhouse without Ophelia for protection, someone had come calling. His presence was either one heck of a coincidence or near-perfect timing. Unless I missed my guess, this was the infamous Duane, but after all the suspicions his visit to the hospital had aroused, I wasn't going to make it easy for him. Nor did I come any closer.

Folding my arms, I stood my ground. Waiting.

"Oh, right," he said after a long pause. "My name is Duane Evans. I'm—or *was*—a friend of Mr. Douglas's sister, Jeannine Caruthers."

Figuring it would be best to let him do the talking, I opted to play dumb. "Was?"

"She died this past January."

"Sorry for your loss," I said. "Would've been nice if someone told Calvin about it." That much was true, anyway.

"Yeah, well, that's why I'm here. Jeannine asked me to try to find him."

"Her dying wish?"

"Something like that." He stepped down from the porch and approached me. He hadn't gone far when Ophelia growled a warning.

Duane raised his hands, palms forward, and backed off slightly. "Your dog won't attack, will it?"

"That depends on you," I replied. "Might be best if you don't come any closer." Especially considering the nature of the papers I held in my hand. I hesitated, choosing my words with care. "So how did you know Jeannine?"

"I'm on the board of one of her favorite charities—a support service for single mothers. I have an interest in that sort of thing." His slightly embarrassed, even apologetic smile struck me as reasonably genuine. "You see, my parents never married and my mother had to raise me on her own. Anyway, I promised Jeannine I would try to find her brother. She said there'd been some bad blood between them and that they hadn't seen each other for nearly thirty years."

Although at least part of what he said was true, I still didn't trust him. After all, we had yet to figure out how he could have known Calvin was in the hospital. "How come she waited until she was dying to try to find him? Why not before that, when they might've had the chance to reconcile, maybe even visit each other?"

"Oh, you know how it is…" His smile seemed less genuine this time—the sort of condescending smirk that made me want to smack him. "Family ties seem more important when you're nearing the end."

"I suppose they do. How did she die?"

"Heart attack," Duane replied. "She'd had angina for years—had bypass surgery twice—but she hadn't been doing well for several months before that last episode."

Calvin's health history was similar, minus the bypass surgeries, and anyone who knew Jeannine's history could have made the same assumptions about her brother, especially after going through Calvin's meds and seeing what he'd been taking—or rather, was *supposed* to be taking. Perhaps it truly was as simple as dumping out his nitro tablets.

Or not.

Calvin had claimed he didn't remember much about what happened that evening, which put me in mind of what that nurse had said about Calvin acting like someone who had overdosed.

But what on earth could he have taken? If a drug screen had been done when he was first admitted, something might've shown up, but I seriously doubted there would be any lingering traces now. I didn't know how long hospital laboratories normally kept specimens, but surely they wouldn't have kept them this long unless there was evidence of foul play.

"So tell me, why keep looking for him even after she's dead? Just to let him know she was sorry for the 'bad blood' between them?"

For the first time, he seemed evasive, casting a furtive glance toward the bunkhouse. "I'd, um, rather tell Mr. Douglas that."

"I see." I wasn't about to let Duane inside until the rest of the men—the young, healthy, and possibly armed men—returned. I checked my watch. Duane had been trying to find Calvin for months; he could wait a little while longer. "Think you could come back later this evening? Around seven, perhaps?"

To his credit, he took that suggestion fairly well. "Sure thing." With a brief nod, he headed for his car. "See you then, Miss…"

He was obviously hoping I'd introduce myself, but I wasn't telling him anything. "We'll be here."

Every last one of us.

I watched as he got in his car and headed back down the drive, waiting until the dust cleared and the sound of his tires on the gravel had died away before turning toward the bunkhouse. I reached the porch easily enough, but was a little surprised at how wobbly my knees were as I climbed the steps. My hands trembled as I tried to put the key in the lock, missing twice before finally getting it right.

So that was Duane. Murderer or not, he sure had me rattled. I wondered if Angela had seen him from the house.

Once inside, I closed the door and locked it before checking on Calvin and Jack, both of whom were snoring loud enough to assure me they were still breathing. Having made my "rounds," I picked up the phone and called Angela.

"You can bet your boots I'll be joining you all for dinner tonight," she declared after I related the details of Duane's visit. "Glad you didn't invite him to dinner, by the way. What did you make of him?"

"I honestly don't know. There were a couple of times

when I thought he might be lying, but that could've been my imagination."

Her giggle sounded more grim than usual. "Yeah. It's pretty hard to trust someone once you've pegged them as a murder suspect."

"I sure didn't trust him enough to tell him anything. Come to think of it, I never actually admitted that Calvin lived here."

"Way to go, Tina," Angela said, now chuckling with genuine amusement. "This should be a very interesting evening."

"No kidding." It would be especially interesting seeing as how I hadn't even thought about what to fix for dinner.

If Monday night was pork chop night, Tuesday must be…

"Meat loaf," I said aloud.

"Huh?"

"That's what we're having for dinner. Meat loaf with, um, mashed potatoes and onion gravy, and"—I was grasping at straws now—"peas and carrots."

"Sounds great. What's for dessert?"

"Dessert?" I echoed in dismay. "Oh, bloody hell…" This might turn out to be the night when the sugar-free Jigglers finally made an appearance. Nick would forgive me. Eventually. "Don't worry. I'll think of something."

"I'm sure you will." Sighing, she added, "Meanwhile, back to the bookkeeping. I'm so far behind it isn't even funny. Thanks again for looking after Dad. I'm actually getting some work done today. It isn't so much that he's a lot of trouble, but I just…worry."

"I know how that is," I said. "I couldn't concentrate on much of anything wondering if Grandpa was up to something—especially after I caught him taking a pair of scissors to his PICC line."

"That'd do it," Angela agreed. "I haven't had to deal with that sort of thing yet."

"I hope you never do. It…changes how you feel about someone you thought you knew. Makes you realize you never really knew them at all." On that cheery note, I figured it was best to get back to less thought-provoking issues, such as the dessert menu. "Guess I'd better get started on dinner."

"See you at six?"

"Sounds good."

I hung up the phone wishing I'd told Duane to come back at eight instead of seven. An hour's worth of dinner-table discussion prior to his arrival didn't seem like much. I just hoped he didn't show up early.

Chapter 28

IN THE END, I BAKED A CAKE. DELVING MORE DEEPLY into the pantry than ever, I managed to unearth a box of spice cake mix and some ready-made cream cheese frosting. God only knew how long it had been in there, but I couldn't imagine cake mix ever going bad, and after sampling the frosting, I deemed it safe to eat, if indeed such things ever are.

I was icing the cake when Calvin shuffled into the kitchen.

"Have a nice nap?"

"Yeah. I could get used to that," he said. "Probably should've retired a long time ago."

I wasn't completely sure how to answer that because after my chat with Duane, I suspected Calvin was about to retire in style, rather than having to scrimp and save to make ends meet. "Speaking of which, guess who was banging on the door when I got back from the main house?"

His brow rose. "Somebody named Duane?"

"You got it." I scraped the last of the frosting from the tub and spread it on the cake. "Turns out his last name is Evans. He claims to have worked with Jeannine on her single mothers' support charity. Says she asked him to try to find you."

"Well now, isn't that interesting." His sarcastic tone mirrored my own feelings precisely.

"That's what I thought. He wouldn't tell me why, so

I told him to come back at seven this evening. Figured it would be best for everyone to be here."

"Just in case, you mean?"

"Yeah. Especially since he was trying to open the door when I spotted him."

"Which you'd locked when you left, right?"

I nodded. "Although it would've been interesting to see what he would have done if the door had been open. Catching him red-handed would've been a nice touch— depending on what he had planned, of course." I paused, licking a stray dab of frosting from the back of my hand. "What has me intrigued is his timing. He picked the one time you and Jack were alone in the bunkhouse."

"Think he actually knew we were asleep?"

"Maybe. Even if he didn't, if he was watching from up on that ridge, he could have seen me leave and then hurried back to wherever he'd parked his car. I was up at the house for the better part of an hour—Angela gave me a tour of the place—so he would've had time. He was wearing a suit and tie, but I suppose he could've changed clothes before he drove up here."

Calvin nodded in agreement. "Not the sort of outfit I'd want to wear clambering around on that ridge."

"No, it isn't. A better detective would've paid more attention to his shoes—you know, to notice how dirty they were and such. Me, all I did was focus on not telling him anything." I couldn't help but laugh. "If Duane really is who he says he is and has a legitimate reason for trying to find you, he'd probably freak if he had any idea what we suspect."

"Might be best if we don't tell him that. Maybe we can catch him in a lie."

"That's what I'm hoping. With all of us here asking questions, he's bound to be nervous." I giggled again, realizing we had one of the most intimidating men to ever don a Stetson on our side. "We should let Wyatt do the talking. He'd probably scare the pants off him."

"Good cop, bad cop?"

"You betcha." That being said, the strategy session now seemed more important than ever. The trick would be to keep Bull from spilling the beans.

But then, Wyatt was also better at that than anyone else.

Among other things…

The problem would lie in deciding who should play the good cop role. Given my already adversarial treatment of our visitor, I doubted it would be me.

———

I had just picked up my spiffy new oven mitts to take the meat loaf out of the oven when a stealthy footstep behind me made me smile.

I know he's there without even turning around.

I could've called him on it, but opted to let the scene play out. Heat enveloped me. Strong arms surrounded me. Sensuous lips brushed my ear. A deep, purring "mmm…" sent a thrill racing toward my heart and every erogenous zone I possessed.

I sighed with utter contentment. "You know what happens when you pester the cook."

"Hey, I caught you before you opened the oven, so I figure I'm safe."

The mere sound of his voice eased the tension in my neck and shoulders—tension I hadn't realized was there until it was gone. And to think, this man had turned me into a bundle of nerves when we first met.

My, how times change...

I was beginning to understand the change in him as well as myself. He'd even said the word a moment ago. Safe. Not only was there passion between us, but a sense of belonging—that safe port in a storm where nothing could harm either of us as long as we were together. I would keep him from dwelling on the past while he kept me from worrying about the future. I wondered if that was what love was: finding that certain someone who could take your worst nightmare and turn it into pleasant dreams.

"How was your day?" I asked. "Cattle and horses and fences behave themselves?"

"For the most part," he replied. "But from what Calvin tells me, your day was more eventful."

"No kidding. Boy, do we have a lot to talk about over dinner."

"Over dinner, hell. The summit meeting has already started. Calvin and Jack were hashing over the story when we came in." He turned me around in his embrace. "How about you? You okay?"

"I was a little shaken afterward, but I'm all right now."

The hug he gave me lingered long enough to show his concern. "Sounds like you did a good job of thinking on your feet. I'm really glad you told him to come back later."

I shuddered slightly. "I wasn't about to let him in the bunkhouse. Especially after Ophelia growled at him."

"Her testimony alone should be enough to convict him."

Despite the way his comment might've sounded to a casual observer, Wyatt didn't appear to be kidding.

Yet another point in his favor.

"He asked me if she would attack him, which gave me the perfect excuse to warn him to keep his distance." I was just glad he hadn't been waving a gun around—not that he'd struck me as that type of villain. Devious and underhanded, perhaps, but not blatantly violent. Prior to his illness, Calvin had spent a good deal of time alone in the bunkhouse kitchen. A determined gunman could've barged right in and shot him dead with no witnesses and very little interference.

On that rather unsettling thought, I pulled Wyatt down for a kiss only a moment before Dean and Nick sauntered into the kitchen.

"Just have to rub it in, don't you?" Dean teased as he picked up a stack of plates.

"Hey, dude, timing is everything," Nick said. "They can kiss all they want as long as I get fed." His hands flew to his mouth. "Holy cow. She baked a cake." Appearing somewhat dazed, he picked up the bowl of mashed potatoes and headed toward the mess hall, shaking his head. "She baked a fuckin' cake."

I glanced at Wyatt for enlightenment.

"Um, cake is a pretty rare commodity around here," he said.

"I can't imagine why. It's a lot easier than making a pie." I'd made a sheet cake from a mix, for heaven's sake. It wasn't like I'd baked a six-layer confection from scratch.

Go figure.

"Here, let me get that," Wyatt said as I opened the oven door.

"Thanks." I handed him the oven mitts, recalling another time when he'd simply assumed the task and had snatched the pot holders right out of my hands. I didn't mind it now. He was being helpful—and bless him, I didn't even have to ask.

Lifting the pan of sizzling meat loaf, he inhaled deeply. "Smells great."

"You're not fooling me, Wyatt McCabe," I said with a slow wag of my head. "You just wanted the first sniff."

"You caught me," he said, chuckling. "Although to be honest, we all smelled it as soon as we came through the back door."

"Nice." I shooed him out of the kitchen, then poured the peas and carrots into a bowl, which I handed to Sonny as he came in to lend a hand.

"I see Nick wasn't kidding," he said. "You really did bake a cake."

"And it isn't even your birthday," I quipped. "Lucky you."

"Lucky us, you mean. We never have cake."

"Yeah, yeah," I said with a dismissive wave. "So I've heard."

I took up the gravy, marveling at how easy it was to make a bunch of cowboys happy—unless they were laying it on thick to discourage me from serving up canned pork and beans for dinner. Then again, they'd never had my beans and ham with cornbread before—a menu idea that brought to mind the "campfire scene" from *Blazing Saddles*, along with a serious bout of the giggles.

Bull stopped short in the doorway. "What's so damned funny?"

I handed him the gravy, biting my lip to keep from laughing. His quizzical expression added to the fact that I could easily picture him as one of the cowboys in that scene triggered an explosion of hysteria I couldn't even begin to control.

Bull stared at me for a long time before doing an abrupt about-face and heading back to the mess hall.

"Wyatt, you need to take her out on a date or something," Bull said, his loud, ringing tones clearly audible from the kitchen. "Big-city woman like that stuck out here in the middle of Bumfuck, Wyoming… I think she's gone stir-crazy."

———

Dinner was a rousing success, despite our preoccupation with real or imagined crimes. After I'd related the afternoon's events to the gang at large, Wyatt was the unanimous choice for the bad cop role, and it didn't take us long to decide who should be the good cop.

"Gotta be Angela," Dusty said with absolute conviction. "I mean, look at her."

He was right. With her long dark braids, big brown eyes, and sweet smile, she was the epitome of the kid-sister/girl-next-door-who-wouldn't-hurt-a-fly type. Plus, she'd already proven her concern for Calvin by being the one to stay with him at the hospital. If anyone would encourage him to accept his inheritance, it would be her.

We had almost finished dessert when headlights flashed in the mess hall window.

"Here we go," Angela said. "Now remember. To start off with, we're gonna let him do the talking. Glare at him all you like, but hear him out."

Nick answered the door and showed him in.

Not surprisingly, Duane seemed a tad nervous, especially after Ophelia growled at him, although finding a
lot more people in the room than he'd expected might've
had more to do with his mood.

As rattled as I'd been when I'd first seen him, I hadn't
noticed what an attractive fellow he was. Tall, dark-
haired, and urbane in appearance, he didn't seem like
the type to be out cutting fences and spying on us from
the eastern ridge—although he was just the sort of man
who could charm an elderly widow.

His gaze swept the room as he took a seat in the
chair Nick indicated, touching briefly on Jack before
finally settling on Calvin. "Mr. Douglas?" he asked.
"Calvin Douglas?"

Calvin nodded. "That's right. And who might you be?"

I pressed my lips together, stifling a smile. Apparently
Calvin didn't intend to let Wyatt have all the fun playing
bad cop. Or maybe he was simply the justifiably terse
would-be victim—a part he could easily play without a
script or any coaching.

I met the questioning glance Duane shot at me with a
suitably blank expression. He probably had me pegged
as a real bitch for withholding what little information
he'd passed on to me, but I was okay with that.

He turned toward Calvin again. "My name is
Duane Evans," he said. "I was a friend of your sister,
Jeannine Caruthers."

Calvin leaned back in his chair, his jaw set and his
lips pressed in a firm line, fixing Duane with a steely-
eyed glare. "Go on."

Duane let out a fair imitation of a regretful sigh. "I'm

sorry to be the one to tell you this, Mr. Douglas, but Jeannine died of a heart attack this past January. Her death wasn't unexpected—she hadn't been doing well for several months—and she asked me to try to locate you. She said she regretted the estrangement between the two of you and wanted to make amends."

"That's nice," Calvin said. "Been nicer if you'd found me before she died."

"Well, you see, sir, that was something of a problem. Jeannine had no idea where you might be or even if you were still living. Anyway, that's why I'm here. To offer her apologies and to tell you that she named you as her heir."

Calvin rubbed a hand slowly across his chin. "And if you hadn't found me? Where would the money have gone then?"

"To charity," Duane replied. "Jeannine was very interested in support for single mothers. In fact, that's how I met her." Smiling, he seemed to relax slightly. "She would've been very happy to know I'd found you, Mr. Douglas. She seemed very determined for you to inherit her assets." His gaze focused on me for the space of a heartbeat or two, obviously annoyed that I hadn't shared his sob story about being raised by a single parent with anyone—a story I was finding harder to believe with each passing moment. "Although to be honest, I was hoping the money would wind up going to the foundation."

"And when would that have been?" Calvin asked.

"If you hadn't come forward or been located within two years of her death, her entire estate would have reverted to the foundation."

If Duane had kept quiet and waited, he probably would've gotten his wish, eventually. Still, two years was a long time, and if the foundation was in dire need of funds, Jeannine's request had left him with quite a dilemma. I wondered why he'd even bothered to look for Calvin. After all, a promise made to a dying woman wasn't exactly a binding contract. I hated to admit it, but perhaps he was actually telling the truth.

I waited for the guys to chime in with their two cents' worth—Bull in particular. I couldn't believe he was keeping quiet.

Stunned, perhaps.

"How did you know where to find Calvin?"

Wyatt's satyr-like frown and intimidating tone should have had Duane shaking in his shoes, but Duane simply smiled—a perfectly sincere, disarming smile.

"I'd tracked him down to Wyoming. Believe it or not, there are actually three men named Calvin Douglas living in this state. I was checking the newspapers trying to decide who to contact first when I saw the report of the problem you'd been having with your fences."

"That was in the *newspaper*?" Even in a small-town paper, I doubted a story like that would have made the front page. Duane really must've been scouring the news.

"It was in the police log," he replied. "Apparently they'd spoken to Mr. Douglas."

Calvin nodded his agreement, but Wyatt was undeterred. "That still doesn't explain how you knew Calvin was in the hospital."

Duane's unruffled demeanor never wavered. "I looked up the number for the ranch and called. The man who answered the phone told me he was in the hospital in Salt Lake City."

Once again, I searched the faces of everyone present,

not seeing anyone who appeared to remember taking the call.

Then it hit me. He'd called the main house. With Angela gone, Jack had been alone up there for at least part of each day. He wasn't claiming responsibility, but that didn't necessarily mean he hadn't spoken with Duane. At this stage of his life, he wasn't exactly a reliable witness, nor would he have had any reason to be suspicious of anyone trying to contact Calvin.

Angela darted a glance toward her father, suggesting that she and I had reached a similar conclusion. Still, the fact that Duane had called the house—if indeed he had—didn't necessarily mean he was innocent.

I wanted to slap some sense into myself. We now had a perfectly reasonable chain of events to explain how Duane knew Calvin's whereabouts.

Why couldn't I believe it?

Because we still don't know why the fences were being cut.

Ah, yes... The fences. I couldn't quash the notion that there was a connection.

Angela cleared her throat. *Good cop's turn.* "We wondered about that. The nurses told me that someone named Duane had tried to visit Calvin. You see, we were trying to find his next of kin ourselves. He was unconscious for a good while, and I was uncomfortable making decisions for him so I asked Tina to try to track down his family."

My turn. "We read through some old letters and discovered the names of his sister and her husband. With that information, I did an online search to see if he had any living relatives. As it turned out, he didn't."

Color flooded Duane's cheeks. "You mean to say you already knew Jeannine had died?"

"We only found out a few days ago," I said. "Since then, we've been in touch with her lawyers." I gave him what I hoped was an equally sincere, albeit apologetic smile. "They've already told us she left her estate to Calvin. He's trying to decide if he wants it or not."

There, I thought. Let him chew on that for a bit.

I was having a hard time maintaining my suspicions until I remembered what Duane had said about being a board member. Although support for single mothers was a worthy cause, I couldn't imagine anyone resorting to murder to fund it, even if they *were* on the board. Still, if Duane was the CFO, he would certainly have the opportunity to get his hands on the money.

The only motive required was greed.

Chapter 29

"WELL THEN," DUANE SAID. "I GUESS I'VE GONE TO A lot of trouble for nothing."

Angela gave him a warm smile. "If Calvin hadn't been incapacitated, we never would've gone looking for his family, in which case, you would've been the one to bring him the news."

Duane nodded slowly, then darted a quick look at Calvin. "You are going to accept the money, aren't you? I mean, I can't imagine why you wouldn't."

"Dunno yet," Calvin said with a shrug. "Depends on how much it is, I guess."

Duane let out a shaky laugh. "I don't know the exact sum, but it has to be in the millions."

"Millions, eh?" Calvin echoed. "No idea what I'd do with that kind of money."

Expelling a laugh even shakier than the last, Duane said, "Donate it to charity?"

I'd been wondering why Duane had bothered to pay Calvin a visit. If he'd truly wanted the money to go to charity, he should've kept his mouth shut. Now I understood. He was here to talk Calvin into sharing his inheritance with the single moms.

And him.

My gaze met Wyatt's. The twitch of his brow and nearly imperceptible shake of his head suggested he was still suspicious. Convincing him of the murder plot had taken some doing. Therefore, I could only assume it would take a ton of proof to get him to believe otherwise.

"I suppose I could do that," Calvin mused, stroking his chin. "Have to inherit it first, though."

"I'd appreciate it if you'd think about it," Duane said, sounding reasonably sincere. "I know she wanted you to have the money, but she also felt very strongly about support for single mothers."

"I'm sure she did," Calvin said. "Which makes me wonder why she left her entire estate to me."

Duane spread his hands. "I can't answer that. We'll probably never know her exact reasoning, but those were her wishes."

"Well then, I'll give it some thought," Calvin said. "Thank you for coming."

As dismissals went, it was a tad abrupt, but Duane seemed to take it well. "Thank you for agreeing to see me." His gaze passed over everyone present as he stood, the *even if it wasn't as private as I would have liked* left unsaid. "I'll take myself off, then."

Nick escorted him to the door and I heard the lock click behind him. Just as I'd done earlier that day, I didn't breathe easy until I heard his car drive away.

"What do you make of that?" Calvin asked no one in particular.

"I think he's lying through his goddamned teeth." The words seemed to burst from Bull's mouth. Evidently the effort of keeping quiet had cost him a great deal.

"He sounded reasonable enough," Dean said. "Can't say I trust him, though."

I nodded. "He's too smooth."

"He was until you rattled his cage, Tina," Wyatt said. "He sure wasn't expecting to hear that."

"No shit," Angela said. "I thought he was gonna have a cow."

"What do we do now?" Sonny asked.

"We email Calvin's forms and identification papers to that law firm right now." I glanced at Calvin. "Got that form filled out?"

"Sure do," Calvin replied. "Took care of that while you were getting supper on the table."

"Great," I said. "I'll need to use your scanner again, Angela."

She hopped to her feet. "No problem. Let's do it."

—⁕—

I was back at the bunkhouse and getting ready for bed before I remembered the one thing we hadn't discussed in the wake of Duane's visit: the phone call he claimed to have made to the ranch. A search of the phone records might prove his story, although I wasn't sure they could *dis*prove it.

Climbing in beside Wyatt, I asked, "Any idea how hard it is to get phone records?"

"No clue," he replied, pulling me close. "I'm guessing you'd need a court order to get someone else's records. Dunno how it works when it's your own phone."

Resting my head on the hollow of his shoulder, I draped an arm across his chest. "Jack is the logical person to have taken that call, and even if he'd forgotten about it, hearing what Duane had to say should've jogged his memory."

"Maybe he wasn't too keen on admitting it—or maybe he couldn't remember one way or the other."

"Either of those would explain why he didn't speak up," I said, stifling a yawn. "I'm sure Angela will ask him about it."

The occasional hand Jack had cupped around his ear proved he'd been listening to the conversation, but he hadn't said much of anything after dinner beyond a quick good night when he left the bunkhouse with Angela, Dusty, and me. He'd headed off to bed as soon as we reached the house. Perhaps he'd simply been too tired to think straight.

Jack wasn't the only one; I was pretty well exhausted myself—until Wyatt rolled over and kissed me.

And not just any old kiss. It was one of those I-know-the-world-has-gone-crazy-but-we-still-have-each-other kinds of kisses.

"Tired?"

"Not anymore." I had considered simply giving him a hand job that night, but since my current visit from Aunt Flo had faded to the point where only a pantyliner was required, I didn't think I needed to go that route. Now all I had to do was figure out how to phrase my decision. After a moment's reflection, I opted to take the direct approach. "Better keep a condom handy."

"No problem."

As easy as that. I was getting better at this sex stuff all the time. One of these days I might even try saying something more graphic, like…

Hmm… Maybe I still had some learning to do.

Didn't matter, really. Wyatt's kisses and his slow, sensuous removal of my pajamas and undies proved he didn't need me to talk dirty to get him in the mood. Actually, I was pretty sure he was in the mood before

I ever came to bed. The way the sheet had been tented over his groin was proof of that.

Reaching down, I wrapped my hand around his penis, marveling at the smoothness of the skin stretched over his turgid flesh. I traced a fingertip over the engorged veins crisscrossing his shaft, then on to the thicker vessel that ran the length of the underside. I loved feeling that, seeing it, proving he wanted me as much as I wanted him.

Easing lower, I kissed his cockhead, sipping the salty nectar flowing from his slit—so slick, so smooth, so delightful on my tongue. I sucked him in and savored him slowly, completely. Rolling onto my side, I lay with my head pillowed on his stomach, my free hand massaging his balls while I devoured his cock.

I backed off slightly, running his shiny, plum-shaped glans over my lips before discovering the truly marvelous feel of his cock gliding over my cheek. My softly uttered "Ohhh…" must have encouraged him, for he took his cock in his hand and began stroking my face with it.

The transition was shockingly erotic, and my body responded with a swift contraction centered deep within my pelvis. Pressing my fingertips on the space between his scrotum and anus, I urged him on as more of that luscious fluid poured from his penis, coating my face. My legs writhed seemingly of their own accord, as though trying to soothe the desperate thirst in my core, a thirst only Wyatt could quench.

His stomach muscles tensed beneath my head, and I heard the drawer open, followed by rustling sounds as he rummaged through the contents. A slight breeze wafted over my face as he placed a condom packet on his thigh. "Whenever you're ready."

I was more than ready. I was dying to have him inside me again, dying to keep him there until long after he'd reached his climax. We had so many wonderful encounters ahead of us. Would I ever know every move he could make, every sound? Would loving him ever get old?

I doubted it. Even tonight, when I'd been so worn out that all I really wanted was sleep, one kiss brought the desire surging back to fill me with need and want and lust and passion.

Sitting up, I ripped open the packet with my teeth before rolling it down over his pulsating cock. My patience exhausted, I lay back on the bed, dragging him down over me, demanding his kisses, beckoning to him with my parted thighs.

Although Wyatt hadn't been deprived of sexual release for several nights, he'd clearly been anticipating this moment as much as I had. His first push was gentle, but that nudge soon became a plunge, followed by another and another…

"Oh my…"

I raised a hand to his cheek, bestowing a delicate caress. He was as tough as any man could be, yet he leaned into my touch, his soft groan proving how much that simple gesture meant to him. He rose up on his hands and knees, altering the angle and undulating his spine as though determined to discover new ways to give me pleasure.

No, this would never get old, would never be the slightest bit dull. Those who complained it was boring had never been with Wyatt—or had never been in love.

Wrapping my legs around his waist, I locked my ankles near the small of his back. I reveled in the strength, the heat, the sheer joy of it all as he rocked into me, his rhythm as steady as waves crashing against the shore.

I could have lain there enjoying the ride for the rest of the night, but Wyatt obviously had other ideas. With a quick shove, he pushed himself upright and arched his back. My legs were still locked in place as he grasped my thighs, lifting me until only my head, shoulders, and outstretched arms rested on the mattress. His penetration was complete, and his balls brushed my bottom as he drove me to the brink of nirvana with short, powerful thrusts. Days spent on horseback must've been responsible for that ability, for only his hips moved. Nothing else.

Picturing the flexing of his buttocks triggered an unbelievably powerful orgasm. As my inner muscles gripped his cock, a guttural cry signaled Wyatt's climax, and his hips lurched upward, taking me with him as he reached the pinnacle of ecstasy.

My clitoris hovered near the flash point; one touch would detonate it. I didn't say a word, but somehow Wyatt knew what I needed. With one slow, circular sweep of his thumb, he blasted me into oblivion once more.

But he didn't leave it at that. Maintaining pressure on my clit intensified and prolonged my orgasm, keeping me suspended and breathless as time stood still. Nothing existed in the universe beyond the two of us.

Not one single thing.

———

The next morning I woke up early, let Ophelia out, and had my teeth brushed and hair combed before Wyatt even began to stir. I felt absolutely marvelous—even adventurous enough to try something new for breakfast.

A breakfast casserole? Hmm...

Grabbing my laptop, I headed for the kitchen. After a quick perusal of a few recipes, most of which needed to be put together the night before, I finally found a version that could be made on the spot and seemed easy enough, although I would, of course, have to double the amounts.

Pretty soon I was sautéing sausage, onions, and peppers with joyous abandon, all the worries of the previous evening completely expunged from my mind. Damn, I loved that man. He could make me forget all the bad karma our cold, cruel world could dish out.

All I needed to do now was feed my wonderful pack of cowboys and keep them happy. Simple enough job. Much more rewarding than cleaning viruses out of computers.

I lined two baking dishes with sliced bread and added the sausage mixture. After stirring milk and eggs together with a few added spices and seasonings, I poured it over the bread and sausage, topped both casseroles with grated cheese, and popped them in the oven.

Easy peasy.

I stuck my head out the door and called for Ophelia. When she didn't come right away, I set her breakfast out on the porch. The weather was clear, although still slightly chilly. I wondered if Wyoming nights were ever truly warm.

Maybe in late July.

Deciding that smoothies also sounded good, I dumped a bunch of fresh fruit and juice into the blender and switched it on. Not surprisingly, the blender was loud enough to wake up the guys. Or maybe it was the delicious aroma wafting from the oven that did it. Whatever the reason, they began stumbling into the kitchen about the time the casserole was done.

Dean put the coffee on while Nick went off to set the table. I divvied up the smoothies into eight glasses.

"That looks tasty," Dean said. "What's in it?"

"Strawberries, blueberries, orange juice, pineapple juice, bananas, and a few dollops of plain yogurt. Not allergic to any of that, are you?"

"Nope. Don't think any of us have any allergies."

"*I* sure do," I declared. "I'm allergic to all sorts of things—" I stopped there, realizing once again that Wyoming seemed to agree with me, at least in that respect. I shrugged. "Not bothering me much at the moment, though."

"Guess that means you belong here."

I smiled at him. "I guess it does."

Wyatt came in from my room, running a hand through his tousled locks and looking like every hot, sexy dream I'd ever had—awake or asleep.

Our room, I corrected myself.

"Hey, babe," he said. "Something sure smells fantastic." Hooking an arm around my waist, he tugged me closer for a kiss. "Must be you."

"Yeah, well, you *taste* good." Given that we had an audience, I thought it best to clarify. "Minty fresh."

"Uh-huh," Dean scoffed, obviously not believing that toothpaste had anything to do with Wyatt's flavor. "Sure."

He was right, of course, but that didn't stop me from retaliating. "The rest of him tastes even better."

Dean let out a long, tortured groan. "Guess I deserved that."

"Yes, you did." Still gloriously wrapped up in Wyatt's embrace, I refused to let anyone get me riled, not even Dean. "If you'll take those smoothies into the mess hall, Wyatt and I will bring in the casseroles."

"Yes, ma'am." Dean's wicked grin belied his contrite response. "Whatever you say."

Wyatt waited until Dean disappeared through the doorway. "Looks like you've got us all coming to heel, don't you?"

"Not likely," I said with a snort. "I can't even get my dog to mind this morning. I hope she hasn't gotten lost."

He shrugged. "I doubt it. She's lived here long enough to know her way around. Maybe she found a rabbit to chase."

"You're probably right." Donning my oven mitts, I took one of the casseroles out and set it on the stove. Wyatt grabbed some pot holders and carried it into the mess hall, leaving me to follow with the second one.

The guys were sipping their smoothies. Bull's glass was already empty, his mustache speckled with frothy pink foam.

"Great stuff," he said. "High in carbs, but damned healthy."

"Uh-huh," Nick said. "Thanks for the nutritional analysis." He shot me a grin. "It's delicious, but I bet that casserole is even better."

"I hope you're right. This is the first time I've tried it."

After tasting it, I thought it needed a touch more sage, but the guys were more enthusiastic.

"Definitely a keeper," Joe announced. "Think you could write down the recipe so I can give it to Jenny?"

"Sure," I replied. "Be easier to email her the link, though."

Calvin chuckled, shaking his head. "Technology…"

"Hey, it's made me the cook I am today. A whole world of possibilities at my fingertips." I flexed my fingers for emphasis. "I'm thinking teriyaki chicken wings for dinner."

"Awesome," Sonny said. "I haven't had Chinese food in ages."

I shrugged. "Technically, teriyaki is Japanese, although my version won't be truly authentic. Guess I could make some fried rice to go with it and call it Asian Fusion."

"Doesn't matter what you call it," Wyatt said. "I'm sure it'll be good."

Adorable man.

———

After the guys left for the day, I went out and called for Ophelia again, but received no response. I was starting to get worried.

To pass the time and take my mind off what she might be up to, I went online and found a basic fried rice recipe and several versions of teriyaki chicken wings. I put my own spin on the marinade and was in the process of cutting up the wings when Angela brought Jack down from the main house. After getting him settled in the mess hall with Calvin, she joined me in the kitchen.

"I asked Dad about that phone call from Duane," she began. "He claims it never happened, but his memory isn't what it used to be. Wish we knew for sure."

"Me too." I poured the marinade over the wings, put a lid on the bowl, and stuck it in the fridge. "I still can't decide if I trust Duane. One minute I think he's legit, and the next, he's Public Enemy Number One."

"I'm having the same problem. I mean, what he said seemed reasonable, but there's something odd about him."

"Yeah. Ophelia didn't like him, and she's a pretty good judge of character. Speaking of which, have you seen her this morning? I let her out early and haven't seen her since."

"No, but I'll keep an eye out for her. Let me know if you hear from the lawyers."

"Will do."

Angela went back to the house, and I had just come back inside after yelling for Ophelia until my throat was sore when the phone rang. I answered it, but immediately handed it off to Calvin.

"It's Jeannine's lawyer," I whispered, not wanting to disturb Jack, who was already dozing in his recliner.

Calvin took the phone. "Hello, this is Calvin Douglas." Ten minutes passed before he said another word, making me toy with the idea of picking up the extension.

"Is that right?" he finally said. "Didn't seem that way to me... Yes, well, thank you for your time... Good-bye."

"Okay," I prompted as soon as he switched off the phone. "Spill it. What did he say?"

He shook his head slowly. "According to that lawyer, Jeannine originally meant for all of her money to go to that charity of hers. Then about six months ago, she changed her will, making me her primary beneficiary."

"That's interesting. Did he say why?"

"I don't think he knew, although he did say Jeannine hadn't been doing well for a long time. Duane was right about that much." Arching a brow, he leaned forward in his chair. "He also said that Duane Evans didn't know I existed until the will was read."

"Even more interesting," I said. "Looks like we're back to square one, but we know one thing we didn't know before."

"Yeah," Calvin said. "That Duane fellow is a damned liar."

Chapter 30

I WASN'T TOO SURPRISED TO HEAR THAT, PARTICULARLY since it confirmed many of our suspicions. "What else did he say?"

"He said Jeannine never expected them to find me and told them not to try very hard."

"That's weird."

"I thought so too, and so did the lawyer, but you know how it is. Rich old ladies sometimes have strange ideas."

Then again, it might have been a very shrewd move on her part. It would certainly keep Duane or anyone else from embezzling money from the foundation. At least for a while. "I guess the next question is what would happen if you weren't around to inherit."

His smile was grim. "That's where it really gets interesting. Proof of my death would mean the money goes to the charity in a year."

One year versus two, and five months had already passed. *Hmm…* "And if you refuse the inheritance?"

"They didn't say anything about that—mainly because I didn't ask."

"Might be a good question for next time."

"I suppose so. Anyway, they're in the process of making sure I am who I say I am. Said they'd call me back in a day or two."

In the meantime, our vigilance needed to be continuous. Unfortunately, I had a missing dog.

"Listen, I hate to leave you and Jack here alone, but

do you think you could hold the fort for a while if I let Angela know I'm going out to look for Ophelia? She's been gone all morning."

"Sure thing, but you'd better take a pistol with you," Calvin advised, pointing to the holsters hanging on pegs near the door. "No telling what you might run across out there."

Never having fired a gun in my life, I wasn't terribly pleased about carrying one, but I couldn't argue with his suggestion. My aim was what concerned me. "I wouldn't be able to hit anything smaller than the barn."

"The noise is enough to scare off most things," he said with a grin. "Just be careful you don't shoot the dog."

"I'll try not to."

After a quick lesson in gun safety and a call to Angela, I tossed the chicken wings in the slow cooker, then put on a jacket and holster and set out.

The only trouble was, I had absolutely no idea which direction to take.

Think like a dog, Tina.

After a quick check of the barn and other outbuildings, I went off through the open gate to the nearest pasture. The quiet voice of reason in my head told me I should check that eastern ridge, but I ignored it. Just because I thought Duane might be watching from up there didn't necessarily mean he had Ophelia with him. For one thing, she didn't like him. For another, as steep and rough as that hillside was, I wasn't too keen on trying to climb it. Stepping gingerly over the cattle bars, I headed north up the dirt track behind the barn.

Judging from the ruts, the men drove the truck up that way fairly often, and the track continued on for quite a ways before petering out. By the time I'd reached the summit of the third hill, I had no voice left whatsoever. I did a slow three-sixty turn, taking in the landscape, which was pretty much the same in every direction. Green shoots were beginning to peek through the dead grasses, and I saw the occasional bird, but not much else.

As I stood there, listening, I finally heard it: a distant bark, which—as luck would have it—was off to the southeast.

Bloody hell...

I started off in that direction, but it wasn't long before I regretted my decision as the terrain grew increasingly rugged. What looked like a reasonable path from a distance was actually crisscrossed with deep gullies and treacherous, rocky slopes. I stopped for a moment and called again.

No bark.

"Damn it all to hell and back." Now was obviously the time to start cursing a blue streak, but that was the best I could do. I called out again, and received no bark in reply.

By that time, I was so turned around I wasn't even sure which direction I was headed. The sun, being almost directly overhead, was no help at all. I was exhausted, footsore, thirsty, and hoarse.

Not to mention stupid. I should never have come this far on my own, although for all I knew the bunkhouse was just over the next hill. Considering how far north I had walked, then back toward the southeast, I figured if I turned to my right, I should get back to the house eventually.

Maybe.

Purely through force of habit, I had my cell phone

with me. I even had the bunkhouse phone number programmed into it, but of course, there was no signal whatsoever. I started off on my new heading, wishing I had brought a compass with me instead of a phone.

I bet there's an app for that. Too bad I'd never seen the need to download one. However, I had every intention of doing so. Just as soon as I had Internet access again.

Then I remembered the WiFi. The signal from the bunkhouse probably wasn't very strong, but even a weak signal would give me some idea of the right direction. Normally, I kept the WiFi receiver turned off because my phone tended to get carried away with signal searching and run down its battery. I enabled the setting and turned around slowly.

Nothing.

With no other options, I resumed my trek in the direction I'd already chosen, checking for a signal every so often. Unfortunately, I soon discovered a drawback to staring at your phone while hiking across uneven terrain. I have no idea what I stepped on, but one moment I was trucking along at a decent pace, and the next, my ankle turned so sharply I went down on my knees. Excruciating pain shot through my ankle and what was left of my breakfast threatened to make a comeback.

"Great. Juuussst great." I sat back and massaged my ankle for a bit, then tried to stand. That time I really did throw up.

No phone signal, no Internet connection, no dog, and now, little or no mobility. I didn't consider crawling back to the bunkhouse to be a viable alternative. Having Wyatt come riding up on a white horse was preferable, but at the time, I would have settled for Duane. Where

was our fence-cutting, charity-embezzling, attempted
murderer when I needed him? If he'd been skulking
around as much as we suspected, it was a wonder I
hadn't run into him.

I sat there for about ten minutes, trying in vain to
solve my dilemma when the obvious solution finally
occurred to me.

*You dummy. You're carrying the Wild West equiva-
lent of a flare.*

Drawing the pistol, I released the safety, cocked
the hammer, pointed the business end toward a rather
innocuous grassy spot on the opposite hillside, and fired.

As weak as I was from pain and exertion, the recoil
nearly dislocated my shoulder. The report echoed across
the vast, empty spaces. Surely someone would hear it.
I was on top of a hill, for heaven's sake, not down at
the bottom of a ravine. Nevertheless, I couldn't help
wondering how long I should wait before firing another
shot. There were plenty of extra bullets in the holster,
and Calvin had shown me how to load it. He knew I
was carrying a gun too, and though I couldn't very well
count on him or Jack hearing anything, the other men
should have. The sound probably carried for miles.

Not hearing a single sound that would indicate help
was on the way, I began massaging my ankle again.

If nothing else, the guys would come in for supper,
realize I was gone, and start searching for me. Calvin
knew I was out here, and so did Angela. Surely I would
be rescued before dark. Even if wolves or coyotes came
prowling around, I had a weapon. I wished I'd known
how big the ranch was and how far away the guys were.
That way I would have some idea of when they might

find me. Funny how you never know what you need to know until you need to know it.

Okay. I'm delirious now.

I was also getting cold. My jacket and jeans had kept me warm enough while I was walking. Now they seemed woefully inadequate. There were gloves in the pockets, and I put them on, but I'd have given a lot for a knitted cap and a blanket.

Shivering, I lay down on my side and curled up as best I could while trying to keep my ankle straight and elevated. I doubted I would fall asleep—surely the pain would keep me awake—but passing out was a distinct possibility. Maybe after a little rest, I would be able to walk.

I was lying there, slowly becoming resigned to my fate when I realized what I'd done. I'd fallen right in with Duane's plot to get me out of the way. Knowing I would go out searching for her, the conniving creep had taken my dog.

I reminded myself that Calvin wasn't alone, nor was he defenseless. I wasn't so sure about Ophelia. After attempting to kill a man, I couldn't imagine Duane would have any qualms about doing away with a dog, especially one that didn't like him.

I tried standing again and found I could hobble a bit. I was almost to a large, flat rock that appeared to be a nice place to sit down and rest for a while when Wyatt came riding up the hill. The horse was brown rather than white, but I wasn't about to complain, especially when I spotted Ophelia trotting along beside him.

Bringing his horse to a halt, Wyatt dismounted with practiced ease. "I'd have been here sooner if you'd fired another shot." To my surprise, he didn't seem at all angry with me, simply sliding his arms around the small of my back and pulling me up close to him. His soft, lingering kiss conveyed his relief perfectly. "The first one got my attention. The second would've helped me to actually find you."

"I'll remember that the next time I twist an ankle," I said grimly.

"I thought you were limping." His frown displayed his concern and sent his eyebrows flying into the vertical position. That expression had unnerved me at one time. Now it gave me the warm fuzzies. "How bad is it?"

"Better than it was. I was beginning to think I was gonna have to crawl home." I reached down and gave Ophelia a pat on the head, ruffling her fur. "I see you found my dog."

"Nick and I have been searching for her all morning." He nodded toward the eastern ridge. "About an hour ago, Nick found her tied up in a thicket about half a mile on the other side of that ridge. She seemed kinda groggy. I'm guessing she'd been fed some sort of sedative."

I didn't have to think very hard to figure out who might've done such a thing—or how. "Duane could've left a pill in a piece of meat right outside the door. She would've gobbled it up as soon as I let her out this morning."

"Yeah. That's what we thought." His smile intensified the warmth already surrounding my heart. "Anyway, when I took her back to the house, Calvin said you'd gone out, so I came out to tell you we'd found her. I heard the shot not long after that." With a glint of mischief in his eyes, he went on, "Nick might've rescued your dog, but I'm really glad I got to be the one to rescue *you*." He flicked a suggestive eyebrow. "So...should I carry you or put you up on my horse?"

"Better let the horse carry me. I wouldn't want you to mess up an ankle too. Would it be okay if we rode double? I could sit behind you." I was enough of a romantic to want to ride off into the sunset with my studly cowboy, but I wasn't about to let him sling me in front of the saddle like a sack of feed.

"Sure. Think you can stand up on that outcropping?"

I had my doubts, but I nodded anyway. Wyatt scooped me up in his arms and put me up on the slab of stone. Still somewhat dizzy, I was afraid I would keel over at any moment, but Wyatt held on to me until I felt reasonably steady.

"Okay," I said. "What's next?"

"I'll mount up and move in close to the downhill side. From there, you should be able to get on without too much trouble."

Considering I was now on much higher ground and therefore taller than the horse, I thought I might have a chance. The pain in my ankle made my head swim a bit as I inched closer to the edge, but Wyatt was right there to keep me from falling. Bracing myself with a firm grip on his shoulder, I swung my leg over the horse's rump and sat down on the rear edge of the saddle pad.

First time for everything.

"I should warn you, I've never been on a horse in my life."

"Don't worry," he said as we started off. "We'll go slow. Just hold on to me and keep your legs close behind mine so you don't kick Hal in the flanks."

"Hal? Your horse's name is Hal?" Seemed an odd choice to me for some reason.

"Hey, if you can name your dog after a Shakespearean character, I can name my horse after a rogue computer."

"Touché," I said, although I couldn't help wondering if this particular Hal had as much of a mind of his own as the original.

Wrapping my arms around Wyatt's waist, I gave him a hug and rested my head against his back, feeling the urge to say something along the lines of "My hero!" I didn't, of course. "Thanks for coming after me. And for finding Ophelia."

"You should've known we'd go looking for her," he said. "We all know how much she means to you."

The tears stinging my eyes had nothing to do with my sore ankle. I hugged him again. "You guys are so sweet to me. To think, I was almost too chicken to sit down to dinner with you that first night."

He placed his right hand over mine and gave it a meaningful squeeze. "I was a little afraid of you myself. Afraid of how you made me feel."

"Still scared?"

"A bit. But I'm doing better. One of these days I might even get the nerve to ask you to marry me."

I had no idea what to say to that. It sounded like a proposal—sort of. I already knew the answer. All he had to do was ask the question. "Not feeling particularly brave today?"

"Mmm…maybe, maybe not."

I sighed. "I think you're *very* brave. Searching for possible prowlers in the middle of the night. Rescuing damsels in distress. Finding lost dogs. Grilling murder suspects."

"None of those things required much courage," he pointed out. "Nothing like asking the kindest, most beautiful, wonderful woman in the world to marry you when you're nothing but a cowboy who doesn't even own the horse he rides."

"Hmm, well, when the woman in question is the bunkhouse cook and doesn't even own the pans she cooks with, I'm not sure being a cowboy—rich or penniless—matters."

"Not quite rich, not quite penniless. Somewhere in between—although closer to penniless than rich."

"Ah. Just the way I like my cowboys. Hungry."

He might not have been able to see my smile, but his grin creased his cheeks and crinkled the corner of his eyes—the ones I could see, anyway. "Is that a yes?"

"Depends on who's asking the question."

"I am," he said. "I'm asking you to marry me, Tina. Will you?"

I could have hemmed and hawed for the rest of the journey back to the bunkhouse, but I didn't see the point. Adding a lifetime of wedded bliss to what I already felt for my handsome cowboy was guaranteed to make my happiness complete. Why would I want to put it off?

"Yes, Wyatt. I will marry you. And I don't care where we live or how much money we have. As far as I'm concerned, it's all good."

Chapter 31

WE RODE IN SILENCE FOR MOST OF THE JOURNEY, allowing me to simply enjoy the moment with all its delightful minutiae: the murmur of the wind through the tall grasses, the creak of the saddle, Hal's muffled hoofbeats and the shifting of my weight from side to side as he walked. But most of all, the warm strength of the man I had my arms around. If it hadn't been for my twisted ankle, I would've counted it as one of the most perfect days of my life. I really didn't want Duane or anyone else to spoil it, even though it was possible that I owed him one. After all, Wyatt had just proposed to me, which might have been the result of some sort of rescuing-the-damsel-in-distress syndrome. God only knew whether he would have asked that same question if I'd been making sandwiches at the time.

Still, this new turn of events made me long to wrap up our recent bouts of intrigue and speculation and get on with our lives. It also reminded me of some rather pertinent information I had neglected to pass along.

"Guess what? Jeannine's attorney called this morning. Apparently Duane didn't know Calvin existed until the will was read. What do you say we bite the bullet and confront him with our suspicions?"

"You'll get no arguments from me. I'm getting really tired of all this dognapping and fence-cutting crap."

"Same here," I agreed. "I'm sure he'll deny

everything—might even be a bit huffy about it—but at least he would know we're on to him."

"Yeah. Did you notice the change in him when Calvin said he wasn't sure he would accept his inheritance?"

"He seemed very relieved."

Wyatt nodded. "Which makes me wonder how desperate he is for that money."

"You mean like loan sharks threatening to break his arm or something?"

"Or worse. That would explain a lot, but it also makes me wonder if he had something to do with Jeannine's death."

"Hurried it along, you mean?"

"Yeah, although I doubt he had the kind of access to Jeannine he would need to do that. I can't see him sneaking into her house and dumping out her nitroglycerine unless he had an accomplice. I wonder how good a *friend* he was to her."

"I dunno," I said. "If he were to visit her and ask to use the restroom…"

"True, but I'm guessing she had more than one bathroom in her house, and she wouldn't have kept her medications in the one a visitor would use."

I was about to voice my agreement when the horse came to a rather abrupt halt, causing me to bump my nose on the middle of Wyatt's back.

"Looks like we might get that confrontation sooner than you think," he said.

Peering around Wyatt's shoulder, I could see that we were headed down the track to the pasture gate. Then I spotted Duane exiting the bunkhouse through the rear door to Calvin's quarters.

Unfortunately, Duane saw us a second later. If he'd stood his ground and given us a plausible explanation for being there, he might've talked his way out of it, but like most wrongdoers caught in the act, he opted to make a run for it.

"Nothing quite like catching the varmint red-handed, is there?" Wyatt reached back and took my hand. "Try to land on your good foot."

"What? Oh, right."

With Wyatt's assistance, I slid off the horse with a lot less grace than I'd mounted him.

Not that it mattered. No one could have seen my dismount for the cloud of dust Hal kicked up as Wyatt launched him into a full gallop. Duane never looked back as he rounded the end of the bunkhouse and high-tailed it down the drive. Ophelia had a head start, but the horse and rider quickly overtook her, leaping the cattle bars and scattering gravel as they thundered across the stable yard.

Fortunately, Duane didn't appear to be armed. Wyatt had a pistol in the holster strapped to his thigh, but he didn't resort to drawing a gun on his quarry. No, in classic rodeo style, he leaped from the saddle and wrestled Duane to the ground like a runaway steer. Three seconds later, he had Duane facedown with his hands tied neatly behind his back; a calf-roping champion couldn't have done it faster. I half expected him to throw up his hands to stop the clock.

Ophelia joined in the fray, barking her head off. Hal stopped a few strides away before turning and trotting back to Wyatt. I, of course, approached the scene much more slowly.

Duane's slick, assured manner was gone, his expression of frank dismay clearly evident as Wyatt jerked him to his feet and marched him toward me. From the look of him, it wouldn't take much encouragement to get him to talk.

At about the same time, Calvin came out onto the porch through the kitchen door. "What's all the ruckus about?"

"Caught this varmint coming out the back door to your quarters," Wyatt replied. "Better call the police— and Angela. I think they need to hear what he has to say for himself."

"Sure thing," Calvin said.

Calvin had no sooner retreated through the doorway when Jack came outside, his lips stretched into a broad grin and his eyes alight with excitement. "I was standing by the window when you came flying across the yard. That was some damn fine ridin' and ropin'—like something out of a John Wayne movie." With a slow wag of his head, he added, "Shoulda been taking pictures."

"Me too. That was totally awesome!" My phone had a decent camera on it—I could've even taken a video— but by the time I'd fished it out of my pocket and started filming, I would have missed seeing my hero do his stuff.

Wyatt's grin spoke volumes. Duane offered no resistance as Wyatt aimed him toward the bunkhouse. Ophelia walked alongside him, her menacing growl undoubtedly contributing to his docility.

Jack came down the steps and took Hal's reins. "I'll put him up for you. Just don't do anything 'til I get back. Don't want to miss this."

Neither did I. Too bad the rest of the guys weren't there to see it. A glance at my watch informed me that it was one fifteen, although I could've made a pretty good guess based on how hungry I was. Limping along as quickly as I could, I reached the steps just as Angela came running down from the main house.

"Thank God you're all safe," she exclaimed. "I was getting worried." Her gaze traveled downward to my bum ankle. "You're hurt."

"Not too bad." I waved a deprecating hand. "A little horse liniment should fix me right up."

Angela giggled. "You're turning into a real rough-and-tumble cowgirl, aren't you?"

Wyatt and I exchanged a glance that had me chuckling along with her. *If she only knew.*

"No kidding. I've even been on a horse—*and* fired a gun." I nodded at Wyatt. "Not sure I could ever top what he did, though. Did you see it?"

She shook her head. "I was in the office. Thought I'd better come down and see if you were back yet." With a nod toward Duane, she added, "Looks like you found more than your dog. You'll have to tell me all about it."

"Believe me, it'll be a pleasure."

———

The local sheriff and his deputy arrived in a surprisingly short time. Sheriff Carlson was tall and lean with iron-gray hair and a bristly mustache, and his dark-haired, smooth-cheeked deputy appeared to be a capable young man—young being the operative word. However, neither of them fit the part of a Western lawman quite the way Wyatt did. All he needed was a badge. I was so proud of him I couldn't stop smiling.

I stretched out in one of the recliners while Wyatt rubbed liniment on my ankle, which had swelled considerably and was already turning all sorts of interesting colors. The officers took statements from those who were witnesses, after which, Duane proceeded to spill his guts. As fast as he was talking, I hoped the sheriff was taking notes in shorthand.

Filthy dirty and soaked with sweat, Duane Evans sat alone in a straight-backed wooden chair in the middle of the room, his shoulders hunched forward as he picked at the inseams of his jeans. The only things missing from the classic interrogation scene were the glaring overhead lights and a hard-bitten detective with rolled-up sleeves and a battered fedora.

"I needed that money to pay gambling debts and cover up what I'd already stolen from the foundation," Duane began. "The loan sharks were threatening me. I couldn't wait two years. I needed the money *now*. I had no idea Jeannine was going to leave her estate to her brother. Hell, I didn't even know she *had* a brother. When I heard how the will was worded, I-I panicked. I had to make sure he didn't inherit."

"And how did you plan to do that?" Sheriff Carlson asked.

"Cocaine," Duane replied. "I got it from a guy who swore a high enough dose would cause a heart attack— said he'd seen it happen. Jeannine had a bad heart, and after I'd seen the sort of medicines her brother was taking, it was obvious that he did too. I switched some of his pills for cocaine tablets. When that didn't work, I dumped out his nitroglycerine."

Calvin snorted his disgust. "The cocaine didn't work

because I hadn't taken any pills in months. It wasn't until Tina showed up that I decided I wasn't quite ready to give up on life. I honestly don't remember doing it, but I must've taken one of each like I was supposed to—which, as it turned out, was a mistake."

A momentary chill shook me as I remembered how close Calvin had come to dying that night—and all because he'd decided he wanted to live.

How ironic. "I have all of Calvin's old meds in a bag in my desk. Some of them didn't match the label descriptions, and since I didn't have any idea what they were, I'd planned to take them to a pharmacy for disposal. Never quite got around to it, though."

The sheriff nodded. "Good. We'll take those as evidence." He returned his attention to Duane. "That explains how Mr. Douglas wound up in the hospital, but not what you were doing here today."

"Doesn't explain how you got into Calvin's room with the door locked, either," Wyatt put in. "Especially with Calvin and Jack sitting right here in the mess hall."

Duane actually smiled. "I figured you might lock up at some point, so I stole a key and had a duplicate made. The way you people leave this place unlocked made it so easy. As for coming in when they were here, after last night, I realized they were both deaf as posts, so I thought I'd give it another try. The cocaine almost worked the last time." He paused, giving me a look that made me want to slap him. "Once I got you and your damned dog out of the way, I knew they'd be here alone."

I could scarcely believe what I was hearing, especially given the smug manner in which he'd said it.

The creep actually seemed proud of his ingenuity. How could anyone be that cold and unfeeling? "But why would you do that after Calvin said he wasn't sure he wanted the money?"

"I figured he'd change his mind once he realized how much money he would be giving away."

"What about the fences?" Wyatt asked. "I take it you're the one who's been cutting them."

"Yeah," Duane said with an insolent shrug. "That was just to keep you guys busy."

Wyatt turned toward the sheriff. "We can probably prove that, if necessary. There was blood on the last wire that was cut. I covered it up in case we needed it for comparison."

"Good thinking," Sheriff Carlson said. "Although we may not need it."

Having heard Duane's confession, I thought we all deserved a pat on the back for our intuitive detective work. We'd already figured out everything except for the gambling and the cocaine. Wyatt and I had even hit on the loan shark angle, which was probably why Duane was being relatively cooperative. He must've realized he was safer in police custody than tangling with a bunch of vindictive loan sharks.

Of course, the fact that Calvin was still alive was the most important result of our involvement. Perhaps Jeannine hadn't been as lucky.

"What about my sister?" Calvin asked, giving voice to my thoughts. "Her death was mighty opportune."

"Believe me, killing Jeannine was the last thing I wanted to do," Duane replied. "She was donating to the foundation on a regular basis. When she died, the

donations stopped." With an expression of utter mystification, he stared at the floor, shaking his head slowly.
"She always said she was going to leave her estate to
the foundation. I still can't figure out why she didn't."

My derisive laughter diverted Duane's downcast
gaze. "Couldn't possibly have been because she suspected you of embezzling, could it? She might not have
been able to prove you'd been stealing, but cutting the
funding for two years might've made it more obvious
that something fishy was going on and at least gotten
you kicked off the board."

Judging from his openmouthed reaction, that explanation hadn't occurred to Duane.

Sheriff Carlson closed his notebook and got to his
feet. "Kinda reminds me of the night I was chasing a
suspect who was wearing shoes with flashing red lights
in the heels." With a grin, he added, "We don't catch
the smart ones."

Evidently Duane Evans didn't belong in that category.

———

Dinner that evening was a relaxed and festive occasion.
Festive for obvious reasons, and relaxed because the
chicken wings were already done and Wyatt had made
the fried rice, deeming me too injured to stand in front of
the stove. I could've done it, of course, but he insisted,
so I let him. He even made a fruit salad for dessert.

Everyone seemed happy and relieved that the mystery had finally been solved, until Wyatt let it slip that
he and I were engaged to be married.

After we'd received hearty congratulations from the
group as a whole, Calvin spoke up. "If it hadn't been for

you two, I might not have been alive to inherit anything. I'm thinkin' I oughta give you a big chunk of my inheritance as a wedding present."

As touched as I was by his generous offer, it was a moment before I could control my emotions enough to speak. "That's very kind of you, Calvin, but you might want to wait and see how much money you'll get before you start giving it away. Duane might be wrong about the amount. It might not even be enough for your own retirement."

"I dunno," Calvin said. "Must be quite a bundle for a man to resort to murder. Don't want anyone else trying to bump me off to get their hands on it. Might be best to spread it around."

Wyatt chuckled. "If that's the case, I'm not sure we'd want it, either. Seems jinxed to me—kinda like the Hope Diamond."

"Yeah, right," Dean scoffed. "I think I'd be willing to take that chance."

Sonny elbowed him in the ribs. "You *would*."

By that time, we were all laughing.

Everyone, that is, except Nick.

"How could you do this to us, Wyatt?" he lamented. "We have a cook we all love who makes the best pies in the whole wide world, and you want to marry her and take her away from us?"

"Now, Nick," I began, "nothing's been decided yet. I don't think we'll be moving away anytime soon." Especially since, prior to Calvin's offer, I'd been prepared to go right on living in the bunkhouse.

I glanced at Wyatt, who shrugged. "We don't have to go anywhere, or even buy our own place if you don't want to."

Angela spoke up. "We could sell you a few acres. That way you could build a house of your own and still be close enough to feel like part of the Circle Bar K family." She sniffled as though tears were imminent. "I really hate it when people leave."

That sounded like a good plan to me, unless Wyatt and I had a bajillion kids and I didn't have time to cook for the men. Then again, I figured two kids would be plenty, and they wouldn't stay babies for long. The question was whether Wyatt would want to keep on working for someone else when he could be the boss of his own spread.

"We'll think about it," I said. "No need to do anything rash."

Bull let out a guffaw. "You mean like getting engaged after only knowing each other for a week?"

"Um, yeah," I said with unruffled calm. "Something like that—although we haven't set a date. Might be a while before we actually tie the knot."

Giggling, Angela leaned closer to me, keeping her voice down, her tears already forgotten. "You watch, he's gonna offer to perform the ceremony."

"Would it be legal?" Somehow I didn't think it would be.

"Probably not," she replied. "But would you want him to?"

"No. Not really."

To be honest, I hadn't given the particulars much thought. I was so happy to be engaged to Wyatt and no longer worrying about who might be trying to kill Calvin and why, I didn't really care what happened next. I was perfectly content to let the future take its course, and it felt wonderful. Even a sprained ankle couldn't diminish my idyllic state, especially since it gave Wyatt the perfect excuse to put his hands on me in public.

Our eyes met, and he smiled—a smile I felt all the way to my soul.

I'd begun this journey filled with shyness and apprehension. Those qualms had been put to rest by a man who'd shown me the softer, gentler side of himself, an aspect of his character that made him seem no less masculine, no less appealing, and certainly more human. The hurt and pain beneath the intimidating glare from a pair of brooding hazel eyes had given way to love and joy that I was convinced would last for a long, long time.

Had Grandpa known how much this adventure would change me? That it would give me the courage I never dreamed I would find anywhere, let alone on a Wyoming ranch?

I suppose the how or why didn't matter in the greater scheme of things, but I had an idea Wyatt wasn't the only one smiling at me.

Thanks, Grandpa.

Acknowledgments

My sincere thanks go out to:

My loving husband, Budley

My handsome sons, Mike and Sam

My pals from my nursing days

My talented critique partners, Sandy James, Nan Reinhardt, and TC Winters

My keen-eyed beta reader, Mellanie Szereto

My supportive agent, Melissa Jeglinski

My longtime editor, Deb Werksman

My amazing blog followers

My fellow IRWA members

My insane cats, Kate and Allie

My normal cat, Jade

My barn cat, Kitty Cat

My trusty horses, Kes and Jadzia

My peachy little dog, Peaches

Google Earth for helping me find my way around Wyoming

And last, but certainly not least, I'd like to thank my wonderful readers for following me from the far reaches of outer space to the wide-open spaces of Wyoming. I hope you enjoyed the ride!

Read on for an excerpt from *Cowboy Heaven* by Cheryl Brooks

THERE HE WAS AGAIN. THAT SAME COWBOY I'D SEEN on the drive into town, still walking, still carrying a big green duffel bag on one shoulder and a saddle slung over the other. He'd been traveling in the opposite direction and hadn't bothered to look up as I'd passed him earlier. I'd barely glimpsed his face then, but I saw it quite clearly now. A glance over his shoulder revealed his bleak, exhausted expression. He might have been near the point of collapse, but he obviously wasn't prepared to admit defeat.

Not yet, anyway.

I couldn't believe no one had picked him up in the three hours since I'd last seen him. He hadn't looked very fresh even then. I had no idea where he was headed, but in the middle of Wyoming, there wasn't much within walking distance, no matter where you were going.

He turned toward me, sticking out a halfhearted thumb as I came closer, his face streaked with dirt and sweat and what might have been tears. A black Stetson shadowed his eyes, and his boots and jeans were dusty and worn. His sweat-soaked denim shirt clung to his chest, unbuttoned halfway to his waist, the sleeves ripped out. He probably wasn't trying to look cool, even though he did. No, he was likely trying to *get* cool, in any way he possibly could. My truck was air-conditioned and comfortable, and there was plenty of room for him and his meager belongings. I could no more have left him there than I could have ignored a starving child.

As I pulled over to stop, his eyes closed and his lips moved as though uttering a prayer of thanks. His knees buckled slightly, and for a moment, I thought he truly would collapse. Instead, he took a deep breath and stood up straight. Lifting his chin, he aimed luminous blue eyes at me and flashed a dazzling smile. His silver belt buckle suggested this man was no ordinary ranch hand but a down-on-his-luck rodeo cowboy who, unless I missed my guess, was heading for Jackson Hole.

A real heartbreaker of a rodeo cowboy, too. Up close, he was even more handsome than he'd been from a distance. Long and lean with tanned, muscular arms, dimples creased his cheeks and black hair curled enticingly from the open edges of his shirt. Several days' growth of dark beard surrounded full, sensuous lips, darkening a jaw that my fingertips ached to caress. More ebony curls peeked from beneath his hat, making me long to yank off that Stetson to discover what else it was hiding. Oh yes, there was enough gorgeous cowboy to sway a much stronger woman than I ever claimed to be. Tears stung my eyes as something in his expression reminded me of Cody.

My dear, sweet Cody... He'd been gone for two years now, but I hadn't forgotten that look, and I doubted I ever would.

Determined to mask my roiling emotions, I searched for something amusing to say as I rolled down my window. "Lost your horse?"

My clever tongue was rewarded with another

heart-stopping smile. Cody used to say funny things just to make me giggle—which wasn't difficult since I tend to find humor in nearly any situation—but brushing up on my own repertoire of one-liners to keep this guy smiling seemed like an excellent idea.

His grin was sheepish as he tipped up the brim of his hat. "He sort of drove off without me."

"*Drove* off?" I scoffed. "Somehow I doubt that. Seems like he would've needed help."

My handsome cowboy gave me a grim nod. "Oh, he had help all right. My girlfriend dumped me on the highway and took off with the truck, the trailer, and the horse—all of which were actually hers, by the way. She was kind enough to leave me my saddle and my clothes, although a cell phone would've been nice."

I shook my head. "Nice, yes. Helpful, no. They don't work very well around here. Which kinda makes me mad—I mean, where would you need a phone more than if you were stranded out in the middle of nowhere?"

He glanced around at the vast expanse of sunbaked rangeland. "Is that the name of this place? Nowhere?"

"Sure is." I couldn't help giggling. "Want to get out of nowhere?"

"Yes, please," he replied. "And as quickly as possible."

"Throw your stuff in the back and hop in," I said. "We'll leave nowhere and go…somewhere."

He did as I suggested, and suddenly the interior of my truck was filled with the pungent aroma of hot, sweaty, dusty—but cologned—cowboy. He'd most likely showered that morning, but it had been one helluva day. The forecast called for the upper nineties—quite a heat wave even for mid-August—and though the humidity was low, some temperatures are best avoided no matter how dry the air.

"You're a lifesaver," he said. "I thought that sun was gonna roast me alive."

"As hot as it gets in these parts, I never go anywhere without water, enough food for a couple of meals, and an umbrella in case I'm ever forced to hike. Want a sandwich?"

"You bet."

I tossed a nod over my shoulder. "The cooler's on the backseat. Help yourself. There's plenty of water." Although, at that point, a cold beer probably would have been his first choice.

He pulled out two bottles of water and a sandwich, downing the first bottle in three swallows.

"Better now?"

"Much."

"Let's see now…" I said as he unwrapped the sandwich. "A cowboy dumped in the middle of nowhere with a saddle and no horse. There's got to be a country song in that."

"If you mean a song about a guy bein' picked up by a girl in a flatbed Ford, I think the Eagles already did that one."

"I love that song," I said wistfully. "Guess I always wanted to be that girl."

"Well, now you are." He took a bite of the sandwich, chewing it quickly. "How does it feel?"

"Not much different." This wasn't entirely true. I wasn't in the habit of picking up gorgeous cowboys—and this particular cowboy's presence had me feeling strangely excited. Oh yes, I was very aware of him, and if my brain hadn't noticed him, my erogenous zones were there to remind me. "For one thing, this isn't a flatbed Ford, and I'm not what anyone would call a girl anymore."

He paused in mid-bite. "Why? Have you had a sex-change operation?"

"Nope," I replied with another giggle. "You can't call a forty-two-year-old a girl. Well, maybe you could if you happened to be eighty-two yourself, but I'm pretty sure I outgrew the girl category a long time ago—about the time that song was popular."

Despite the fact that I never once took my eyes off the road, I was aware of his prolonged scrutiny—an assessing gaze that left delightful tingles in its wake.

"Some things improve with age." He turned toward the window. "You don't seem like the type to dump a guy in the middle of nowhere."

Having heard the catch in his voice, I did my best to keep my tone light. Bursting into tears in front of a perfect stranger probably wasn't on his bucket list. "True—unless he was really obnoxious."

This particular cowboy would have to have been homicidal or, at the very least, abusive for me to throw *him* out. He was the most adorable cowboy I'd ever laid eyes on, including the one I'd married.

"I wasn't being obnoxious." He fairly bristled with indignation, which seemed to have won out over heart-break. "I was *asleep*. I thought she was stopping for gas when I felt the truck slow down. She asked me to take a look at the tires on the trailer, said she thought one had gone flat. While I was checking the tires, she dumped my saddle and duffel bag on the side of the road and drove off. I found this tucked into the saddle." Reaching into his shirt pocket, he handed me a torn, sweat-soaked scrap of paper.

It's not working out. Sorry.

"Ouch," I said with a sympathetic wince. "That's pretty hard."

"Yeah." With an absent nod, he stuffed the note back into his pocket. "I don't even know what I did wrong. Don't guess I ever will."

He seemed nice enough, and he certainly wasn't ugly. Maybe his girl had breakup issues. As irresistible as he was, I couldn't imagine breaking his heart while gazing into those eyes of his, and I didn't even know his name.

She'd probably gone about it the best way possible—a quick, clean break before losing her nerve completely. One glance, one smile, and she'd have forgotten why their relationship wasn't working. I wasn't looking forward to dropping him off at the crossroad to the ranch, myself. I had a sudden, overwhelming urge to take him home and wash him, feed him, and tuck him into bed—*my* bed, to be precise.

I had my doubts about that part. He couldn't have been more than thirty, and young men generally didn't seek solace from older women—not that kind of solace, anyway. Consoling him seemed impossible, so I changed the subject.

"Where were you headed?"

"The rodeo in Jackson Hole," he replied. "I'm a rodeo cowboy."

"No shit," I drawled. "I'd never have guessed that.

I don't suppose your girl left you with any money, did she? I mean, I'm not going to charge you for the ride or the lunch, but I'm not going all the way to Jackson Hole, either."

"I didn't figure you were." His downcast expression suggested his hope that he'd been wrong about that. "But at the time, I didn't really care."

"Neither did I. I wouldn't have left you there no matter where you were going. It was…well, let's just say it was something I couldn't bring myself to do."

"Pick up lots of strays, do you?" Turning sideways, he leaned back against the door, a move that not only drew my eye, but also gave me a full-frontal view that made my breath catch in my throat. Oh yes, I'd taken in lots of strays, but none that were anywhere near as attractive.

I shook my head. "Actually picking them up usually isn't necessary. They all seem to know where I live."

"If you don't mind my asking, where *do* you live? I mean, are we close?"

Obviously, he hoped I lived somewhere near Jackson Hole. I hated to disappoint him. "It's about another twenty miles—most of which are *not* on the main highway. I'll let you out at the turnoff, if that's okay with you."

His face fell, but he nodded, apparently resigned to the fact that this ride wasn't going to be more than a brief respite. "Not much choice, is there?" He gave a fatalistic shrug. "I don't have enough money on me to pay you to take me to Jackson Hole. I really should pay you for what you've already done."

I caught myself wishing that he *did* have enough money—or that he would ask me to run off with him and follow the rodeo circuit, never going home at all. I would have loved to throw caution to the wind and do just that, but I had too many responsibilities. Not only did I have a ranch to run, but I also had my father and my kids to look after.

No, scratch that. Chris and Will were both in college. I had a hard time remembering that except when confronted with the sight of their empty rooms as I passed by them every day. Out on the highway I could pretend they were both there at home waiting for me—and Cody, too.

No, regardless of how much money this man might offer to pay me, I couldn't shirk my duties and simply up and disappear. Nor would I accept his money. He obviously needed to hold on to what little he had stashed in those jeans.

"I couldn't possibly take money from you," I protested. "I wouldn't be much of a Good Samaritan if I did, would I?"

"I suppose not."

He shrugged again and we drove on in silence. Remaining slouched against the door, he draped his left arm across the headrest and bent up one knee, stretching his legs apart enough that my eyes were continually landing on that section of blue jeans due south of that big, silver belt buckle. From time to time he shifted his hips as though my glances made him uncomfortable, and while I *did* try to keep my eyes on the road, every once in a while they would stray back to him—and that enticing bulge in his jeans…

"What would it take to get you to drive me all the way to Jackson Hole?" The hint of suggestion in his voice startled me almost as much as the abrupt nature of his query.

Suddenly, my mouth was as dry as a gulch. Reaching for my bottle of water, I took a sip and stole another peek at him. Those luminous eyes peered at me from beneath lids that were heavy with sensuous intent.

His lips curled into a provocative smile. "I'd be willing to bet there's *something* I could do for you that would pay you back—or at least make it worth your while."

I'll just bet you could. Something quite remarkably wonderful...

Aloud, I said, "Such as?" hoping that my voice sounded more innocent than my thoughts.

He shifted his butt on the truck seat with a slow pelvic thrust. "Pull over and I'll show you." Glancing over his shoulder at the road ahead, he nodded toward the big cottonwood that was as much of a landmark for the turnoff as the road sign. "There. Under that tree."

My brain told me to keep driving, but my hands and feet ignored that directive, choosing instead to follow orders from my more primal body parts. I parked the truck in the shade and turned to face him. "This is where I let you out." Despite having cleared my throat before speaking, my voice still sounded a tad hoarse.

"You're not dumping me, are you?" His tone was teasing, but at the same time he managed to sound rather hurt that I would ever do such an awful thing to him. "I couldn't possibly get dumped again. Not twice in one day."

"No, this is where I make the turn toward home," I replied with a trace of regret. "This is where I said I'd let you off."

He nodded slowly, tipping his hat back with a finger to the brim. "Mind if we sit here and talk for a minute?"

"I suppose not. I'm not in any big rush to get home." Quite honestly, I could have sat there gazing at him for at least another hour or two. He was candy for the eyes, and I was starving to death.

He nodded again, reaching for that huge, shining belt buckle. "Let me show you something. Since you plan to leave me here anyway, I don't have much to lose."

I gasped in surprise. "You're not thinking about trading your belt buckle for a ride to Jackson Hole, are you? I can't imagine you'd want to part with something like that." Closer scrutiny proved it was no ordinary belt buckle, but a trophy buckle—the kind you can't buy, but have to win at the rodeo.

"I don't plan to." Releasing the buckle, he flipped open the button on his jeans. "What I intend to give you I can easily afford to lose." He unzipped his fly and pushed the fabric back away from his briefs. I could see the reason for the bulge now. His dick was rock hard and oozing all over his underwear. "You've been staring at this for miles. I thought you might like a better look." With that, he pushed off his jeans and briefs in one long, slow sensuous thrust. His stiff rod escaped its confinement and stood erect, taunting me—daring me not to look, not to touch…

I believe I gasped, and I know my jaw dropped in amazement. His handsome face, incredible eyes, and terrific body had already rendered him irresistible. The addition of a fabulous dick—thick and long with a tight, shiny head—created a truly lethal combination. All I could do was stare, breathlessly waiting to see what he would do next.

Pulsing his cock, he pumped out rivers of pre-come

that poured over the head and down the shaft like hot fudge over vanilla ice cream. With a wicked smirk, he slid his fingertips up and down the shaft. "Want a ride?"

I let out a pent-up breath as my tongue swept involuntarily over my lips. I'd never dreamed anything like this would happen when I picked him up—would've bet money he was too exhausted for any funny business—which only goes to show how much a sandwich, a bottle of water, and air-conditioning will do for a guy. Not to mention a place to sit down and rest.

Or some strong incentive.

He obviously wanted a ride to the rodeo badly enough to sell himself for it—and to me, of all people. I had to be at least ten years his senior, and I probably outweighed him—although he *was* a good bit taller than me. Perhaps he was heavier than he looked.

Not having enough spit in my mouth to lick a stamp, I swallowed with a great deal of difficulty.

"Maybe you'd rather have a drink." His voice was a seductive purr as he pumped out more fluid. "You look a little on the dry side."

My hand flew to my lips, and I tried to swallow again but couldn't. Every ounce of excess fluid in my body had gone south, along with my reason. I couldn't help it. Powerless to resist and ignoring the protests of my normally reasonable brain, I leaned forward and kissed his cockhead, sliding my tongue over the slick surface while inhaling his intoxicating scent. Salty to the taste and smooth as silk to the touch, he robbed me of every inhibition I had. I went down on his cock, capturing as much as I could inside my hungry mouth.

Laughing softly, he stretched out his right leg and

jacked off his boot using the stick for the four-wheel drive. Then he slid his leg out of his jeans. "Maybe you'd like some ass too." Raising his leg, he pushed me away with a foot on my shoulder before bracing it against the seat to flip himself over onto his knees.

Damn. Somehow, this man—this stranger—seemed to know my every weakness. His tight cheeks waved back and forth in front of my face as an orgasm struck, doubling me over. Falling forward, I kissed his sweet buns, giving myself sufficient recovery time to move on to lick his succulent balls.

He'd certainly chosen the right currency. For a little more of this, I'd have driven him all the way to California, given him my truck, hitchhiked my way back home, and considered myself the lucky one. I devoured him, licking my way underneath him before turning onto my back. His tasty cock dangled above my waiting lips.

"Fuck me in the mouth," I whispered. "I want you to come in my mouth."

"How far is it to Jackson Hole from here?" Groaning, he slid his thick head past my parted lips. How in the world he thought I was supposed to answer him, I have no idea. I couldn't possibly be expected to carry on a conversation with a cock that size in my mouth.

"Not that it matters," he went on. "I'll fuck you every twenty miles and twice when we get there. You can have it any way you want."

Giggling around his penis, I pushed it aside on the upstroke. "You are *such* a slut."

"Yeah. Doncha just love a slutty cowboy?" He came down on me again, sliding his wet cock across my cheek. "And you're just the kind of sweet little woman that brings out the man-whore in me. As cute and round as a robin, with big, brown eyes and long, dark braids like an Apache maiden." He groaned again and pressed his cock to my lips. "Suck me, baby. I'm ready to fill you up with my cream."

He punctuated those words with a push past my lips. His hard cock filled my mouth, and I licked the underside of his shaft as he pumped in and out. Cupping his swinging balls in my hand, I fondled them gently, massaging them while tugging on the long, curly hair adorning his scrotum.

"You like my nuts, baby?" he asked breathlessly. "I like what you're doing to them. It makes me feel like I'm gonna explode all over you."

That prospect was too much for me. Moaning, I came again, grabbing his ass in a desperate attempt to pull his dick farther into my mouth. My fingers crept to the cleft of his buttocks, seeking his soft, velvety hole. Putting a hand to his mouth, he spit on his fingers before reaching back to lubricate himself.

My massage of his slick, tight hole made him fuck even harder until at last, a sharp exhale heralded his climax. His body tensed as his breath hissed back in through his teeth. Semen shot straight down my throat, filling my mouth with spurt after spurt of warm juice. As he slowly withdrew, I sucked the cream from his cock, savoring its tangy sweetness before swallowing every last drop.

"That was payment for the ride so far." He twisted around to land heavily in the passenger seat. "To get more, you have to keep driving. I'll be hard again in another twenty miles."

I stared mutely through the windshield at the highway stretched out before me, that huge cottonwood tree a mere speck in the distance. Barely visible on the horizon, it moved closer with each passing moment. Breathing deeply in an attempt to restore harmony to my riotous emotions, I fixed an unwavering gaze on the tree—the familiar landmark steadily bringing me back into reality.

I blinked as a hand passed up and down in front of my eyes.

"Hey." His voice was overly loud, as though I hadn't been listening and he was trying to recapture my attention. "Are you always this quiet?"

As I glanced in his direction, I noted that, unlike the man in my fantasy, this cowboy remained fully dressed, his cock still an enigma, well hidden behind stout layers of blue denim.

Not quite trusting my voice, I cleared my throat. "Sometimes."

"Thought I'd lost you there for a minute." He smiled, seeming somewhat relieved. "Do you know how far it is from here to Jackson Hole?"

If you like Cheryl Brooks's cowboys,
then you'll enjoy this sneak peek
at Victoria Vane's *Saddle Up*

WITH SPEAKERS BLASTING AEROSMITH'S "BACK IN THE
Saddle," the buckskin-clad rider vaulted onto the
horse's back. Squeezing moccasin-covered heels into
the animal's flanks, he pierced the air with a war cry
and entered the arena at a hand gallop, crouched low
over the pinto stallion's neck.

Bareback and bridle-less, he performed an intricate
series of maneuvers—flying lead changes, spins, and
piaffes—before circling one last time and sliding to a
stop in the center of the arena. Leaping to the ground,
he strode the length of white-rail fence separating him
from his enraptured spectators, leather fringe softly
slapping long, muscular legs as his horse trailed
closely behind.

His black eyes were piercing, his cheekbones
prominent, and his features, chiseled perfection. His
physique was equally mouthwatering, honed of lean,
hard muscle. "I'm not here to teach you how to train a
horse," he said, black eyes dancing over his captivated
audience. "That's not what this is about. I'm here to tell
you how you can forge a lifelong partnership, a spiri-
tual bond that is virtually unbreakable." He paused, the
connection with his spectators almost palpable.

"Just as in love," he continued, "there are three possible kinds of relationships you can have with your
equine partner. The first is much like a stale marriage.

You barely tolerate one another. When you speak, he mostly ignores you. Like a passionless husband, this horse is completely indifferent to you."

He glanced over his shoulder.

Cued to his movement, the horse turned his hindquarters and walked off.

The audience snickered.

"Unless, of course, he wants something from you."

The horse came sauntering back to nudge his pocket, snatched a treat, and then promptly trotted away again with its head in the air.

"As you might guess, this one-way relationship can lead only to frustration and ultimate dissatisfaction."

He paused again, this time for effect.

"The second kind of relationship is confrontational and combative. You fight all the time, exchange harsh words, maybe even blows. You use the crop, and he reciprocates with his teeth. You are almost fearful of him. When you ride, he bucks and rears, employing any tactic to get you off his back. You beg and plead, becoming euphoric with the least crumb of cooperation."

He reached out tentatively toward the horse. It reared, baring its teeth, then kicked out and bolted across the arena.

"The third kind of relationship is what we all seek— the romance and passion. The magical relationship when your two souls become one. Like a good lover, he not only responds to your sounds, moods, and body cues, but even comes to anticipate your innermost thoughts and unspoken desires."

He looked over his shoulder with a smile. The horse came trotting up, offering his muzzle with a soft nicker as he once more scanned the spellbound faces, before his mouth stretched into a slow, seductive smile. "Now I ask, which kind of relationship do you want?"

Miranda glanced up from the video monitor as her roommate, Lexi, passed by, exclaiming with a double take, "Whoa, Nelly! *Who. Is. That?*"

Miranda paused the video. "*That's* the guy I'm filming tomorrow. He calls himself Two Wolves. He's supposed to be some sort of equine behaviorist."

Leaning over Miranda's shoulder for a better look, Lexi gave a low whistle. "Man, just look at that ass."

Miranda rolled her eyes. "Don't drool all over my keyboard, Lex."

Lexi peered closer, clearly appreciating the glittering eyes, silky black hair, and delicious hard body. "Rawrrr." Lexi gave a throaty growl. "I'd do him in a heartbeat."

"By the look of it, so would half the women in his audience," Miranda replied dryly, not about to admit she was just as enthralled. She'd never seen anyone quite like him. From the top of his head to the tips of his beaded moccasins, everything about the guy oozed raw sensuality. One thing for certain: he sure knew how to work a crowd. No wonder he'd caught Bibi's eye.

Lexi popped the top of her Dr. Pepper. "Randa, honey," she chided in her native West Texas drawl, "just because you aren't gettin' any doesn't mean you have to begrudge the rest of the world."

"My love life, or lack thereof, is none of your business, Lex."

"Someone needs to make it their business, because you certainly aren't doing anything about it."

"I don't have time—"

"No time?" Lexi snorted, nearly choking on her

drink. "You have nothing *but* time. How many hours a week do you spend vegging in front of the tube, watching old movies?"

"It's work!" Miranda protested. "How can I learn anything if I don't study my craft?"

"All right, I'll bite, but why not take one lousy night off just to play? Go out and mingle with the other half, spread some pheromones."

"Like where?"

"I don't know." Lexi shrugged. "How about the beach?"

"Are you kidding?" Miranda snorted. "With this skin? I have to wear SPF 40 just to walk out to my car."

"Then go clubbing with me."

"You're kidding, right? No offense, but I'm really uncomfortable in those kinds of places. I don't have the right look, or wear the right clothes. I don't fit in with all the 'beautiful' people here."

In four years she'd had no real dates to speak of. Not that she hadn't wanted to date, but she'd never been all that comfortable meeting new people, let alone Lexi's flamboyant crowd of actors and musicians. No matter how hard she'd tried, she always felt like a fish out of water. That was the one thing she hated most about LA, feeling insecure. She knew she didn't fit here. Although she'd accepted that long ago, acceptance didn't alleviate loneliness. Lexi had just about given up on her. Then again, who had time for a real relationship anyway?

Lexi laughed. "Honey, this is Southern California. Anyone can be beautiful. All you need is a credit card. Do you think this nose came naturally?" She turned her head to display a pert, perfect profile. "So what's the story with this hottie horse whisperer, anyway?"

"I don't really know," Miranda said. "Bibi called a couple of hours ago, telling me to drop whatever I had going on this weekend to go down to Rancho Santa Fe. Marty was supposed to video for her, but he's in the ER with a kidney stone. She wants me to fill in for him."

Bibi was a big name in indie filmmaking and long accustomed to everyone jumping at her command—not that Miranda had any plans this weekend, or any other. She didn't care that Bibi was giving her the assignment only because her lead videographer had called in sick. The reason didn't matter. All that counted was that she'd finally have a chance to get behind a camera and prove herself.

"In Rancho Santa Fe?" Lexi's brows rose. "Not quite slumming it, are you?"

"It's only a promo video," Miranda said. "But I'm hoping she'll finally let me have some creative input."

"Don't get your hopes up too high," Lexi warned. "You know how tough this business is."

"I know." Miranda sighed. "But I can't help hoping for a chance. Hey, do you want to go with me? We haven't done anything together in ages. It could be really fun."

"Wish I could," Lexi answered. "I'd love the chance to get up close and personal with him." She nodded to the paused image. "But I got a callback yesterday on the new zombie flick. I have to memorize the script."

"You actually have lines in this one? I thought zombies didn't talk."

Lexi grimaced. "No lines exactly. But I plan to raise my grunts and groans to an art form."

"Good luck with that," Miranda remarked.

Lexi's brows met in a scowl. "Need I remind you that Jamie Lee Curtis got her big break by screaming?"

"I'm sorry, Lex. I didn't mean to sound disparaging," Miranda replied, adding with an apologetic smile, "Break a leg, okay?"

In truth, she couldn't help a pang of envy. Like her aspiring-actress roommate, Miranda had arrived in Hollywood with stars in her eyes. Lexi was at least getting callbacks, but thus far, the closest Miranda had come to fulfilling her own dream was fetching lattes for the camera crew.

After Lexi disappeared into her room, Miranda went back to the video. She'd initially hoped this would finally be her chance to prove herself, but put little hope in a project featuring a man decked out in Native American regalia, doing a bunch of circus tricks. It was unlikely to win her any professional accolades, no matter how smoking hot he was.

Determined not to go into the project blindly, she spent the rest of the afternoon researching her subject, but Google gave her almost nothing besides his appearance schedule and clinic videos. Other than a brief bio on his website, the man in the ass-hugging buckskin was a complete mystery.

The following morning, Miranda tossed her overnight bag in the back seat of her VW Jetta, and rolled down all four windows before pulling out of the drive. The AC had quit working months ago, but rather than wallowing in misery, she chose to fantasize that she was behind the wheel of the shiny red Mustang convertible she'd promised herself once she got her big break. It was the car she'd vowed to drive in the entire length of the Pacific

Coast Highway—still another unfulfilled promise she'd made herself the day she'd arrived in LA.

Everything about California had been so exotic and exciting back then, but over time, disappointment and disillusionment had begun to tarnish the glitter of Tinsel Town. Passing the historic Studio City Theatre on Ventura, she was vividly reminded of the dream that had driven her west in the first place—the chance to make movies. Would she ever get a break? Statistics weighed heavily against it. Only stubborn pride had kept her from hanging it all up and going back home to Ohio.

Hedged in by traffic on all sides, she crept along, lost in her thoughts, until finally merging onto the Hollywood Freeway. Although this assignment wasn't quite what she'd hoped for, she was determined to make the best of it. She consoled herself that it was at least a step up from the weddings and bar mitzvahs that normally filled her weekends. The drive would also give her the chance to escape the monotony of her real life for a few days.

Approaching the junction of Interstates 5 and 710 in East LA, she suddenly felt like she'd come to a fork in her life. For five years she'd been too blinded by ambition to enjoy herself, and what had it gotten her? An overpriced apartment the size of a postage stamp and a lonely single bed.

Seconds passed.

Her hands tightened on the wheel.

A horn blasted as she swerved right into the lane leading to the Long Beach Freeway as she veered west toward the beach. The ocean route would add at least two hours to her drive, but she was determined to fulfill at least part of her dream.

Slow Hand

Hot Cowboy Nights Series
by Victoria Vane

—⁓—

In rural Montana...

Wade Knowlton is a hardworking lawyer who's torn between his small-town Montana law practice and a struggling family ranch. He's on the brink of exhaustion from trying to save everybody and everything, when gorgeous Nicole Powell walks into his office. She's a damsel in distress and the breath of fresh air he needs.

Even the lawyers wear boots...

Nicole Powell is a sassy Southern girl who has officially sworn off cowboys after a spate of bad seeds—until her father's death sends her to Montana and into the arms of a man who seems too good to be true. Her instincts tell her to hightail it out of Montana, but she can't resist a cowboy with a slow hand.

—⁓—

"A red-hot cowboy tale... Their sexual chemistry crackles." —*Publishers Weekly*

"Delightful, funny, page-turning steamy sexy, and the romance makes you wish you could pull Victoria's characters straight off the page." —*Unwrapping Romance*

For more Victoria Vane, visit:

www.sourcebooks.com

Rough Rider

Hot Cowboy Nights Series

by Victoria Vane

———

Old flames burn the hottest...

Janice Combes has adored Dirk Knowlton from the rodeo sidelines for years. She knows she'll never be able to compete with the dazzling all-American rodeo queen who's set her sights on Dirk. Playful banter is all Janice and Dirk will ever have...

Until the stormy night when he shows up at her door, injured and alone. Dirk's dripping wet, needs a place to stay, and Janice remembers why she could never settle for any other cowboy...

———

Praise for Victoria Vane:

"Erotic and sexy...absolutely marvelous." — *Library Journal* on the Devil DeVere series

"The Mistress of Sensuality does it again!" —*Swept Away by Romance*

For more Victoria Vane, visit:

www.sourcebooks.com